# BRUSH
## WITH
# DARKNESS

## JAMIE MALTMAN

## ARTS REBORN: BOOK I

TESTUDO

PRESS

Library and Archives Canada Cataloguing in Publication

Maltman, Jamie, author
    Brush With Darkness/Jamie Maltman.

Issued in Print and Electronic Formats.

ISBN 978-0-9921474-1-9 (bound).-- ISBN 978-0-9921474-0-2 (epub)

    I.Title.

Cover Design by Keri Knutsen, Alchemy Book Covers

Maps © 2013 Jamie Maltman

Published in 2014 by Testudo Press

To Monica, my wife and first reader

VALTARI

Rantusha

RANDESH

Betrosh

Jalut

Avjat
BENJEA

Agben

GALAT
Aldas

Bulla

GREAT
OCEAN

FAR
SEA

ALKAZY

Valera

Melaxa

Stoba

Novoxa

PAZH

Gazara

Nahuz

Sarea
Pazh

Malayus

THE GAP

Keura

Saqur
Laogas Thegos

Ras-Dura
Nea

EGARAS

Sulw

Dougga

J. MALTMAN 2013

REPUBLIC
of
PAZH
and surrounding nations

# I

## Ambition

It started with a dream, and Simon's life would never be the same again.

*The world was gray—not just the sky, but the field, the trees and the corpses. As if the life had been drained from both the land and his fallen comrades, leaving a pale imitation. Where was the green of the trees? The blue of the sky? The red of their legionary tunics?*

*Of their blood.*

*Gone too was the angry black of the arrows littering thousands of corpses. Only form remained, as if carved from pale lifeless stone. Where was the color? The soul?*

*His mind screamed out in opposition. He had to do something.*

*Heat trickled up from the ground between his hobnailed sandals, a gentle current escaping from a hole. A pale branch sprouted from the gap, growing up to touch his hand. Sparks of golden light flared from the contact, so warm as his fingers closed around the wood, the comforting radiance spreading down his arm to engulf his heart.*

*He had never felt so alive, so vibrant. He saw the world with new clarity: what was missing and how to bring it out. To bring it back.*

*The stick was above his head now, dancing in his hand through the air, colors leaping forth; swirling, splashing, beautiful colors. Vivid greens sprayed the ground, erupting into new life. The air buzzed around him in waves of azure glory as he spun, enraptured. Pure happiness shone yellow through his skin.*

*If only he could find his friends among the dead, and give them back their color, he could—*

*Sudden cold washed over him, raising the hairs on his other arm. He turned to face the source.*

*Darkness, an inky malignant blackness, billowed over the battleground toward him. Smoky wisps swirled around the bodies; seeking, searching, devouring.*

*The light in his hand flickered, frail and defenseless, shrinking from the advancing evil.*

*He had to get away. To protect the light. Or it would be lost.*

*He turned to run, but stumbled, the stick thrown from his grasp, skittering away across the gray scrub. On hands and knees he scrambled after the branch, but it continued to roll further and further from his reach.*

*Despairing, he looked back, and the darkness was nearer now, inhaling the last vestiges of color he had returned to the world.*

*He threw up his hands to ward the darkness away, but it surged around his fingers, enveloping them as it sought to extinguish his spark. He averted his face, turning back to the branch one last time.*

*A scream escaped his lips and the fiery blackness rushed in through his open mouth, burning and choking. The darkness reached the branch and the light winked out of existence, just as the black covered his eyes. The world became night and death and he was spiraling down, down, down...*

Simon woke up, drenched with sweat and shivering against the cold. *There will be no more sleep this night.*

Squinting through the first rays of early morning light, Simon saw no sign of sinister Scentari horse archers lurking in the gloomy steppe below. Were they still out there, waiting to prey on the column once they got moving again? Yesterday's attack had been the worst yet, and the most deadly. Simon would never forget the sightless eyes of the dead legionaries. Success no longer seemed assured as the legion struck north into this barbarian homeland, despite the superiority of their numbers, organization and weaponry.

Simon sat atop a small hill at the center of the 7th Legion's temporary camp, looking north into the gray unknown. Tendrils of icy mist hung in the air, transforming the vast plains beyond the palisade wall into a ghostly forest. They seemed almost alive, reaching out to drain the blood from his fingers and leave only bones freezing in the wind. As he blew in his hands to try to coax back a spark of life, hope itself was fading.

Was this how every soldier felt? And was he even crazier to have chosen this? Wouldn't he prefer to be warm in his own bed back in the city of Pazh? Where his biggest worry was enduring his father's next wine-addled tongue lashing.

He was drawn to the legions by the promise of some greater destiny. He'd enlisted what, six months ago? The day after he turned twenty. He'd wanted to see the world and make a name for himself and his family. He was not content to cling desperately to the bottom rung of the *mercati* merchant class. His father may have stopped dreaming long ago, but Simon knew there was more in this world for him. And he meant to prove it.

The legions offered a man from any part of the Republic of Pazh the chance for advancement, from the lowest freed slave or *mundati* worker to the wealthiest *suprati* and *digniti*. The legions were the embodiment of the Pazian ideals of devotion, duty, and success through personal achievement, ideals that every citizen held dear. Like every Pazian boy Simon idolized the noble legionary, defending the Republic from her enemies and bringing civilization to far flung provinces all around the Near Sea. To be a part of striking down tyrannical despots and bestowing upon new citizens the opportunity to vote for their rulers. The ideals of his father's Republic were woven into the fabric of daily life in the legion. By comparison his former life looked selfish and hollow; toiling in his father's failing business for the hope of meager profit.

Noble idealism had burned bright while he was first training on the Pazian mainland and kept burning through his assignment to the 7th Legion for garrison duty in Sal Dar, capital of the Pazian province of Pelusia. But now, with the entire Near Sea separating him from his home in the capital of Pazh, out here on the wind-blown steppe of western Scentar—beyond the furthest borders of civilization—that spark of inspiration was as elusive as the warmth in his fingers. How anyone could live here in the long winter was beyond him. No wonder these barbarians had made their attack on Pelusia, perhaps as a foolish attempt to reclaim their former lands in the much warmer province.

When the provincial Governor Jasun Suboras got word of the Scentari sack of the Pelusian frontier town of Jamad, he had assumed generalship of the 7th Legion and driven them hard to the northeast, where they found the burned and mangled remains of the town and all its people. The invading force of Scentari horsemen had fled before the much larger force. The legion had been marching north in pursuit for eight days now without coming close to catching the faster mounted Scentari. After crossing the northern border of the Republic into Scentar proper there were no roads, just barren steppe, and the barbarians knew their homeland and didn't have to worry about protecting a wagon train. That's when the raids had started.

The tail end of their force had been hit hard in the latest surprise attack. The Scentari horse archers were just too fast, and accurate from well beyond the range of the legionary javelins. Garas said they'd lost at least thirty-five men to those wicked barbed arrows before the charge of the auxiliary cavalry drove them off.

It was the first time Simon had been there when they buried the dead. Garas had sent him around to make sure the equipment got back to the proper storage wagons. The grizzled camp prefect counseled Simon: *Never trust a soldier to bring back a shovel when he just buried the rest of his squad.* Simon thought it was pretty practical advice, like everything he was learning from the veteran. Almost three decades in the legions had taught Garas much about how death affected men, even the men of the greatest military force the world had ever seen. Simon had barely been able to concentrate on the equipment manifest after seeing the lifeless eyes and twisted torsos of men his own age and younger disappear into the cold, unforgiving clay. At least the cold masked the smell of death.

*I shouldn't complain. I could be one of those unfortunate souls.*

And likely would have been, if it weren't for Garas Numeno. All because of the details.

He'd seen from his father's business how neglecting the details was disastrous in any sort of endeavor. When his father was sober, he was as fastidious as any. *When* he was sober… which was far too infrequent. *Especially since Mother died.* So Simon went easy on the drink and heavy on paying attention.

Garas had recognized that quality in Simon and raised him from just another newly enlisted legionary to a junior aide in his prefectural retinue. While not the most glorious position, once in hostile territory it was far better to be making sure tents were straight and shovels accounted for than to be on the receiving end of a Scentari arrow. And there was far more to be learned at the table of Garas in his role as third in command of the entire army, than from nine other raw recruits around their nightly campfire.

The rest of the camp was stirring to life with the clanking of pots and armor and the smell of cooking fires for the morning porridge. Simon had been awake for an hour already, sunk deep in his melancholy reflection. As tired as he was, he didn't want to face any more of those dreams. He'd climbed the hill to clear his head with a view of this grim gray country. He shuddered, an unnatural chill amplifying the cold in his bones.

Normally he was too busy to appreciate the incredible logistical and engineering marvel of a Pazian legionary traveling camp, but on this morning he had a view of its perfection. Six thousand men organized down to the last tent. The central hill housed the command tent and the quarters of the general, the legate, his second command, Garas as camp prefect, and the tribunes who served as junior officers. In front of him lay the supply wagons, as well as his own tent that he shared with Garas' other aides. Beyond them several hundred horsemen from the province of Kawan made up the auxiliary cavalry, and they also tended the officers' horses. Each of the ten cohorts, the main organizational unit of the legion, had its own section of the camp, like self-contained villages. Six hundred of the finest veterans made up the first cohort, taking pride of place just north of the command center. Every cohort was subdivided into six centuries of one hundred men, each led by a centurion. It was so perfectly coordinated that even from here, Simon could pick out the exact tent where his nine (or ten if he'd been replaced) former squadmates of the 9th squad, 6th century, 9th cohort were already moving in a flash of polished iron and red wool to tear down their tent for the day's march.

In more than five centuries of the Pazian Republic, times of complete peace were few and far between. The logistics of war depended on discipline, organization and order. Only with these could an army be prepared for the chaos that came in the heat of battle. And this was imparted by the career soldiers like Garas Numeno, men who learned their craft through years in the field with preceding generations just like themselves.

Under the direction of the camp prefect, the legion would set up a complete fortified camp every night in hostile territory, surrounded by a freshly dug trench and the earth piled into an embankment topped with sharpened stakes. And it didn't get much more hostile than invading a barbarian homeland. At night at least, they were safe from attack.

"Legionary Baroba?" said a familiar voice from behind him. "You are up early."

"As are you, Tribune Scribora."

Kyso Scribora was always so formal that it bordered on ridiculous. The tribune, one of the junior officers, was stiff with his friends, and positively wooden with superiors. He was five years older than Simon, with close-cropped sandy hair, a gray cast to his skin, and a bookish and unsmiling face.

Kyso always looked out of place in his full legionary attire, like he was trying too hard to fit in his father's equipment. It was almost identical to what Simon wore as a rank and file legionary: a red woolen tunic under armor of overlapping iron bands that deflected arrows and sword blows as well as any, topped off with a rounded helmet with additional plates that covered the cheeks and the back of the neck. Set on the ground, his rectangular curved shield stood waist-high, and was painted red with a stylized number 7 for their legion number. A javelin, short sword and dagger completed his armaments. All the weapons and armor perfectly formed from top quality Pazian iron, the finest in the world. To signify his rank, Kyso wore a red cape with a thin purple border. Simon preferred the heavy woolen cloak he'd been issued for the colder weather.

Kyso did not mix well with the rest of the tribunes, but he and Simon were becoming fast friends. He was a lot smarter than the others, and his uncommon diffidence was a result of his family's very recent rise to the ranks of the *suprati*—new members of the senatorial class who had made it on the back of military, economic or other success. In his case it was his uncle Akeri Scribora's illustrious military career that paved the way, though his lower standing meant that he got the appointment at a more advanced age than more noble tribunes, and he had only been with the legion for a year. Kyso was determined to make good on the opportunity, and the family story inspired Simon.

"Can't sleep?" Kyso asked.

Simon shook his head. "Does it get any easier? Seeing…" His voice trailed off as he thought again of those cold dead eyes.

"I do not know. This was my first time in a hostile situation. My uncle said it haunts him still."

"So what's the latest plan?" Simon asked Kyso. Garas hadn't filled him in on last night's council.

Kyso brightened up, like he always did when speaking of strategy and tactics. "A brilliant plan by the general. It is pointless to keep chasing them, with their superior mobility. They have stayed ahead of us ever since we left Pelusia, and now are using their knowledge of the terrain to raid us with increasingly dire results."

Simon knew this, but nodded, encouraging his friend.

"General Suboras has decided to strike into the Sentusi River valley—the heart of Scentar. It is the best grazing land, with more moderate weather than up here on the steppe. With winter fast approaching, the Scentari women and children will be there with the flocks. That will force their warriors to meet us in battle to protect them, and our superior arms and discipline will carry the day. He hopes to force them to submit now, so we can be back before the snow comes."

"It sounds like a good idea."

"It is a much better prospect than either continuing the chase until supplies run short, or pulling back and encouraging these raiding parties to wreak havoc all over northern Pelusia."

"I think I understand now why they attacked in the first place. Would you want to spend every winter here? I'd want to retake Pelusia if I were them."

Kyso resumed a very serious expression. "It was a grave mistake. They should not have broken the treaty. It very clearly marked the borders, and any breach of the line would be met with lethal force. It has held for twenty years. But word is the squabbling clans have united again, under a new grand thane."

"Shouldn't you be making sure the wagons are ready to move, *Benjai*?" said Tribune Persei Lokuta from behind them. Simon fought to hide his anger at the insult to his mother's faith as he turned to behold the self-satisfied smirk on the tribune's chiseled jaw. Standing tall and muscular in the early morning light, with a head of blond curls, he looked ready to model for a painting of the quintessential Pazian hero. And while Kyso gave the impression of a youth trying in vain to fill grown up armor, Persei's looked made for him. Which of course it was, with additional ornamentation rivaling even that of the general's. *Any chance to show off his wealth.*

"Or," Persei continued, "have you decided to observe your day of rest?"

Conceited second son of the fabulously wealthy *digniti* house of Lokuta, Persei never tired of reminding others of his superiority, whether based on his rank, inherited wealth, aristocratic lineage, swordsmanship, success with women or in this case, Simon's inferior heritage. While Kyso was delightfully humble and earnest, Persei exemplified the worst of the haughty noble families of Pazh. Most of the tribunes and generals of the Pazian armies, as well as the lion's share of the high elected officials, came from eminent families such as the house of Lokuta. Simon had little choice but to endure the barbs. One had to respect them, or else.

While Simon resented the easy arrogance of those born to privilege, Persei's vile epithet was technically accurate. Simon's permanently bronzed skin, though lighter than his mother's, betrayed him as half-Benjish among the much paler Pazians. But it wasn't his color that made him the object of scorn, as the citizens of the Republic varied widely, and the city of Pazh itself was as multicultural as any. Simon's mother's followed an ancient faith that originally hailed from Benjea, west across the Far Sea from mainland Pazh. Always outsiders in the city where her ancestors had settled, the common Pazians and especially the aristocrats scoffed at their veneration of one single god, a sharp contrast to the multitude of deities in the ever expanding Pazian pantheon. The Benjish observance of a scripturally mandated day of rest generally excluded them from public office and the military. The Pazian generals believed this to be a lazy and even dangerous tradition in times of war and allowed them to be exempt from mandatory service. Common Pazians generally considered them cowards.

Though Simon was only half-Benjish, with a Pazian father whose faith rested mainly in whoever was pouring the wine, this noble officer liked to remind him of what he considered an indelible stain. For the second time this morning Simon questioned why he had repudiated his late mother's heritage and willingly enlisted in the service of his father's. But he would prove that he was as brave and as Pazian as any Lokuta.

Kyso backed off, deferring as always to his superiors. He looked past them to the command tent. "I was just leaving. I must meet with the prefect. Good day, Tribune Lokuta. Legionary Baroba." He clasped his hands together before him. "For Pazh."

Simon stood up, which meant he was now looking down at Persei. Though Persei was already tall at six feet, Simon had a couple of inches on him, no doubt another reason the tribune felt the need to knock him down at every opportunity.

"Good morning Tribune," he responded with a slight bow of his head, the expected deference to a superior. "My only faith is in the glory of Pazh. Like many here, I did not sleep well last night, and was heading down to help break camp."

Persei's blue eyes betrayed an echo of Simon's own mix of fear and exhaustion. He wasn't the only one with nightmares. And no wonder, he and Persei had both joined the legion just three months before the attack on Jamad.

*We are not as different as you believe.*

Persei was also in his twentieth year, and neither man was ready for the grinding toll of a real campaign.

"There is much to do," Simon said. "The general wants us to make the Sentusi by nightfall."

A scowl crossed Persei's face. He probably assumed he knew more than this poor merchant's son, with only a lucky accident elevating him above his rightful place as a common soldier. While Simon's service in Garas' personal retinue afforded him an uncommon status here, he had to tread carefully to make sure he didn't anger these spoiled sons that had the ear of the general. How that irked him.

Persei scoffed. "You'd best be going to your *labor*. I must meet General Suboras and the rest of the commanders for one last council before we march." The smirk returned, with the young nobleman satisfied that he had twisted a barb in the upstart's side.

Simon nodded. "Good day, Tribune. For Pazh."

*Oh to have all the doors in the world opened by your ancestors.* He reaffirmed his vow to one day see his name, Baroba, in the annals with names like Sarrinai and Lokuta, Pollian and Marcona. He was no less Pazian than the others, and the Republic and its ideals were his birthright too.

How would he make his mark? If the god of his mother's ancestors knew, he'd never given Simon even a hint.

But some good came from the encounter with Persei; the spark of rekindled ambition would keep him warm on the day's march.

# II

## Flames

The light of the central fire cast its flickering glow on the collected throng of Scentari warriors as they sat under the stars of their ancestral homeland. The Sentusi River flowed past them, the rippling of the water joining the crackle of flame to pierce the silence of night.

Shadush, Grand Thane of the Scentari, looked on his people with pride. These were hardened men of the steppe, living their lives on horseback in the open air, faces weathered like the fur-trimmed leathers they wore. Before him sat all the power of his people: the thanes as heads of each clan with their banners, the generals and captains of his army including his five adult sons, his closest bloodriders, and the spiritual heads—the high priests of Mija, goddess of the flame who watched over her people. All were here, answering his call.

But not yet united. It was mere months since he was elected as their leader, the first grand thane in twenty years, in a long and difficult contest. Even his election was a breach of the treaty with the Pazian Republic. That hated treaty would bind him and his people no longer, keeping them fractured, divided, and weak. He had already completed the first step, pushing past internal opposition to bring them together once more.

Next he would avenge their humiliation at the hands of the Pazians twenty years ago. The dishonor of his uncle's capitulation. The loss of the fertile grazing land in what the Pazians now called their province of Pelusia. Shadush would lead his people to reclaim their land. And more.

His people only knew he burned for revenge. They weren't ready to see the glory that was possible. To bequeath a new and glorious Scentar to his children. His oldest son, now twenty-five, was just a boy when they suffered the humiliating defeat. He had never known anything but captivity. So Shadush did this for them. For their future.

Nervous shouts from the edge of the circle announced the return of the scouts with news of the Pazian legion that had been following them north. Shadush looked up from his maps just as Kazash, his most favored captain, reached his side. Well over six feet of solid muscle, Kazash stood more than a head taller than Shadush. Kazash's lip curled in a vicious broken-toothed smile under his long black mustache, the ends braided together below his chin, marking him as a captain among their people.

"The Pazian legion continues to follow us," Kazash said, "but we stay out of reach. Our raids bleed them, inflicting minor casualties, and they're too slow to cause us any losses. They will descend into the upper reaches of the Sentusi tomorrow, my lord." His dark eyes burned with the bloodlust that had simmered dully within them for far too long. "Just as you prophesied they would. They are following us right into the river valley. Right where you want them. We will make it the largest Pazian grave ever seen."

He was a good warrior, but impatient, and like many of the assembled war leaders was ready to charge out to meet the Pazians here and now, while others looked like beaten dogs cowering from the return of a cruel master.

"We must have patience," Shadush replied in that cold, deep voice that chilled the hearts of any who heard him. "The trap is set, but we must stay upwind of the hare until he sets his foot in the noose." It was the voice of one supremely confident in his power. Though he preached cool restraint, Shadush's blood also boiled at the prospect of the coming slaughter.

Many years of preparation were finally nearing fruition. His submission, his sacrifice, everything had worked toward this end. Tonight he would reveal his power to his people. Tomorrow he would turn it on his enemies, with the victory heralding the dawn of a golden future for the Scentari.

Shadush stood up at the edge of the fire, his long bearskin cape cascading behind him. The flames glinted off the iron breastplate he wore over the traditional studded leathers of his people, reflecting flickering shafts of light onto his own braids, two strands of mustache worked into two more from his beard, signifying his position as ruler over all the Scentari clans. He did not tower over his captains in stature, but their fire-illuminated eyes belied their mixed feelings: respect for their grand thane, but trepidation for the plan he had yet to reveal.

To succeed, he needed them to each do their part exactly, to become warriors once again, and not degenerate into a mangy pack of ravening wolves. These were men who had lived their adult lives in fear of the Pazian legions, slinking around these wild plains that were but a shadow of their former range.

*Time to show them who was worthy of respect. And fear.*

"My brothers," Shadush said, his words reverberating around the throng of collected warriors. He withdrew a scroll from a case by his chair. He projected his voice with almost supernatural authority. "Do you know what this is?" He sneered. "This is the treaty signed twenty years ago by my uncle Gazush when he submitted like a dog at the foot of the Pazian master. When he gave up not just our lands and our vassals, but our dignity. While too many of our people accept these chains, skulking about in the muck, I have burned to restore our glory. And with our new might, we shall throw off the yoke and take back what is rightfully ours. We are great warriors, but now we are much more."

He unrolled the scroll in the air in front of him, turning it to face the crowd. What began as a low rumble in his throat came out as a guttural, spidery incantation in a language that none of them understood. He felt the seductive warmth smolder deep in his heart before shooting down his arms into his hands with a mix of searing pain and ecstasy. Wisps of black flame crackled out from his fingertips to devour the hated document.

The more fearful among them erupted in wide-eyed gasps. None had ever witnessed these dark arts, which were the stuff of stories told by old crones to scare children into obedience. His inner circle looked on in admiration and even awe of their dark deliverer. At least two looked furious, the Mijazi—high priests of Mija. He had anticipated the challenge, and relished what was to come. Their grip on the people was the last bond holding them captive. Jagaz, the senior of the two priests, stood and pointed toward the dark flames burning through the script.

"What manner of dark sorcery is this?" Jagaz asked. He wore the red cassock of his station with authority and confidence, as one who communed with nature itself and could call forth the power of the flames. Natural flames. He stabbed a finger toward the burning document. "You are not one of Mija's faithful, and *that* is not the work of our goddess!"

Shadush wore an evil smile. Jagaz turned to his comrade and then to the rest of the warriors, his hands indicating the fire before them. His voice pinched with furious condemnation. "Will you allow this blasphemy to violate Mija's sacred hearth of war?"

"You are correct," Shadush said. "This is not Mija's work. Mija's work has led us into a cage. A cage of Pazian manufacture. We should all be ashamed as we huddle around a fading fire that can hardly keep our women and children warm. We have followed your ways too long."

Jagaz' eyes burned with a rage of their own, and his fellow Mijazi rose, shaking, to join him in confronting Shadush. More than a few other faces reflected their shock and outrage. The two Mijazi extended their hands to draw on the power of the sacred fire at the center of the circle, their eyes burning like the flames flickering at their fingertips. A corona of fire blazed forth around their hands.

"Blasphemer!" they cried out. "Mija, burn this heretic!" A streak of fire sizzled toward Shadush, and he raised the remains of the burning scroll to meet the hurtling fireballs, which struck with a thunderclap that shook the ground beneath them. Black sparks sprayed outward, searing the faces and singeing the hair of the nearest warriors, as the fireballs and the scroll disappeared in a cloud of oily black smoke. The fury in Jagaz' face drained away, replaced with powerless terror.

"Mija's flames won't save you now," Shadush said, shaking his head in mock sadness. He continued on in that unknown tongue, faster than before, while pointing his now empty hands at the faces of the two priests. Their pupils first widened, then darkened, melting into pools of burning agony as they clutched at the pain. The sickening aroma of scorching fat permeated the air; a sibilant hiss erupting from their eyes as the black conflagration boiled within their sockets. Spreading to their faces and beyond, the unholy dark flames burned flesh and bone as easily as they had consumed the scroll. With a final blood-curdling scream, their lungs were consumed from within, and the two men fell silent, their remains crumpling to the ground.

A hush fell over the mix of cowed and exultant faces, broken only by the low crackle of dark flames burning away the remnants.

Shadush basked in the exhilaration of this demonstration of power, a power that coursed fiercely through his body like new life. His strength was growing, and demanded to be fed. And feed it he would. There would be no more opposition among his people.

"Tomorrow, we burn Pazians."

# III

## ꙋꙌꙋꙌꙋꙌꙋ

## *Eruption*

Simon stood high on the escarpment with Garas and Kyso, watching the last of the general's force wind down the path into the basin of the Sentusi, like a serpent flashing red and metallic gray. Creases of worry intersected with the scar across Garas' brow, one of many he bore after thirty years of active duty. Simon had never seen him this concerned, and it set him on edge.

"This is too easy," Garas said. "I would have expected serious opposition, or at least more raids. General Suboras assumes that the herdsmen are fleeing only as we advance on their grazing lands, and that the Scentari would have evacuated the women and children much earlier if they intended to fight us here. But it doesn't feel right to me."

The anxiety made Garas look older than his forty-six years. He could still keep pace with the best of them with sword or javelin, as he kept his stocky build in impeccable shape. His hair was still thick and dark, and he might even be handsome if he ever smiled, but lines in his face betrayed too many years of experience.

General Suboras had taken the first seven cohorts into the river valley, and the slow descent took them most of the day. They needed to move fast to put pressure on the main herds before the Scentari could withdraw them.

Along with Kyso as his lone tribune, that left Garas in command of the remaining three cohorts of the 7th and the Kawanian auxiliary cavalry. Their orders were to guard the southern passes of the escarpment and the main wagon train.

"Think of the victory over the western Macatri from the *Campaigns of Porruna Macator*," Kyso said. "His use of the river to limit their cavalry was genius, and Suboras is right to use the same tactics here to the benefit of our heavy infantry." He never missed a chance to demonstrate his knowledge of military history and the tactics of the great generals of the past. Simon didn't mind the lesson, but Persei might have decked him for it.

Garas kept an eye out for Kyso, since his uncle Akeri had been the prefect's commanding tribune in his earlier campaigns under General Marcus Sarrinai. Relationships were as important in the hierarchy of the Pazian legions as they were in the Senate or the markets. Simon stood with both of his allies.

"Is it truly a good plan if it doesn't sit well with the gut of an old veteran?" asked Simon with a wink to Garas.

"Their behavior just doesn't make sense," Garas said. "We left them alone for twenty years. Pelusia was our province, and it was common knowledge that there was a legion at Sal Dar, not just the usual garrisons. Why burn a town to the ground, and make such a spectacle of it, then turn around and run home? They'd have to know we'd come after them in force, to make them pay for breaking the treaty."

"You think they want us to come after them?" Simon asked.

"If they do, they've got a death wish. I just hope everything goes according to the general's plan. Well, let's get the boys to work on extra fortifications. If those horse riding bastards decide to hit us up here, I want to be ready for them. Simon, when you're finished drawing up a better picture of those new traps you came up with, show each centurion and direct them to have their men build them out in the tall grass outside the camp—but just inside arrow range. We've got to get this right if we want a chance against another surprise attack. Or at least a better chance than your mates who fell in the raid."

Simon enjoyed drawing sketches of whatever Garas needed, whether a camp plan, fortifications or the inner workings of a siege engine. They especially praised his maps, like the rough one they pored over to review the impact of the terrain on the plans the general had set in motion.

While nice to be respected as a draftsman, it was so boring and technical compared to the joyful sketches he used to create. Still, getting any respect for his artistic talent was something new. When he was in school, he filled his margins with fanciful drawings. His father never had any time for it. "No money in your kind of art," was his usual mocking refrain whenever he caught Simon doodling creatures of legend. But that was still better than the rap on the knuckles, or full paddling he'd get if the teacher went through his schoolbooks. With its focus on the mundane subjects needed by a merchant's son, his school left him little time for the arts. When he did get to draw, they demanded rote copying of the designs of the ancient masters. Simon knew he could do so much more, but why bother, when it went unappreciated?

At least here a little creativity proved useful, as long as you stayed within the parameters. And being able to communicate visually sure did help with the tasks Garas assigned him. *I don't mind this kind of labor one bit.*

"After that, ride down to let the general know we're all set up here, and to send you back when he's ready to move on."

It was with more than a little pride that Simon rode down into the valley with his message for the general. The traps were coming together exactly as he drew them out, with that familiar sense of wonder as he transferred something from his mind, onto parchment, and from there to reality. Even though it wasn't his hands that brought it together in the physical world, he felt the thrill of creation. And to be entrusted with a message for the general himself? This was shaping up to be a very good day.

He looked down at his map, amazed by just how accurately it described his descent. It was as if he could see himself on the craggy sloping track in his drawing. The area was picturesque in its barren beauty, with interesting rock formations intermittently flanked by patches of low vegetation and not a tree in sight. Their view of the troops at the bottom was blocked, but in the distance they could see the Sentusi. The cold late autumn sun shone on the fast-flowing river, reflecting like countless sapphires.

"Unnatural," said Jarom, one of the two legionaries sent as extra muscle on this little courier mission. His mouth turned down at the corners, giving him a permanent frown. He had the golden skin of a Maruthan, but not the sunny disposition to match. Jarom put that stereotype to rest. "I feel like these cliffs are closing in on me."

"Quit your whining, Jarom," said Tark, the swarthy Myraki, "or would you rather be breaking your back making Simon's new fortifications all day? I don't mind the chance to get away from camp for a bit."

"Garas thought the general would set up his command center here," Simon said, indicating a rocky outcropping drawn in on the map, on the near shore of the river. "It gives a good vantage point across the whole valley, and since the river is too wide at this point their back is covered. The scouts report the nearest ford is almost a day's journey downstream."

*It's a shame Kyso can't see the setup, and compare it to the classical tactics he holds so dear.*

After a few minutes ride the path opened up and the full valley and their forces came into view. Black mist blanketed the river, obscuring the far side.

"Does that mist look strange to you?" Simon said.

The cry of a distant horn echoed off the cliff face, spooking Jarom's pony. "That's not one of ours," he said as he righted himself. The three of them exchanged worried glances and drew their swords.

"We should get down there right away, shouldn't we?" Simon said, nominally in charge. His eyes sought out their destination. "What is that?" He pointed to the rocky promontory that housed the command tents, bustling with activity and giving the general staff a good view of the surrounding area. A strange moving shadow covered the wall that faced the river, and was… growing? Flickering like black… flames? The sight of it filled him with dread. It was unnatural—an abomination. The other two strained to follow what he indicated but looked blank. *Why can't they see it?*

Inky fire continued to pour forth, angry and devouring. It exploded in a thunderclap that shook the entire valley with deafening echoes. A dark plume of smoke shot up in front of the command center, obscuring it from view.

Everything went to hell.

A hail of arrows burst through the mist on the river, raining death on the legionaries as they scrambled into battle formations.

Further down the Pazian side of the river, a storm of dust whirling in the air announced a charging horde of Scentari riders screaming in unison as they crashed into the disorganized front lines. From Simon's vantage point, the threat was clear. *The general and his staff have a good view and will—*

"Salar save them," said Tark, pointing back to the cloud where the command tent had stood.

A huge smoking gash covered the far face of the rocky promontory, and the top listed badly toward the river. With a terrible crack it broke loose and skated down to splash like a giant ship dropping into the water. Terrified horses thrashed about, dragging officers and fallen tents over the side into the roiling river.

"That would make a good... bridge," Simon said. No sooner had the word escaped his mouth, when arrows filled the air on the rocky bridge, piercing officers, tents and horses alike. Torrents of swirling water washed away more of the tents, and Scentari riders surged out of the mist, hewing down any Pazians who had found their feet.

The surprise assault hit every part of the Pazian camp at once. Hundreds of Scentari riders galloped over the bridge, cutting into the confusion of the Pazian rear.

Simon broke free of his shocked paralysis. Battered by this scene he could barely comprehend, he defaulted to his orders. "We must get the message to the general!" He kicked his mount to go forward, but both soldiers hung back.

Jarom put up his hand. "We'd be dead long before we reach him. If he even lives."

"We must observe and report back to Garas," said Tark. "That bridge is overrun. We have to hope the others can form their lines and give them a chance to get out of there."

Simon surveyed the scene, looking for glimmers of hope. He found few. The screaming Scentari force was tearing through terrified new recruits at the original front. The veterans behind them would normally enforce discipline, but the sheer volume of routed soldiers shattered even their lines. The unrelenting rain of arrows felled legionaries everywhere Simon looked. Without commanders to coordinate the legion as a whole, each century—each individual squad—was fighting their own battle, to predictably poor results. A few small islands were holding their own, but would soon be engulfed by the Scentari tide.

This was slaughter on a grand scale.

"You think they'll be able to get up these paths?" asked Jarom. He pointed to where riders were tearing through the rear. "They'll be surrounded in minutes, cutting off any escape. Look at that group breaking off, they're heading for the bottom of this path!"

Tark nodded. "We have to move before they come for us too.

They know these routes far better than we do, and their horses are faster both on the trails and in the open. I don't want one of those arrows in my back. Simon? Are you with us?"

"The mist... those flames... the earthquake... can the Scentari move nature against us?" *It was impossible—magic was a myth.* But how else could he explain what his eyes had seen?

And it was far too similar to his terrible dream, only with no light to show him the way, just his mind screaming for escape. *Fall back... run!*

"Whatever it is, Garas needs to know," Jarom said. "I'm going. I hope you can join me so I'm not in breach of any orders."

Simon nodded. "But we tell only Garas. If the men panic, we're all dead. Understood?" The two men exchanged a worried look, then nodded. They started up the treacherous path back to their camp.

One final scan of the scene burned an image of the horror into Simon's mind. *Would Garas be able to lead us to safety, or are we doomed like our fallen brothers?*

ᏨᏋᏨᏋᏨᏋᏨ

Shadush surveyed the valley, Kazash at his right hand. Much was already aflame, lighting up the dusk. His plan had worked almost to perfection and caused such chaos as even the vaunted discipline of the Pazian legions could not overcome. *Scentar will know a new glory, but we all must bear the cost.*

He nodded his assent for Kazash to begin directing the men. "Tents, bodies, everything we don't need, pile it high. Our grand thane wants the biggest fire this valley has ever seen! And he wants any survivors brought in chains to enjoy the heat."

Shadush turned his horse and rode back to the bridge that had featured so decisively in the battle. Given some time, the river had diverted around it on both sides, turning it into more of an island, but enough debris littered the banks that it could be forded on horseback.

Shadush mounted the highest point, and called out to the assembled warlords, survivors and selected few who had distinguished themselves in battle.

"Noble warriors of Scentar, today you have won a great victory for our homeland. The Sentusi runs freely over our fallen enemies, as is right and good. This would be enough to please Mija. But we must do more." He nodded to Kazash, who signaled to the warriors holding the most important captives. They brought the prisoners forth, forcing them to kneel. Shadush approached the Pazian general, still wearing his breastplate and long red cape. He held his head high in proud defiance. *A shame I can't save the armor. Such craftsmanship. But a small sacrifice for the greater show.*

"General Suboras." Shadush rolled his tongue over the sounds of the foreign name, then continued in his own language. "Your name will not be one raised in the pantheon of Pazian heroes, I'm afraid. Instead, your honor and passion will burn for the glory of Scentar!"

*Understanding in this one's eyes? Clever, learning the language of the enemy. Which traitor to our people assisted him? Let him understand the cost of failure.*

He pointed three fingers at the head of one of the general's aides. Shadush savored the words of that dark ancient tongue as the power escaped through his hand and into the aide. A blood-curdling scream emanated from the man's lips as black flames licked out from inside his eyes, burning him from within.

The previously composed general blanched. "You monster!" he said in rough Scentari. "Perversion of Mij—" Kazash's fist smacked the back of his head.

The aide's torso blazed with black fire, his life force draining away from the charred husk of a body to flow unseen through the air into Shadush, filling him with power.

Shadush beckoned to his warrior, then pointed at the pyre. "Light this beacon for the new Scentar!" he cried out, and the warrior tossed the corpse onto the tower. The flames licked greedily across tent, equipment and bodies alike, rising into a terrible black inferno. The surge of energy into Shadush was like downing a full jug of fiery spirits. And he thirsted for more.

Shadush walked down the line of captives, and each jerk of his head toward the pyre committed another screaming and terrified man to the unholy flames. The ecstasy threatened to knock Shadush off his feet, and twice he almost fell, unnoticed, as all eyes were on the burning men.

Only the general and a young officer remained. *A tribune, in the Pazian tongue.* Shadush stopped in front of the quivering man.

*Weak. All of them.* "Name?" he said in Pazian.

The young man's head snapped up. "Tribune Persei Lokuta."

*Too much pride here. He would burn all the same.*

"Wait," said his daughter Mirasha, forestalling his order.

He acknowledged her with surprise. *Only sixteen, yet she never shies from the grim reality of conquest.* Dressed elegantly in fox furs, she strode like a queen through the staring Scentari leaders.

"Grand Thane!" she said, all eyes fixed on her. She evaluated the young Pazian officer with strange intensity before looking back to her father. "Keep him alive."

His warrior, grabbing Persei's quivering shoulders, looked to Shadush for instructions.

Even though she was his daughter, his favorite, she should not be challenging his orders in front of the men. Shadush gritted his teeth, the volatile mix of dark power and anger churning inside him. "Why?"

"They need to know of our power. He will do."

She walked to the fire and grabbed the end of a tent pole that now made a slender torch. She carried it to Persei. Shadush watched in silence, nodding at his daughter's leadership and foresight, but filled with foreboding. It was moments like this that reminded him of what he'd done. Of what had changed. What he'd forced himself to forget. He blinked away the memory, focusing on what she had in store for them.

She addressed the prisoner. "You have never been so scared, yet your eyes betray your own thirst for power. And more. Let me give you a taste." She licked her lips. The terrified tribune looked on, uncomprehending, but animal desire shone through in his eyes. Shadush wanted to throw him into the fire himself for his temerity, but deferred to his daughter's performance. He marveled at the crudity of such a man; even when faced with death, he was still thinking with his loins.

Mirasha tore open Persei's tunic and slowly traced the burning pole across his chest, leaving a cruel black mark. The man steeled himself against the pain, never looking away from his tormentor. Mirasha smiled at him again, now an enchanting young woman, then finished with a kiss on his cheek. She turned to her father. "Make him watch the general's death, then let him go."

Shadush saw the wisdom in her plan. He was proud. So precocious. And more beautiful by the day. The Pazian prisoner wasn't the only one who noticed. Even Kazash looked on her as a woman now. She was already starting to cause him worry.

He walked over to the general, and Kazash jerked his head up by the hair.

"So you see, general, that you got more than you bargained for when you trespassed in our homeland. No awards for you. You're just fodder for our fire, and my power."

"Your dark sorcery will damn you to destruction!" the general responded, spitting in his face.

Snarling, Shadush grabbed the bound general and tossed him into the center of the pyre. He sat for a while, watching him burn, the warmth of power pouring into him from the heat of the black flames.

Finally he turned back to the lone remaining Pazian. The fear was still there, but Shadush saw something more, something base. *She's right. This one thirsts for power, power such as I have.*

Shadush stepped forward to address him, knowing that none of his words would be understood. "You enjoyed our little show! Well that is enough for you. You have seen our power, and it only grows after consuming so many of your people. We have our homeland. Soon we will recover what you stole. Then we will come for more." He switched to broken Pazian for the last command. "Go, now, tell them what you saw."

He waved his hand, dismissing Persei to be lashed to of one of the Pazian horses. His man slapped the terrified beast on the rump to send it galloping up the winding path to the remaining Pazian camp.

Shadush motioned for Mirasha, Kazash and his warriors to follow him down the hill to the shore. As they crossed the waters, the rock itself began to smoke, and with a huge crack, it split asunder and the river flowed free once more.

ᎶᏋ᏶Ꮛ᏶Ꮛ᏶Ꮾ

Persei's head jostled painfully against his horse's galloping flank as it fled the evil scene. He couldn't believe he was still alive. But he wouldn't question why. That wasn't his nature.

No, he planned his revenge. Personal revenge. The deaths of generals, officers and soldiers he'd known for months registered with him, but were no longer his focus.

No pagan barbarians with their dark sorcery could do this to a son of the house of Lokuta. Not without suffering his wrath.

But the sorcerer's might left him impressed. *If I wielded such magic, the world would be mine.* The thought fueled his burning ambition. He would return, discover the source of their power, claim it as his own, and make them suffer.

All of them except the girl with those dark eyes; captivating, smoldering with an intensity that he yearned to explore. She looked young, but there was more than enough body there to provide nights of pleasure. He would find her, and he would take her as his prize. He didn't know who she was and he didn't understand anything she said, but he could tell she wanted him. *Didn't they all?* He smiled to himself. *That's why she kept me alive.*

He twisted against his bonds to try to get free, but instead was forced to bite his lip against the pain; his charred chest flared in agony with each galloping stride. She'd have to pay for what she had done to him. But in a very different way. His vivid imagination conjured thoughts of what he would make her do, stirring his loins to keep him warm on the cold ride back.

# IV
ᎾᏋᎾᏋᎾᏋᎾ
## *Retreat*

An aide poked his head through the flap of the command tent, interrupting Garas as he outlined potential next steps to Kyso and Simon.

"Sir! Tribune Lokuta is here, and you must see him right away."

Simon exchanged a look with Kyso. *Persei? But he was with the main force...*

"Send him in," said Garas. The aide saluted, and returned with the shocking form of Persei supported on his arm. He was stripped down to a torn and dirty tunic, his hair matted with sweat. But worst of all was his face: haunted, like a man who had seen too much death, or worse. After what Simon had witnessed that morning, he felt no satisfaction seeing the vain noble in such a state.

"Persei, you look terrible," Garas said "Sit down and share your news." He motioned him to one of the chairs as the others seated themselves, concern etched on their already tired faces.

"Do you have wine?" Persei asked, his voice a dry croak. "I need it, but so will you." Garas, who normally showed admirable restraint, went to a chest and produced a small jug of wine. He reached for the water jug to add to it. "Unwatered," Persei said.

"Simon watched the start of the battle from afar," Garas said, "but they rode back as soon as they saw the battle turning, to warn the rest of us. How did it happen, and how did you get away?"

Persei drank deep, getting some of his color back. "They let me leave. *He* did."

"Who?" Kyso asked, out of turn. "The sorcerer? Simon said there must be some kind of dark sorcerer with them, but there is no historical mention of the Scentari controlling such power, and their priests of Mija have long forbidden any meddling in the dark arts. They can work with natural fire, but what Simon described—the explosion—that is far beyond them. How could a sorcerer be at the forefront of their battle plans?"

"I only heard the explosion," Persei said. "But I saw the one who did it. Shadush is their sorcerer."

Simon gasped, and Kyso and Garas exchanged very worried glances.

"Can you be certain?" Garas asked.

"He started a pyre by burning Tribune Brellas from the inside out with those... black flames. I've never seen anything like it. The fire burned like any other, only hotter, and as black as night. Then they burned the rest of them."

"Why did they let you escape?" Simon asked. *It didn't make sense.*

Persei kept his eyes on Garas. "I think he wanted a witness. To his power."

"What about General Suboras?" Kyso asked.

"He was the last one thrown into the fire, and admirably defiant to the very end. A true Pazian nobleman." He raised his cup in a toast. "The Scentari are not looking for slaves, only revenge."

"What about the other survivors?" Simon asked.

"If any were taken, I didn't see them."

"None? So many lost..." Simon said.

"Over four thousand men," Kyso said. "But the strategy was sound!"

"In a normal world, yes," Persei said, "but not when the rules have changed. They waited for us to set up, and against any normal attack we would have destroyed them. The fog on the river did seem strange at first, but then it turned dark, more like smoke, and everyone started to feel a kind of creeping dread. But we never imagined they could topple our command tent! Dark magic, that's what it was. You would never believe it unless you were there."

"I saw," said Simon, nodding. "It was that same dark fire. Cracked the rocks right beneath—"

Persei cut him off, betraying irritation. "Then they were upon us, gathering up the entire general staff. They didn't have much fight in them, most being unarmed or unconscious after the violence of the blast. I had my sword, but my legs were trapped under a table. The whole thing was a trap."

Simon looked at Garas, who swore to himself. He had felt it from the beginning.

"So you never saw the rest of the battle?" Kyso asked. "I still can't believe that our men couldn't take most of the Scentari with them. We were set to receive the charge, and have our discipline."

"Discipline is overrated when you've just seen an act of the gods turn against you and remove your leaders. I don't think they broke and fled, but there was no way to escape, and they weren't prepared for riders to come flying over a bridge. When you feel it's impossible to be outflanked, it comes as quite a shock when there are riders instead of commanders at your back."

"Do you think they'll be riding after us tonight?" Simon asked.

"No. They're celebrating their victory and enjoying much of what we brought with us. And the burning... so much fire." His eyes closed and he withdraw inside himself, unwilling or unable to continue.

Garas was the one to break the grim silence. "Simon. Send word to the centurions. We move at first light. We don't know enough about the size of their force, but we can't stay here on their doorstep. Not with less than two thousand men. We must return to Pelusia. Kyso, send riders ahead of us to the frontier to the south to warn them of the possible attack. And send word to the men guarding the passes down to the valley. Have them ready to ride to us with warning the moment they see any of those barbarians coming up the trails."

Persei interrupted once more. "One more thing. I think he needs to burn things... people, with the dark fire, and that's where his power comes from. He may be more powerful than ever after... harvesting so many."

"I've seen a lot of things in my career, but this is far beyond me. I don't like it one bit. You have my orders, men, get to it. I want to be far away from here as fast as possible. Don't give them a chance to turn even greater power against our men."

"Yes, General Numeno," Kyso said, with the now appropriate salute. Simon started, and even Garas flinched with the truth of it.

Simon left the tent to deliver the orders. *None of us will sleep well tonight, or any other night until we're safe back in Pelusia.*

*The darkness surrounded Simon again, rising from the river and covering the army of screaming, dying brothers. Pain and horror contorted their faces. He was with them, but could only join in the screaming crescendo.*

*Now he stood on the bridge, looking into a wall of black fire—a wall with heads protruding: tribunes with their features melting away like wax and General Suboras' eyes burning with dark flame.*

*He had to run.*

*Up, up the trail to the top, but when he turned back he could see countless black fiery riders rising from the valley, coming closer and closer. Cold fire almost touching his skin.*

*Simon felt naked, powerless, falling down to the hard ground. He scraped his hands backward, trying to get away, but hit something. Solid wood. He raised his hand, brandishing it in the air. Colors, wondrous colors in a trail to the left and right, sweeping back and forth. Hope leaped into his heart with the warm light on his face... a sound...*

"Simon!"

He awoke to see Kyso standing over him, fully equipped for the march.

"Time to move!"

*The likeness is uncanny.* Simon held up his map to compare with the foliage. If anything, there was even more than he remembered, making it the perfect defense against their Scentari pursuers. The hardy low-lying bushes obscured both rocky outcroppings and gentle gravelly slopes. This made the going slow for the infantry, and treacherous even at a glacial pace for their remaining horses. Even the hardy Scentari mounts couldn't navigate this terrain at any kind of speed, which let Simon relax his guard. Or at least redirect it. That attention was better spent watching his next step. More than a few men were nursing turned ankles or cut feet from lapses in focus.

They had made good time from the camp to the scrubland, and it seemed that the Scentari had not expected this course of action. Kyso had worried aloud that a full mounted assault on their way could overwhelm them, but for the first time in days luck, or something, favored them. The scouts and engineers worked together to guide the wagons through, sparing them from carrying the rest of their supplies on their backs.

Small Scentari patrols had been shadowing them from a distance, but to press for a battle in this country would be somewhere between foolhardy and suicidal. And with little forage, a large Scentari force would be hard pressed to feed themselves, while the supplies for a full legion would feed their remnant force for a long time yet.

The scrub spread for many miles to the west, far into the Nahar Hills according to the only scouts who had been through the area. It meant a tough slog for the better part of the week, but they should be able to avoid combat.

It was more difficult to pitch a good camp, but despite that they felt more secure that night than they had in weeks. Simon sat in their makeshift command tent with Garas, Kyso and Persei, sketching out a new map of the hills from intelligence the scouts had given him.

"The hills should let us keep our advantage," said Kyso. "But where to next, General?"

Garas bristled, still not comfortable with the unasked command. "Simon, show me the maps." He pointed to the newly drawn hills, and swept to the south.

"They'll likely be expecting us to head directly to one of the fortified cities. In isolation, that might make sense, but isolation is not to our advantage. They can encircle us, and then use our roads to strike deep into the province, and beyond. But our Republic is our strength. We have forces in other provinces that could be summoned quickly. All we need is to send the word."

Now he drew his finger across the hills that continued all the way west to the coast. "If we stay in the hills, we neutralize both their horse and their knowledge of the area. With that relative safety we can continue west to the coast at the port city of Tamar. From there, I intend to send word by sea to Pazh, and the governors at Myrak, Bor, and the garrisons across Pelusia."

"Do you think they will follow us?" Simon asked. "Why wouldn't they turn east, and strike south through the plains into eastern Pelusia, as they did before?"

Garas looked grim. "Persei, what do you think? You were with them. Do you have any idea of their motivation?"

"Revenge, at least at first. They want their lands, and they want to humble the Pazian legions."

Kyso nodded. "In that case, they will surely strike east, to reclaim the lands they ceded to us by treaty. But what then?"

"That's the Senate's worry, not ours," Garas said.

"But aren't we charged to defend the cities? Jamad was burned to the ground, and with just the garrisons to defend them, more will fall. Many Pelusian and Pazian lives will be lost! We can't just abandon them."

"We help them by getting word to Pazh as quickly as we can," Garas said.

"The Senate is not easily moved," Kyso said. "Who will you send? They will need to know the full import of the situation if they are to act accordingly. Someone who speaks with some level of authority."

Garas nodded. "I cannot send you, I need you here." Kyso shifted slightly, relieved. Garas turned to Simon and Persei. "Authority does not come only from rank. In this case, the eyewitness accounts will be most powerful, and most important. Persei, Simon, I'll be sending both of you."

Persei's look somehow combined both pride and affront, while Simon stood numb with shock. A journey with Persei Lokuta all the way to address the Senate in Pazh? He was just starting to get comfortable working with Garas. The thought of facing the leaders of the Republic filled him with terror.

"Surely I should be able to address the Senate on my own," Persei said, making no effort to hide his scorn. "And I was there."

"Yes, but so was Simon. And he had a better view of the overall scene, and could draw them a better picture both of what we face, and of the lands around here. My decision is final, I'll be sending both of you. We'll reach the far side of these hills in a few days, and then it will be safe to send you riding ahead." He rolled up the map. "That will be all, you'd better get some rest."

Persei left without a further word or any gesture of respect. Kyso gave a slight bow and left for his quarters. Simon held back, and Garas nodded for him to speak.

"General? Couldn't Persei go on his own? I'm learning so much from you, and I know nothing of addressing politicians."

"Exactly. Persei was bred for this, and I don't trust the Lokuta to do anything but twist this to their advantage. In fact, I don't trust Persei at all. There are many in the Senate who would feel the same way about his family. Your account will be taken at face value, and will lend full weight to how dire the situation is now, and could become. This is no ordinary band of barbarians, as so many of our brothers have learned. And not only can you tell them, you can use your talent to show them." He pointed to the maps. "You'll have a lot of time on the return sea voyage. You draw well. Better than anyone I've ever seen. I want you to draw what you remember, of the battle, of the magic, and these lands. To show the Senate what really happened, and what they're facing."

That thought excited him, but the full implications were weighing on Simon's mind. Garas had been his anchor, and now he was cast adrift into raging waters that he could not navigate on his own.

"Simon, Pazh needs you. That is your duty. And I think you'll surprise yourself." His rare smile of encouragement calmed Simon a little, but as he bowed, he knew he would get little rest that night.

*Simon stood before the august fathers of the Senate. They were cold stone, like the marble columns that surrounded them, the Senate Hall a silent mausoleum. There was no life in this room, no hope.*

*A sound drew his gaze to the heavy doors—the ominous sound of darkness beating down the door. It seeped under, around, and into the hall.*

*He looked back to the seated men for help. Fear haunted most of the faces, frozen and powerless. A few looked on with delight, and matching darkness oozed forth from deep within them. Darkness, in the Senate?*

*"Do something!" he said.*

*His pleading gaze was met by a cowering multitude, and an enraptured few.*

*He threw up his hands to ward against the encroaching darkness.*

*A glint of light, a glimmer of hope sprang forth from his fingertips. A golden spark like candlelight. Color and life in this dead place.*

*I must act.*

Simon awoke to the first light of morning on his face.

"Ride with me Simon," Garas said as they crested another hill. The men and especially their feet were happy to reach the hills after the painfully slow scrub, and it had been days since they had seen even a Scentari scout.

While unsettled about the upcoming voyage, Simon welcomed the opportunity. *The name Baroba is moving up in the world after all.*

"I have been many years away from Pazh," Garas said, "but that doesn't mean I don't have allies of my own. Allies you will need. You aren't useful to Persei, and he doesn't like you. He doesn't like me either. Thinks we're both below him." He spat. "No Pazian citizen is below another, and the gods know I've spilled more blood for the Republic than most."

Garas pulled out a satchel, and opened it to reveal a number of letters stamped with his military seal.

"You'll need these. Letters of introduction, each with a name and address." He handed it to Simon.

"Numeno may not be one of the leading families, but I've served under many generals, and can call in a favor when I need it.

"First, Markus Sentollus. I served under him against the Gandari nomads in the south. A good man, and fair. He's only the second generation of his family in the Senate, and he grew up with people like us. Go to him as soon as you reach Pazh. He will make sure you are protected."

Simon's worry returned. "You don't think Persei would harm me, do you?"

Garas' mouth was a tight line. "I doubt it, but I wouldn't put it past his family. If they feel you could hinder their cause, which I believe you do, then you won't be safe until you've said your piece to the Senate. As I said, Markus will protect you.

"Next you'll need to see Lokas Lepilla."

"The great orator?" Simon's eyes went wide.

"The same. I served under his father Polas in the garrison of Egaras when he was governor. Lokas was there as an aide and asked many questions. I was happy to answer them and we forged a good bond. He will be our voice in the Senate.

"Third, is Genaro Morichea. He's a good general, and an even better friend. Still not quite done his prime, and my hope is Lokas can angle to send him as the new general. I want you to give him all the details personally, along with this letter. He needs to know firsthand what's going on."

"I still don't know if I'm up to this. I met a general for the first time only this month, and he's... I still can't believe he's dead."

"This wasn't your career plan, I know. You shared your aspirations, and you're young enough that you may yet live to see them. With your help, we're still alive to see another day. If you want to make a name for yourself, you'll need to move in the company of generals and orators. I'm happy just knowing the generals on the field myself, and I don't envy your tasks.

"But I think you can do it. And I need you to. My life, and the lives of the rest of our men hang in the balance. I will not desert Pelusia and her people. But you are our best chance." Garas placed his hand on Simon's shoulder, a rare physical display of reassurance, solidifying the fatherly dynamic growing between them.

"I won't let you down," Simon said, and they rode on in a comfortable silence.

Through the five days it took for the legion to cross through the hill country, Simon had barely seen Persei. Not a word had passed between them. Simon wasn't sure whether he was scheming or still stinging from being made to share the duty with a mere *mercati*. Either way, the excitement Simon felt for the coming trip was matched with an equal measure of foreboding. Garas didn't need to warn him that Persei would take any opportunity to prove his superiority, but had cautioned him not to let the barbs through to the bone. He must remain above reproach, to best serve the interests of Pazh, and for his own safety. An attack on a noble tribune could easily lead to court martial, or at the very least detainment while Persei faced the Senate alone. No, Simon would need to continue turning the other cheek.

The smell of salt on the breeze induced a sense of real relief mixed with the weight of duty, as Simon first experienced their proximity to the sea. That afternoon the two of them would ride ahead to Tamar, with two more scouts accompanying them.

It was Kyso who hailed him when the time had come. They rode together to the edge of the formation where Garas and Persei were waiting.

"I am honored to call you my fellow son of Pazh," Kyso said with his usual formality, clasping his arm in farewell. "Safe journey, and may the gods smile on you to see you true."

"And upon you," Simon said, with more warmth. "You are a credit to your family, and the Republic, Kyso. I will not fail you."

"For Pazh."

They approached Garas, who indicated two other riders.

"Simon, Rydar and Malem will ride with you to Tamar, then return to confirm that you have safely set sail for Pazh. They know this country better, and will show you true. Persei, I formally relieve you as Tribune of the 7th Legion, and charge you to lead this important mission. Work with Simon, and Salar will see you through. We will await further orders and reinforcements from Pazh." He nodded to Simon, the gruff career soldier in every facet except a slight hint of a smile at the corner of one eye.

"For Pazh!" Simon said, with a final salute that the others joined.

"Onward," Persei commanded, breaking his horse into a canter. Simon and the scouts matched his pace, and Rydar took the lead.

Simon looked back and nodded to Garas one more time as the others sped up to a full gallop. *I'll get you the help you need. It's the least I can do.*

# V

ᘒᘓᘒᘓᘒ

## *Creation*

Only Malem spoke to Simon during the first day's ride. Persei barely said a word to any of them, and Rydar, the silent Kawanian auxiliary, rode alone at the front of their group.

Malem was a typically tawny Pelusian, both in hair and skin tone, though less stocky—which made sense as a rider. The Pelusians in the infantry were a solid bunch. Malem's mother was from Tamar, and he'd been there many times to visit family. Since Simon had previously landed at the military port of Sal Pratta, he was curious to see a new city, and asked Malem what he knew.

Tamar was the commercial heart of the province of Pelusia, and famous for their red dyes, known as the "Blood of Tamar". The merchants prized peace and stability and were willing to pay the Pazian taxes to keep their trade routes open. Already prosperous, the city had seen a boom in the time since Pelusia became a full province. With a constant stream of ships to the large harbor, Malem said it should be easy to find swift passage to the west. Having grown up among the *mercati*, Simon was sure he would feel right at home in the bustling trading port, and felt a pang of disappointment at the likely shortness of their stay.

That night as they waited for Malem to ready the evening meal, Persei approached Simon with sword drawn, flexing his muscles, and challenged him to spar.

"Come on, Benjai! I know you'd love another go at me after I embarrassed you back in training." He turned to the others for

35

effect. "Though you wouldn't have wanted to see it. It was rather pathetic."

Simon didn't take the bait, and just stared into the fire. While Persei embellished their former duel, his swordsmanship did far surpass Simon's own. He'd gained more bruises than he cared to remember, from Persei and too many others in his training.

When no answer was forthcoming, Persei egged him on. "Or would you prefer we duel with your preferred weapon, the pen?"

This time he got the riders laughing with him. Persei was good at that kind of camaraderie when he wanted to be—usually at the expense of someone else. Simon fought the fire that burned inside him. *Give me strength, Garas.*

The second day Simon rode in silence through the more gently rolling coastal hills, with the others preferring Persei's company. Their well-traveled track fed into a straight Pazian road. After hill and scrub and treacherous pass, Simon appreciated the handiwork of his people. Wherever they settled, the Pazians upgraded the road system. Moving troops and trade goods at maximum speed was another national advantage.

They passed a steady stream of travelers, mostly fully laden wagons of the merchants who traded with the major commercial city. It might yet be Pelusia, but the feeling of being back home was very strong.

It was early evening when they reached the high stone walls of the city of Tamar. Archers trained arrows on them from above. Simon tensed, hoping some nervous young recruit didn't kill them by accident.

"I am a Tribune of Pazh," Persei called out to the guards at the gate.

The guard captain came out to meet them. "Sorry, Sir," he said. "We heard about what happened at Jamad. Can't be too careful. Please report to the garrison commander, he'll want news."

"I'll see him at the docks," said Persei. "The mission of a Tribune of Pazh waits for no mere garrison commander."

The captain sent a runner to pass on the curt message.

Once inside they merged with the throng of people going about their business on this main artery of the city. Two and three story buildings lined the street, with walls of plastered timber topped with thatched roofs—in sharp contrast to Pazh, where the poor lived in tall apartment complexes of brick and mortar, and the homes of the wealthy and the gods were stone and marble. *Different local supplies or just different levels of wealth?*

Shops at street level were busy selling every manner of food, drink and trade good. *Father would love this kind of traffic.* Little details like the fine cloth curtains revealed the upper story apartments housed successful merchants, rather than the urban poor like in Pazh.

Simon breathed deep the aroma of civilization, that mix of sweat, spices and sewage. Of home.

His smile was a magnet for Persei's scorn. "Safe at home, are we? Very like *your* people. Not fit to serve in the legions." Amazing how civilization brought back the contemptuous sneer that had been mostly absent since his mount had dragged him back from the battle.

Simon bowed his head and took on the expression of a mule.

Persei laid out the plan. "We head for the port first, and once we secure our passage, I plan to avail myself of the comforts of a civilized town for at least one night." Persei winked at a passing woman, who blushed. Stocky for the Pelusian men translated to buxom for the women. The two scouts flanked him, leering as they shared his laugh. They knew on which side to curry favor. Nobles over nobodies.

*Once again alone, surrounded by so many.*

The garrison commander was a tall, dark-haired Pazian with a long nose by the name of Karr Mykander. Simon wasn't sure why, but Karr went to great lengths to demonstrate his pedigree as a dutiful Pazian soldier and share his life story. He had married a local girl and settled here in Tamar, and risen up to his current post swiftly due to his skill, and his wife's father's connections. When Persei gave him their news, he blanched, likely considering how this easy post might put him on the wrong end of a Scentari scimitar if things took a turn for the worse. Persei once again took the opportunity to show off his rank and his lineage, snubbing Karr further by declining the inevitable dinner offer. The commander left with furrowed brow, setting his men on a more vigilant watch, and sending messengers to his counterparts in the cities to the east and south.

The port was even busier than advertised, with no shortage of options for ships departing for all corners of the Republic. On Malem's advice, they booked passage on the *Sunrise*, a fast merchantman setting sail the next afternoon. It would sail first to Attarsus in the Izar Archipelago, and after swapping their cargo would head on to the city of Pazh. *Back to my own bed in less than two weeks.*

At least he had an actual bed, in an inn for the night—a luxury after so many weeks in a legionary tent. Simon declined Malem's offer to join them for a night on the town, engendering a slur from Persei directed at his Benjish manhood, or the shortcomings thereof. Simon didn't mind some wine, but having seen the damaging effects of too much drink on his father's business and marriage, he was careful with his own consumption. He also wanted a clear mind for the journey the next day. And at least one part of him wanted to make sure he didn't get left in a ditch here in Tamar.

What he really wanted to focus on in the morning was getting a good supply of parchment, treated panels, paints and brushes. Drawings were good, but nothing less than his finest painting would do justice to the images burned into his brain of the battle and its aftermath, and the Senate needed to understand.

*When was the last time I painted? Years.* He had always loved the feel of a brush in his hand, and how he could work the colors together to create something beautiful and filled with emotion. At least, that's what he did in his mind, because any painting required in his father's shop was purely functional, and in his schooling they only ever allowed him to paint in the highly stylized and formulaic ways of the great masters. Oh how that frustrated him. There always seemed to be something wrong with the Pazian notion of art. He hadn't thought about it for many years, but now he recalled how he was almost expelled from his academy for daring to defy those imprisoning conventions. Every stroke circumscribed, every color combination dictated by the works of men from hundreds of years before. He always felt art should feel, and be a new act of creation. But the schoolmasters would have none of it, rejecting Simon's creative ideas, and charging his father to beat some sense into him. But that was a time when a beating would mean more presence than normal, with the wine jug his father's main companion.

His mother was the only one who ever appreciated his work,

but she cautioned him that he needed his education, and his father paid good money to make sure he received it. He mourned the loss of his early dreams. But those thoughts were soon buried beneath an increasing workload and noticing girls for the first time. It had been a long time since he'd thought of painting.

Until now. *My duty to the Republic calls on me to revisit this talent. They need to see this.*

That night, he went to sleep with anticipation he hadn't felt in years.

Rydar and Malem saw them off at the pier, following Garas' instructions to the letter. They boarded the *Sunrise* after the noon meal, with Captain Melchior welcoming them aboard. He owned the deep gold complexion of the province of Marutha, far south of Pelusia. A face well worn by years on the open sea, it looked to Simon as lined and creased as his maritime charts. This was no amateur, and that boded well for their journey across the capricious sea.

The ship was heavily laden with the Blood of Tamar and other goods, but the captain assured them that with the favorable winds this time of year, they would land at Attarsus by the fifth day.

Garas had sent a little extra coin to ensure Simon would have private quarters to work on his commission, away from the watchful eye and barbed tongue of Persei. Not that Persei would deign to bunk with him. Lokutan gold had secured him the use of the first mate's room for the duration of the voyage, something that had not earned him any points with the crew. But he'd already started to win them back with several amphorae of good wine he'd brought to share.

They set off in the afternoon, and Simon took the opportunity to watch their passage out from the protected harbor into the open water. This was only the second sea voyage of his life, with the last one on a cramped military galley. He savored the iridescent beauty of sunlight dancing on the cresting waves. The sea fascinated him with its mysterious depths. A calm washed over him as he basked in the reflected rays of endless possibilities.

"Benjai!" Persei's tone broke the sanctity of the moment. Simon met his cold stare. "It is time I made it clear how things will proceed. When we return to Pazh, I will meet my brother Daymar and he will call the Senate to order as quickly as possible. You will attend me, and I will speak for our mission. I will call upon you to recount what you saw from the pass at the time of the unfortunate attack, and that is all. No mention of my state when I returned to the camp. Do I make myself perfectly clear?"

Simon nodded. "May I give my regards to my father while you meet your brother?" Persei waved his hand, dismissing any possible importance of Simon's actions.

"He won't have time for you anyway, and you certainly are not welcome in our home. You should remain there so that I can send for you when our time has come to address the Senate."

Simon thought quickly. Garas needed him to meet his allies, but how to ensure Persei didn't somehow force the meeting without him? He had to meet Sentollus as quickly as possible to set their side in motion. The elder Lokuta would move swiftly.

"Of course, you can find me there." Simon cast his face down.

"You have learned some respect. I may have use for you yet, Benjai."

*I will never be your pawn.*

Persei clicked his heels and strode away.

*And you have no control over what I create. It is my own.*


Back in his cramped cabin, sunlight streaming through the small porthole, Simon set up his materials. That morning he'd found his way to a merchant who supplied the artisans working at a temple nearby, and was able to acquire the right pigments, charcoal, parchment, good hog's hair brushes, and several plaster panels. The market provided the eggs, oil and vinegar.

For as long as he could remember, Simon had possessed the ability to vividly recall an emotional scene. He had longed to use this talent for his art, but until this requisition from Garas, the situation never presented itself. Now, while he performed the laborious task of mixing his first batch of paint, he set the scene in his mind.

Sitting down, he let his eyes unfocus while the rays hit his face. The oaken panels of the cabin faded, replaced by the banks of the Sentusi and the Pazian legion deployed on the near bank. He gazed upon the rocky promontory at the river's edge where the banners flew above the command tent. The dread rolled in with the mist, followed by the deep-seated terror of the inky blackness. That was the moment: immediately after the explosion, with the dark flames at their peak, the chaos of the two fronts opening up, and the command tent being thrown into the river as the Scentari boiled over the spell-crafted bridge. His mind's eye captured the colors, the emotion, the action, and the danger. *Now to transfer this to the surface.* He decided one panel would be too cramped, and only a triptych would provide the required panoramic view.

He always started with a rough sketch to capture the perspective, and in his hand the charcoal leapt to life, forming lines on the parchment effortlessly. Oh, it felt good to create. In a very short time his plan was ready. He grasped the first of his brushes. It just felt right, like an extension of his body. He daubed it in black paint and began filling in the darkness. When he studied the works of the great Izari masters, he gravitated to those who built up from a base of color. Start with the darkest parts, and build up to the light. It sounded like something out of Benjish scripture. *We start as blank, are painted with the darkness of the sins of our forefathers, and must every day strive again for the light. I don't suppose the elders would appreciate my mixing of the arts and their faith. Or maybe they would?*

The darks in the river, the cliffs, and the areas where the soldiers would later appear were easy, and natural. It flowed as it had for any painting he'd ever worked on. He was bringing his memory to life, with no regard for the conventions and strictures of the classical style. This would be a work that the masters would cast into the fire, and that spurred him on with the zeal of a heretic.

As he moved his hand to bring forth the darkness of the evil sorcerous flames, the work took on a life of its own, and he felt the cold hands of fear close upon his limbs, raising goosebumps wherever they touched. The air grew thicker, and the sensation of being watched pricked his back, to the point where he checked to confirm that he was indeed alone in the cabin. There was a power to the darkness, an evil power even in his memory, and especially in this painting. And he had only just begun.

It was unlike anything he had ever experienced, this exhilarating connection to his work. It banished the cold, and drove him forward. Grays and browns built up the next coat. The paints dried quickly, which allowed him to build layer upon layer with little pause. Stroke by stroke, the colors melted together, his memory forming on the page. His whole body tingled, as if waking after a long sleep. More alive than ever, he worked until the light began to dim, and the dinner hour arrived. As he looked down to survey his

work, he felt a satisfaction that had proven so elusive in his life.
*This is the moment I was made for, and this is exactly where I should be.*

On each of the following days he started his morning by clearing his mind with the sea breeze and the low sun on the water, and after breaking his fast would spend most of the daylight hours at work in his room.

He was proud of how he captured the chaos, the tension, the emotion. But each time he returned to look, he was slowly, inexorably drawn to the horror of the darkness splitting the rock, and the command tent lurching into the mist-covered river. There was not just power in the scene, but the power to move the Senate.

A knock at his cabin door interrupted his detail work on the legionaries. It was the first mate.

"Baroba, we will be sailing into Attarsus in the next hour, and the captain thought you might want to watch the approach." And he was right.

# VI

## ᏩᎬᏚᎬᏚᎬᏩ

## *Elysia*

$A$ttarsus was one of the great city states of the Izar Archipelago, but more famous for the arts and trade than for philosophy. Simon grew up dreaming about exploring the city. *Funny how dreams were becoming a reality of late.* The thought struck him like a note out of tune, and left him unsettled.

The mate told him they were arriving too late in the day to conduct their business, but should be ready to push off by noon the following day. Not much time for exploration, but Simon meant to make the best of it.

A busy port, steady ship traffic moved in both directions as they approached. The city was, as the Izari preferred, built around a central hill reserved for their temple complex. In the waning sun the temples shimmered as if covered in molten gold, surrounded by the sea of orange-red tiled roofs of the houses below. Simon imagined the hands that could create such a wonder. Hands such as those could almost bring gods to life, not just pay homage to them.

Persei was off the ship quickly, eager to sample the local pleasures of another port of call. Simon headed instead for a good vantage point of the temple complex, having decided that it deserved at least a good sketch, if not a future painting. *It's amazing how once you start to paint, every scene becomes one you'd like to capture.* While sailing in to port he had noticed the large open space of the agora, a short walk away from the waterfront, which looked to offer a good angle of the hill and its splendor. He gathered his drawing tools and sped out before the light faded.

He passed Attarsan people dressed in variations of the styles one would see in any Pazian city, men in simple tunic or toga, and women in longer tunics or dresses. There were more beards and hats for the men and most of the women covered their hair. And any conversations Simon heard on the way were totally unintelligible, with the Izari language completely unrelated to Pazian.

At least a quarter of the people in the streets were ethnic Pazians, which he imagined had quite an influence on fashion, but hoped that the other arts were allowed to flourish. And he spotted far more people from other provinces and beyond than had been present in Tamar. The Izar Archipelago sat at the center of most of the major trade routes and had been dealing with every nation since before Pazh was founded, while Tamar was an upstart off in one corner of the trading world.

Much of the architecture was familiar, featuring the same kind of mud-brick construction popular in Pazh, with a lot of columns and arches and the beautiful functionality of fiery terracotta roofs. Height was the main difference: other than the temples, none of the buildings had even a third story. If there was height to Attarsus, it came from the contours of the land, not the construction.

He remembered from school that architecture was another area where Pazh borrowed heavily, if not outright copied the Izari styles. That fact had passed by him much as any other he was made to memorize in his classes, but now it prompted a deeper thought: *did Pazh create anything new? Art, music, poetry, architecture... all endless copies of the Izari originals, with only minor refinements. Has our Republic lost its ability to create? Were we too busy trading, administrating and warring to have time for these more aesthetic pursuits? Or did it leave us without a true appreciation of the arts? Them, not us, because I believe we're still capable.*

The market stalls had almost completely cleared out for the day, leaving the agora much emptier than it would be through most of the daylight hours. There were still men gathered in discussion along the main colonnade, a few pedlars trying to make some extra coin, and a handful of people buying. A young couple walked by, hand in hand, and a youth chased a dog.

Simon checked the view of the temple complex, judged it satisfactory, and sat down on the ground to begin his sketch. Most people gave him a cursory glance, but didn't find him interesting enough to approach, not even the pedlars. He sketched away in happy silence bathed in the muted gold early evening light.

After completing the lines for the base and a few of the temples, he sensed a figure pass through the corner of his vision, then stop. Someone was watching him.

He turned slowly, alert but not feeling any danger. A young woman stood several paces behind him with her head cocked to the side to better see his drawing. Dark hair danced freely in waves around her smooth cheeks before spilling upon bare shoulders, not tied up in the prevailing fashion. Her long linen tunic was more typical, clasped at the shoulders but slightly off-center, hanging awkwardly. A light powder dusted the material on her chest in several places, which drew his gaze to note the hint of curves below.

She didn't seem to notice, totally oblivious to both his look and her disheveled state. Her lips were drawn together in concentration, evidently judging his work from afar, with a hint of a smirk at the corner.

Meeting his gaze, her dark eyes sparkled with a playful light. With a raised eyebrow she shot him a questioning smile, punctuated with the most endearing dimple on her right cheek. The smile lit up her face—a striking transformation. He found himself smiling back.

"Battle plans?" she asked, stepping toward him.

Bewildered, he almost dropped his charcoal as he stood up, then remembered his drawing.

"No, just admiring your, uh... beautiful temples," he said.

"So are you a soldier, or an artist?" She was close enough now that he could smell her scent. It was familiar, delicious... like fresh-baked bread?

"Soldier?" he said, before looking down at his military cloak and understanding. He hadn't been dressed in full armor while sailing, having heard tales of how quickly you'd drown if thrown overboard. Instead he wore his standard issue legionary cloak over his ordinary tunic. "Right. I guess you could say a bit of both, but I certainly prefer the visual arts to the military." He smiled again. "And you?"

"An artist? Yes. But not drawing. I do appreciate it, though. You speak Pazian like a native, but you're..." She gestured toward his arm.

The bronze of his skin made hers look so pale by comparison.

"Lived there all my life. Pazian on my father's side. But my mother was Benjish."

She cocked her head sideways again, this time inspecting him. Her attention was unsettling, like he was a piece of art, rather than a man. "I can see the Pazian in the nose." She pointed to the drawing again. "Can I see that a little closer?"

"I don't think I have much of a choice here, do I?"

She received it with her full attention, absorbed in her scrutiny of his work. Without meaning to, Simon took in the rest of her form. She was slender, and a head and a half shorter than him, but held herself straight. He'd initially thought she was older, but with a closer look at her features realized she was about his age. Something about the Izari style was so graceful, even askew, and accentuated those curves. He flushed when she spoke again.

"You show some skill here. And not stuck on the usual conventions. I like that." He felt himself blush, and she laughed. "Not used to the compliment?"

"No, actually. It's been a long time since I've been able to draw, or paint. Though I've recently taken it up again."

"I'd love to see more of your work." He felt himself frown, and she answered before he could speak. "You're not staying long, are you? On your way to battle?" It was like she could read his face somehow.

"Heading home. We're on our way back to Pazh from battle on the frontier." He stopped himself from saying more, although it felt natural to tell her. Share his burden? There was something so intriguing about her... more than just her physical appearance. "If the ship is finished its business in the morning, then we leave tomorrow afternoon."

"That doesn't leave much time. When can I see your work?" She looked right into his eyes, like she was searching for something deep inside him. It aroused his curiosity.

"Yes, uh, I... I've always wanted to come to Izar to learn more about your arts. I'd like to come back when I can, after my mission is complete." Why was she so easy to open up to? He shouldn't be sharing this.

"Mission?"

"I don't even know your name. I'm Simon, Simon Baroba."

"You can call me Elysia." She turned, as if to go.

"Could I see your work?" he asked, trying to prolong the encounter. She glanced back, the smile dancing in her eyes for a moment, then hidden away in that serious appraising look.

"A man comes in from the sea, and is only staying the night. How can I be sure of his intentions?"

"I apologize, I didn't mean…"

Her laugh was like a bell ringing the tension away. "No, you're much more of a hopeless romantic. I can see that from your drawing, how the temples look how you wish they could be. Come with me, I would like to show you something."

Elysia waited with mock impatience for him to put his things away, then walked lightly in the opposite direction of the ship. He kept pace with her, stealing a glance every few moments as they walked. She looked straight ahead.

"Where are we going?"

"You'll see."


After leaving the agora, they walked down the main waterfront street for a few blocks before turning to one of the side streets. With each turn the light faded further in the deepening dusk. A thousand thoughts buzzed around the back of Simon's mind, but mostly muted and blurred by the warm hazy feeling of connection. Whoever this Elysia was, he wanted to know more. He couldn't figure out why she smelled like a bakery, but each time he caught a whiff his stomach reminded him that it was empty. *Maybe I should have bothered the remaining pedlars, after all.*

A flight of steps took them to a lower part of the town, through narrow twisting roads lined with two-story apartments. After the open sea and the plains of Scentar, the alleys were almost suffocating. She turned into one beside what appeared to be a bakery. Producing a key, she opened an unadorned door and lit an oil lamp inside to illuminate a set of stairs. With the smile of a co-conspirator, she led Simon down.

He had to stoop slightly to avoid bumping his head in the basement. The lamplight revealed a forest of shrouded shapes. His mind screamed warning, and his hand went reflexively to where his sword would be, but instead found the satchel with his charcoal. Not much good in a fight.

She hung the lamp from a hook on the wall.

"Are you ready?" she said, with a hint of excitement, and for the first time looked a little unsure of herself. He nodded, wondering what was to come. She walked over to the largest shape, an irregular mound taller than Simon, and whisked away the linen shroud with a grand flourish. A cloud of dust puffed into the air, and through the haze, the flickering light revealed a perfect white stallion, except that it wasn't just a horse. Wings grew out from the shoulders on the forelegs. The noble face looked straight at him.

Did his eyes betray him? Was the gorgeous creature swaying slightly? Or was it the light? But it had no smell. The smell of horses was something he had become all too familiar with in the recent months. Then it dawned on him, and his mouth opened in wonder.

"This is your work? A statue?" He looked at her, asking permission as he reached out his hand to touch the majestic animal. She nodded, at once shy and proud.

He stroked the mane, and felt the coolness of the marble. The detail and the texture were remarkable. A true original, no pale imitation of the great masters of the past. It was worthy of them, except she'd imbued it with even more feeling. His heart leaped, reaching out for that connection.

"It's exquisite. You're... amazing," he said, his eyes meeting hers again in the flickering lamplight. "Did you do this all yourself? All these are yours?"

She nodded, beaming.

"Do you have a teacher? Why is this hidden?"

"So many questions, Simon." She returned the shroud and picked up the lamp, then walked to the door.

"But I'd like to see more... of you." He whispered the final word, before catching himself.

She didn't turn back. "Then first, I'd like to see more of your work."

Panicked thoughts rushed through his head. *Who is she, really? My work? But I can't! My mission? I need to keep this a secret. What if she is a spy? Or working for the Lokuta?*

By now she had reached the steps, and the light was moving with her. He hurried to catch up, careful not to crash into any of the mysterious shapes around him. With the light receding, they looked like dark guardians of the space.

They ascended in silence, and she locked the door at the top without looking at him.

*Is this a test? Trading her secret for mine? But this is also real work, mine was just a mediocre scribble by comparison. What if my greatest work falls short of her expectations? But she did like my sketch, enough to show me here. She has to like something. This connection, artist to artist, and one who can create such wonder. I can't let her get away. Can't let these moments escape in silence. But can I really trust her?* Gnawing doubt coursed through him. Or was that hunger? It had been many hours since his noon meal, and here he was in a strange city with this striking sculptress, with no idea where to find food.

"First, some dinner?" he asked.

"And then you'll show me your work?"

He sighed. "Yes."

She smiled again and his heart stirred.

"Wait here." She walked to the front of the bakery, and knocked quietly. A minute later a light approached the front, the door opened, and she ducked inside. She returned with a wicker basket, and covered by a cloak of her own. He shivered at the late autumn cool, present even here in Attarsus. He'd take it over the cold of the steppe, now half a world away.

As they walked to a destination only she knew, he was the first to break the silence. "Do you work there, the bakery?"

"When Father needs me to."

"He's the baker? Actually, I can relate, my father is a merchant as well."

She stopped and looked at him, her eyes earnest. "Does he appreciate your painting?"

Simon spent a few moments in pained silence. "No. He never has. His appreciation of the arts starts and ends with vintages." He shot her a rueful smile, and she touched his hand in sympathy. The unexpected contact made his heart leap. "My mother always liked them, but couldn't encourage me when I ran into challenges at school."

She withdrew the hand, her eyes looking down.

"My mother had no interest. She was Pazian after all. Father was the one who found me the tools and space to work. It's everything to him." She wiped away a sudden tear. "He's my inspiration. I do my work to bring the beauty and emotion of our world back to him. He's never been the same since my mother died."

"I'm sorry." Now it was his turn to reach out to touch her, to capture that electric feeling again. She didn't flinch. "That's so inspiring, having someone to appreciate your work. I wish my mother could see what I'm working on. We laid her to rest three years ago."

"I'm so sorry."

They resumed the walk in silence. It still hurt. His mother had been a moderating influence on his father when he was drunk, and good for his business as a result. Without her, he had been floundering in every way, not least of which in his relationship with Simon. They barely spoke, and when they did, it generally turned angry. Neither had really dealt with the loss. *But maybe she could relate, could understand?*

Soon they reached a small public park on the edge of the water. The sight of the sea brought him a measure of peace.

"Simon, would you care to join me for dinner?" Elysia asked, beckoning to some rocks by the shore.

"I would love to."

"It's not much, but hopefully better than what you've been eating on the ship, or on the march." She produced savory Izari flatbread, olives, watered wine and a tangy ivory spread he didn't recognize. Simple, but the freshest meal he'd eaten in months.

"It's wonderful, thank you. My compliments to the baker." He paused, then with a quizzical look asked, "Doesn't your father worry about his daughter dining with strange soldiers late at night?"

She laughed, the sound like sweet nectar to his ears, and his heart.

"Not unless *I'm* worried." Her expression turned melancholy. "My mother's dying wish was for me to find a man to take care of me. It infuriated her that I never showed any interest."

"Well in that case, I am very honored," he said with a slight bow. It earned him a scowl and an olive flicked against his forehead.

Taken aback, he rubbed away the juice and started to apologize, when her stern expression collapsed again into an impish grin, and she laughed again.

"You have *some* talent. Let's leave it at potential. Which is far more than most. But you still haven't shown me your *real* work."

Whether it was her charm, beauty, talent, wine or a combination of them all, his inhibitions had melted away.

"It's for a mission," he said as seriously as he could. "For my legion."

"What are you, the General's Sketch Artist?"

"Yes, and in this case painter as well. And my work is to be shown to the august fathers of the Senate. Can you believe it?"

She appeared more curious than awed by the thought of his work being destined for the most powerful group of men in the world. "But why? What could be so important?"

He recounted the story, and she listened, rapt, until he came to the explosion of the dark flames. She sat bolt upright, her whole body tense and brown eyes piercing.

"Dark flames? You're certain?" He nodded. "Simon, you have to be sure. It was not some trick of the light? *Black* flames?"

"That's what I saw—I was the only one of our group who saw it in the battle, but Persei, the one I'm traveling with, he saw the Scentari grand thane call the dark fire."

She was shaking. "You must tell Master Xelos."

"Who? Why? You've heard of such a thing?" Had he said too much? "General Numeno would be angry that I've told you, I really shouldn't speak of this with anyone else. Not until after I report to the Senate."

"This is what you're reporting to the Senate? Why do they want you to paint it?"

"Garas... General Numeno, sent both of us. He doesn't trust Persei, so he believes that if I paint the scene, it will better capture the emotion and the threat. Then the Senate will take it more seriously."

"Master Xelos, we must see him. But he's not back until tomorrow night. This is very important."

"But I will already be on my way to Pazh. Who is this Master Xelos, and why is it so important?"

She was silent for a while, then in a small voice said: "I need to see the painting first."

"Before you can tell me? Elysia, this doesn't make any sense. I've told you far more about my secret military mission than I have any right to, and I just met you. And you can't tell me who this man is and why he needs to know?"

Crestfallen and shaking her head, she suddenly looked much younger. The transformation from the confident young woman who had so enthralled him was disheartening. Whatever the reason, this was very important to her.

Her reply came as barely a whisper. "I'm sorry Simon, I must see your painting first."

His mind was racing. He wanted to show her. He had to show her. To get some answers. And out of... pride. This artistic connection, with a fellow creator. Only she could really appreciate his work. And maybe it would... impress her. But her urgency resonated in his gut. There was something important here, and he needed to understand it.

"It's too late tonight, it will raise too many questions if I go back on board when they think I'm in... a cozy inn somewhere. And if I came back out again carrying my work... too many questions. No, tonight won't work. But I could go back for the night and come meet you in the morning?" It was the right thing to do, though he wished she would share what she knew right now, especially when he had to leave the city tomorrow afternoon. He felt drawn to her, to learn more about her art, and what she knew about this magic, and...

"Thank you for understanding, it means a lot to me." She grasped his hand and squeezed it, and in that moment he felt peace. How quickly she regained her former decisive bearing. "You should go. I'll walk you back as far as the agora, and you can meet me there when the market opens. I have to help Father first, or I would come at dawn. I'll find you in the same spot where you were sketching."

He began to protest, but she was right. Instead he nodded, and helped her to her feet. Every touch begged for another moment together, and her scent mixed with the gentle sea breeze made him feel like he was on the verge of swooning.

"But be careful not to approach the bread stall at the north end, unless you'd like to meet my brother Alexander. I'd rather you didn't at this point. He doesn't approve of much of anything I do."

"I've always wondered what it would be like to have a brother."

"You can have him. He'd rather I was married off so Father would stop doting on me. Spoiling me by encouraging my carving. But I think there's more to life than just being the wife of some minor merchant."

The life he left behind.

"What do you want to do?" he asked.

Her eyes shone in the reflected moonlight. "Simon, have you been to the temples on the acropolis?"

He shook his head.

"The sculptures there, what the masters created hundreds of

years ago. They're beyond anything that people carve today. So much is possible!"

She picked up a rock and held it up.

"Alexander says I should spend more time accepting what is in front of me, instead of dreaming about what could be. But it's not a dream. I pick up a piece of stone and I see what's inside, and I take away everything else to let it out. I can't help it if others can't see it."

She was so alive, so passionate, drawing Simon into her perspective of the world.

"That's incredible. Is there something in... in that rock?"

She squinted, her brows drawn together in concentration. Simon leaned in, and she burst out laughing.

"No, it's just a rock." She tossed it into the sea.

"I... my art works a little differently," Simon said. "I have to capture it from what I can see in the moment, or what I remember or can imagine. But the joy when I get it just right—"

"Exactly! I could spend all day on the finest little details, just to get them exactly right. But when I do, it's the greatest feeling in the world. It's almost like—" She cut herself off and was serious again. Distant, like she'd taken a step back emotionally.

"Like what?"

"I'll... just wait until after I see your painting tomorrow."

What was it she kept approaching, but pulling back from? He could hardly stand not knowing. But he let it drop.

The rest of the leisurely seaside walk was spent in conversation about family, their fathers' businesses, and Elysia pointing out local landmarks or peculiarities. Simon was careful to avoid anything to do with Xelos or either of their art, preferring to wait until he passed what he felt was the looming test in the morning. Conversation was so easy and natural. He had always been nervous around girls he found attractive, never like this.

When they reached the agora, he turned to her.

"Elysia?" He paused. *I've never met anyone like you before.*

"What?" Her expression was earnest.

"I look forward to seeing you again."

"Good. So you'll be sure to meet me again tomorrow. As long as you bring your work. And remember, avoid my brother!" One more smile, and she turned to leave before he could reply.

"Until tomorrow," he whispered, watching her as she walked

off into the shadows. Who was this girl? *Mercati* like him, and a mix of Pazian and more Izari by far than he was Benjish. Someone he could share his thoughts and words with. And maybe more? *Fortune, are you smiling with me, or laughing at me? To cast this incredible woman into my life, but only for a day.*

Without the warmth of her proximity, the damp autumn cool crept in. Pulling his cloak a little tighter, he made for the ship, alone once more.

# VII
## ୧ଓଓଓଓଓ
## *Talent*

Simon set out as the sun rose the next morning. His pack was heavier this time, laden with all three panels of his work. He left his cloak behind, wearing merely a simple homespun tunic. Something told him that he wouldn't want to appear the Pazian soldier today.

"Looks like we've made you quite the sailor," said Jawad, one of the crew members, as Simon was crossing to the pier.

"The sea is a jealous mistress. I decided I couldn't sleep without *her* gentle caress."

"If you need help, let me point you in the right direction for a good stroke in the city. There's still time!" Jawad laughed at his joke, and Simon shook his head with a slightly embarrassed smile as he waved him off.

"Maybe next time."

Mytar on the evening watch had also chided him for his lack of success with the ladies, when he returned so late. *Rather they question my skill with women than what I'm actually doing, lest Persei get their tongues wagging.*

"Be back by noon, we should be ready soon after," Jawad said. Simon nodded and went on his way.

It took all his self-control to keep an ordinary pace as he left the pier and headed for the agora. He had barely slept, he was so excited and anxious about Elysia viewing his work. And judging it. Only once had his work ever been on display to be judged, and he shuddered as the memory surfaced, replaying itself in his mind.

He was twelve, and there was a contest at his school. He hadn't yet submitted to playing by the rules. Willful, yet ignorant, he had worked on his piece in secret. They were expected to copy one of the scenes of the gods, and most chose from one of the ubiquitous friezes in the temple complex that housed the school. His chosen scene showed Meliax, king of the gods, forced by his wife Harina to cast away his latest dalliance, a girl named Metria, with the goddess turning her into a tree. The scene they expected was in the classic style, balanced and proportioned, but the centuries had drained away any feeling in the original work.

Simon's treatment was raw, with a weeping Meliax, a raging Harina, and Metria's look of terror as her feet transformed into roots drilling into the ground. His colors were vibrant and daring, his brush-strokes conveying the movement of the transformation. There was passion, life, and a kind of raw power to it. A piece of him had come to life in the picture; he'd never been more proud.

On the day of the contest, each student brought their piece to the section of the temple that housed the original, to unveil it before Headmaster Corellus, the teachers and the other students. Piece after piece was revealed to be somewhere on the continuum from crude, lifeless imitation to a soullessly perfect match, while the masters made comments. Praise was scarce, criticism bountiful. One of the better students, Tyron, son of a wealthy slave dealer, was the assumed leader as they came to the last few pieces, Simon's among them. Simon had no time for Tyron's talent as an artist. He was an exemplary copyist, but had never formed an original idea in his life.

Simon was excited, sure that his inspiration would overwhelm them to claim the prize. Not just the wreath of victory, but a new set of expensive Izari brushes to keep. He had done his best with the worn school supplies, and imagined new heights his artistry would reach with better tools.

The masters assembled before his piece.

"Interesting choice," muttered Master Granus, an accomplished copyist himself. "A challenging scene." He nodded to Simon, giving him his cue.

With a showman's flourish, Simon whisked the shroud from the painting and stood before them, beaming with youthful pride.

The masters gasped in unison. His fellow students were stunned to silence. Simon's pride turned to bewilderment, tinged with fear as purple mottled the face of Corellus.

"You dare mock us?" the headmaster said. "Meliax himself will strike you down for your impertinence!" Apoplectic, he charged forward to grab the panel in one hand, Simon with the other. He shoved his student roughly forward. Simon slumped down, numb, as the walls of his world crashed down. Corellus' voice regained some of its composure, resuming its customary hectoring tone. "Let this be a lesson to you all! None of you are fit to consider yourselves among the great masters. We can only walk in their shadows. They have shown us the way to perfection in the arts, and the best we can do is a pale imitation of their glory. Yet this... this young peacock deigns to put himself above them. Peacock, are the works of the masters so beneath you that you feel compelled to improve them in your own way?"

Simon's tongue hung dead in his mouth.

"You think this is beauty? You consider this art? This is deviant, and worthless." Corellus broke the panel across Simon's back, eliciting a whimpering gasp as he slumped to his knees with the force. The greater pain stabbed at his heart, leaving a void.

"Get up, peacock," Corellus commanded. "Marcinus, a lamp." The teacher handed the lamp to Simon. "Burn your abomination. Absolve yourself of your transgression."

Simon could not even feel the warmth as he poured burning oil from the lamp onto the panel, crackling flames devouring his masterpiece. A part of his spirit died that day, with his dreams going up in the acrid smoke.

Was this spirit now reborn? Or had it merely been dormant, forced into a dark place in the corner of his heart where not even he could recollect it? Somehow this commission had brought it new life, and Elysia was fanning the flames of hope. Except this time he was not nearly so confident in the outcome.

The agora looked completely different buzzing with morning business, with all manner of foods, spices and crafts available for purchase. The Izar Archipelago was perfectly situated in the middle of the Near Sea, and trade had enriched these shores for a thousand years, long before joining the Republic.

Simon picked up some honeyed bread, figuring Elysia would have eaten before coming, and he didn't want to waste any of his brief time with her. When he passed a woman selling flowers and considered buying some, swirling mixed emotions stayed his hand.

He wasn't just nervous about her judgment of his work. His rational mind was worried about her level of familiarity with the dark magic. What if she or this Xelos were practitioners of these dark arts? Such magic was officially outlawed throughout the Republic, barely more than rumor for the past half-millennium. For hundreds of years, many had been imprisoned based merely on suspicion of pursuing that path, or put to the pyre when confirmed. There hadn't been an execution in his father's lifetime, but vivid stories were passed along and no child of Pazh would ever want to even think about the dark arts. And the priests of Salar railed against the pernicious effects of exploring such power, warning that it consumed the user's years, aging and damaging their body.

But what of these formerly foreign provinces, with their own people and traditions? Could they be continuing those practices in secret? No part of his heart felt Elysia could have anything to do with such perversion, but his head couldn't fully dismiss the possibility. But even then, what was the danger? She couldn't possibly be in league with the Scentari. Could she? As hungry as he was, the sweetness of the honey was lost on him as these conflicting thoughts churned within him. *No, flowers can wait.*

It was difficult to work back from the sightline of the temples to find the same spot where he had been sketching, while dodging people in the far busier public space. It took all his focus and recollection to finally get it right. In the cool morning light the marble offerings to the co-opted Izari-Pazian gods looked solemn and watchful, but still beautiful. He was framing the scene for another potential picture when he felt someone brush against his shoulder.

He could scarcely recognize Elysia, if not for the same striking eyes smiling back within a serious face. Gone was the slightly wild and disheveled look of the night before. She looked the part of a young Pazian lady. Her braided hair was pinned up in a circle around her head in the current fashion, with a curl playfully escaping down each side of her face and a shawl partially covering it all. She wore a simple flowing dress clasped at the shoulders and cinched at a high waist with a cord. The outfit wrong-footed him, and he stumbled to keep up with her when she walked away. Between her different garb and a night spent alone with his thoughts, the sense of connection had faded like an elusive dream after a sudden awakening. He followed her at a reasonable distance as he jostled people in the thickening market crowd, keeping an eye out for anyone selling bread who just might be her brother.

When he left the agora and reached an ordinary street, his heart pounded as he lost sight of her rounding a bend. Near panic, he rushed to the spot where she'd disappeared from view and passed the two story shop, but she was still nowhere to be seen.

His eyes jumped from figure to figure like a fly evading a striking hand.

A mother with two daughters.

Two togate men.

A boy playing with a dog.

An elderly couple.

Had his eyes failed him? Did she turn another way?

A flash of sunlight from the metal sign on a closing door spurred him forward. The moments rushed by as he closed the gap and looked upon the sign, written in the indecipherable Izari script. He felt for the handle and pulled, but the lock withstood him. Momentarily defeated, he threw up his hands and turned back. And across the street in a similar doorway stood Elysia, biting her lip to suppress a smile. Relief washed over him, and his excitement built as he crossed to her.

"You would make a horrible spy," she said.

"Let's hope I never have to play the role. You make quite the fetching noblewoman," he said and smiled.

She shifted uncomfortably, frowning. "Really? You like it? It's not very practical for my work. It gets all dusty. Don't get used to it. I don't like dressing up. I told Father I'm going to visit Xelos and had to look the part."

"So that's where we're going? I thought you said he wasn't back?"

"No, his workshop. Where we can see your work, without any nosy eyes. Most people have nothing better to do than gossip and go out of their way to look for it."

"Lead on, milady," he said with a bow, offering his hand. She rolled her eyes but accepted it, pulling him onward along the street. Though her fingers were graceful and elegant, her grip was surprisingly strong. His heart fluttered at the renewed connection as he kept up with her brisk pace.

This time they headed in a different direction, leading up to a higher part of town. There were no apartments here, only large dwellings, with facades and entrances that were progressively more ornate in their decoration. Unease set in, as Simon was not used to such wealthy surroundings. He felt under-dressed in his simple tunic.

"Don't worry, nobody will judge you," she said, reading his expression.

"But don't you think I'll look out of place?"

"Simon, you already do." She held up his much darker hand. "You don't look at all Izari. Pazians are pretty accepting of people no matter where they're from, but unfortunately my people are a little less open minded. But luckily Xelos' servants come from all over, and you're dressed well enough to fit in with that crowd. He treats his servants well, and doesn't have slaves."

"Is he some Izari version of a *digniti*?"

"We don't have those official classes here, but I think he'd be more of a *suprati*? He's quite wealthy but made most of it himself. He has a company of stone carvers—he's the retired master tradesman—and a bunch of other businesses that he doesn't really talk about. He treats me as the daughter he always wished he had, and lets me use his studio. His steward will let us in."

Simon was more nervous now. "But won't they think it's unusual that I'm accompanying you? Are you in the habit of bringing strange men over here?"

She released his hand and glared at him.

"Of course not! In fact, I've never brought a friend, but… well I'll explain afterward. I'll leave a message for him, because he needs to know about you."

*Enough with these cryptic answers.* At least judgment was close at hand.

They walked in silence, slightly apart for a few more blocks before she approached a majestic set of double doors. Simon stopped, his mouth agape. While most of the buildings they passed had featured variations on the same basic columns with little decoration, these doors and everything around them were worthy of the finest temple. Fluted columns of flawless white marble stood at attention on either side, with green acanthus leaves growing up from the top to nestle gently against the entablature. They looked so real that he wanted to touch them to make sure. A mythical scene adorned the frieze above the great doors, with the pantheon of Izari gods defeating all manner of realistically portrayed mythical beasts. Was that blood dripping from the stroke of a hero beheading one particularly fearsome monstrosity? He had to squint to make sure. His eyes drank in every detail, but swallowed deep the emotion underlying the scene. *No evil is safe, but a friend is well protected.* Yet he felt secure, like the leaves and columns reached out to surround him in a protective embrace.

Elysia watched him with her head tilted slightly to one side, carefully studying his reaction. Seeing her broke the spell of the exquisite craftsmanship, and he stepped forward to her, still wondering at the cost of such an incredible facade. She gave a barely perceptible nod before knocking on the huge iron door knocker, shaped like a hammer striking a chisel.

A small window slid open, and the eyes behind it twinkled when they met Elysia's, but his eyebrow raised upon spotting Simon. She nodded confidently, and was greeted by the sound of a heavy bar scraping aside, then a large lock turning. The giant door swung open, and they were faced with a middle-aged Izari man with a shrewd yet kind face.

He spoke in confident Pazian. "Miss Elysia, I regret to say that Master Xelos has not yet returned. Will you be wanting to use the studio?"

"Yes, Ycastros, thank you. My friend Simon Baroba will be coming too."

"This is highly unusual, milady. Does Master Xelos know he is coming?"

"No, but he would wish to be informed right away. He will understand."

"Ah. He trusts your judgment, milady. I defer to his wisdom in such matters. Will you require any refreshments?"

"No, Ycastros. And thank you. I will be leaving a message for Master Xelos in the studio when we leave. Please make sure he reads it immediately upon his return."

"Of course. Simon, welcome to the house of Master Xelos, milady will lead the way, she knows it well."

"Thank you," Simon said, feeling very awkward. Ycastros nodded formally, and left them.

"Are you sure this is proper? I don't want to cause any alarm."

"Don't worry, just follow me."

She led him through the open reception chamber, a beautiful atrium garden with a fountain as ornately carved as the front doors, but this one lined with scenes of beautiful women chased by satyrs and other spirits, so real that Simon blushed.

"The work is incredible," he whispered to her. "Who did it?"

"Master Xelos keeps his best work." She pointed to a barely visible mark on each piece, like a stylized Izari X with wings. It was worked into the design so naturally, in the foliage or the fabric.

As they passed through a colonnade, he began to doubt himself again. *Who am I? Were my teachers right? Compared to a living master like this, she'll think I'm nothing.*

She led him to a door, produced a key, and unlocked it, letting them in before locking it again behind them.

It was indeed the studio of a master, with partially carved marbles on plinths, benches or tables all around the room. It was well lit with strategically cut windows and skylights bathing all the major working areas in abundant light. There must have been at least a dozen statues of varying sizes and stages of completion. Stoneworking tools were carefully arranged by several of the nascent pieces, including a bust of a noble looking Izari with a kind face that particularly drew his attention.

"We're quite safe here," Elysia said and led him to an empty table with two stools in front. She indicated his pack. "Now show me what you've got there, I've been waiting all night for this."

So had he.

His hands moved on their own, with his mind blank after running through all the possible negative responses. He withdrew the first of the wrapped boards and laid it out to the left. Her eyes widened, enthralled, as they traced the lines of Pazian legionaries facing the brunt of the Scentari assault. The look of pure wonder made her even more beautiful. Her eyes darted back to the bag, and he withdrew the second, showing the river mist enveloping the reserves, and the panic evident in the individuals and their mounts.

He paused, at first wanting to let her soak it in, but there was also the slightest sensation of resistance to showing her the final piece of the triptych. But he had started down that road and there was no turning back. With heavier hands he produced the scene of the command tent falling into the river, the hordes boiling over the new bridge, and the dark flames. In the full light of day, its power washed over him, fresh and terrible. It was an unfinished painting, yet he could feel the flames reaching out to engulf him in terror.

She gasped and clutched at his arm, strong fingers digging into the flesh. She fought to turn her head away from the picture, straining to face him and block his view of the powerful scene. Sweat beaded on her brow, her eyes tired and haunted.

That his work had so moved her filled him with awe. *Was such a thing possible?* Yes, since it had almost the same effect on him. And would do the same in the halls of the Senate.

"Simon, this is very bad. We have to stop them!" Her grip on his arm was insistent, the disquiet in her voice palpable.

He wanted to take her in his arms, to show her that there was nothing to fear. *But is there?*

"We? But how?" His mind was alert and engaged, even if his body was yearning for the conversation to move in a different direction.

"You must stay to see Master Xelos. He needs to see this. There is so much he can explain." She released him, and looked to the door, imploring her mentor to step through and reassure her.

Hope welled up inside him. He had passed her test, but couldn't make any rational connection between the things she was implying and his situation.

"All I know is that I have to do my duty, to finish this and bring it to the Senate. They will know what to do."

She shook her head, her mouth tight.

"They will only be sending more armies to their death. Master Xelos suspected that the dark arts were returning, but even his worst fears did not go this far, not yet."

"What are you talking about? Elysia? You know more than you're telling me. What is it?" His resolve to leave was weakening. What if there was something they could do here? What could this Xelos tell him? On curiosity alone he wished he could stay. And the thought of spending more time with her, whatever the circumstances, was making him lightheaded.

"You saw the power that this…"

"Shadush. Grand Thane of the Scentari."

"Right, that Shadush wields. I can only tell you the little I have learned from Master Xelos. He warned me to keep watch for any sign of dark magic anywhere, and let him know right away.

"There have always been those who would seek the power of the dark arts, but always in secret. And most are consumed by it before they reach any level of power. It… it does that. But for the leader of a nation to display this kind of command, this is grave news. Master Xelos was seeing signs of a shift in the balance, which must mean…"

"The balance?" She had totally lost him.

"The dark arts are the magic of destruction. You saw how it destroyed the rocks, right? And the flames must have consumed the water to create the mist. That magic can't create anything—as far as I understand it, something must always be destroyed to generate the power it needs. This is destructive magic. Master Xelos said that it is constrained by what matter is available, so there are limits to what is possible."

"But can it be stored up?"

Her frown deepened. "What do you mean?"

"That tribune, Persei Lokuta, the one that I was sent with. Before he was released he was made to witness some kind of ritual. Shadush was burning the prisoners alive on a giant pyre made of those dark flames. It was consuming them."

All color drained from her face. She released his arm and covered her mouth, mumbling something in Izari.

"All of Pelusia is in serious trouble. And Garas!" Part of him wanted to run out of there to warn his mentor, his friend, but his mind knew it was folly. "I must send word to him!"

She reached out to touch his shoulder.

"The whole world would be in danger if this power is left unchecked."

"But how can Master Xelos help, if the Senate and the entire Pazian army can't face this threat?" He pulled back, coldly appraising her. "Who are you, and who is Master Xelos? How do you know so much about this?"

She sighed. "Let me try to explain. I wish Master Xelos was here." She closed her eyes for a moment, as if preparing to recite a verse from memory.

"You have seen the magic of destruction, the dark arts."

"Yes."

"There must be balance in the world. A creative power to match the destructive. The two forces are in constant struggle."

"But most people think magic is just a myth. There has been no magic in the Republic for hundreds of years."

She gave him a knowing smile. "Officially, no. In reality, there are always pockets of the creative, what we call Talent. Talent such as yours."

He gasped, the wind knocked out of him by the weight of her statement.

"Magic?" he whispered. "Me?"

"Simon, you have the Talent. You can create. Your skills are far from refined, but I thought I could see it in you, there in the agora."

*Was he some sort of curiosity?* "So you weren't interested in my looks?"

"Don't be disappointed, but I saw something much more special. Much more intriguing, to me." She reached for his hand, but he drew back.

"Why were you looking for me?"

She laughed. "I wasn't. It was a lucky accident. I had just finished helping my brother pack up the stall. But then, I saw something. I... let me try to explain."

She sat up straight, squarely in front of him, holding out her hands. This time he took them. "Simon, look at me. No, really look. Or sense is a better word. Use all your senses. Do you feel something different?"

Her closeness distracted him, and he struggled to follow her meaning. *Different?* Her smell, her dark eyes, the warm feel of her skin in his hand, the sound of her voice, and... he started. There was some kind of... presence.

"What is that?"

"You feel it?"

"It's like there's a glow around you, but it's barely there. I don't see it, but I feel... I sense it. It's like I need all of my senses together to notice it, but once combined there is something special there. And it feels..."

"Like you knew it was there all along. Only you didn't know."

"Exactly."

"You learn quickly, Simon. That's good. There is so much you need to know, and I fear there is little time."

"So you saw this in me, from afar?"

"Not... not exactly. First I saw that you were drawing, which was interesting enough to take a look. I'm curious whenever I see any artist in action. But when I got closer, I felt a prickle, a faint hint. Master Xelos tried to teach me to be attuned to that feeling."

"So you, and Master Xelos have this Talent as well?"

She waited for him to continue.

"Of course you do. I've already seen it. In your work. But let me guess, it's not visible to everyone in your work, is it?"

"No."

"Almost like a secret trail only those with the Talent can follow."

"Exactly. You're very quick." She smiled again, this time with a hint of something more. "I like that too. And I have no problem with the way you look."

He leaned in closer, his mind struggling to deal with a whole new level of attraction. He wanted to know more, about her, about the magic. How she understood him more than he did himself...

"Elysia, you've turned my world on its head. I was just a simple messenger, but now you're telling me that I'm playing a part in the fate of all of Pazh, and beyond? But being here with you, all I can think about is..." He paused.

"Is what?"

He leaned in to kiss those soft lips, closing his eyes, warmth from the contact streaking through his body like lightning...

Elysia recoiled, withdrawing lips and hands in unison. Her eyes darted around, searching for any observers. When she looked at him again, she chewed at her lip, her brows drawn together.

"Simon, I..."

He felt himself flush. Was it all in his mind? "I'm... I thought... I'm sorry... I didn't mean to—"

"No, you just... you surprised me. And if any of the servants saw, Master Xelos would be angry. He's... in that way he's very traditional. Protective. But it... was wonderful. I just can't get the threat out of my mind."

"I know... it's just that I've never felt so connected to someone before. Like you truly understand me. Do you feel it too?" He reached out his hand again.

She looked down at it for what seemed like an eternity. She took a deep breath and tentatively offered her own. He leaned down so that he could meet her eyes.

She relaxed, but only a little. "But I've only just met you... and you're leaving... and... I never expected any of this..."

"What if I promised you I'd come back, as soon as I can?"

"You would do that?"

"There's nothing I would rather do. I want to learn from you… with you. I've just started getting back in touch with my artistic side… Talent as you called it. Now you're saying this is just the very beginning. I want to meet Master Xelos. He seems to know so much, and I want to understand all of it. I want to help Garas and Pelusia. And… I can't bear the thought of never seeing you again."

Her eyes softened, a shy smile lighting up her face.

He lifted her hand to his mouth, and she didn't resist as he kissed the back. This time she leaned in and he kissed her yielding lips. There was nothing else in that moment, only beautiful shared desire. He stroked her face, then her soft dark hair. She pressed against him and the stirring in his loins was almost unbearable. His hands moved down the sweep of her neck to her bare shoulder, but she broke away, breathing heavily.

"Simon, don't go…"

The taste of her lips lingered as he shut his eyes and took a deep breath. Cold reality crashed in, and the space between them grew wider with every moment. When would they see each other again?

"What can I do? The ship sails in a few short hours." The thought of leaving her was intensely painful.

"Stay with me." She locked her eyes on his, entreating him.

This new grip on his heart was sweet agony, but his mind was already pulling away.

"But I have my duty, to Pazh, and to Garas. I gave him my word. I believe you, in how great the danger is, but Garas, my friend, is right in its path."

"Can you delay the ship?"

His head snapped up. "I hadn't thought of that. But how? I'm just a passenger. And not even the one with the money, or the rank. How can I do it in such a way that Persei suspects nothing?"

"You must try. Even if it is only until tonight. So you can meet Master Xelos."

"I want to stay, I will do what I can. I…" He took her hands again. She smiled, and craned her head up to kiss him lightly on the lips once more.

"You must find a way. I'm not ready to let you go, either. But we must get you back to the ship. First, let me leave a message for Master Xelos."

"What will you say to him?"

"A storm blows in from the East, send for me, Elysia."

"He'll understand?"

"It was his orders." She stood up and inspected his work once more before motioning for him to pack up.

"So he is your teacher?"

"He has taken me under his wing."

A sudden pang, like a snake had bitten his heart.

"His wing…" he said before he could stop himself. She scowled at him.

"In the *arts*?" She rolled her eyes. "Men. Already trying to claim me?"

"I'm sorry Elysia, I didn't mean…"

"Yes you did." She broke out in a smile. "Simon, you're sweet. No, it's not like that at all. I already told you he's more like a grandfather. My mentor. He has shown me so much about how to use my Talent to create, for good. He will show you too, in time. You must return so that he can help you to see your potential, and how you can use it. I can't wait to explore what we can do together. You may be the key to saving Garas in more ways than one. But for now we speak no more of this. Not even to his staff."

She urged him out of the workshop and locked the door behind them.

"Our big secret," he said.

She waved to Ycastros when they left, and they spent the rest of the brisk walk back to the pier working on ideas to try to delay the ship, but nothing seemed plausible. Each step took him further away from Attarsus.

They were getting close to the harbor area when Simon heard a shout. Directed at him.

"Benjai!"

He winced. Persei sat in front of a tavern with a flagon in his hand.

The tribune looked Elysia up and down, lingering on her chest, finally meeting her eyes. She pulled her shawl tighter over her head, her look defiant. He laughed. "I'll have to apologize to the crew. I had told them you had that typical taste in Izari boys." He guffawed to himself, rising to approach them. "I've had better. Twice last night, in fact. But I guess she'll do for the likes of you."

He reached for her chin, and she slapped his hand away.

That brought out a leering smile. "How much is he paying you,

I'll pay double. I like them with spirit!" Persei saluted her with his flagon, spilling wine near her feet.

Simon seethed, but she caught his arm before he could raise it, and linked it in hers.

"He's been good to me. So I'm afraid I'm not available, at least not until tonight. Would you care to stay and meet me?"

She squeezed Simon's arm harder, quelling his protest.

"Sorry honey," Persei responded with a wink. "Our ship is about to sail. I've had just about enough of this backwater of a town, even if your sisters have been lovely company for a man of my great needs."

Simon tried to be properly polite. "Enjoy your drink, Tribune. See you back at the ship."

"Enjoy your last taste of the local produce, Benjai. But be quick about it. The captain is almost ready, and they've got some urgent cargo. We'll be making great time. He wants to leave in an hour. Plenty of time for a drink!" He laughed and almost missed his step as he returned to his seat. He winked at her again, then whistled at the young serving girl. "Another of your finest Pelari for the road!"

His blood still boiling, Simon made his way down the street with Elysia on his arm.

"I can't bear another hour with that noble swine." He looked into Elysia's eyes. "And for you to even imply that you are a..." He couldn't even say the word. "If I were armed..."

"Simon, stop. Your gallant defense of my virtue is quite flattering, but the important thing is that he suspect nothing. Didn't Garas warn you it wouldn't be easy?"

The general's name cooled him off; the heat replaced with anguish at his duty pulling him away from Elysia and new avenues of discovery she'd opened for him.

She put her finger to his lips to stop him from speaking.

"Simon, I know you have to go. I see why. You can't let *that* be what the Senate sees. They need to understand the danger. The need is far greater for our power to fight this. Swords are secondary. But still necessary."

"But I don't want to leave you." He felt like a petulant child who knew better. "And what about Master Xelos?"

"Our fates are linked, and this will not be the last you see of me. But for now, you are being drawn west." She looked suddenly vulnerable. "But promise me, Simon Baroba, that you will fly back to me as soon as you can."

"On the grave of my mother."

She nodded, accepting his pledge.

"Where should I find you when I return? I don't dare come to your father's house."

"No. Come for Master Xelos. Ycastros will remember you. And he'll be waiting." She looked thoughtful. "He may send someone to you in Pazh, once he hears me recount your story. Remember his sign. You can trust anyone bearing it."

Simon nodded. They had reached the pier. He felt a tear escape, and she wiped it away, before adding one of her own.

"Simon, you've changed my world too, and for the better. Together, we will make a difference for the rest, for the cause of creation, of good."

"I'll miss you, Elysia."

"I will count the hours until you return to find me. Be strong, and serve the Republic of our fathers well." She leaned in and kissed him one last time with soft intensity, before releasing him and backing away. His hand touched his lips, desperately trying to capture that feeling to accompany him on the journey to come. She smiled one last time before disappearing into the busy streets of Attarsus.

# VIII

⦿⦿⦿⦿⦿⦿⦿

## *Pazh*

With leaden feet Simon retraced his route to the *Sunrise*. To Pazh, to duty, to destiny. But away from Elysia. Away from answers. So much of him wanted to turn and chase after her, to leave this fool's errand behind and stay to explore their Talent and feelings together. For a moment he stopped, reeling on the precipice. But duty reasserted control and forced his heavy steps onward. He would keep his promise to her, and to Garas, by completing this mission and then returning to Attarsus. She would never trust him if he broke this first vow.

The crew appeared to have finished loading their cargo onto the ship, and were bringing the last of it down to the hold. Simon returned his precious pack to his cabin, then surfaced again to watch their departure. He had a particular spot he favored just off the bow on the port side, where he was able to keep out of the way but have an ideal view of the sea ahead. And in this case, of the port as they left.

Persei swaggered up the pier and onto the ship, merrily slapping the back of any of the crew he met on his tipsy way. He spotted Simon and approached with lurching steps. His face looked different; welcoming even.

"You surprised me today, Benjai. What was the wench's name? Too thin for my liking—I like something to hold on to. More curves. But I saw some spirit in her eyes..." He grinned at Simon, who shrugged in return. Persei laughed. "I knew it! A wild one! I like that! Well maybe I'll make an exception and pay her a visit on my way back to the battlefront. We're partners in this mission, so we might as well share even more, what do you say?"

"You mean to return to Pelusia after we face the Senate?" Simon asked.

Persei's face sobered, his eyes burning with a new intensity. "Of course! A Lokuta never forgets an enemy. You would be wise to remember that. I will return with the mightiest host Pazh has ever produced, and gain revenge on that Scentari dog!"

"Of course. For the glory of Pazh may you succeed!"

"For Pazh, and for Lokuta!" He raised his arm in a clumsy salute. "But for now, to sleep. I tire of this maritime travel. So tedious. I far prefer the city myself, and my own bed. With a woman or two. You should join me in my revels sometime. You could learn a lot!" He smirked, and stumbled back to his quarters.

Simon sighed with relief. Persei being friendly was far more disturbing than his usual arrogant self.

The captain barked out orders and the crew pushed off. Simon scanned the pier and its surroundings, seeing dozens of ships coming and going, sailors, pedlars, dock workers and merchants. It wasn't until they were just about to leave the sheltered harbor that he spotted what he was looking for: past the pier, on a wall at the top of a small hill, stood a lone woman with her hair covered in a shawl and her hand raised in farewell. Simon's heart soared out to her, leaving him alone once again. With duty and promises binding his path.

With only six days before landfall in Pazh, his commission dominated his focus. He spent very little time on deck, claiming slight illness, and instead threw himself into his secret work. The fine details and subtle layers of light and darkness that gave the work depth took time, but not as much as the emotion. Every tiny face, every eye had to reflect the emotions of the scene, to capture the essence and deliver it to the viewer. He channeled his own promises and desires into becoming one with his Talent, with the brush, the paint and the panels. He became bolder again by far, completely disregarding every stricture and rule held dear by his oppressive teachers. He would claim his place among the masters, but in a way none had ever envisioned for him. None save Elysia, and her faith in his Talent drove him forward to create; to capture thoughts in an image powerful enough to move the world.

He avoided the darkness. If he came too close, it seemed to absorb the light and the colors on his brush. Did his Talent open a gateway for darkness? Was he really in control at all? Or was he a danger to himself, without proper guidance? How he wished his path could have crossed Xelos in time to advise him. He covered the disturbing third panel and focused on the other two, to keep the darkness out of his mind.

The act of creation consumed him, exhausting both mind and body. Each night he fell asleep as soon as laid his head to rest, entering into a welcome dreamless slumber. The lights and sounds of the morning that would normally wake him could not penetrate this almost supernatural recovery. Upon awakening he would survey his work, plan the day's mixing of paint, and then set off to break his fast quickly before returning to work until dinner. He kept quiet, and avoided conversation with Persei, even though the tribune had ended the constant barrage of pejoratives and was almost cordial. After dinner he would light a candle and continue until sleep overcame him.

The night before they were due in Pazh he was finally satisfied with his work, and laid out the completed triptych. Stepping back to see the whole for the first time staggered him; first the enormity of the loss of so much Pazian life, then the individual suffering and terror. The void drew his eyes like a lodestone—a dark stain on not just the painting, but the very fabric of the world. Completion brought a new kind of exhilaration: of culmination, of release. Completely spent, he collapsed into the bunk and slept like the dead.

Insistent knocking on the door woke him up, groggy and disoriented. His ears struggled to make sense of the words.

"Simon, we've arrived, and Tribune Lokuta commands your presence on the pier!"

While his eyes attempted to bring the surrounding scene into focus, his limbs didn't respond initially, but with great effort he was able to prop himself up on his bunk.

His voice came out as little more than a croak: "Ten minutes, tell him ten minutes."

The knocking ceased and his mind shed the webs of sleep as he put on his armor and military traveling clothes.

In a flash of realization, he snapped to full attention. While focusing on his work he hadn't considered his next steps. Here he was, returning to the city of his birth, his life, his father, but with all these new experiences that made home feel distant, even after only a few months. And today the city would not be filled with old memories of his former life, but the new and secret connections vital to his mission.

He carefully wrapped his panels and remaining materials and checked to make sure the letters of introduction were safe, reviewing the addresses. It would be a busy day. As he walked into the sunlight, carrying the heavy pack with all his possessions, he felt refreshed, invigorated, and ready to face any challenge. The first appeared before him, dressed in formal toga. Persei Lokuta scowled at him.

"It is past noon. You had better not keep the Senate waiting, or I may have to see them without you, Simon."

Hearing his name from Persei's lips was a shock, but a welcome one. Had he changed so much? Or was he just getting in practice so he didn't slip and use an epithet while addressing the Senate?

"I have sent a runner to my brother already, while you slept in. Do you still mean to see your father first?" Simon nodded. "It is impossible that we will see the Senate today, and I have changed my mind. My brother and I will receive you in the evening, so we can be fully prepared for what is to come, likely on the morrow. You have no experience in such matters, but Daymar will make a fine coach. He has served in our family's seat since our father died when he was eighteen. We grew up with this. You, have not, *mercati*. Not that you'll be speaking much, regardless. But you need to understand how these things work."

"How will I find you?" His mind attempted to plot a course. Would there be sufficient time for the three stops that Garas entrusted to him in the six hours before evening?

"The House Lokuta is on the Arenial of course. Ask anyone, and they will point the way. Be there for seven. I can't guarantee Daymar will be ready for you, but the servants will know you're coming."

"It is my honor, Tribune."

Persei smiled with smug satisfaction. "Excellent. Well, I'm off. I must speak with my brother." He snapped his fingers, and two heavily laden porters followed as he strutted away. The noble scion had returned to the city of his birthright.

Simon traced his route through a mental map of the city, while his eyes scanned the mass of tile-roofed buildings rising up in stages on the hills, peaking with the Temple Mount in the northwest. He had lived all his life in Salamis, the low-lying yet high-rising district on the south side of the Narunis River. The river flowed through the city from the Island in the west to the port lands where he now stood. All of his list of four destinations were high in the hills on the north bank, areas with which he had little familiarity. Markus Sentollus lived in the district of Janiar, on the eastern face of the hill that rose up to the temple complex. Most of the newer senatorial families, the *suprati*, lived there, along with the richest of the *mercati*. The Mazial neighborhood where Lokas Lepilla lived was out of the way on the north side. The houses were large, but it was the least accessible. Perfect for someone who didn't want to be bothered at home. Finally, Genaro Morichea lived near the Lokuta in the exclusive Arenial district where the *digniti*, descendants of the oldest noble families, had been living for hundreds of years. *As long as each man is at home and doesn't keep me too long, I should be able to make the circuit in time.*

As busy as the ports of Tamar and Attarsus had been, the continuously busy port of Pazh dwarfed them as a hive of frenzied activity. Trade was the lifeblood of the Republic, and the city of Pazh was the beating heart, as the political and commercial capital of lands spanning three coasts of the Near Sea. Cargo of every kind flowed in and out all day and night, along with many people. These passengers included not just lighter native Pazian citizens, but free men and slaves of the entire rainbow spectrum, from all over the Republic and beyond. The diversity made Simon feel at home.

After his long absence, the port and the city beyond looked unimaginably vast. Home to a million people and almost one quarter of the population of the entire Republic, it was easy to lose one's way on the teeming streets. Luckily Simon's talents extended to his excellent sense of direction.

At the crossroads he headed right, along the broad avenue of Temple Way, which led up to the Great Forum. From there he could take the road to Janiar and Sentollus.

But he stopped. His ears pricked up, along with a nagging urge to reconsider. Whether it was the weight of his pack, the thought of being followed, or some vestige of filial piety, he turned west instead, toward Salamis and the house of his father.

He marveled at the feel of his sandals on a real Pazian road, smooth and firm despite the millions of steps that had preceded his. His eyes darted around to see if he could catch anyone following, but it was impossible to tell with people moving in every possible direction.

Was that sailor following him? Another headed in the direction he'd initially intended to go. Was he jumping at shadows? Surely Persei had not sent someone after him? Or would he? *In the same circumstances, what would I do?* Where before he saw unknown faces and familiar sights, now he imagined spies, informants, and the possibility of a trap. Was it even safe to meet with the Lokuta tonight, on his own? This was a world he didn't understand. Could he ever? Would Garas' allies be enough to keep him afloat? Or would he be swept away by the political currents of the capital? At this point, nothing was certain except that he wanted to finish his tasks quickly and extricate himself from the situation. The sooner he could return to Elysia and Attarsus, the better.

He shook off his misgivings, and resolutely struck out for the home of his father. His route took him through the market square, where the pungent aroma of onion and garlic made it painfully clear that he hadn't eaten since dinner the previous day. The rumbling of his stomach could be mistaken for the rattle of wheels from one of the passing oxcarts, heavily laden with goods for sale. He spied an old favorite stall, and parted with a few coins in return for bread brushed with roasted garlic and a handful of figs, which he chewed as he walked.

The familiar tastes of home made his worries seem as far away as the cities he had left across the sea. The densely packed apartment complexes soared to six, seven and even ten stories, surrounding him like a warm embrace. The hawker extolling the virtues of his wares, the crier bringing news of the day, children coming home from their lessons, and the peal of the blacksmith's hammer: all were the sights and sounds of his home. Inspiration for a hundred pictures swarmed in his mind, to capture the life of the metropolis and its people—to illustrate the lot of the common man, removed not just by a river and a hill from the machinations of the ruling elite. Yet the nostalgia was tinged with something new, something different. Things had changed for Simon, on the plains of Scentar, and in hidden rooms in Attarsus. He had grown beyond these roots. It was like an old familiar tunic that no longer fit quite right, no matter how comforting the smell and the feel.

*I always wanted to leave this all behind, and strive for something more. But am I ready for this? Am I getting what I asked for?*

As he rounded the corner to his father's shop, the walk through memory emerged upon a cliff of apprehension. He hadn't left on the best terms, many months ago. Would his father even want to see his son? Would he want to know about the danger? *I'll drop my pack, make sure he is well, and take steps so that nobody can follow me. If he wants to talk, we can talk.*

Shutters covered the front door, unusual for this time of day.

*You should be open for business.*

Simon shook his head as he ran his hand over the carved wooden sign that bore his family name. Worry bubbled to the surface. Simon fumbled for the key, looking around once more for any signs of someone following, then opened the lock and stepped inside. As his eyes adjusted to the darkness, he recognized familiar shapes. The racks of goods, the counter where customers paid, and the door behind that led to their apartment all appeared to be in regular use, just not today. And it wasn't a feast day, with the rest of the district open for business.

*Out for supplies or an early dinner? Hopefully you're not drinking at this hour. It's a wonder you can still afford the rent on the shop.*

The familiar bitterness crept back. Business looked to be flagging, with the shelves too well stocked.

He used another key to let himself into their apartment behind the shop. The side door was locked. He'd never liked living on the ground floor, with all the noise, but it could be useful today for getting out unnoticed. The remains of a midday meal were on the main table, along with a half-full jug of wine. His father wasn't in his room either, and Simon found himself relieved. He lacked the energy for a battle, with so many stops still to come.

A thin layer of dust covered his own room, which remained exactly as he had left it. He lowered his heavy pack at the side of the bed. Although used to the weight, it still felt good to set it down. He rummaged through to find the smaller pack containing his artwork. Hanging up his armor, traveling cloak and military tunic, he looked through the rest of his clothes. *Do I own a single garment appropriate for visiting four senators in a day?* He took out his best tunic, a finer weave of soft white wool, which he wore for funerals and festivals. It would have to do. He had the good sense to hang it when he wasn't wearing it. *Was it slightly more snug?* He had always been thin, but life in the army had firmed and toned what had previously been skinny. *I'd rather be going to see Elysia like this.* He combed his hair, washed and shaved quickly, and found the three letters. *Sentollus and the Janiar first.*

He shouldered the pack and returned to the shop. Peering through the shutters, he surveyed the scene outside—a street typical of Salamis. There were other shops on the opposite side; Marced still selling flowers, Burkhan the weaver, Lintarus the collier. An ordinary number of people passing by. *Still, I can't be too careful.* He locked the front door, and found a wax tablet in the shop to leave a note for his father, warning him he was in town, but not back until after dinner. Back in the apartment he locked the shop door and left through the side door to the laneway. A quick look confirmed it was empty as usual, and dim with six stories blocking out the sun. He turned right, away from the main street and toward the junction where the lanes met, following the empty route all the way to Key Street that ran parallel to the north. *Nobody following, good.*

After merging into the early afternoon traffic he made his way west to Senate Way, the central north-south thoroughfare. Crossing the President's bridge north over the widest part of the Narunis River was like traveling to another country. Where Salamis bustled with the busy disorder of vibrant mercantile life, the Valley beyond lived in barely contained squalor. The poorest of all the neighborhoods, it sat in the shadow of the Arenial Hill and the Senate Hall itself looked down over the ridge like the *digniti* looking down their noses at the *mundati* housed below. The rickety buildings were taller, but none allowed to reach the lowest plateau of the Arenial. The lanes between were clogged with the filth of hundreds of thousands living too close together. The majority were workers continuing the lot of their families for generations, but their numbers swelled with migrants from other regions of the Republic, drawn here to make their fortune, and the occasional bankrupt former merchant or penurious *dissati* family far removed from their former senatorial splendor. And it was also the only part of the city that most freedmen, former slaves, could ever hope to afford. What it lacked in sophistication, it made up for in dynamic energy. The people worked hard just to survive. The upper classes might recline languorously on a fine afternoon like this, but the lower classes were hard at work.

Only the Senate Way itself was kept clear, along with the Arenial steps that led up to the Great Forum, home of the Senate Hall. Old and imposing, the stairway demonstrated just how far above the fray the ruling class lived and worked. While free movement up and down was permitted, it was rare to see the lowest climbing those steps, or the highest descending them. But Simon, firmly in the middle, didn't look out of place in his ascent.

The Great Forum fascinated him as a child, and remained a marvel. The majestic buildings that delineated the square were the highest points of Pazian architectural splendor. Pazians might not have the greatest appreciation for most visual arts, but they made sure public buildings were structures both fine and functional, if never innovative. That part of his history lessons he vividly remembered, with the physical manifestations present in all their glory.

He passed through the Valley Gate, in between the Temples of Salar the Iron One, patron God of the city of Pazh, and Choron of the Secrets, which doubled as the hall of records.

The Senate Hall, covering the northwestern side of the open square was built four centuries prior by President Marcos Lukken to replace an earlier much smaller hall. In classical Pazian style, its majestic pure white marble steps led up to a towering colonnade, topped with a frieze depicting the victory of the *digniti* families over the tyrant King Suenas VII. The iconic melting of his crown as the founding moment of the Republic formed the central scene, one that always made Simon uneasy. Pazh was founded on virtuous ideals, but established and maintained through might. Might seriously challenged by barbarians conversant in the dark arts.

On the northeast side lay two important buildings divided by the Janiar Gate. The Basilica Marcona housed the law courts, named after Lucas Marcona, the famed general and president, who built it a century before the new Senate Hall. The second was the stately Temple of Hasur, God of Wisdom. Their gold-leaf roofs shone in the afternoon sun.

At the southeast corner facing the Senate Hall stood the Podium, where officials were sworn into office, major speeches delivered, and the culmination of the triumphal march of a victorious general celebrated.

This was the center of Pazh; the city, the Republic, and the ideal. A political and civic brain that sent out laws, judgments and leaders to every corner of the Republic. It exuded power; the power of civilized society triumphant.

On a day like today, when not in use for a parade, speech or public spectacle, the space filled with all manner of market stalls, giving it an additional commercial life. A crier on the Podium called out the news of the day to all that would listen.

Before he passed through, Simon asked a wine merchant whether the Senate was currently in session. It could complicate his timeline considerably.

"They left this morning," the man said. "Word is that there will be a report from the East on the morrow. Yarkses over there heard it's about a setback in the campaign to relieve Pelusia."

"Oh? I hadn't heard," Simon replied, feigning ignorance. News traveled fast. He did his best not to frown. If only this vendor knew he bore these ill tidings.

"Nothing official. We'll find out more tomorrow, I'd wager." All the classes voraciously consumed the latest news, from the greatest matters of state to the basest rumors, especially those regarding the peccadilloes of the ruling class.

Simon nodded, and made his way quickly to the Janiar Gate, toward Markus Sentollus' home. *Garas called him the protector? If I can only meet one of the three today, I hope to the gods it's him.*

# IX
## ᏧᏲᏥᏲᏥᏲᏥ
### *Allies*

Simon only had to stop once to get directions, since the building he sought was on the main road. With nowhere near the elaborate decoration of Master Xelos' house in Attarsus, it was nevertheless an imposing sight. More impressive than any other he'd had the opportunity to visit in Pazh. On this day he'd get a chance to see not only how the upper class lived, but how they compared with each other.

Mustering up his courage, he approached the main doors and knocked. Almost too quickly, a small window opened and a pair of bored eyes peered out.

"What business do you have with the Sentolli?"

"My name is Simon Baroba, and I come bearing a letter from General Garas Numeno in Pelusia. He sent me to hand-deliver it to Markus Sentollus himself. Is your master in?"

"Garas, a general?" Momentary shock was evident in the voice, and Simon winced. He hoped he could trust this servant of Garas' friend, having already revealed too much. More composed, the man continued: "Come in, and I will bring your news to Master Sentollus."

The door opened, and the graying man led him to a seat in a receiving room. He looked Izari, and definitely a slave, but likely the head of household staff. Before he left, he summoned a young boy and gave him an order in Izari.

"The boy will bring you wine while you wait. Can I take your pack?"

Simon clutched it protectively. "No, I have need of it, thank you."

The steward tipped his head, Simon not meriting a full bow, and left to find his master. Simon settled himself comfortably on the smaller of the two couches to wait for his erstwhile protector.

The receiving room was tastefully lavish, showing someone comfortable with their wealth. Sentollus might not be one of the *digniti*, but his family had been wealthy for several centuries and done their best to make the home worthy of its location in Janiar. An exquisite tapestry on the far wall caught Simon's eye: a particularly well rendered map of the Pazian Republic, with legionary standards marking locations across the provinces and hinterlands. *The victories of Sentollus perhaps? A man quite proud of his accomplishments?*

The boy returned with two cups and the wine as promised and poured both. The wine was robust and flavorful even well-watered. Better than anything he'd had in a long while, and possibly ever. *I could get used to this.*

Before he could collect his thoughts, a tall man walked in wearing the red tunic of a senator under his bright white toga. With a businesslike stride and a stern expression on a narrow face, Markus looked to be in his late fifties. His straight back and impeccably trimmed gray hair marked him as a disciplined military man. Simon stood instinctively to salute and the man waved him back to his seat.

"The letter from Garas," the senator said as he sat down, grasping his glass.

"Yes, sir." Simon handed over the letter.

The senator broke the seal and maintained a clinical expression as he reviewed the contents. He sipped absently at his wine without looking up, and Simon covered his nerves by matching him sip for sip.

The man's look was unchanged when his eyes met Simon's again. "You'll stay here tonight." His tone was perfectly level, making it sound more command than question.

Simon felt like he was a boat on the edge of an untamed ocean, and had come unmoored.

"But I had planned to see my father—"

Markus cut him off. "Too dangerous."

The winds were picking up.

"But Garas charged me to see…"

"I will call on Lepilla and Morichea."

"Persei asked that I attend his brother for dinner tonight."

"Unacceptable."

"He is still technically my commanding officer." It was one last attempt to keep control of this vessel he called self.

The first chink in Markus' stoic armor was consternation. He stretched the fingers on both hands together then stood up, pacing.

"He knows you're seeing the three of us."

Simon hesitated for a moment. *Was this a question?* Markus didn't seem to be continuing, so he responded. "No. He doesn't know about the letters. Not specifically. But wouldn't he guess that Garas would have me contact someone?"

"Are you committed to him." The look was piercing, demanding a response.

"No!" It came out a little more defiant than he intended.

Markus nodded. "Galcius. Fetch Xander, parchment and my seal." The slave boy bowed before hurrying off to find the steward. Markus took a deep draft from his cup.

"I would rather be with Garas in the open field, facing that monster, than dealing with the Lokuta and their like in the forum. He trusts your judgment. What do you think of young Persei."

Simon was getting used to the statements as questions. He took a deep breath. He was committed here, now.

Markus sensed the hesitation.

"You have no love for him. Speak freely." His voice was even, but the clarity commanded military obedience.

"No. He is everything my father and his drinking mates would say are the ills that afflict the upper classes. No offense intended." Markus nodded again to continue. "He lords his station over the common soldier, even other tribunes. Yet he can be charming and inclusive if he sees an advantage. Petulant if he doesn't get his way, or his due. Ambitious. Very ambitious."

"He bears watching. I recommend that you rebuff their invitation, but my friends will weigh in."

Xander from the front door returned with the supplies. Markus took the offered parchment, and drafted two short letters. "Xander, send these separately with our two fastest runners. You were right to summon me immediately."

Xander bowed low.

"Let the kitchen know that Lepilla and Morichea will be here shortly, and likely for dinner." The steward nodded, bowed once again and was off. Markus waved to the boy, who refilled their cups.

"Persei. You don't know his brother."

"Until today, the only senator I had ever spoken with personally was the late General Suboras." His voice wavered.

"Facing the Senate troubles you. Lepilla will prepare you for tomorrow. The elder Lokuta may be just shy of thirty, but he is shrewd, and dangerous in his own right. Is the younger a tactician. Clever."

"Not especially so. More cunning. He fancies himself strategic, but it is mainly the ambition speaking." He hesitated, before revealing what had been told to him in confidence. "He is also vengeful. He has been humiliated by the Scentari, and I think his desire for revenge might be even greater than his ambition."

Markus' sudden laugh startled Simon and changed his bearing entirely. "That family keeps a book of slights as large as the hall of records. They have no love for my family, or Lepilla for that matter. You were not followed here."

"No, I had a feeling I should be careful about that."

Markus nodded his approval. "Garas made a good choice. Did you have any other plans for the day."

"No, just delivering the three letters, seeing the Lokuta, and hopefully my father. I understand your reasons for changing my itinerary. And I thank you for your assistance. This is all new to me."

"The lady Pazh is fortunate to have good men like Garas, and yourself. To defend her from those who believe they can best protect her by bending her to their will. Of course those inbred bastards would likely say their way is right. Now tell me of the campaign."

Markus had a keen military mind, and was quite engaging and even verbose when in his element, drinking in every detail of the troop movements, battles, and especially their innovations in camp defense. *Obviously wistful for the glory days.* He regaled Simon with his own martial exploits, pointing out the sites of his victories over various barbarian clans or rebels commemorated on the tapestry map.

After some time, Xander returned to announce the arrival of Senator Genaro Morichea.

"Markus, who is this emissary from our friend in the East?" the guest asked as he entered. He was even taller than Markus, and radiated an air of easy command. A full head of auburn hair topped his tanned face, and he was strong, muscular and looked to be in the prime of life. *Forty, if that.* Even his eyes smiled as he walked over to embrace his friend, who received him with a more dignified and understated contentment. Where Markus was spare and efficient, this man was confident and engaging. Handsome, powerful and vibrant, Genaro was the very picture of the ideal Pazian man, and likely sent the women swooning. *Worthy subject for a portrait someday.*

Genaro clasped Simon's arm. "What may I call this friend of Garas Numeno?"

"Simon Baroba, Sir."

Even Genaro's laugh was hearty, but inclusive. "I am not your commanding officer today, my young friend." He winked at Markus. "Call me Genaro, as a fellow conspirator." He looked Simon over. "Is your mother Benjish by any chance? Certainly wasn't your father. Baroba is as Pazian as they come."

"Yes." This man was perceptive, and infinitely likable. If he was as intelligent as he was personable, he would make a fine leader of men. And Simon doubted many women would decline to follow his lead.

"Give him his letter," Markus said. Simon did as asked as they returned to the couches. A third and fourth glass had appeared and Genaro drank lustily, then made a face.

"Still cheap as ever. Can you at least break out the good stuff for your friends?" Genaro asked Markus with a laugh. "Well, we'll need clear minds to figure this out."

His expression darkened as he read. A few times he looked over to Markus, quite concerned. "At least our friend Garas is the general now. Jasun was a very good man, but he was woefully unprepared for this. He walked right into their trap." He shook his head, and sat back, exhaling deeply. "I could have saved us a lot of good men. Don't get me wrong, Simon, I have no counter to that dark abomination, but I wouldn't have let my men get slaughtered like pigs in a pen."

Xander led the third guest to meet them, and Genaro's face lit up as he walked over to meet the large man. "Speaking of pigs!"

The new man scowled, and his jowls puffed out to look even rounder. This was no military man, nor athlete, but one who evidently enjoyed all the epicurean delights Pazh had to offer. His toga sagged awkwardly over a huge belly. But the sunken eyes were keen and intelligent.

His voice was rich and smooth, full of life. "Genaro, Markus, and who did Garas send to us?"

"Lokas Lepilla," Markus said, "this is Simon Baroba. He has your letter," Simon handed it over. "Have a seat."

"You'll need it," added Genaro, which elicited a wry smile from Lokas.

"Swine of a certain quality always do. I take it the news is bad?"

"Worse," said Genaro. "Just read and catch up with the rest of us. Good thing you read fast, with how long you kept us waiting. Whatever possessed you to buy that place up on the far side of the Mazial?"

"The brisk walk keeps a man the very picture of good health."

"True," Genaro said. "Your litter bearers are in top condition with the toil you put them through." He winked to Simon.

How casually they included him in their banter: two great generals and a master orator. Markus Sentollus' brevity and austere manner had matched more closely with the picture of a senator he held in his mind, and his questions hadn't left him much time to adjust to the circumstances. His most famous campaigns predated Simon.

But here stood a decorated general whose triumphal parades Simon had witnessed as a gawking teen. And another man whose speeches he'd studied at school, who now turned his barbed wit to friendly jibes. They were so much more human than deity, but he would have to pay close attention to everything they had to say. These three had control over his vessel like two winds and the sea beneath him. They could help him navigate through the rocky straits in the Senate tomorrow, but where was he now headed? Far from Attarsus, for the time being, and his mind needed to stay alert.

Lokas read faster and more expressively than the others. His running commentary was insightful and entertaining.

"Oh Jasun you buffoon, even I can see that you were charging headlong to your doom.

"Oh ho! I would have liked to see the Lokutan whelp arriving in camp, an ass across a horse!

"Garas, a general! Well, he's as good a choice as any man, present company excepted, and far better than most other candidates!"

When he finished, he drank deep of the wine laid before him, sighed, and then sat forward.

"I'll need most of the evening to prepare my speeches for tomorrow, so let's not waste any more time before we get our plans together. I'm sure you've thought of the details, Markus, plus you've had the most time to consider."

"Before we do, my friends," Genaro interrupted, "I'd like to hear a little more about these dark arts that are at play. Simon, you were there but quite a distance away. Can you be sure this was some evil magic?"

And so it began. Fear welled up inside him.

"The mists were unnaturally thick along the river, but I can't confirm that it was out of the ordinary for the area. There were three of us, and I was the only one who saw it. It was like a flash of pure darkness, and an explosion as the rocks were burned away to change the course of the battle. I would swear on my mother's grave that this was no natural phenomenon."

"You paint quite the vivid picture with your mind's eye, young Baroba," Lokas said, looking intently at him. "I'll have a few more questions for you later about that, but I think you've shown us enough to give us the full picture." Simon had been unconsciously touching the clasp on his pack, but now withdrew his hand with a nod. None of the others had made any mention of the picture, so perhaps Garas intended it for Lokas only, at least for now? He longed to share this burden, but had to bear it alone for at least a few more steps. Now was not the time.

Lokas continued: "Simon has established, and Persei will be confirming to a much greater extent, that this is no ordinary barbarian chief we face. This is a dark sorcerer bent on tearing apart the fabric of our very Republic!" The others were nodding as his voice rose. "We cannot leave this to incompetent generals like another Suboras. We need forward thinking men with the requisite experience to come up with a strategy. Men exactly like... yourselves!" His exaggerated gesture encompassed the other two senators.

"But unfortunately, widespread panic would not be at all helpful, and that's what we'll have if the people of Pazh were to know there was an agent of the dark arts in the East, capable of destroying entire legions.

"Yet if we understate the urgency, then we risk a majority in the Senate charging some other idiot to lead more of the young men of Pazh to their deaths on a black pyre.

"And what if this Shadush grows in power with each victory? Is that possible Simon?"

Simon shrank from the question, struggling to compose a response when Lokas resumed. "How would you know? But if he never used his powers in their first foray in our province, or not to the same degree until he had some success in his raids, then I think we can deduce that either the power of his magic is tied directly to his success, or that he is gaining in skill and control over this evil. Either way, the threat is ever increasing."

Simon was awed by how quickly Lepilla was able to process so many possibilities and expound upon them immediately. His legendary wit was no exaggeration.

"So I ask again, Markus, what practicalities are at the forefront of your mind? I take it Simon is staying here tonight and will have an escort to the Senate tomorrow?"

"That is the right course. However—"

Genaro cut him off with a guess. "The Lokuta wish to entertain our young friend tonight?"

"And I told him this is out of the question. The danger—"

This time it was Lokas who interjected. "Have you considered how things will look if he does not arrive for the invitation? The young one will be rabid, and the elder not just slighted, but preparing for the worst. And we all know how bitterly those dogs feel anger. We obviously need Simon to be ready to report to the Senate tomorrow, and not to come to any misfortune that would preclude his involvement. That would be in the best interests of the Republic we serve." He paused as they all nodded their agreement.

Simon could almost see the shore.

"But he absolutely must not miss this dinner."

Dashed on the rocks.

"But Lokas," Markus said, "if we leave him alone in their clutches, we may never see him again."

"Unless they know he is under our protection," Genaro said.

"Ah, but that won't do," said Lokas, clearly enjoying himself as he whisked them about as the tour guide on this suppositional journey. "He must go, and under no circumstances can they know he has spent any time with us at all. In fact, it might be best if he spent the night there, should the offer be forthcoming. And once again, declining is not an option when they do in fact ask you to stay." He chuckled at Simon's gaping mouth, his eyes twinkling. Markus frowned, but Genaro appreciated the show.

"How do we ensure that he comes out of House Lokuta," Markus asked in his usual way.

"Oh Markus, you're no fun, always wanting to cut right to the grand finale." Lokas pouted like a young girl for a few moments, then let his face settle into a cherubic grin. "The letters. Simon, here's where your real coaching begins. So the letters, or one single letter in this case. Who among us is known to be closest to Garas Numeno?" He looked between the two senators. Markus looked at Genaro.

"So you're saying he'd surely contact me, especially since he'd want me to be the one the Senate sends in command. But how do we preserve the illusion that our friend Simon here is not tainted by too close a connection?"

"Simon my boy, you're not very familiar with the Arenial are you?" Lokas asked.

Simon nodded.

"Quite an imposing place, and not somewhere that you just meander about trying to deliver ill tidings. And this being your first sojourn away from Pazh, you desperately wanted to spend some time with your family before the big day tomorrow, am I right?"

A slower nod.

"And all this talk of senatorial business is quite beyond your humble education, and not something you take well to, not before some quality coaching from the friendly Lokutan brothers. So quite naturally, you would find the harbor courier Garas recommended to send the letter he entrusted to you, with the money he gave you specifically for that purpose. Your letter sent, you went to spend the day with...?" He looked to Simon.

"My father."

"And then excitedly prepare your finest tunic for a dinner date with your new patrons. Do I have that right?" His ear to ear smile was contagious.

Simon nodded with a smile of his own, finding he quite liked Lokas Lepilla, and the way his mind and tongue worked together in unison.

Genaro clapped his appreciation for both performance and plan. "And once you're done giving our young friend here an education, they'll be quite certain that he's their pawn to be used to their ends, and certainly not discarded. Those arrogant pricks won't suspect a thing, and then you pull the rug out from under them tomorrow. Maybe we should be getting Garas a seat in the Senate House? He has orchestrated this perfectly."

Markus was still grumbling. "Garas asked me to protect the boy, and he is far safer here. Now we have to get him back to Salamis by six, which barely leaves time to get agents in place to protect his walk. Then we lose him completely when he's inside their complex. Lokas, you realize the weak point is the walk to House Lokuta."

"Absolutely, my dear Markus. But that's why Garas sent him here first. Your agents will need to be in precisely the right places to ensure he lets the Lokuta know others are expecting him to appear with young Persei tomorrow."

His every move under surveillance? *Was nowhere safe?* All eyes turned to Simon as he opened his mouth, and he keenly felt the attention. "But there's another problem. If they had me followed from the *Sunrise*, then they'll know I never met a courier in the harbor."

"I'm sure you had the foresight to stop somewhere along your way home?" Genaro asked.

Simon thought for a moment, then brightened. "I stopped at one of my favorite food vendors. Money changed hands, so it would have been easy for me to pass him a letter for his son to deliver."

"Then this portion of the matter is settled," Lokas said. "Markus has work to do to cover your evening stroll. Battle plans for the Senate proposals will be the subject of our dinner tonight, and I'd imagine you'll need to compose your thoughts, Genaro. Good thing our cartographical collector here will have just what you need. I'll work on the speeches after dinner. But first, Markus, can you find Simon and myself somewhere quiet where I can prepare him for his performances for the Lokuta tonight and the rest of our august colleagues tomorrow?"

Markus barked a command to the slave boy, who beckoned toward a doorway. Lokas nodded as he rose and put his soft arm around Simon as they followed. "It is a pity you won't be able to join us for the dinner, Simon. I know you'd enjoy our company much better. Though if I'm critical of the Lokuta in most respects, they will make sure you eat well tonight." He looked wistful.

The quiet room appeared to be a study, with the walls lined with books and scrolls, and a desk with a chair for reading.

"Excellent," said Lokas, seating himself as the slave left them alone. "Now let's see what you have for us." He indicated Simon's pack.

Fear and excitement vied for supremacy as Simon's trembling hands withdrew his work, setting it face down in three parts before the portly senator, who waited with a quizzical look.

Lokas laughed as Simon turned them over with a flourish. "Quite the showman!" His eyes traced the lines of the image from the sloping walls of the valley at the left, twinkling as they took in the details. "This is exquis—" He gasped as his gaze reached the dark flaming void. The folds parted and his eyes looked like they might fall out. Beads of sweat rolled down from his thinning gray hair. He sat, transfixed, his mouth open in a terrified grimace.

"Senator?" Simon asked, worrying for his health. Lokas did not respond, even as Simon shook his arm. Near panic, he covered Lokas' eyes, and the senator breathed again. He looked very old, and shaken to his core. Lokas stared at the ceiling, brooding.

Baffled, Simon covered the panel with his pack.

An eternity passed before Lokas spoke, his voice filled with caution. "This complicates matters tremendously." His eyes narrowed as he regarded Simon like a potential threat. "This is no ordinary work. You have *Talent*. And I fear far too much of it. There are those who would consider you to be at least as great of a danger to the Republic as this darkness from the East. Imagine this were to happen to a gaggle of senators in the middle of the debate? What are we to do with you, my boy? How can we make use of this, yet protect you in the process?"

He paused, as if inviting Simon to give a response, but none was forthcoming.

Lokas sighed, opening up one hand. "We could conceal this from the Senate, which weakens our position, and may work in favor of the designs of the Lokuta. And that would be a shame, with this being such an incredible work, and sure to move the Senate with the gravity of the situation. We cannot hold you back from addressing the Senate, or your work will be lacking authentication. The Lokuta will certainly not take my word for it. But if you are there, some may condemn *you* as a sorcerer, and have you locked away for the good of the Republic, or worse yet, for later attempts to bend you to their own devices."

Lokas lost himself again in silent thought.

The words were a maelstrom rushing through Simon's mind. He had never considered any of these possibilities. He was so far out of his element. Had his work brought him into far greater danger than the blades of the Scentari?

"Our time is short," Lokas said. "Entrust these weapons to me, and I will ensure they are used to maximum effect on the morrow. I will meditate on this, and if our cause is true, may Choron bestow upon me some clue as to what course we should follow. If you value your life, speak to no other about this unless I ask in the Senate chamber.

"I will lead you with my questions, and you will give clear and honest answers. Are you nervous?"

Simon's face betrayed him.

"Of course you are. But never forget that every viper in this foul pit we call the Senate is still a man. The food and water goes in and out of each of them with the same noises as any other. Never forget that. Fate may have elevated them above you in our Republic, but they are still men. If the collection of them brings fear into your heart, imagine the individuals bent over in the latrine." He smirked, then proceeded to give Simon some advice about how to stand and breathe and project his voice.

Simon's stomach churned. He hadn't spoken in public since his school days, and then it was to his fellow students, not the most powerful men in the world. The thought of all their eyes on him made him shudder. And then they would all know him. Would his life ever be the same? He would have his chance to stand out, but did he want it?

"As for your engagement tonight, enjoy the hospitality of the Lokuta to the fullest extent of a solider returning home on leave. They will treat you as an honored guest and will assume they have your allegiance. Let them believe that fact and we will lead them to a delicious surprise tomorrow." He closely observed Simon's worried face.

"Yes, you *will* be making them your enemy. But it is either Pazh and your friend Garas Numeno, or the Lokuta. You have made your choice?"

Simon gulped, and nodded once more.

"I say again, enjoy the delights for at least one night, and tomorrow the real work begins. Your work and your life is safe with me. Now get yourself home so their spies can watch you approach."

# X
ᎶᏋᎶᏋᎶᏋᎶ
## *Lokuta*

On his walk home from the Janiar he reveled in the return to anonymity, imagining himself just another faceless citizen thronging the streets of the capital with only the mundane worries of the day to trouble him. He mulled over the seductive possibility of slipping away. Of escape. They might be looking for him on the route to the Arenial, but at the harbor or city gates he might still pass unnoticed. Tomorrow he would be known to the entire Senate. Was this his final chance for a third option? His mind screamed at him to run, to fly from this place, this spider's web of intrigue. Just the briefest glimpse of this new world was far, far beyond his faculties. He could leave, one lone man, and start a new life. Perhaps in Attarsus?

But at what cost? A traitor to not just the Lokuta, but Garas and his allies. Would he be condemning a friend to his death? And what about his father? He was the only family he had, and retaliation was not out of the question. A drunken man might come to any manner of unfortunate endings in Pazh.

But where did this road of duty leave his Talent? And the mystery of Elysia? Mind and heart both yearned to return to Attarsus, now far away and unattainable.

No, heavy steps led him home, committed for now to a world where others dictated his fate. He stole in through the side door and found the house still empty. He locked up again and left through the front.

If he'd been cautious on his way to the Janiar, it took his full conscious effort to walk at a normal pace to the House of Lokuta. The senators had not only confirmed his fears, but amplified them to new heights of paranoia. Even with hidden agents watching out for him the evening shadows drew in ever closer.

While the Janiar was a world of varied opulence, displaying newfound riches to any who cared to notice, the Arenial bore the weight of centuries of wealth and power with nobility. Architects of the distant past had created urban palaces for the founding families of Pazh, and these loomed over Simon as he walked with mounting dread to his next appointment.

House Lokuta, as one of the original *digniti* families, had one of the best locations, with stunning views of both the city and the Forum. The house was massive, with a sweeping facade of perfectly finished marble columns in the serious and unadorned style of centuries ago. Approaching the mighty doors gave Simon a whole new perspective of Persei. He'd always resented his rival's arrogance as empty and undeserved, but when faced with the physical manifestation of half a millennium of history and ancestors, Simon felt very, very small. When the massive doors opened for him, the mouse walked into the lion's mouth.

With a look of moderate disdain, the steward showed him in past four guards to sit and wait in the reception hall. While the ornamentation of Master Xelos invited you in with beautiful artistry, that of House Lokuta kept their visitors firmly in their place. The surroundings were cold and regal, appearing impossibly tall through a trick of perspective—with only his artist's eye breaking the spell. The original builders had designed the house with purpose, and those previous generations might have even been worthy of his respect. Persei however...

"Young Master Lokuta," the steward announced from behind him.

Simon immediately stood, cursing inwardly at being caught off guard. After looking him over, Persei sniffed at his simple tunic.

"You were right," he said to the steward. "No toga, but at least the tunic will do. Get him ready."

The steward nodded to one of a pair of pretty serving girls. The first, with skin of dark mahogany and bearing a tunic, bowed and left. The other, with dark hair and pale complexion, carried a toga over to Simon. He began to reach out, but caught himself when the girl looked startled. Persei's smirk brought color to Simon's face, and he stood stiffly, letting the beautiful girl dress him while he dealt with an awkward stew of emotions.

Being dressed by a woman made him think with sorrow of his mother. She was the only woman who had ever helped him get dressed, and not since his coming of age ceremony, the last time he'd worn a toga. That memory battled with the awareness of the warmth of soft young hands arranging the folds of the unwieldy formal garment, and a nagging guilt that he only wanted to allow Elysia this close.

The servant girl stood in front of him to appraise her work. Finding fault, she stepped forward, intent on the toga as she leaned in. The sweet scent of flowers tickled his nose as her fingers deftly adjusted one last fold. Was it his imagination, or did her hand caress him as she pulled it away? The moment hung suspended in time until she stepped back, gave an approving nod and shared a secret smile with him. He exhaled abruptly, realizing he'd been holding his breath. She suppressed a chuckle, then bowed to Persei. The young master's eyes lingered on her chest, then met Simon's and winked.

"Be good Simon, and maybe you'll see her again later?"

A part of him definitely wanted to. The girl hurried out without a backward glance.

Persei put his arm around Simon's shoulders like an old friend and led him out. "Our allies always enjoy a stay at House Lokuta. And now you at least look worthy of meeting Daymar. Let's not keep him waiting." He leaned closer for a whisper. "It makes him even more of an ass than usual!"

The dining room was as lavish as the reception hall was cold. Frescoes adorned the walls and ceiling with scenes of gods bestowing gifts of riches and power upon men whom Simon assumed were some of the first Lokuta. Long couches loaded with silk cushions formed three sides of a square with low tables spread out in front of them. Beside each couch and at the far corner beside a door stood four more beauties clothed in their native styles, showing off the diversity of their native Pazian provinces, like a living addition to the artwork. Simon tried not to stare, but couldn't help but marvel at how radically different features and dress could result in such uniquely stunning women.

The first was a willowy Maruthan, with matching hair and skin like amber. A white knee-length dress with an interesting texture—linen perhaps?—hugged surprisingly ample curves and left thin shoulders bare but for delicate straps. Her shy smile through long lashes was for Persei and he responded with a wink.

Next to the middle couch was a defiant Myraki woman in flowing red robes that draped all the way to her wrists and the floor, other than a plunging neckline. With her hair tied back in a loose ponytail it exposed more of her enchanting skin—it wasn't tanned, or truly dark, but had a cast to it like dark clouds partially obscuring a sunset. She stared at Simon, as if challenging him to look.

Simon's father had a few Borathi women as clients, unusual for their dominant place in the province's society. But while those merchant women were plain and almost mannish with their short hair and formless unisex tunics, this example at the third couch was very much a woman. Black hair bobbed behind the ears framed a round, inviting face the color of fresh cut oak. Large, dark eyes were full of life, and awareness of her femininity. Instead of traditional rough wool, her tunic was cut from sky blue silk that clung to a swelling chest and wide hips like a second skin.

An Egarasi flanked the door, her skin shining like polished copper. She stood straighter than the rest, with an air of superiority. She might have been more covered than the others, but her garb was no less seductive. Her form-fitting indigo silk shirt featured dainty sleeves cut off below the shoulder with cuffs of lighter purple silk. Her waist was bare between the jacket and a matching silk wrap sitting right below the navel and reaching all the way to the floor. In the dark coil of hair behind her head sat a single flower of the same deep blue.

Simon had never seen so many beautiful women in his life, and cursed himself for noticing that the toga girl was not among them. The Lokutan staffing preferences were abundantly clear.

Opulent feasts among the wealthy were well known in Pazh, but it was a facet of *digniti* life Simon had only dreamed about. Until now.

"Master Daymar Lokuta," the steward announced, once again surprising Simon. A more mature version of Persei entered. This was a young man of supreme confidence, just entering the prime of his thirties. Slightly shorter than his brother, he was handsome in his own way, with clear blue eyes that sparkled with intellect, even burgeoning wisdom. He wore the senatorial toga like he'd been born in it, and looked in every respect a powerful ally. Or worthy adversary.

The servants looked on not in fear or desire, but in attentive respect, waiting for his command.

"Welcome to my house," Daymar said, no trace of arrogance in what looked like a genuine smile. "I am pleased you could join me for dinner." Persei stiffened enough for Simon to notice the change.

Daymar took the host's middle couch, and gestured for Simon to take the seat of honor to his right. This time Persei's scowl was visible, but only to Simon, as he lay down opposite.

"You must be tired after your long journey, Simon," Daymar said. "And with a big day tomorrow. We hope you can relax and enjoy yourself tonight as our honored guest." He waved to the Egarasi beauty by the door, and she and the other serving girls began to flutter in and out of the room like precious butterflies bearing cups, jugs of wine and steaming trays overflowing with food.

Simon cleared his head and mumbled a courteous response as the Maruthan girl filled his cup with a golden wine. The smell was tantalizingly sweet. The girl or the wine? Or the bounty in front of them?

The servants filled the table with delicacies Simon had never seen before. Daymar started with the herb-encrusted leg of some delicately small fowl, while Persei took a shank of meat so soft that it slid sensuously off the bone as he bit into it. Simon fought off bewilderment at the array of courses laid out before him and followed his nose to a dish of meat swimming in a rich, aromatic sauce. The first taste was rapture. Subtle fruity flavors with an undertone of pepper infused the meat. After soldier's rations and a simple life before that, his mouth was transported to the heavens. He couldn't stifle a moan of pleasure.

"Ah, the boar is spectacular," Daymar said, his mouth half full. He lifted the tiny leg. "And try the thrush. Perfectly in season."

"If you don't know what something is, just ask," Persei added, helpful yet once again making Simon feel inferior. "Not much of this in Salamis?"

"Persei tells me you share a room with your father?" Daymar

asked. "That must be… crowded."

Simon washed his mouth out with some of the wine. The warm, heady nectar caressed his throat as he swallowed. He breathed deep, nodding. "It's only a temporary stop while I'm serving in the legions. This is my first time home."

"With the right friends, maybe you could do better for yourself. Or for him."

Simon's mind considered the new possibilities. He'd never imagined…

A woman's sweet voice from the doorway interrupted his thoughts. "I've decided to join you and meet your new friend, brother."

Another beauty entered the room, the glow of blonde braids twisted into a crown on her head contrasting with the deep green of her low-cut gown, clasped at the shoulders with delicate gold chain. She was a classic buxom Pazian beauty, with full lips expertly rouged and lashes accented with a hint of black. Her seductive walk blended the authority of high birth with knowledge of her beauty. She half-smiled as blue eyes snared Simon's, and he fought a losing battle to resist the generous curves beckoning for attention as she walked over to his couch.

Daymar introduced her. "Welcome Lokilla, Simon would be honored to have you join us. We're just getting started."

She offered her hand, soft and inviting. "May I sit with you, honored guest?" She settled in to lie beside him on the couch, not quite in contact but tantalizingly close, with her plunging neckline in full view. Simon looked into his cup, hoping he wasn't blushing.

Picking up a fish dish, she waved for wine of her own, then toasted him with a beguiling smile. "Sorry for interrupting your business, please go on. Simon, were you telling us of little Persei's acts of *heroism* in Scentar?" She chuckled, and Daymar shared her amusement. Persei's teeth clenched in suppressed fury.

*This night, this family is too complex for me.*

Persei broke the uncomfortable silence. "The first you saw me after the battle was when I safely escaped back to camp."

"Yes. When you rode back into camp. You were one of the few to escape."

"Where were you during the battle, Simon?" Daymar asked.

He recounted how he'd been sent as a courier from the rearguard, and had retreated when they saw how the battle fared.

"So you didn't specifically see what happened to the command tent after... the explosion?"

"No, Persei will have to fill in those details."

Daymar took a slice of boar for himself, making satisfied noises as he ate. "Then you really do not have much to add. Persei will give his account first, and then we can trust you to exactly corroborate the portions that you were able to see, and that you greeted him as he rode in on horseback to the camp?"

Simon looked into his host's eyes while taking another long sip of wine, digesting the words that so deftly mixed request and command, offer and threat.

"We treat our friends well, Simon."

"Very well..." Lokilla whispered in his ear, her arm brushing his. He tingled at her touch, feeling lightheaded.

*I could get used to this life. There's no harm in enjoying myself. And maybe I don't have to make a decision yet?*

"It is my honor to be called your friend."

The three Lokuta siblings all nodded, and for once smiled as one.

With business settled, Lokilla spent the rest of dinner asking him about Attarsus, Pelusia, his father and his business as they ate through more courses of fish, game, and the crowning glory: peacock. Lokilla tickled him with a feather as he sampled the succulent flesh. Already too full, but he couldn't resist. It was the best meat he'd ever tasted.

Lokilla demanded specific descriptions of the Scentari warriors. She sat, rapt, as Persei described Shadush in terrifying detail. He painted a vivid picture with his words, and the resulting image in Simon's mind was very, very real.

His couch-mate waved for more wine for Simon and herself, then ordered the servants to bring out the sweets. In moments, the main courses were gone, and replaced with dishes piled with fruits, cakes and iced treats. She reached for a small flaky cake drizzled with a sticky sauce. "You have to try this, it is to die for." Gracefully, but with surprising speed she placed the cake in his mouth, her finger glazing his lip with honey. Involuntarily, he closed his mouth around it, which she very slowly withdrew. The sweetness intermingled with exotic spices as the cake dissolved in his mouth.

"Exquisite," was all he could say. She teased him with her eyes while her tongue lingered on her finger. The warmth of the wine intensified her radiance and the result was intoxicating. *I could stay like this forever...*

Persei lifted his cup. "A toast to a victory for House Lokuta at the Senate tomorrow." They all raised theirs in answer and drained them.

*A victory for Pazh.* Simon's head cleared as he matched them in form, but not feeling.

As advised by Lokas, Simon took the offer of a room for the night. Predictably, his guide to the sumptuous guest suite was another beauty, this one with the tawny skin and mysterious slit-like eyes of the people of Kawan. Most of the auxiliary cavalry were Kawanian so he'd known quite a few, and Simon had to admit that the features were much more attractive in a woman.

Once again, the quality of the room far surpassed anything Simon had ever experienced. The bed was soft and immaculate, making Simon feel dirty by comparison, though he was cleaner than he'd been in months.

He stepped in front of a full-length polished metal mirror and appraised what he saw. In this fine toga he looked the part of at least a prosperous *mercati*, if not some *digniti* heir like Persei himself. With the right backing, was he destined for something more? And Daymar had certainly offered far more certainty than Garas' friends. Might he aspire to a life previously beyond imagining?

But looking around at his rich surroundings, a new thought struggled for attention. This Republic that he defended, who did it really defend? Was it the common folk who lived in cramped and dangerous apartments, tended the fields, or fought in the armies? Or was it these ancient families who enjoyed untold splendor in huge private palaces, surrounded by servants—no, slaves—to care for their every whim?

Why judge these people for enjoying what they had? Or others for aspiring to attain the same? Business with the right backers would launch him into ever higher circles, and even make him eligible for lower public office. An esteemed political and military career could open the door for his descendants to enjoy this kind of life, defended by legions of soldiers and slaves.

Men like Garas. Men who risked decades of their lives, accepting the bargain in return for the tiniest sliver of glory and the chance at comfortable retirement after honored service. They walked into it willingly, did they not? And the Senate would act to relieve them, no matter what part he played tomorrow. So why not maximize the return for the Baroba? Why not enjoy the fruits of this roll of the dice Fortune had called in his favor?

A knock at his door interrupted his musing. "You may enter," he said.

The door opened without a sound, and the raven-haired girl who had dressed him earlier stepped through.

"Master Persei said you would need help... *undressing* for bed," she said, her eyes asking for permission to approach him. A slight accent and skin so pale it was nearly translucent marked her as belonging to the tribes north of the mountains.

His mouth was dry as he nodded, and she closed the door. The flickering lamplight illuminated every detail of her form, and he realized he'd been mistaken. She was young, but this was no girl. *Was it the clothes? What had she worn before?* All he knew was that this dress showed off curves rivaling any of the other women at dinner.

Blue eyes met his and she smiled again, approaching him. This time she started from the front, her hands gracefully unraveling the folds of his formal garment. Her sweet scent teased his nostrils. He stood very still, and followed her with his eyes until she circled around behind him.

His mind wandered.

*I've barely ever talked to girls my age. Not as romantic interests... and never with such beauties.*

During his schooling he'd spent most of his days surrounded by old priests and other boys his age. While he met women daily in his father's business, they were generally older slaves sent for specific purchases, or matrons from lower class families.

Of course some neighborhood girls had caught his eye, like Tarina that he'd even kissed that one time in the alley behind the apartment building where she lived. The memory of her breast scant layers away from his chest still brought a flush to his face. Wincing, his back remembered the beating her father had administered when he caught them. He never had another opportunity to be alone with her.

"Did I hurt you?" she asked, peering around to meet his eyes.

"No... just a memory," he said, flushing. He tried to smile away the awkwardness, and she smiled back.

With the extra layer gone and almost naked, he became excruciatingly aware of the effect of her proximity. She folded the toga with care and placed it on a table next to the mirror. He stole a view from behind, but she caught his smile in the mirror, and he blushed.

"Do you need my help with the rest?" she asked.

*I need so much more than that.* He nodded.

She approached again, kneeling down to untie the corded belt on his tunic. The belt fell to the floor, and the fabric now hung loosely down at his sides, except for the bulge right in front of her. She chuckled and took up a position behind him. He raised his arms, and watched her in the mirror as she slid her hands up along his ribs, ever so slightly caressing the muscles as she raised the tunic up and over his head. Her touch was like lightning crackling across his skin. Still he restrained himself as she returned to the front, just out of reach. She looked straight down to his crotch, then back to his eyes, a flush painting her face a light pink.

"Master, do you wish to *see* more?"

Her words sent a bolt through him, awakening him from the passionate dream.

*Master? No!* His body desired nothing more than to see her naked before him and take her in his arms, but his mind and heart screamed out in opposition.

"I will have no *slave* abase herself before me."

Startled, she flushed with... shame? No. Anger? Disdain? Fear?

"Thank you for your help, you may go."

She turned her back on him, and walked over to the toga.

The heat of the moment evaporated, leaving the cold of night upon his bare skin. Simon sat down on the bed and rubbed his face with his hands.

He exhaled loudly. *No. Whether this beauty finds me attractive or not, I don't have her heart, just her true Master's obedience.*

Simon was a man, but his Mother's faith and care had engendered in him a respect for women. For love. While the other soldiers spent their last coin on camp followers or the women in the towns, Simon never joined them. It was why Persei's jibe about finding himself the right whore had so rankled him. Elysia was no base prostitute, nor a slave. Her disapproving face filled his mind, and shame flooded through him, at how his body so readily reacted to this pale imitation. He could blame the wine, or how she threw herself at him, but it still came back to shame.

What would Elysia think of this place? Of these people? If he were to give his soul over to be the client of the Lokuta, and enjoy all their gifts, would there be a place in his life for her? Would he still be able to connect to his Talent, or would that chance be gone forever?

No, he would cast away all these things for the chance to explore their Talents together. Along with a taste of those lips...

But by rejecting this *gift*...

"Wait!" he called out before she opened the door, reason and compassion returning. And strategy.

She turned back, scowling.

His voice was more gentle: "Persei commanded you to lie with me, if I wished?"

She nodded, eyebrow raised.

"I don't wish for him to be angry. You've done your duty well. Go tell him that and I'll confirm it."

She hesitated to speak, and he bid her continue, still unused to having any kind of control over another person.

"I... have not been here long. He will suspect something is wrong between us, or..." she said, nodding toward his lower half, "with you."

Simon's momentary confusion was replaced with proud indignation. "There's nothing wrong with him—me!" When he saw that she was laughing with him, he joined her. "Maybe you can stay a while... and talk?" He grabbed a towel to wrap around himself, then arranged a chair facing the bed and gestured for her to sit.

Still looking suspicious, she took the seat. "Master, what would you—"

"Simon, please. I'm nobody's master. What's your name?"

"Mysena."

It turned out she was indeed from the north, taken into slavery as a girl of nine in a campaign against the Valtari, her people, and Persei's family had bought her soon after. Simon had almost as little experience with the life of slaves as he did with women, and was genuinely curious.

"Do you like life here?"

"It could be much worse. The Lokuta feed and clothe and keep us well, as long as we are... obedient." She sighed. "But at least the Masters are young, and handsome. You're a lot nicer than most of their friends."

The thought of many others sharing this room—this bed—with her in the past filled him first with revulsion, followed by pity.

"I'm sorry, you deserve better."

She cocked her head to one side, considering. "Like you? I wouldn't have minded... I still wouldn't." She reached out a tentative hand.

He flinched. "No... That's not what I meant... I..."

She smiled, realization filling her face. "There's another girl? Aren't you the faithful one!" Her whole bearing changed to that of an older sister who had been let in on a secret. "Tell me about her! She's a lucky girl. What's her name?"

"Elysia," he said, savoring the taste of saying it out loud. "We just met."

"Here in Pazh?"

"No, in Attarsus."

"You are faithful then, to a girl in some foreign port that you've only just met. She must have made some impression on you."

"She... she understood me in a way nobody ever has. It was like... magic." His eyes stared, unfocused, imagining being close to her again. "I have... little... almost no experience with women. Can you tell me what they like?"

"I could show you...." She arched her brow, then laughed at his discomfort. "You are too innocent. Sure, you helped me here, so I'll share what I know, for the benefit of your love, Elysia."

She spent the next thirty minutes explaining more about romance and physical love than he could learn from any book.

"Has this been enough time?" he asked.

"I could stay with you all night."

"No, you've been wonderful. Thank you Mysena."

"As long as you tell that to Persei, when he asks. And he will certainly ask."

"I will."

She smiled again. "You're a good man, Simon. Will I see you here again?"

"I don't know."

"I have a feeling I won't. Be careful."

She let herself out, carrying the toga with her.

After the intensity of the day, sleep came quickly.

*Simon was in the Senate Hall again, but this time completely naked and fully aroused. Beautiful women in togas filled the benches. They were talking about him. Staring at him, his manhood, and trying to lure him in with their eyes.*

*One beckoned to him, and her mouth opened to speak but her forked tongue stretched toward him like a snake.*

*He recoiled in horror, but more of the women advanced toward him on the central dais.*

*Nowhere to turn. Nowhere to run, their hands closing in on him, caressing, wanting, needing. They laid him down on the floor and vied to be the one to climb on top and take him...*

He awoke with a gasp, to a body looming over him in the darkness, hips pressed against his heated groin. The intoxicating scent was familiar somehow... recent... the chuckle was...

"Lokilla?"

She purred in response. "Did you miss me, Simon? I wanted to see more of you."

He retreated, covering himself. As his eyes adjusted to the light, he could make out that she was, thankfully, clothed in sheer fabric.

"You... shouldn't be here. Your brothers..."

"Are not my masters. I do what I want, with whomever I want." She laughed. "And tonight, I want you."

"But I'm..."

"Just a lowly *mercati*? Don't be silly. I'm not marrying you. But life here is so boring. Daymar's friends are mostly crusty old senators and officials. I'll have to spend too much time with that sort when I do marry. And I want nothing to do with Persei's boorish friends. And they only ever find *girls* to serve us." She pouted. "But you... you're interesting. Would you be *my* ally Simon?" She leaned in close, with the loose garment providing an enchanting view of her chest.

*Will this night of pitfalls ever end? Can I escape this house with my morals intact? With my head?*

"Lokilla, I must sleep. The Senate tomorrow..."

"Let me help you relax. Turn around."

Confident there wasn't much she could do with his back turned, Simon obeyed.

Lokilla removed the sheet, and her soft hands stroked his back, kneading the muscles. The massage felt so good, unwinding months of uncomfortable bedding, riding, and stress.

He was becoming aroused again, and hated himself for it.

"Anywhere else I can help with?" she said, her hands wrapping around his chest and fingers walking playfully down... down...

He had an idea.

"My turn." He faced her and gestured for her to turn around. *Thank you Mysena.* Lokilla did as he asked, then raised her arms. Inch by inch Simon lifted the gauzy fabric up to her shoulders to expose her back. Steeling himself, he rubbed his hands together to warm them up before grasping the base of her neck with a light touch. The skin was soft, flawless, and delicately warm as he worked her muscles. *Like painting, just like painting.*

"I hope my soldier's hands aren't too rough?"

"No... Mmmmm... Please... go on."

He massaged first neck then shoulders, slowly making his way down her spine to the small of her back and the top of her hips. The act was so seductive it took all his willpower not to give her what she so obviously wanted from him. The air felt heavy.

"Does this please you, Lokilla?" he asked, hoping it was enough for her.

"Keep going," she said, her voice hungry. She reached to grasp his hands, drawing them up and around to her breasts.

While a small voice inside told him to stop, his flesh shouted it down before he could pull away. He yielded, her fingers clutching his against the soft roundness, and the surprise of erect nipples.

"Here," she said, her voice commanding.

It pushed him over the edge of control into a chasm of desire. His hands found new life, enjoying the sensation as much as she did, her hair cascading back across his chest as he felt every inch of hers. He breathed into her ear as one hand moved slowly down her smooth belly. She arched her lower back, pushing round cheeks against his loincloth, and the sensation drove him into oblivion with a groan. His hands fell to the bed, limp.

She pouted. "That's it? You're done?" She let her shift fall back to cover herself. Her voice regained its haughty confidence. "I guess I'm too much woman for you."

He struggled to respond, his body weak, spent.

She kissed him, firmly in control, then pulled back, looking satisfied at reasserting her dominance. "Next time, you will show me that you know how to use more than just your hands." She patted him on the shoulder before standing up. "Get some sleep. Daymar needs you tomorrow." She blew him a kiss as she opened the door. "Come back soon."

Shame showed no mercy, pounding him into dreamless sleep.

# XI

## ᏭᏊᏭᏊᏭᏊᏭ

## *Allegiance*

Simon's morning wakeup call came from another new young lady, this one notable for her shining reddish-gold hair. After his last experience he kept carefully aloof. She brought him a tray of bread and fruit to break his fast, and handed him a note with his itinerary for the day. He was first to accompany Persei and Daymar to the baths, then head home to don his armor so he could look the part of the returning soldier, and finally go to the Senate.

Luckily for him, wine didn't seem to leave him with a hangover. Maybe his father's blood had some benefits? His head was clear as he picked at his food, carefully considering this day of decision. *Is there a way forward that keeps options open on all sides?* He just couldn't see one. Some potential actions would be neutral for a time, but all too soon he would be forced off the fence. Which one was best for him? For his father? For Garas? For exploring his Talent? For seeing Elysia again? And for fulfilling his duty to the Republic? Which gained the most useful or powerful allies? And which choice would create the most dangerous enemies? Just considering the interrelated possibilities was a complicated logistical exercise. Every promise confirmed meant another broken. That dilemma weighed on Simon the most.

Life was much simpler in the legion. Those few short months seemed like a lifetime already. Now the Lokuta were offering him a track faster than he had ever imagined. But the path of Garas and his allies would keep him true to the principles he held dear. Sitting alone, surrounded by finery and the uncomfortable memory of last night's shame, none of that mattered so much as following the road back to Elysia and Attarsus. Following the promise of a deeper understanding of himself, this Talent that had been lurking dormant for so many years, and love. Which roads would even lead him back there?

Persei opened the door to interrupt his reflection. "Ready for the big day?"

It was a new experience, walking through the streets of Pazh with a senator and his brother, surrounded by their bodyguards. The Gathaki warriors with their long golden hair and beards stood half a head taller than even Simon, and so powerfully-built as to make Persei look ordinary by comparison. They might technically be barbarians from the far north but they also made some of the best and most expensive bodyguards money could buy. Even on a busy street, the crowds parted instinctively to give room. Or if they didn't, a light reminder from the cudgel of one of the leading guards would do the trick.

Daymar took this time to brief Simon on the procedural aspects of what was to come today. Barring any unforeseen emergencies, they would be the first order of business on the senatorial agenda. He would introduce the two of them to some of the senators at the baths, and more when they assembled outside the Senate Hall. Simon and Persei would be off in a high gallery until called upon, but would have a view of the proceedings. Official priests would open with prayers, then turn things over to the president, who would call on Daymar to lead the discussion. Daymar would lead Persei through his statement first, then Simon. Questions might arise during the statement, and certainly afterward. The two of them would be dismissed before matters got to a vote.

Simon wondered where Lokas Lepilla and his allies would enter the picture, and could only imagine the anger his current companions would turn in his direction as a result. Had his choice already been made by even seeing them? Doubt gnawed at him.

The baths were the one luxury that wasn't foreign to Simon. Each district boasted at least one major bathing complex, and they were one of the great civic achievements that had been exported to all major cities of the Pazian Republic. Mornings were reserved for men. Daymar paid for the three of them and chose their attendants as they entered the marble edifice.

The massive public baths in the Arenial were less crowded than those he was used to in Salamis, with a far more homogeneous clientele. It was one of the first times Simon felt self-conscious of his own skin. He'd become quite accustomed to the diversity of the neighborhood he grew up in, and especially the legions, calling as they did upon people of every color from all provinces of the Republic. Naked, the upper classes of the Republic looked quite similar: whether new *suprati* or old money *digniti*, they were almost uniformly older and light-skinned. These families had roots going back centuries to the land in and around the city of Pazh. *Yet they speak for all of us.* Another chink opened in the previously formidable wall of his faith in a youthfully idealized Pazh.

Daymar led them through a cloud of steam to the room containing the hot baths, where the attendants took their clothes and started them off with a close shave and haircut. Next they rubbed their skin with delicately perfumed oils before scraping off the resulting grime with large curved metal strigils. It was the decadent version of a very Pazian ritual, and with the residue of foreign experiences gently scoured away, Simon was truly home.

Daymar followed it with a massage, while Persei headed to the pools with Simon.

Feeling five pounds lighter, Simon was like a young boy as he plunged into the cleansing portion of the hot pool. It still amazed him how they could get so much water this hot on a cool day, spouting out through a fountain shaped like a leaping dolphin. He luxuriated as the oil melted away under spray so hot that his skin tingled. Scooping up water with his hands, he washed his face and worries away for at least a few moments.

"Your first since you got back?" Persei asked. "It was the first place I came after seeing Daymar yesterday. Would have thought you'd do the same. I'm surprised you didn't join me in Tamar. You seem born for the baths!" He clapped Simon on the back.

"I was still tired yesterday, and it was nice to be home. I'd forgotten how much I missed this until just now."

"I always remember. And so do the ladies." Persei winked. "Speaking of which, maybe if you'd bathed, Mysena would have begged to stay the night!"

The few moments of pure relaxation were over. He tensed up again at the implication. "I needed to save a little strength for today," Simon said, trying to match his companion's bravado.

"It *gives* me strength," Persei said, puffing out his chest. "Speaking of women, which did you like better from dinner? Your personal servant, or mine?" Simon could barely remember which was which after his eventful night, so he shrugged. "Can't choose? Well I didn't have to, I had them both for dessert. Would you like to come back for more tonight? We could share!"

"Perhaps our new friend wants to develop his tastes slowly," Daymar said, wading over to them. "This is all new to him, is it not?" He gave Simon a knowing look. Shocked, Simon could only nod. "It would take him years to develop as keen an appetite as yours, brother."

Persei guffawed in response. "You're right, of course. I have yet to find a single one that can keep up with me." He indicated his groin with a grand flourish.

*Nothing I do or say around these two will go unnoticed. Or even... unscripted?* Simon was imagining himself as a fly trapped in a web filled with Lokutan spiders.

"What worries you, Simon?" Daymar asked.

*This one is far more perceptive, and dangerous.*

He revealed a far secondary concern. "I've never faced the Senate before."

"Myself excepted, they are just a bunch of old men. They love to hear stories about battles, so just tell your version and they'll hang on your every word. They'll be the ones worried about the decisions they will have to make as a result. Or rather, my decision that I will have them confirm."

"Which is?" Simon asked, curiosity spitting out the words before he could stop himself.

Daymar looked around, then drew them in closer with a quiet voice. "Since we are the only ones that know what has taken place, we have the advantage. I have already conferred with my allies, and they will put my name forward for election as general to prosecute the campaign. Persei will come as a tribune with my legions, since he is the only one who can identify this Shadush that leads them."

"But you're young; won't they want someone with more experience?"

Persei scowled and opened his mouth in rebuke, but Daymar stayed him. "You're thinking. Good. I have a great many allies, and I am of an age when I should have my first command. I am no fool like that dead Suboras, who only got the province because of his uncle's name, and the command quite by accident. While I have served under some great generals, including Daras Vanatri Marassano."

"Daras Vanatri!" Simon said, in awe. He was old, but possibly the greatest general of the past century. His campaigns against the Marassani in the East had yielded the provinces of Myrak and Bor. Kyso was fond of quoting his stratagems in their meetings back with Garas and the other general staff.

"Yes, and I count him a dear family friend." Daymar waved over to an old man on the far side of the pool. "Why that's him there. He served under our grandfather, and our father served with him as well. He is too old to lead a legion himself these days, but when asked for advice, he will endorse me as a star student and ready for command, offering to come along as my adviser. And another of my esteemed friends will extol the virtues of a dynamic young leader against a frightful new opponent."

Simon was impressed. *Maybe these are the right people to lead Pazh.*

"And of course, after I drive the Scentari to destruction, I will return for my triumphal parade, and ride the adoration of the people all the way to next year's Presidency."

*Or maybe everything serves his own path to power.*

"I would love to introduce you to him now, but you really should be heading home for your armor. Best not keep the Senate waiting. Our guard Galax will escort you."

"Thank you for the dinner, the baths, and the bed for the night," Simon said.

Both brothers smiled, and held out their right arms. Daymar clasped Simon's as he spoke. "You are an important new friend to the Lokuta, Simon Baroba. Do well for us today, and there is no telling how high you might rise. Perhaps I could find you a good position in my army as well?"

Persei added with a naughty grin: "And maybe we can find more women together like that fox in Attarsus. You'll have to take me to her when we go there together."

Simon forced a smile as he clasped his former—and future?—rival's arm in farewell. *Not while I still draw breath.*

Walking home to Salamis accompanied by the burly Gathaki drew more than a few stares, especially in his immediate neighborhood. He had to admit that it made him feel safer. The paranoid part of his mind had briefly considered the possibility of Galax being an assassin, but the combination of daylight, being seen together with the Lokuta in the baths, and the current positive state of his relationship with the brothers made that worry too far-fetched. He wondered what Markus' men thought of the arrangement, assuming they were still watching him.

His father's shop was open for business, which shouldn't have surprised Simon but did add a whole new unexpected angle for the morning. Not wanting to drive away a potential customer, Simon didn't protest when Galax escorted him inside.

"Welcome!" came his father's cheery automatic greeting when they stepped across the threshold. "Oh, Simon. And a friend?" He harrumphed, realizing there was no business to be had.

"Hello father. Good to see that you are well."

His father looked up, distrust in his eyes. "Why are you here? I thought you were pursuing your *dream* of getting yourself killed in the East?"

Galax busied himself with inspecting the wares on the shelves opposite Simon and his father.

"I was. I am. I… I was sent back on a special mission."

"You? Special mission? Must be some serious danger if they sent the likes of *you*."

"I can't talk about it."

"Well you never did share much with me. Why *are* you here?"

"I need my armor. I dropped it off last night. They want me to wear it for when I address the Senate this afternoon."

His father's eyes bulged out, his mouth trying unsuccessfully to voice the word Senate. As Simon started past him to the living quarters in the back, his father fumbled to find his sign indicating to sound the little gong for service.

Simon shut the door behind them.

Now alone together, his father found his voice. "Senate? Who is that man? He's a guard, but not one from the Senate, I'd reckon."

Simon spoke quietly as he changed into his armor. "He's from the Lokuta. I stayed the night at their house."

"House Lokuta?" His father looked on him in awe, then spoke to himself. "My son, guest of one of the oldest *digniti* families." Then back to Simon: "Have they taken you as their client? This could be great business."

"They would like to."

"Oh, Simon, this is wonderful news. It calls for a drink!" He reached for a jug of wine on the table.

"Not now, Father. I need my wits about me to answer the questions of the senators. This is a new world I don't understand."

"Have you even met a senator before this? I did once, but he barely deigned to speak to the likes of me."

"I met four yesterday."

"Four? The young Lokuta, and some of his allies?"

"More complicated than that. I'm just a fly caught in their web. With the fate of many hanging in the balance."

"So why are you here in Pazh? Surely you can tell me something. I'm your father, and my tongue won't wag."

Simon took away the jug and cups before his father started pouring. "Not if you keep your mouth dry it won't."

His father looked hurt, and a little surprised at Simon's commanding tone. "Fine. I'll go without, if it means hearing your tale."

Partially convinced, Simon continued. "There have been complications in the campaign in the East, in Pelusia, where I served. I have to report back to the Senate, so they can decide what to do to relieve the situation."

"Simon, you look haunted. There's something more to this. Don't give me the official version. What is troubling you? Are you in danger?"

Simon just stared back at him. The walls were too high, had been there too long. He couldn't let him back in.

His father looked uncomfortably at the wine jug, then shook his head. "Simon… I understand things haven't been good between us. Not for a long time. Not since…" He wiped a tear from the corner of his eye. "I'm horrible at this. I miss your mother more than anything. I know I've failed you." He looked up with new resolve. "But I'm here now. And I've always done everything I can to keep you safe. More than you'll ever know. You can trust me."

Simon sat down, and considered briefly. *If there's anyone I can trust here, it's family.* And he was out of options. He started slowly. "There's several factions involved. Thanks to you, I was elevated to aide to the Camp Prefect Garas Numeno. Some of the skills I learned from your business helped me get a position helping with logistics." He was surprised to see his father smile, swelling with pride. "Garas is the one who sent me to report to his friends and allies."

"The Lokuta?"

"No, young Persei Lokuta was also sent to report as an eye-witness. But he might prefer to give a different account that better supports their aims. Garas' friends are from a different faction."

"Anyone I've heard of?" His father hungered for delicious details of more famous names.

"Genaro Morichea? Markus Sentollus? Lokas Lepilla?" His father's eyes grew wider with each name.

"Simon! These are some of the leading names of our time!" He hugged his son around the shoulders, his excitement overflowing. Simon was again shocked, almost to tears. This was the first loving touch from his father in... as long as he could remember. He . looked into Simon's eyes with genuine concern. "So where is the problem?"

"The Lokuta want me as their client, so long as I confirm their account. Garas' allies want me to report accurately, and I've given them... a painting that shows what really happened."

Color drained from his father's face, followed by an oncoming storm.

"I thought I told you to give up that fool hobby of yours."

Old wounds torn open. *Again trying to control me?* "I have a talent for this, Father! Garas liked my maps! That helped me gain the favor of the general and his staff! That's what got me out of there, otherwise I could be dead!" He was more savage, more confident in his words than he'd ever been.

His father recoiled into a chair, looking old, beaten and small. He closed his eyes and sighed. "I fear you may have put yourself in even more danger. Who has this painting?"

It wasn't the reaction Simon was expecting.

"Lokas Lepilla. But why? What are you not telling me?"

Another sigh as his father began to pour himself a drink. This time Simon didn't stop him. He looked so old clutching that cup, swirling it around a few times, and finally looking up without taking a sip.

"I know you're good. You're very good. I used to love seeing what you would create."

Incredulous anger flared up. "You? Mother praised me for my work, but you always tried to stop me!"

"I did it to protect you."

"Protect?"

"The headmaster warned me. He and I often shared a drink together, and had a good relationship. He saw your talent, and didn't want any bad to come of it. Especially with your rebellious streak. He told me that if I truly loved you, I'd have to be hard on you, and discourage your dabbling in something you didn't understand."

Simon was dumbfounded. His father knew there was more to it? Stopped him?

"But Father, there's so much possible... I'm only now starting to learn—"

"I don't want to hear about it. I don't understand any of this, but what the headmaster told me is that if you were to go further with this, at any point in your life here in Pazh, that you would put us all in very grave danger. It hurt me to shut down that part of you. I saw the joy it brought you. Your mother disagreed with my stance, naturally... but she didn't hear the *fear* in the headmaster's voice."

Simon's whole view of the relationship was turned on its head with just a few words. *He was protecting me? Hiding this from me?*

"I wish I had done a better job. I'm sorry I have failed you." His father shook his head in sorrow. "So now you've created something new, and Garas' friends have it. *That* is the biggest danger here. So have you made a decision?"

"I... well... I've been trying to weigh the options. On one side there's patronage and support and luxuries that the Lokuta have promised. Higher rank, a house, and I could help care for you, Father." He felt like a small boy offering his father a gift he'd stolen for him. "But now you're saying my work itself is dangerous... that Lepilla, or another, might use it against me?"

His father nodded, his lips a tight line.

"Or I could spurn the Lokuta, but they are dangerous enemies in their own right, and not unwilling to cut our throats. Your business and our lives would be in danger. And they hold grudges, even for generations."

"But Garas did so much for me, and I gave my word to him first that I would support his cause. There is honor and right on that path."

"But also danger." His father stood and paced the room.

Simon voiced another option. "I could flee."

"Flee? To where? You would be a deserter, enemy of the state, and you would anger both sides. That wouldn't help anyone."

"Then Father, what should I do?"

"Do you trust Lepilla?"

"He seems a good man, with the interests of Pazh and his respect for Garas and his men at the forefront."

"Then I think you have already made your choice, in your heart. Lokas and his people should help you against the Lokuta, but I fear that greater forces could be at play if your work comes under scrutiny."

"But the Lokuta would give us everything you ever wanted!"

"Yes, my son. But that's not worth losing you."

His father took him in his arms, and this time Simon hugged him back, relief and vulnerability washing like a torrent over the crumbling walls of so many years of painful distance.

With his head on his father's shoulder, Simon saw the situation with new clarity. He had cast his lot with Garas and his allies when he'd presented the picture to Lokas. His brow furrowed.

"Father, no matter how things go today, *you're* in danger."

Simon looked to his sword, thought better of it, and strapped on his hidden dagger instead.

"I know, my son. Leave that to me. Perhaps I should leave the city, or go stay with friends. I was thinking of taking a vacation..." A spark lit his eye, bringing back life to his face. "My cousin in Sarea. Yes, the Far Sea air would do me good. I'll go there first, and let him know where I end up."

"But your business?"

"Things haven't been good for a while now, I'm afraid. I filled the shelves but then... I know I'm at fault." He poured the untouched wine back in the pitcher. "I'll leave a notice for customers to contact Jory. He's a good neighbor. I'll get to it right now."

"But... I'll miss you Father." The words sounded foreign coming out of his mouth. A few short minutes ago he didn't care if he ever saw his father again, but now with this fragile new connection, he couldn't bear to be apart, to risk it slipping away. His father hugged him again.

"You'll do the right thing. For Pazh, for your friends, and for yourself."

That reminded Simon.

"One more thing, Father... there's... a woman."

His father mocked a scowl. "Aren't things complicated enough for you already? Which side is she on?"

"Neither. She's in Attarsus. I want to return to her. More than anything."

Was there a twinkle in his father's eye as he appraised Simon's face? "Attarsus? How long were you stationed there?"

Simon avoided his father's gaze, feeling sheepish. "One night."

His father's voice began to rise. "One night?" His tone softened as Simon bristled at the challenge. "She must be a very special girl. I don't know if she's your first, or what. But be careful. You have a lot on your mind, and while she may seem like the most important... you're no use to her dead, or in prison. Or worse."

It was the last comment that stopped Simon from speaking of Elysia's Talent as well. He swallowed the words, and nodded instead.

"I don't know when I'll see you again."

"Just know that you will," his father said, with surprising certainty. He kissed Simon on the cheek, then straightened a fold of his cloak. Stepping back, he looked at his son the legionary. "You certainly look the part of a soldier."

"Thank you Father." Simon reached for the door.

His father's voice cracked as he bid him farewell. "I truly am proud of you, son. Your Mother raised you well. You honor the Baroba name." His last words were a whisper. "Be safe."

Simon let him go before he broke down. He steeled himself before facing the impassive Galax, who opened the front door for their departure.

ᕋᕐᕋᕐᕋᕐᕋ

Elysia rushed into the arms of her mentor.

"I sent for you as soon as I returned," Xelos said.

"Master Xelos, there's so much I need to tell you."

Ever since their first encounter, when she first showed him her work and he in turn opened her eyes to new possibilities with her Talent, she had trusted him implicitly. Her father loved her, but Master Xelos understood her in a way no other ever had, or seemed capable of. Until... Simon. She flushed at the thought of him. Of the power of his painting. And of the feel of his lips.

She'd always ignored the young men in her life, usually friends of Alexander's or sons of other merchants from the agora. Which was very unlike other girls her age who were either married or

119

angling for a partner. The young women weren't enjoyable company either, being completely dismissive of her vocation as man's work. Izari society believed a woman's place was in the home, doing womanly things like raising children, weaving, cooking and keeping the house or managing the servants and slaves who did those tasks. Sculpture certainly wasn't on the list of approved activities. So she'd rebuffed the advances of any man seeking to make her his captive wife and hide her away from her art. And that had been just fine with her.

Until now. Simon had stirred something. He appreciated her Talent. She'd never imagined a partner who would. The thought made her heart race. She'd worried about him constantly this past week. Would she ever see him again? Somehow she knew she would. But what then?

"Tell me, Elysia. What news from the East?"

"The young man I brought here. He has Talent."

His kind old eyes narrowed with interest. He bid her sit with him on one of the couches in workshop.

"Yes, they told me he was about your age, and well-mannered. One of the girls even said he was handsome?"

Handsome? Yes, she supposed so. With kind, noble lines in his face and a tall, lean physique. He'd make a fine subject for a sculpture. But not in marble. In bronze, to do justice to the depth of color of his skin. So different from the pale bearded men of Attarsus. She'd never worked in bronze but it inspired her to learn.

"Elysia?" Xelos said.

"What? Oh, I found him in the agora, a man, a Pazian soldier, drawing freehand. The acropolis."

"That is quite a surprise. A soldier you say?"

"Yes. But so much more." She winced inside. *Have to keep this interest professional.* "His name is Simon Baroba. His father is Pazian, his late mother Benjish. He wants to learn more about his Talent. He has only just begun to connect to it."

"What did he know about his Talent? And you're sure?"

"I... I saw it in him when he was drawing. When I got closer. And then his paintings confirmed it. I wasn't going to say anything, but he was cooperative, and getting worried. I gave him a very basic explanation, and said he must meet you."

"So when can you bring him to me?"

She frowned. "He left a week ago. I begged him to stay, to meet you first. But thank the gods that he didn't, since you were delayed so long. But he vowed to return," she said, looking down for a moment, reluctant for the first time that she'd known him to share full details with her mentor, "after he completes his mission. He was to report to the Senate about what he saw in the East. Dark magic!"

Her words etched lines of deep concern into his usually calm face. When he finally spoke again, his voice was grave and commanding. "Tell me all you know."

She recounted everything Simon had shared with her. Every detail that had been racing around in her head these days since he left. About the battle, the darkness, his art, the emotion it carried, and the Talent evident throughout. She felt horrible, but she skirted around mentioning the dinner shared, the emotional connection, and especially the kisses.

He sat silent, his eyes staring, unseeing while he stroked his neatly trimmed white beard like he always did while thinking.

"Everything is in danger. I pray this Simon returns to us, so we can work together to confront the peril. You were right to bring this news to me as quickly as possible. I must contact the others. Who else knows about this? And has anyone made a connection between the two of you?"

"No... well there was one man from his ship who saw us together." She sighed. "He... assumed I was the type of woman Simon might have picked up for the night."

"We may be in danger. Simon *will* be in danger. Not just from the machinations of the politicians of Pazh. No, we must be very careful. Spend time only here or at your home and workshop. Avoid public spaces."

Elysia was confused. The anxiety of the usually peaceful old man was contagious, and frightening.

"But what about Father? He will worry. And he needs my help."

"I will send one of the servants to let him know, and will send him any assistance he needs."

This was serious. She invoked the name of a goddess she hadn't prayed to in many years. Not since that night when she had discovered her first love, the one that brought magic into her life: working with marble. *Oh Simon, Aliata protect you and bring you back. To me.*

121

# XII

## ᏲᏋᏋᏋ

## *Senate*

The Great Forum was even busier that morning, bustling with all manner of commercial activity. The crier called out the news that the Senate would be discussing news from the attack in Pelusia. Flocks of senators in their red tunics and white togas were scattered around the area, chatting, grabbing a last minute snack or making their way toward the Senate Hall.

Simon stood out in his legionary armor, but given his lack of obvious arms, most people didn't give him a second look. More eyes looked askance at Galax towering over him. But strangely, the armor helped him feel like he belonged here. As a child he'd loved the sights and sounds and wonders, but as he got to better understand his lesser standing in the Pazian world he became more uncomfortable. But now, assuming the role of an honorable soldier defending Pazh from her enemies swelled him with pride at his greater stature. And in a role that finally had his father's backing.

Persei waved them over, looking even more splendid in his tribune dress regalia—a new and more ornate set of everything, after the Scentari had taken most of it when he was captured. Like Simon, Persei also appeared unarmed, in line with the Senate prohibition on weaponry for any but the presidential guards. Daymar wore his senatorial toga with only a narrow red stripe along the edge, delineating his status as one who had at least one ancestor that had been President of the Republic, but had not personally held higher office. For some reason Simon remembered that from school, but the rest was hazy.

"Nervous, I'd expect?" Daymar asked Simon.

*At peace.* "Less than before. All your coaching has me feeling more settled."

Daymar nodded. "How is your father?"

"Well. And bursting with pride that I've made your esteemed acquaintance." He inclined his head to the brothers in respect.

"Your father is a wise man," Daymar responded. "He'll be well taken care of... don't you worry, Simon Baroba."

Simon nodded again in thanks.

"We still have a few minutes; I'd like to introduce you to a few people before we go in."

"Here comes trouble," Persei said. He sniffed with obvious disdain as a portly senator hobbled up the steps to meet them.

"Senator Lokuta, may I beg a quick word with you," said Lokas Lepilla, breathing hard. He didn't even acknowledge Simon or Persei, dabbing at his face with a cloth to wipe off the sweat from the exertion of the ascent of a few marble steps.

"Of course, honorable Senator Lepilla." They turned away from the two soldiers.

Lokas spoke in a hushed voice, but Simon could still hear him. "Would you mind giving me any indication of what this... special business you're putting forward to the Senate would be about?"

"You'll hear with the rest, soon enough," Daymar responded.

"If there's anything I can do to help..."

"I will certainly let you know. Thank you." Daymar turned and urged Simon and Persei to follow him to another group of senators, leaving Lokas standing awkwardly alone.

The casual way Daymar dismissed his most important ally made Simon uneasy. Or is the talented orator also the equal of the best actors as well? *Have I chosen wisely, after all?* Uncharacteristically, he found himself praying to the Benjish God that he had.

The names and faces of the rest were a blur to Simon, as more and more senators collected around the entrance to the Senate Hall. There were at least five or six famous *digniti* among the ones he met personally, and a member of the *suprati* or two. It surprised him how deferential most were to the much younger Daymar, and even those that weren't treated him as an equal, or at least a favored nephew. He kept an eye out for Genaro and Markus, but failed to locate them in the crowd.

Simon found his excitement building, being so close to the

center of power of the most powerful nation the world had ever known. Or at least that the Pazian historians had ever recorded. And in a few short moments, all their eyes would be on him. With his choice made, he was ready.

A loud gong sounded, drawing everyone's attention to the pair of massive bronze doors cast with images of the gods standing at attention. The doors swung slowly outward, with Senate guards flanking the dark corridor beyond.

The orderly procession of senators filed in, while guards checked Simon and Persei for obvious weapons. Simon felt a pang of guilt at the sheathed dagger under his armor, but its presence was reassuring. Relief washed over him when he was waved through without a more thorough inspection.

The doors opened into a short, dark corridor that funneled them through to a blindingly bright doorway. When Simon's eyes adjusted, he was in the main hall, facing a raised dais containing a single simple chair. Not the throne of the kings rejected many centuries before, but a chair suitable for the first among equals, the current President of the Republic.

Daymar nodded to a pair of guards, who ushered Persei and Simon left and back up one of the two flights of steps that flanked the entrance, leading away from the stage. The stairs accessed rows of seating in a semi-circle like an amphitheater facing a stage. But would he enjoy the show?

Simon counted ten levels as they were led up, with the first containing a single row of ivory chairs, the second simpler wooden seats, and the third through sixth low wooden benches. The remaining levels were shallower, with the senators forced to stand.

The guards led them to a fenced-off space at the back that must have sat right on top of the entrance corridor, then remained to watch over them.

On the wall behind their seats, large open windows with elaborately carved stone patterns of flowers and vines streamed natural light through to shine directly on the dais, illuminating it as the center of attention. The reflection from the smooth marble walls made the whole room far brighter than Simon would have expected, explaining the brightness at the end of the entrance tunnel.

From his high vantage point, Simon could see a map of the entire known world inlaid in the floor. Useful for planning a war. Simon located the circle in Pelusia that stood for Tamar, and thought of Garas. *I'll do my best.*

The higher rows were filling up quickly, while groups of senators remained milling about on the floor. "Looks like a good crowd," Persei whispered. "Normally they're lucky if it's half full. We had spread the word that there would be important business to discuss to make sure our allies were here for the vote, but it looks like almost everyone caught wind of something big. Might even get all the senators currently in the city. Close to the full five hundred! Should make for a lively discussion."

Simon took note of the location of Lokas, Genaro and Markus as they filed in. He was mildly surprised to see them seated with different groups around the hall, all of them near the front. Daymar sat around the middle, with some of those he'd met, while the rest were close by, but closer to the front. Daymar was one of the youngest, with Simon putting the average age closer to fifty, with many near the front considerably older than that. And other than a handful of faces now standing at the back, the high majority were native Pazians. Simon felt even more conspicuous than at the baths.

"Is there any method to the seating?" Simon asked.

"Current office holders get the front row." Simon could see the seats, but none had taken them.

"Those ones?" he said, pointing to one with a red toga with a broad white stripe.

Persei rolled his eyes. "Of course," he said. "That's the Vice-President." He pointed out a few more. "Minister of the City, Minister of the Granary, Minister of the Courts, Censor..."

"So what about the next row?" A few were seated there already, and had the usual white toga, but with a broad red stripe, sometimes accompanied by another colored band.

"Past officials who have held major offices in the second row, then minor offices beyond that. Then those whose families have been president or other past officials." Simon saw Daymar taking a seat in that area. "And then the rest, until finally at the back are new senators recently admitted, or others lucky they haven't been expelled." Persei snorted.

"Expelled?"

"By the censor. If you can't show sufficient assets, he suspends you. Go long enough and you can be expelled. Pazh should only be run by those with more than a mere citizen's interest."

*Who looks after our interests?*

"How old do you have to be to get your seat?"

Persei scowled. "Did you even go to school? What are they teaching the *mercati* these days? Each family gets only one seat by birthright, which Daymar currently occupies. I can only earn one through exemplary service in the army, or taking high public office. And even then I'd only be on the waiting list until one of the five hundred is expelled or one of these old windbags dies with no heir." Unrealized ambition and longing was painted clearly upon his face.

*That explains the tension between you two. The fate of the younger brother.*

"Or you could be adopted—"

"I'm a Lokuta."

One of the guards shushed them, and all eyes converged on an angular man shambling up the steps of the dais in ceremonial robes, leaning on an iron staff for support. The murmur of a hundred conversations died down to silence. He turned to the crowd, and in a surprisingly strong voice began calling out a prayer to the gods: Salar the Iron One, Meliax the King of Gods, and Choron of the Secrets. Simon marveled at the different reactions of the senators. Some looked quite fearful and pious, while others looked disdainful of the ceremony, like Persei next to him with his yawn and rolled eyes. Simon had always been curious about the gods, and listened to all the stories, with a special appreciation for the paintings found all over the temples. But he couldn't reconcile his mother's one solitary deity with the existence of so many in the Pazian pantheon, often adopted from new peoples they welcomed into the Republic.

Another priest brought out a screeching chicken, along with a ceremonial bowl. The first priest drew a wickedly curved dagger, brandishing it for all to see, with his prayers escalating into a crescendo of religious fervor before he struck the killing blow. Blood spurted everywhere, the majority landing in the bowl along with the chicken's head, while the rest brightened the robes of the two priests and the dais below. The priest went silent for a moment as he tore the body apart with his bloody knife, searching for a portent. Grasping a portion of the offal in his other hand, he raised it to the crowd in triumph.

"The gods smile on us, and protect Pazh and all who lead our people!"

With the omens or theatrics complete, a man in a red toga with a wide black band mounted the dais, flanked by ten guards, and took the central seat. The president. Simon had never seen him, and couldn't even recall his name. He looked noble, somewhat rigid in his bearing, but definitely comfortable in authority.

"President Patro Subellius," Persei said. "No general, but *digniti* through and through, and a good administrator. No risk to the public purse."

"Is he... on our side?"

"Generally his interests align with those of our faction, yes. Hasn't opposed us with a veto so far. But keeps himself aloof."

An icy glare from one of the backbenchers forced Persei to lower his voice back to a whisper. "Fair, nonetheless."

The president stood to address the crowd.

"As President of the Republic of Pazh, by the authority of Salar the Iron One, I call this gathering of the Senate to order. I understand we have an urgent matter to discuss before continuing with yesterday's business. Pazh recognizes Senator Lokuta." He sat down.

After a respectful nod to the president, Daymar rose and walked down the steps to the dais. Simon noted the general attitude of curiosity, with several looking excited, and more than a few looks of concern, especially concentrated around Genaro and Markus.

Daymar turned to the crowd, his golden hair shining in the sunlight to give him an almost supernatural authority.

"My brothers, it is with a heavy heart that I bring ill tidings from the East. We received a message sent direct from Pelusia. General Jasun Suboras has fallen in battle."

A collective gasp went up from the crowd. An older man in the second row cried out in grief. Was there some slight resemblance to the late general?

"How?" the man asked, loud enough for all to hear.

"His uncle, Marcus Sarrinai," Persei said. "The one who subdued the Scentari before."

"As we all know," Daymar said, "he was governor of Pelusia, stationed there with the garrison and the 7th Legion. We previously heard reports of a border incursion near Jamad. The Scentari had grown restless, and had attacked the town. We now know they had burned it to the ground, then turned and fled back to their homeland when faced with our legion. General Suboras led his army in pursuit as far as the Sentusi River valley. There, he died after a devastating loss."

"What happened?" Sarrinai said, fury in his voice.

"We have two eye-witnesses who will give their accounts, so that we may decide what action must be taken." Daymar paused. "The first is the reason why I am the one delivering the news. I ask the president to call forward Tribune Persei Lokuta, of the fallen 7th Legion."

"Pazh recognizes Tribune Lokuta, of the 7th Legion."

Persei stood, basking in the attention of a thousand eyes, then marched down to the dais with the utmost confidence. He saluted the president, who nodded in return. Simon took furious mental notes about the finer details of Senate decorum.

Daymar began his questions. "Tribune Lokuta, what was your role in the 7th Legion?"

Persei cleared his throat, and stood straight and confident. "I was a junior tribune, attached to the staff of General Suboras."

"Please share with us the events that led up to the massacre at the River Sentusi."

"The legion was stationed at Sal Dar, the central capital. When word came through of the sack of Jamad, Governor Suboras assumed generalship and took us east."

"What was the state of Jamad?"

Persei didn't flinch as he spoke of the horror. "The city was a ruin. Men, women and children were dead on the roads to and from the town, and everywhere inside. There were signs of abuse. Of ritual slaughter."

Sarrinai interrupted with a question. "But how could a barbarian raiding party breach the walls?" The president held up a hand, but indicated for Persei to respond.

"The outer wall had been torn down by some kind of explosion. General Suboras believed they had discovered some kind of material that could do this."

Whispering broke out among many of the senators.

Sarrinai snorted. "They're little more than savages. They wouldn't know what to do with something like that, even if they found it."

"I can only attest to what my eyes saw. They breached the walls and the city was burning. Yet our scouts reported their withdrawal in the face of our superior numbers as we approached. We chased them north, and they appeared to be in full retreat."

Now most were nodding, caught up in the wave of Pazian military superiority.

"Once we crossed into Scentar proper, the night raids began. Their horsemen would strike at any part of our column that was late getting its camp established, and their arrows would even pick off a few of our sentries each night. The worst was the evening before we reached the Sentusi, when their attack wiped out several squads near the rear of our column. Camp Prefect Garas Numeno convinced the general to strike camp before nightfall each day as a result. He agreed, and combined the scouting groups for safety in numbers, but this meant we were falling behind and lost track of their main force."

"When was the decision made to engage them in the Sentusi River valley?"

"With the weather getting colder, General Suboras had decided that we should strike into the valley, to take away the better winter grazing land. The valley is warmer, and the only place they can feed their horses through the harsh winter. He figured that we would find their women and children there, and that the threat to their safety would bring about a pitched battle. They have some advantage as raiders, but on a field of our choosing should have been no match for more than a full legion."

Solemn nods all around.

"Describe the surroundings."

"The Sentusi is at the bottom of a deep valley, with high cliffs on either side where we approached it. The scouts reported no sign of the Scentari below. There are many tracks leading down, but they wind back and forth, meaning that it took the better part of a day to get our full force down into the valley. At that point, the river is too wide to ford, even on those Scentari horses that are too comfortable in the cold water. We were almost finished regrouping in formation on the near side, and by this time the general had set up the command tent on a rocky promontory on the river's edge."

A shout came up from a senator Simon hadn't met. "That left you trapped with little room to maneuver!"

"The general considered that an advantage. The mounted enemy's superior mobility was constrained when they could only attack us head on."

Daymar again. "Was the entire force in the valley?"

"No, the general had kept back a reserve of three cohorts of the 7th up on the high ground to guard the passes and prevent us from being hit from behind. And to allow for an avenue of escape, but that was very secondary. They also had the cavalry, to ward off raiders on the open high ground. "

"Who was in charge of this second group?"

"Camp Prefect Numeno."

"Where were you?"

"In the command tent, where the general was discussing the next step of the operation with his staff and the senior centurions."

"How did the battle begin?"

"It was late afternoon, but even dimmer with thick mist rolling in to cover the river. We couldn't see anything on the other side. There were signs that the enemy had moved northeast, so the decision had just been made to set up fortifications early, and to continue the pursuit the next day. That's when we felt, and heard, the stone moving beneath us. There was a great noise like a dozen claps of thunder at once, and we were thrown to the floor with the force of the blast, which launched the whole stone platform many feet to the side. Many were injured in the quake, and the tent collapsed upon our group. Then the booming of a thousand drums echoed around us. I was one of the few who had my wits about me, so I crawled to the edge of the tent to look out and was immediately assailed by Scentari horsemen charging across a bridge. A bridge made of the very rock I was standing on. I drew my sword and cut down several before I fell to a blow to my head. I was knocked out."

"So you did not see what happened with the rest of the battle?"

"No. Just that the entire leadership of the legion was silenced before the battle started."

"Was the general killed?"

"Not yet. They took most of us alive: the general, all his tribunes, and the senior centurions. General Suboras liked to include a lot of the lower level leadership in his battle plans."

"A grave error on this day, since the cohorts were leaderless in the ensuing battle."

"Yes, it proved to be one of many fatal errors."

Sarrinai sputtered, livid. "You should show more respect to your commanding officer!"

Daymar intervened. "He is only responding to our questions truthfully. Tribune Lokuta, please tell us what you saw next."

"Night had fallen. My eyelids were caked in blood, so they mistook me for dead. There were so many. At least ten of our own for every one fallen enemy. They had gathered our dead into a huge pile on the side of the river, near the stone bridge. General Suboras and his men were bound in a line facing the largest mound. The tents and everything they didn't steal for their own use was also on the mound." His face turned angry. "The savages were reveling, eating and drinking and laughing. They were pissing on our dead and desecrating their memory."

His anger was mirrored by outraged shouts from the crowd.

"That's when I first saw him. Their leader."

"Tell us about him, this… Grand Thane Shadush."

Sarrinai perked up. "They have no grand thane! We abolished the title when I forced them to submit."

"Well apparently they have a new one. Continue, Tribune."

"He's shorter than most of them, but definitely in charge. The mustache was actually braided into his beard, and he styles himself a bear with the furs to match! He paced back and forth in front of our men, spitting at them, calling out in his vulgar tongue. He had his second in command with him, and…" he paused for a second, looking momentarily unsure. "And his sons." He breathed deeply before continuing, his voice devoid of emotion. "That's when they lit the pyre."

"Were they honoring our men?"

Persei looked haunted. "No. It was a dark heathen ritual. They set fire to the piles of bodies. Shadush himself cast the bodies of our men into the flames, where they were consumed. Most of them screaming. Tribunes, soldiers, auxiliaries. Every prisoner was cast into the flames."

Gasps erupted, and a few of the senators looked sick. One ran from the room holding his mouth.

"And my nephew?" asked Sarrinai, his face ashen.

"He was stalwart to the end. Even spat in the face of their foul leader. Didn't make a sound as he was consumed. He died a most noble Pazian." Persei bowed his head in respect, and others joined him and were silent. Sarrinai shook his clenched fist.

After a respectful few moments, Daymar asked the question on the minds of many. "How did you escape?"

*Escape? But…* Simon's mind raced to prepare himself for addressing this deception in his coming response.

"When the Scentari were well drunk with their revelry, I saw my chance in the darkness. I stayed close to the riverbank, crawling away from the main group. The lone sentry on that side had enjoyed too much of their disgusting fermented horse milk, so it was easy enough to slit his throat and steal his mount. I rode quietly through one of the passes back up to Camp Prefect Numeno and his remaining force."

"Thank the Gods you were safe to deliver your account, Tribune Lokuta." Daymar's face was solemn as he nodded. "So what remains of the 7th Legion?"

"Only those left behind with the camp prefect. No other survivors made it up through the passes. Less than two thousand fighting men."

Grave whispers abounded.

"And how many in the enemy host?"

"Twenty thousand or more."

Simon shook his head at the exaggeration.

"This is grim news. What happened next? How long since the battle?"

"Based on the intelligence I delivered, Garas Numeno assumed the role of general of the rest, and called for the retreat southwest through hill country, to limit the mobility of the enemy horse. They harried us at first, but we successfully reached the coast, where the general sent two of us to deliver this news as fast as we could. We caught a merchant ship at Tamar, overnighted in Attarsus, and found ourselves back here yesterday. Three weeks since the battle by my count."

"Your bravery will be rewarded, when we prepare our response to these barbarians. Thank you."

Hands shot up, senators clamoring for attention. Daymar ignored them, turning to face the president. "I ask that we hold further questions until after the second eye-witness."

The president confirmed with a nod. Persei saluted, and took two steps back. Daymar sought out Simon.

"I would ask the president to call upon Simon Baroba, a soldier from the 7th Legion."

"Pazh recognizes Legionary Baroba of the 7th Legion."

Simon stood up tall at the president's call, his skin prickling as so many eyes turned suddenly in his direction. A single bead of sweat teased its way slowly down his right temple, but he did not flinch. With his back straight, he marched down the stairs toward the dais. He heard the whispers, and felt the questioning glances. He looked straight forward, relying on his military discipline not to seek out the eyes of any of Garas' allies. Instead he focused on walking toward Persei.

Daymar indicated a spot several steps in front and to the left of Persei, and Simon took it. Now facing the crowd, the full weight of their attention was like a fist clenched around his stomach. His mind screamed to run… run from these wolves who would devour him with words. Yet again, only discipline kept him on his feet.

Daymar walked in front of him, breaking contact with the crowd, and drawing Simon's eyes to meet his. They radiated a calm which Simon's nerves gratefully accepted, standing down from full flight mode to mere unease.

"Simon Baroba, when did you join the 7th Legion, and what was your role?"

Simon found his voice more easily than he expected with the simple question. "I had joined at Sal Dar three months before the sack of Jamad. I was a common soldier, but General," a cough from the crowd stalled him, "*Camp Prefect* Garas Numeno chose me to serve as one of his personal aides."

"So you were with the legion for the same journey as Tribune Lokuta?"

"Yes."

"Do you have anything to add for the time up to the day of the *Sentusi Massacre*?" Daymar seemed to be trying out different names for the event, to see which elicited the desired response from the crowd. This one resonated.

"No, I confirm his account."

"Please give us your account of that day, starting with where you were."

Simon breathed deep. He remained on comfortable ground, with his practice in recounting the story several times verbally and many more in his head. "I was with the camp prefect, helping to coordinate some new fortifications we'd designed to better defend our position against Scentari raids. When I was done, he sent me with two soldiers to deliver the message to General Suboras that all was prepared on the high ground."

"From their position on the cliffs above the valley, could the camp prefect's force see the battle?"

"No, the footpaths twist and turn on the descent, and there were no good views. Garas... the camp prefect's scouts had no line of sight of the battle."

"But you did?"

"Yes, but only halfway down, our view opened up and we could see the deployment of our force. And the command tent on a tall flat shelf of rock overlooking the river, just as Persei... the tribune said."

"Please describe what you saw."

He closed his eyes for a moment, and the entire scene came alive, just as he'd painted it. Except moving. He spoke faster, with more confidence once he opened them again.

"The valley was a deep gorge, with the river snaking through the middle. Only the near side, with our forces, was visible. A thick fog had settled in over the river, and it even covered parts of our force. We could see that the formations weren't fully deployed."

"So the battle had not yet begun?"

"That's when we heard the sound of a Scentari horn, followed by the explosion."

"Did you see what caused it?" Daymar's eyes narrowed, the silent command clear.

"Strange flames leapt out of the rocky base under the tent, and I watched in horror as it slid backward into the river."

Shocked looks broke out across the crowd, and Simon's eye was drawn to the corpulent form of Lokas Lepilla, who shook his head ever so slightly.

"That's when the arrows and drums and horns and cries of the Scentari filled the entire valley, and they poured out of the mist... overrunning the confusion in the fallen command tent, and splitting the forces in two. At the same time they came from the north along the river and began driving us back on both flanks. They had laid a trap, and the general walked right into it."

"What were your orders?"

Simon hesitated. "To deliver the message to General Suboras." *Was this a trap?*

"So what did you do next?"

"Our first instinct was to charge down and somehow help, or rescue the general... but we saw the folly in this. To save the rest of the troops, and keep the paths open for survivors, we needed to return to Garas... the prefect, with our reconnaissance."

"So you didn't complete your orders."

Simon looked on, defiant. "No. I did what I could for the many."

"How long did you watch the slaughter?"

"Long enough. We saw the confusion, but couldn't understand why our men didn't form up better to oppose them. We only knew that the command tent had fallen, then saw the full impact of the surprise attack on multiple fronts. The front lines were falling, with the arrows taking their toll, and the confusion impeding the veterans. We were all quite shaken, and we weren't even in the battle. When the Scentari punched through from the command center, part of their force broke off and made for the footpaths to prevent any escape. It became a bloodbath when they surrounded our men. We left before the Scentari could start up our path."

"Tell us the response of the camp prefect when you returned to him."

"He had indicated his misgivings about the general's plan from the beginning, and didn't trust the terrain. He was shocked at the scale of the defeat, but not that we had suffered losses. Based on our report he knew that there was nothing we could do to relieve the attack."

"Did he consider waiting for survivors?"

"Yes, one option was to hold the high ground and see if any could make their way up to us, but when the tribune returned to the camp with his account, it confirmed that retreat was the only option. It was only through the decisive leadership of General Numeno that the rest were saved. He awaits relief from the Senate at Tamar, and has sent word to the Governors of the other eastern provinces and city garrison commanders about what we face."

"Thank you, Legionary Baroba."

Daymar turned to his fellow senators.

"So you heard from two of our brave soldiers how a force of Scentari were able to trick brave General Suboras into a trap, and force our remaining men to cower like dogs. Not only did they violate our treaty, and destroy a Pazian city in our province of Pelusia, they have insulted our people, our honor, our might!" He punctuated these last statements each with a nod, and many in the crowd matched him, getting worked up.

"We should meet this challenge with an overwhelming force!"
Cheers went up.

"We need a strong young general to face this foe! We—"

Simon followed his line of sight to where Lokas Lepilla stood, his hand respectfully raised.

The president spoke. "Pazh recognizes a question from Senator Lokas Lepilla."

"Thank you President Subellius. I am so sorry to interrupt your excellent speech, Senator Lokuta. In fact, I would like to thank you on behalf of the Republic for your fine work in presenting the statements of these brave young soldiers. But you did promise time for more questions. If I may be so bold, I would like to ask a few that are surely on the minds of many of our brothers here. Then we can continue with the very important matter of choosing *appropriate* leadership for a swift response."

Daymar's eyes flashed angry daggers, but his smile remained carefully crafted. Lepilla walked slowly down to join them on the dais, carrying a wax tablet in one hand, and in the other a familiar satchel that snared Simon's eyes.

First Lokas bowed slightly to Persei and Simon. "Thank you, Tribune Lokuta, Legionary Baroba, for your steadfast service in the defense of the Republic. Without your bravery, our people would be caught unprepared." He paused again, allowing for some applause from the crowd. "There are a few details here, however, that I am having trouble piecing together."

He tapped the wax tablet with a stylus.

"First, the explosion. We really do need to understand what weapons these *not-so-savages* are capable of bringing against us. Legionary Baroba, surely the noise attracted your attention to the center of the blast?"

Simon nodded.

"So you got a view of it, and you said..." He read from the tablet: "*strange flames poured out of it*? Can you describe the *strange flames*? What makes a flame strange?" He turned theatrically to the audience with one eyebrow raised.

*There was no turning back.*

"They were black."

"The smoke was black."

"No, the *flames* were black."

Daymar let his control slip for a moment, the blaze in his eyes commanding Simon to stop.

"And of course you reported this to the camp prefect. Did he believe there was any natural explanation for this?"

"He didn't know of any."

"And do you believe it was natural?"

Simon looked Daymar straight in the eyes. "No."

Fury, hatred, and the promise of revenge flashed in response.

Simon felt naked and falling and suddenly alone. He wanted to reach out his hand to Lokas, but had not yet seen any outward sign of support from the man whose side he had chosen.

Rumbling conversations broke out throughout the benches, until at the president's command his guards banged their spears on the floor, demanding silence.

Lokas turned to the crowd again. "So are you saying you believe that the Scentari won the day through the use of the dark arts? With... *magic?*" He let the last word drip off his tongue with incredulity.

One of Daymar's elder allies stood up and protested. "Who is this green soldier to scare us with old crone's tales of evil magic? The Scentari are barbarians! There's no proof!" Many stomped in approval, shouting for proof, and Daymar nodded eagerly.

"Silence!" shouted the president, standing to his own full height. "We will have order!" "Senator Lepilla, this does seem a tenuous line of conjecture. The Scentari have been known to have some ability to control fire through their pagan priests, but this dark magic is only the stuff of myth and legend."

Lokas looked apologetic and nodded his agreement. "I felt the very same. While we have no reason to dispute our brave young soldier here, perhaps his overactive imagination was trying to make sense of the horrors of the slaughter?" He looked on Simon with sadness in his eyes.

Simon's own fury burst out. He spoke out of turn with teeth gritted. "I know what I saw!" He pointed to Persei. "Ask him what happened at the pyre! He saw even more of the magic!"

Persei looked to his brother, then shook his head, his eyes sad. "I'm sorry Simon, the pressure must be getting to you. It was horrible seeing all those people burning in the fires. A tragedy and an insult. But they were *normal* fires."

Every eye turned away as Simon's mind reeled in darkness.

"Is that so, Tribune Lokuta?" Lokas asked, catching Persei's eye. The younger Lokuta was smug as usual. "I have here a letter from General Numeno, in his own hand."

Daymar's head whipped around to Simon. His eyes narrowed and a vein bulged on his neck.

Persei stiffened.

Lokas produced the letter, holding it down in front of his face to review. "Not only did Legionary Simon Baroba attest to seeing dark flames erupting from beneath the command tent, but in his report to the camp prefect, Tribune Persei Lokuta said that *the Grand Thane of the Scentari, Shadush, used his control of the black fire to consume the commanders... including General Suboras.*"

Persei's eyes flashed irritation, before becoming composed once again.

"Why would General Numeno make this up? Or did you lie to him?"

"I only said that so he wouldn't think Simon crazy. We had been getting along so well." He looked at Simon with a good imitation of pity in his eyes. "As you said, a merchant boy can be deeply affected by seeing the deaths of so many of his own age. And furthermore, I was afraid the general was thinking too seriously about a counterattack, when the best course of action was to withdraw, so the Senate could send a *real* leader to bring us to victory."

Simon wished he could slice that smug, arrogant smirk off Persei's face for good. But maybe first he'd crawl into a hole to escape the disgusted censure painted across the faces of the senators.

Lokas looked him in the eye, and there he saw a hint of compassion that deepened into sorrow. The old senator sighed, then held up his hand. The presidential guard resumed their thumping for order and quiet.

"What if I could show you proof?" Lokas called out, his voice resonating throughout the hall. Many of the senators banged their seats, echoing his cry.

Daymar crossed his arms with a bemused expression, while Persei looked from Lokas to Simon in confusion.

Simon slumped his shoulders, resigning himself to his fate. *Every piece is now in play.*

"What if we could view the scene as Legionary Baroba did? Experience the power? See the evil as it happened?"

Daymar laughed derisively. "Are you going to use your own magic to transport us not only vast distances, but back in time as well? Perhaps we can go kill Shadush when he was a child!"

A chorus of laughter and catcalls echoed back from his supporters.

"Alas, but my talents all relate to my mouth, and there is no magic there. Just too large an appetite, I'm afraid." There was a twinkle in Lokas' eyes. "I take no credit here. But if you would like to see the scene, Senator Lokuta, come take a look at *this!*"

Lokas opened the satchel and drew out the three panes of the triptych, laying them on the floor before him.

Senators from all over the room stood and strained to catch a glimpse of the assembled picture, with a few of the more esteemed members queuing for a chance to come up and see.

While the others were angling for a view of Simon's work, one pair of icy eyes evaluated him. Simon felt strangely exposed before the gaunt man's gaze, and wished again he had somewhere to hide. The moment passed when the figure turned to whisper to his neighbor, and the president, Daymar and Persei passed between them to get a better view.

Persei's eyes went wide in surprise and the president looked impressed, Daymar incredulous. Then they froze in place, expressions of fear carved deep onto their features as if they were marble.

Lokas winked at Simon, then passed the satchel over the darkness with a flourish to break the spell.

"The likeness is uncanny," said the president, shaken, looking to Lokas. "Where did you get this, and how?"

"General Numeno commissioned Legionary Baroba to represent what he saw. He felt that we would only comprehend the true import of what we faced if a picture could tell the tale. Simon's work is quite extraordinary, as you can see. He gave it to me for safe-keeping."

"You're a dead man, Benjai!" Persei said, stepping toward Simon before Daymar grabbed his shoulder to restrain him. Simon backed away from the swirl of seething hatred.

Lokas, enjoying the spectacle immensely, leaned close to Persei. He kept his voice low, speaking through the side of his mouth, but making sure Simon could hear it. "Should Simon tell them how proficiently you ride while tied?"

Only Daymar's insistent grip kept Persei from assaulting Lokas.

Lokas addressed the President: "Would you say that Simon's painting conveys the essence of the evil that we face?"

"There is a great evil afoot. Our enemy commands some power that we are not capable of comprehending. Legionary Baroba, you have done our people a great service, and we thank you."

Relief washed over Simon, as if he were finally stepping back onto solid ground. But when he looked up, he was overwhelmed by the far superior numbers of the Lokuta and his allies arrayed against him.

Lokas raised his hand again. "With your permission, President Subellius, I'd like to leave general viewing of the painting until after we make a decision on our response. It would prove to be... a distraction if everyone took a look first?"

The president nodded, and Lokas replaced it carefully in the satchel before handing it to him.

"I have one more question for you Legionary Baroba. General Numeno said in his letter that..." He opened it once again and read: "*this Shadush seems to be growing in power each time he uses his dark arts for human sacrifice. It is my recommendation that the Senate send a strong force immediately to destroy the Scentari before he gets too powerful.*" He looked up. "Strong words! Do you agree with him?"

Simon nodded. "We cannot leave this evil unchecked. We must act, and soon, for the sake not only of our soldiers and citizens in Pelusia, but for the safety of the entire Republic."

Lokas nodded solemnly, then offered his arm to Simon, who clasped it in thanks. As he released it, Lokas slipped a note into Simon's palm. "The blessing of Choron," he murmured cryptically before turning back to the crowd.

"Sorry for the interruption, Senator Lokuta. I wanted to ensure we all understood the gravity of the situation in the East. Now I'm sure you have more to say about what we should do, and who should lead?" Daymar clenched his teeth into a tight line and nodded. "And I'd imagine our brothers in the Senate are ready to get on with that as well? Or do you have any further questions for our soldiers here. We don't wish to bore them with what will likely be a lengthy and *lively* discussion."

With no voices rising in disagreement, the president motioned for his guards to show Simon and the furious Persei out.

A tickle of unease in the back of Simon's mind prompted him to track that gaunt figure. He wasn't in his seat, but Simon spotted him arguing with the Senate guard at the door, who put a hand on him to keep him inside. The man shot Simon a piercing stare, his hunter's eyes locking on prey, before flicking the guard's hand away and returning to his seat with a scowl. Simon sighed with relief, not wanting to be anywhere near him.

# XIII

ᏆᏋᏋᏋᏋᏋᏋᏋ
## *Escape*

The Senate guards shut the bronze doors behind them with a resounding boom, leaving Simon and Persei in the sunshine on the Senate steps.

A hard blow to the back of Simon's skull sent pain flashing through his head.

Persei stepped in front of him, spitting on Simon's sandaled feet. "Benjish dog! I should have known better than to trust one of *you.*"

Simon backed off, rubbing the back of his head. Fighting the dizziness, pain and the blinding sun he surveyed the bustling Forum for avenues of escape. People filled the space, but where were the Lokutan guards? It would be trouble enough to hold his own against Persei, but add Galax and the others to the mix and he'd have no chance.

Persei advanced on him. "I wasted my wine, food and women on *you?* Took you under my wing! I thought I had the measure of you when I saw your taste in Izari whores, but I guess I was right after all. How does it feel to have that fat pig Lokas grunting with pleasure as he mounts you?"

Simon ignored the barbs, having decided on his escape route. He assumed a boxer's pose, with hands raised as he'd been taught in basic training. He hadn't enjoyed being on the losing end nearly every time, but had learned a trick or two. *Wait for the opening.*

"Now you're going to fight me?" Persei raised his own fists. "You're dumber than you look. We promised you so much more.

Now you'll be lucky if I don't break your pretty little face. And your hands too. How will you paint for your porky patron then?" He laughed at his jest, then his smile turned to a sneer as he sprung a lunging jab at Simon's face.

Simon threw his raised elbow forward to deflect the blow, following through with his full weight to strike Persei hard on the shoulder. Persei spun around as Simon sprinted down the steps past him. Simon didn't turn back, trusting the bright sun to give him a head start. His heart beat wildly as he ran.

"Galax, Mylax, get him!" he heard Persei shout, his words not carrying far in the din of the Forum. But far enough. Simon pulled his arm away just as the big brute Galax grabbed for him.

Simon ran to the right, knocking over a food cart and sending apples and pears bouncing across the stones. The livid owner screamed at Simon, but it gave him some room as Galax tried to sidestep the mess. The hulking form of Mylax appeared out of the crowd on the other side. With just a knife, Simon couldn't hope to overcome the huge guard.

But he didn't have to. A burly bald man shoved the advancing Mylax in the arm, shouting obscenities. Mylax pushed him back and again stepped toward Simon, but the other man grabbed him, punching him hard in the head. Mylax turned his full ire on his assailant.

Though not the strongest fighter, Simon did pride himself on being fast. He seized the opening and sprinted past the angry merchant, building a lead on his remaining pursuer through a gap in the crowd, but giving it back when forced to dodge around more people and market stalls.

*Which gate? The stairs to the river? Toward the harbor? Not to the Janiar or the Arenial.*

Just as he gained some breathing space he misjudged an uneven paving stone. His foot caught, gave way, and he landed hard on his right knee. Sparks of pain shot through his leg. He rolled over to face Galax lumbering toward him. Cursing and gritting his teeth, Simon clutched at his side under his armor as if in pain, feeling instead for his knife.

Galax smiled with crooked teeth and unsheathed his sword. The brute leaned down, motioning for Simon to get up.

Simon spat in his face.

The smile turned ugly and Galax swung his sword down at

Simon's leg. Simon rolled just far enough for the blow to strike the stone beneath him with a deafening clang. He kicked his good leg at Galax's ankle, causing him to stumble, then stabbed upward with the hidden knife, sinking it into the soft and exposed groin.

Galax squealed like a sacrificial pig, dropping his sword as he collapsed to his knees, two hands clutching his bleeding crotch.

Simon choked back bile, his hands red and shaking as he sat stunned by the sight of another man's blood. The crowd around them was now a widening ring of fearful shrieks and panicked cries, jerking his thoughts back to the present. There would be others, and even city guards might detain him after this little skirmish.

*I have to get out of here.*

Simon fought the pain in his knee as he regained his feet, limping backwards away from his tortured former pursuer, unable to take his eyes off the agonized face.

*If he dies...*

His back brushed up against solid stone, a column in the portico before one of the big temples. It was empty except for one man with fear in his eyes, and another pointing at him. His legionary armor was too visible; he needed to get out of sight.

Loud voices and charging footsteps approaching behind the wall of the crowd got him moving again. He briefly considered entering the temple, but not with so many watching. And if his enemies didn't respect the sanctity of asylum... No. He ducked around the corner between the two temples. Across from him was the temple of Choron. *Choron? Choron!* What had Lokas said? *His letter!* Simon rushed around behind the temple, hoping to find a place to read it away from prying eyes.

Behind the great structure four majestic trees with mottled bark formed a private grove, the ground below littered with spiky green packets. Chestnuts. Tucked in behind the trees was a door in the back of the temple.

Simon tried the door and was surprised to find it unlocked. With no pursuers or even bystanders in sight, he slipped inside and closed the door. The crash reverberated down the stone hallway. Dim light filtered in from slit-like windows above the door. He withdrew the letter.

"Hello?" A hooded figure stood at the end of the hall, watching him. "Why do you seek Choron through his back door?"

Simon stashed away the letter and felt for the handle on the door behind him. He could run again. The fewer that saw him, the better. And he wouldn't dare harm a priest.

"If you are a thief, remember that Choron sees all, knows all. He sees your heart and the malice that lurks inside, and all will be revealed to the gods when you pass into the afterlife."

"I am no thief," Simon said.

"Good." The man approached. "Why are you here, Legionary?"

How could Simon hope to pass anywhere in this city unnoticed, with his armor betraying him?

"I... I am looking for Choron's blessing. For the secrets I must keep."

"Choron reveals only what should be known. You are welcome here. Especially if you were sent by a friend of Choron."

*What did this man know?*

"Do you know me?" Simon asked.

"What is your name?"

"Wait," Simon said, suddenly on guard. "Why should I trust you?"

"Do you have a letter?" the man said, with a hint of a smile. His eyes remained shrouded.

Simon nodded. Was this what Lokas meant for him to do?

"Come with me and read it. Or go back outside and let their men catch you."

Simon threw his lot in with Lokas' man. He took them to a small room and barred the door. It looked like the bedroom of the resident priest.

The man took off his hooded cloak, revealing a bald middle-aged Pazian face. "Take off your armor, and clean your knife. If you're going to get away when you go back out there, you'll need to be a little less conspicuous."

Simon started to do so, then remembered the letter. He sat down on a chair, hearing Lokas' voice as he read.

*If you have this letter it means your secret was revealed. This will change your life far more than you even know. You have given so much in the service of Pazh, and yet elements here will oppose you even further. You have not just made an enemy of a powerful family, but even greater forces will seek you out. For capture, or worse. For what you can do.*

*Again, I'm sorry. It is impossible for us to keep you safe here in the city.*

*You must flee. Yes, this will also brand you as a deserter when the Senate asks you to return to your unit.*

Simon stopped reading, the weight of desertion hitting him hard. By default he should return to the remains of the 7th Legion to complete the three year term of his enlistment. Deserters were hanged. How long before he would be branded a deserter? Too many threads tangled in his mind, so instead of sorting them he read on.

*I will have told you whose blessing to seek.*

Choron. Lokas' cryptic parting words made sense now.

*Find a friend, and he will help set you on your way. There is money for you. Whatever direction you choose, he will point you to contacts for a boat, horse or cart. You can leave your destination with him and I will arrange for further assistance.*
*All those who are faithful thank you, on behalf of the people of Pazh. We have already asked too much of you. I only hope there comes a day when I can welcome you to my home as an honored guest.*

"You're a priest here?"

"Plinas, Keeper of Secrets."

"What is your connection to the one who gave me this letter?"

"Lokas is my wife's cousin. He was gifted with a silver tongue, while I have steadfast devotion. We both serve Pazh in our own way. Here, this is for you." He handed Simon first a pouch of coins, and then a cloak once Simon was finished removing his armor. Simon wiped his knife clean on his discarded military cloak.

"Thank you."

"A friend of Garas is a friend of mine. But I'd rather not have my name involved."

Plinas took the letter and burned it.

"You know Garas as well?"

"He is like another cousin to me, and I never question his devotion to the Iron One, for the glory of Pazh."

"Is it safe to stay here a while?" Off his foot, the ache in the back of his head was competing with the pain in his leg to dominate his attention. He massaged the painful bruise on his knee.

"If he summons more men, they will likely search all the public places. They should respect the sanctity of my quarters, but I do not trust that to stop them. Like it or not, you should move."

Simon tested his leg in response. It hurt, but grudgingly supported his weight. He put on the nondescript cloak, and pulled the hood over his head. It covered his face to his eyes. It looked foreign, yet familiar. Similar to the Izari style prevalent in Attarsus. Lucky the day was cool so he wouldn't stand out much. And there were many Izari merchants in the Great Forum, and the city at large.

"Do you know where you'll go?"

The word popped out of his mouth. "Attarsus. And if I leave now, they can't possibly cover every way out of the city."

Plinas looked thoughtful. "The port won't work, at least in the city. A few men at the docks could check over anyone coming and going on any ships due to depart imminently. I'd stay away from the main gates as well, at least on foot."

"Do you have contacts for a boat from another town, maybe Nahuz?"

"Of course, but difficult to find one that will take you direct to Attarsus, especially without stopping here first."

"What if I go by land as far as Malayus on the south coast? It was originally Izari, so wouldn't they do more trade with Attarsus or one of the other city states?"

"Good thing you paid attention to your history. That is a good plan; they will not expect you to give yourself less options, down in the peninsula."

"So you can arrange a cart?"

"Not I, but you can see Gleba. Do you know Salamis well?"

"I grew up there. But... they might expect me to go to my house."

"So take a different route. From the main Salamis market on the west road, take the second right and you'll see the Amphora of Gleba. He's a wine-merchant and will arrange to have you shipped to Malayus."

"Shipped?"

"You'll be safer in the back of a cart than on foot."

"Thank you again Plinas."

"Let me check the door." He returned after several minutes, and nodded.

"May Choron keep you hidden, and Salar protect you. For Pazh." He clasped Simon's arm.

"For Pazh."

It might have been the pain in his leg coloring everything, but even the light outside looked different as Simon left the shrine. Every piece of stonework looked somehow sinister now, as if the whole city of his birth, the city he'd been willing to lay down his life to defend, was now seeking to oppose him. Blinking it away as nonsense, Simon silently melted into the crowd.

He tried his best to look for signs of trouble while keeping the hood low over his face. At least that kept his eyes focused on the ground, so he could avoid aggravating his leg with another stumble. Bending his will to give the appearance of a normal gait brought him renewed pain. Fighting it, he made his way to the steps leading down to the bridge to Salamis.

That's when his mind started winding itself in knots. *What about the opposite way, taking the long way around? Misdirection over speed? They're most likely to be watching the obvious routes.* This line of worries joined the already loud chorus throbbing at the back of his head. He took that as a vote for speed.

He fell in behind a pair of Izari merchants wearing similar cloaks, thanking Fortune for the opportunity. He followed them out the Harbor Gate, past two suspicious-looking men whom he'd swear were looking for him. He mentally thanked Plinas again for the change of clothes.

It was as he walked over the bridge to Salamis that his anxious thoughts turned increasingly to his father's safety. *I must warn him!* But when he started down the road toward his house, another internal voice stopped him. *It's too risky to say goodbye, but I just wish I could get my sword at the least.* Instead he took a circling route, bringing him one street to the south, to the laundry run by the parents of Tarina, the first girl he'd kissed. Her mother was inside dealing with a customer.

"Simon?" she asked when she was finished. "I thought you were away fighting our enemies in the East? Your father does worry about you." Her face darkened. "Don't be thinking you're here to see my daughter. Her father will have none of that."

He shook his head. "I was back for just a short stop. I'm in a big hurry, and wanted to get a message to my father."

She looked like a worried mother. "Why can't you go yourself? It's just a block away. Are you in trouble, Simon?"

"No, well... maybe... there might be someone watching for me. It would be best if you forgot that you saw me, unless it's my father you're talking to."

She sighed. "Keep yourself out of trouble. What's the message?"

"Thank you. Tell him I said to make it a rush."

"An order, or?"

"That's it, just make it a rush. I think he'll understand."

She nodded, and that made him feel much better. Thankfully there were some good people he could still trust. "Where are you going?"

"Back where I belong," he said with a grin. "Say hello to Tarina for me. I hope she's well."

"She is. She's engaged to the potter's son, do you remember him?"

Simon didn't, but nodded to end it. "Wish them the best for me. Thank you again!"

Back on the street, he made his way to the main market so he could follow Plinas' directions. He didn't see any uncommonly suspicious characters on the way, and found the Amphora of Gleba easily. The proprietor was middle-aged, balding, and in the midst of negotiating a sale. Simon waited until the current customer had been served and was on his way.

"Can I help you?"

"I'm looking for Gleba. I'm a friend of Plinas."

The man raised an eyebrow. "Would you prefer to speak more privately in the back?"

Simon nodded, and the man yelled through a curtained door and out came a younger version of him to take his place. The man he took for Gleba led Simon to a small room behind.

He was all business. "Where, and when?"

"Malayus, as soon as possible, and unnoticed."

"That goes without saying. Malayus? I've got a cart headed there tonight, so you're in luck. How unnoticed?"

"As much as possible."

"I can have my man lock you in a chest for as long as you'd like, but it's an awful way to travel."

"Just until we get out of the city."

"That would be wise. Wait here until my man comes to pick up the goods after dinner. I'll charge you extra for the food." A sly look came over his face. "This class of travel won't come cheap. But if you... had any useful information for me that could affect my business... maybe I could give you a deal?"

*Everyone wants their piece.* Simon thought for a moment. *The news will be all over by tomorrow, what harm could it do?*

"Do we have an agreement?"

Simon nodded and clasped his arm.

"Let's just say that shipments from Pelusia stand a very high chance of being disrupted. Thank you."

Gleba's eyes lit up.

"Your news and coin is enough thanks, and don't say any more. I'd rather not create any unnecessary entanglements with whoever is looking for you. Have a rest in that chair—I doubt you'll get much sleep in the box tonight."

# XIV
ᏬᏮᏬᏮᏬᏮ
## *Plot*

Daymar glared at Persei. "What do you mean you lost him? You're useless, Persei."

Persei felt the disdain like a whip, beating him with another failure.

"He had help," Persei replied, seething.

Daymar sipped from a glass of wine a servant handed him. "And you still had numbers. We should have had him killed in the first place."

"But he already went to Lepilla. Their version would still have come out."

"Yes, but without his presence it would have been much weaker." Daymar softened slightly. "You have shown you still have a lot to learn about judging character. And letting someone so visibly defy us? You have shamed our family. Now you will fix it."

Persei absolutely hated when Daymar was right, and when he put him down. Which was constantly, leaving few moments he thought well of his older brother. The one who lorded over him, standing firmly in his way.

"Where have you sent our men?"

"To the port, all the major gates... and of course to his father's house. I told the men to bring the father back in chains, or if he's not there to burn the place."

Daymar nodded. "Arson might be a little rash, but the bastard deserves it. Just make sure they don't leave a trail leading back to us."

"If he tries to leave, we'll find him. I also sent men to watch Lepilla's house."

"They're smarter than to hide him there. And the pig owns enough property that they could put him elsewhere. But he won't want to leave the connection open either. Simon will be trying to leave Pazh. Hopefully he does it before he hears the news of the day." Daymar smiled.

Lokilla sauntered into the hall with a smile for Daymar. "What is the news, brother? A victory for our house?"

Daymar brightened as he kissed his sister on the cheek and bid her sit with them. "It was hard fought, thanks to that little stunt Lepilla pulled." He shook his head in a combination of consternation and admiration. "He was ready with his own proposal, to put forward Genaro Morichea with Markus Sentollus as his second. Sure, they'd be good, but none of our faction would support them on their own. It took some serious horse trading, and will cost us more than I'd like, but at least I didn't have to marry you to some shriveled old pervert." He paused to smile at his sister. "And I managed to get myself elected as General of the East!"

Lokilla squealed with delight. "Oh Daymar, this is a great day!" She took her own cup of wine from a servant. "A toast, to our dashing brother, Daymar Lokuta... Scentarus!" She laughed at her own construction. "You'll rid the world of those dirty savages and return home a hero. You could be president!"

Persei tried to marshal his face into a proud smile. "Did you get the legions you wanted? And who is your second?"

Daymar's eyes clouded. "That's where Lepilla's tricks cut both ways. He did manage to saddle me with Morichea as a second. Persei, you'll enjoy him and his taste for the good life. And no, Lokilla, I won't be having him over here." She looked disappointed. The whole family knew she'd long had her eye on Morichea as a suitably handsome and powerful match, despite being nearly twice her age and very married. "His wife wouldn't let you anywhere near him anyway. The Senate wanted him for his solidity to temper my youthful vigor, or something like that. At least he's competent. But this talk of dark sorcery convinced them to send me with four full legions! The 8th and 9th from Egaras will be diverted to Tamar. We're to raise another one here, and then depart when the 3rd comes down from Melaxa."

"We?"

"Yes, You'll be my lead tribune raising veterans and more troops to get the 7th back to full strength. You're not totally useless when it comes to the troops."

Persei winced again, full of resentment.

"What of our dear new friend Simon?" Lokilla asked, her voice innocent.

Daymar looked down his nose at her. "That's where all our judgment failed, dear sister. That half-breed betrayed us. He disappeared before the Senate decreed that he would be the one taking the message back to Garas and the remnants of the 7th. It seems he is already running, and we have no idea where he might be headed."

He turned to Persei with an idea. "That slave you like, the Valtari... with the dark hair. *My...* something. You sent her to him?"

Persei blushed. "You... knew?" Why did Daymar always think one step ahead of him? He hated that. *And why is Lokilla fuming? Did they have their own plans?*

Daymar rolled his eyes. "See what the slave knows. Maybe he told her something. Hurt her if you have to. And if you can't, I'm sure Lokilla here will be happy to assist."

Feeling outmaneuvered again on this day where everything was going wrong, Persei stormed off to take out his frustrations on the slave girl.

He had Mysena brought to him in one of the guest bedrooms. She smiled at him playfully when she entered, but it turned to worry when she saw his face.

"Master?"

"Simon betrayed us. You said you had him under control!"

Her face fell, lip quivering.

"I... I'm sorry Master." She dropped to the floor at his feet.

"Do you wish to still serve me, or should I end this here?"

She looked up, confused and defensive. "I have always been your faithful servant."

"*Slave.*"

She nodded meekly.

"A lesser man would have you whipped. Flayed for all to see." His words were terrifying her. He'd always enjoyed her body, and had an easy power over her... but this was new, and very exciting.

She started sobbing. *Pitiful.* But he needed information.

He reached down and stroked her hair, comforting her. His hand cradled the side of her face, bringing her eyes up. His fingers danced down her neck, and she began to look hopeful.

He clenched her throat, squeezing out a choked gasp. His eyes bore down on her.

"Tell me anything he said. Where might he go? He cannot get away. What do you know?"

Only a gurgle came in response, her eyes pleading in anguish. He relaxed his grip slightly. She coughed.

"A girl... Attarsus."

Persei nodded, the fuzzy image of the beauty on Simon's arm coming back to his mind. He softened his grip, caressing the red marks he'd made on that tender neck.

"A name?"

It was little more than a whisper. "Elysia."

He smiled broadly, and nodded. "That's a start. You're in a good position to continue making it up to me." He began to re-move his loincloth. "I might just forgive you."

## ᏮᏋᏮᏋᏮᏋᏮ

Simon wondered if this was what it felt like to be buried alive. While the Pazians cremated their dead, the Benjish custom was to keep the body whole, usually in a wooden box like this. Was it possible that sometimes they were mistaken? And someone would wake up alive in one of these, unable to get out? A chilling thought, despite the heat. They'd covered the bottom with coarse wool blankets, which barely absorbed the bumps of the ride, more to muffle the sound than to protect his bones. It had the unfortunate side-effect of raising the temperature from late autumn cool to midsummer noon inside. Worse still, he could only fit his height inside by curling into a ball like a small child. Anything bigger would be too far out of the ordinary, Gleba had said.

The only markers of time were the clicking of hooves and rat-tling of wheels on the road. At first he tried to imagine their route toward the south gate, but after the second turn he lost track. As the motion, sound and heat mixed together he started nodding off, but fought it. He wanted to be aware at least until they passed the gates.

Several times they stopped, and Simon caught himself holding his breath. Drenched in sweat, he would exhale in relief once they started moving again. What might be the regular ebb and flow of evening goods traffic on the streets of Pazh became a terrifying mystery on this night.

*Click-clack click-clack click-clack*

On the third stop, he heard commanding voices, too muffled to make out specific words. *This must be it.* Simon prayed once again to a God he barely knew. A few moments passed with back and forth conversation between the driver and the guards. A loud knock on the chest made Simon's heart skip several beats. Lying still and holding his breath, he tried not to make a sound. The driver barked a response, and several men laughed. Another slap on the wood near his head made him cringe, but the cart lurched back into motion. Sweating in the stifling heat, he slowly exhaled.

A new instrument joined the symphony of sound. *Drip... Drip... Drip... Drip.* First occasional, then picking up into a steady rhythm, the rain was comforting. Images of the day danced through his distantly aching head, the pictures becoming indistinct. It had been a long day. Very long...

He awoke, confused, to light streaming in on his face. He'd been dreaming of a deluge washing away bodies... bodies of men he'd killed. When his eyes came into focus, there was an unfamiliar face in front of him.

"Good morning?" the man said.

Starting at the closeness of the unfamiliar surroundings, he finally remembered where he was. It was the first time he'd seen the driver. An extra precaution Gleba had advised, in case of questioning.

"Where are we? How long?"

"You slept all night. You didn't give me the signal to let you out, and with the rain being so bad it would have made a mess. At least this kept you dry. We made good time. Not many on the road in this weather. If we keep this pace we'll be in Malayus tomorrow morning. But I'll need you to take the reins for a while unless you want to stop at an inn?"

Simon nodded. The man handed him some bread and cheese. "Eat up first, I don't want you passing out on me."

As the peaceful, yet unfamiliar, road stretched out before him,

Simon set his chin and kept the pace as the cart trundled on into a very uncertain future.

ᏆᏌᏨᏌᏨᏌᏨ

Another town lay burning at Shadush's feet. He looked on with a measure of pride, but his mood was brooding. He felt somehow empty. *Why?*

The campaign was going well, with a full third of Pelusia falling under their banner. Their losses were minimal, and with their massive burning sacrifice at each settlement, his power was growing daily. There was no challenge, no pleasure in overwhelming these provincial towns. It was like using his sword to crack open a nut. The cost was still gnawing at him, try as he might to lock it away in a dark corner of his mind. But having paid the price, with no turning back, he kept the army moving forward.

"My lord," Kazash said, approaching him from the side. "We have taken everything we need. What are your orders?"

Shadush sighed, and his most loyal captain appeared startled at the melancholy that escaped from his leader. "Kazash, how far have we come?"

"Scentar is almost whole again!" Pride shone through his eyes.

"And then?"

"Then we keep going! We take the rest of this fertile land, and the ripe Pelusian women, and we don't stop until we see the sea!"

"And then?"

Kazash was less sure, pausing for a moment. "Then we run the Pazians into the sea if they ever dare to set foot on our land again!"

Shadush snorted, and caught the flash of anger that it elicited. "Do you think it will be so easy?"

"With our superior horses, and your power... they can't stand before us."

Shadush nodded slowly. "True... very true. With *my* power. But I can't be everywhere."

Kazash nodded, and his eyes burned bright. *With desire for my position? Or my power? Not what I was expecting. And troubling.*

Shadush continued as if he hadn't noticed. "If we take the whole land from here to the sea, all the way south to Marutha, then that gives us a huge border to defend." He took out his sword and began to draw in the dirt. "Here, here, or anywhere along the coast.

Where would you have me stand, to defend all of this?"

Kazash looked uncertain.

"And they will come. They're probably coming already. One force, and we can wheel to meet them anywhere. But what if they send two? Or three? Or more? Or one strikes deep into Scentar to raze our homeland, while another runs us in circles here?" He slashed at his makeshift map, releasing some of his frustration.

The melancholy returned. "Taking these provincial towns is easy, too easy. But now we have set ourselves up as a challenge. A threat. An embarrassment." He pursed his lips. "They won't let us get away with this. They are coming."

"And so we will kill them again," said Kazash, with confidence.

"Yes, we will," came the voice of his daughter, Mirasha. "Again and again, because none can stop you, Father."

Both men stiffened. Shadush looked on her as she approached. So confident, and so beautiful, even in riding leathers, as Kazash was too aware.

"Princess, you shouldn't be here," he fumbled. "It is not safe."

She giggled. "What is the danger? You killed all the soldiers, and sacrificed everyone else. And with two of the greatest warriors of our nation standing here to guard me? There's nowhere safer." She went to Shadush's side and hugged him.

She had caused quite a stir when she rode south with them on the campaign. Yes, she may be sixteen, and rode as well as any of them, demonstrating great skill with a bow... but she was still a woman. Yet there was no denying her. She had always been his favorite. And he couldn't forget that. Not even now. It still felt good to have her here.

"So you think the Pazians will send another force against us soon?" she asked.

"My lord, we can discuss this later..."

"No, Mirasha can speak her mind. Not just a pretty face." Shadush smiled, and Kazash looked down. *Was he blushing?* "And who knows, someday she may be the wife of a future grand thane."

He caught his daughter watching for a reaction, and smiling ever so slightly when she got the one she wanted. Kazash tried hard not to let it show, but both of them knew that he wanted it all. Her hand, and the mantle. He might even make a good leader. Especially with this one at his side. Shadush could trust them both, at least for now. Ambitious, yes, but Kazash would defend his lord to the death, and had come close on more than one occasion.

Shadush continued. "Yes, they will come back to crush us. To make a point. None that challenge Pazh will live. None have, so far."

"We will be the first," Mirasha said. "Your power will make sure of that."

"You're as confident as my captain here. We can defeat a single army here. But how many times? They will raise another. And another. They have the wealth, the men, and they believe in their cause."

"They can't keep doing it forever," Kazash said. "We will bleed them."

"But we also can't keep going forever, in this foreign land. Our warriors thrive on the promise of pillage, but put them on the defensive and they'll long for their land and their women."

It was Mirasha who spoke. "So then we press on. Take more cities. Ports. More pillage."

"We could. We could press them all the way to Pazh itself," Shadush said.

Kazash's eyes went wide. "Cross the sea? With our horses? Is that even possible?" More than a little fear was evident in his voice.

"Pirates," Mirasha said, surprising them again, though Shadush should be used to it by now. "There are many who would wish to throw off Pazian control. They would support us, and then we could capture more merchant ships to take us there. What if we were to destroy their capital? Tear out their heart?"

Kazash nodded in agreement, looking deep into her eyes, the admiration—or was that adulation—plain for Shadush to see. He'd have to keep a closer eye on this. "If we destroy them, then none shall oppose us. The world will bow before us."

Shadush raised one finger. "That is one course. We could continue to destroy every city, including the jewel of the world." He mostly shared their excitement at the prospect, and the power in him burned to forge this reality. "But that would be a waste."

Two pairs of eyes converged on him, shocked.

He spoke faster, seizing the moment with a new fervor. "You have not seen their cities. Not the big ones. These frontier towns barely qualify. They are worthless. But Tamar, Sal Dar, Sal Pratta, and Pazh itself. Make them bow before us in tribute, as our slaves, and they will shower us with riches."

The prospect awed Kazash, and while Mirasha outwardly reflected the same... Shadush detected a hint of darkness, of disagreement. He didn't care. *She doesn't control me.* And this new vision, this new idea might make it all worth it. All he had done. His sacrifice. And hers.

"From now on I want to capture these cities alive. To learn from them. How to rule. How to control them. And how to use their power against them."

"But our men won't allow you to put a roof over their heads," she said.

"I will show them what they've been missing, and let them make the choice. They can have grazing land, or they can have all the wealth of Pazh at their fingertips, and I will honor them equally either way."

Kazash could barely contain his excitement. "Do you wish me to tell the officers?"

"No, bring them to me and I will address them. On the new moon. This is a major change for us. There will be opposition. And we still have to allow some level of pillage to keep them happy. As we take the bigger cities, we will buy off the short-sighted with their portion of the booty, but the remainder will finance the establishment of control—government over our new dominion. And those who stand with us will share in far greater wealth in the future."

"You will still continue the sacrifice," Mirasha said, her voice laced with warning. It struck to his heart, reiterating the difference here. How much she had changed. For him. Because of him. He fought off the memory again.

Kazash laughed. "Has our lord converted you to his new faith?"

She bowed her head, and said a prayer, shooting him a withering look when she finished. "This power is what raised him up, and deserves his respect, and yours."

"We will select an appropriate sacrifice from each city," Shadush said. "But we must leave them populated enough to be useful."

She didn't look satisfied. "I don't agree with this plan, but do what you feel you must."

Shadush shook his head ruefully. *Kazash, You could handle a kingdom before you could handle her.*

# XV

## Pursuit

$A$ktar swayed slightly as he took his first steps on the dock. No matter how many times he'd made the journey, he'd never enjoy sailing. Give him solid ground beneath his feet, any day.

*Mid-afternoon. Plenty of time to do some searching.* He reviewed Persei's notes, which were all he had to go by.

*Simon Baroba*
*Legionary with the 7th*
*20, tall, slight build*
*Half-Benjish, medium dark skin,*
*Short, dark, wavy hair*

*Elysia*
*Izari? Whore?*
*From Attarsus*
*Late teens?*
*Long, curly, dark hair*
*Striking, not classical beauty*

It wasn't much, but Persei paid him well to innovate. And particularly well in this case. He'd been getting his hands dirty for the family for a decade now. And since he could speak Izari he was the natural choice for this mission. *Persei sure wants this guy.* Aktar still couldn't get over the bonus he and the ship's captain had both been paid to leave that very night. The Lokuta would pay much more for Simon to be brought back alive. The girl was just a stepping stone.

*Well, we'll have to start with the brothels.* The sailors had been a fount of information on that front. He smiled and made for the one with the highest recommendation.

ᏬᏋᏬᏋᏬᏋᏬ

As soon as he set foot in Attarsus, Simon made his way to the house of Master Xelos. They'd had favorable winds from Malayus, and he'd been lucky enough to find a ship sailing within hours of his arrival. He'd even slept well on board, and awoke that morning with first light, as they made their way into the harbor. For once, everything seemed to be conspiring to get him where *he* wanted to go, instead of tossing him around like a piece in someone else's game.

He'd kept the Izari cloak, adopting even the traditional wide-brimmed straw hat. This time he intended to blend in. He patted his belt where he kept his knife. Who knew when and where one of Persei's agents might be watching for him?

After the whirlwind two days in Pazh, he'd gratefully accepted the easy pace of the cart ride and following sea voyage. His mind had naturally even returned to thoughts of painting. And exploring the capabilities of this *Talent*. He wished he'd been able to experiment further while confined to his cabin on board the ship.

Still angry that he'd been forced by circumstance to leave his materials at his father's house, he wondered when he'd be able to recover them. If at all. The thought was sobering. He'd expected to have a little time to procure more when he reached Malayus, but another quick turnaround had prevented that. He would seek out supplies soon enough, but after meeting Master Xelos.

As he retraced his steps from his mental map, his anticipation built. He wasn't sure what made him more excited: seeing Elysia again to explore their Talent... and more, or speaking to someone who might actually have some answers for him? Waking or asleep he'd been imagining the coming conversation a hundred ways. He could scarcely breathe as he approached the gates and knocked.

"Simon Baroba, to see Master Xelos." Then he fumbled to add: "Or Elysia if she's here?"

Ycastros showed him in, and in a few moments a balding old

man with kind eyes and a close-cropped silver-gray beard strode to meet him. There was a twinkle in his eye as he patted Simon on the shoulder in a very grandfatherly way.

"Wonderful to meet you Simon! I am Xelos. Welcome to my house. Follow me, we have much to talk about. Have you seen Elysia yet?"

Simon's head snapped to attention. "She's not here?"

"Her brother sent for her. When I saw you, I thought she must have been welcoming you. She speaks very highly of you."

Simon's heart fluttered, and he hoped the hat hid any flush of color.

Xelos looked concerned. "Again, much to discuss. I had asked her to stay here. They'll be looking for you, you know."

The hairs stood up on the back of Simon's neck. "How did you know? And why would Elysia be in danger?"

"If anyone saw you two together, they might come searching for her too. She is under my protection."

"Then we must find her! Where will she be?"

"One step at a time, hmmm? I have an idea. You want to explore your Talent? Follow me."

That was enough to jolt Simon into motion.

"I'm sorry, I didn't bring any paint..."

Xelos waved his hand in dismissal. "I think you'll find my workshop well supplied. We have everything ready for you."

Walking into the workshop was like coming home, with a new desk set up with brushes of every shape and size, and paints in every color. All for him. He was so close to getting answers. But his worry for Elysia tainted the moment.

"How are we going to help her with paints?"

"You are very worried about her?"

"Yes!"

"Then channel that. Strong emotion is important. Very important. When you painted the battle scene, what emotion was dominant?"

Simon didn't hesitate. "Fear. Dread. Of the evil."

"Exactly. And this time it is worry." He pointed to the materials. "Choose any brush that calls to you."

*Calls to me?* Simon reached for the closest brush. But something made him stop short. Out of the corner of his eye, there was something different about one of the brushes. It looked like any other, but with an invisible wave pushing his hand toward it. He chose it. The benevolent twinkle returned to the Master's eye.

"Good. Now you need a window."

"A window?"

Irritation colored the master's voice. "Do you want to learn? Every moment you spend questioning me is another that Elysia remains vulnerable. Paint a window."

Simon set to work with a new intensity. He selected the paints, mixed them and began to work on the frame of an opening. Despite his anxiety, it felt much freer and easier than when he'd been painting in his cabin at sea. When he was about to paint the shutters, Xelos held up a hand.

"Stop there. Just the frame for now. Now close your eyes."

Simon swallowed his protest and obeyed.

The voice permeated his entire being as Xelos continued the instructions. "Now set Elysia in your mind. Picture her inside the window. Channel all your worry, your fear, your... any other emotion you might feel." A hint of a smile in his voice. "Can you see her?"

Simon's anxiety grew, and the image wavered in his mind. As much of an impression as she'd made on him, he'd only seen her for less than a day, and after all that had happened since...

He must have been shaking, but strong, kind hands on his shoulders steadied him without dispelling the emotion. In fact the worry, the care, the... desire intensified. *Those lips. The feel of her lips.* They came into sharp focus, and then her eyes above them, boring into his soul. The curls of her hair, the pale skin looking so soft, he wanted to reach out and touch her.

"You can see her like she's right in front of you now?"

Simon nodded without opening his eyes.

"Now feel that image, and let it flow through your hand, through the brush and into the window frame." Xelos released his shoulders, and Simon let his hand flow free. The strokes came faster and faster, with the black and white image of Elysia beginning to appear inside the window. After the form took shape, the brush strokes leaped unbidden to the white space around her, forming first lines, then shapes. Simon filled with wonder, and a surge of power flowed through him. Steps, columns, pillars, the peaked roof of...

"The acropolis?" he asked.

"Yes, the temple of Attarso to be precise. If we had more time, I could show you how to get there faster. But that will have to wait. You have done well, Simon. Now go to her. You know the way?"

Simon nodded, grabbing the hat and cloak. He flew from the workshop out into the streets of Attarsus.

ᏮᏋᏮᏋᏮᏋᏮ

There were definitely worse places to investigate than a whorehouse, but the idea here was for Aktar to make money, not spend it. Still, his daily expense account afforded him some leeway.

Unfortunately, nobody knew of anyone in their line of work by the name of Elysia. So after several enjoyable, yet ultimately fruitless days and nights, he changed his tack, figuring that particular line of inquiry was a dead end.

The agora was the center of commerce, politics, and generally the place to meet people in Attarsus, so he made his way there mid-morning on the third day. He'd dressed himself as a Pazian merchant, keeping his long knife concealed along his right leg, available at a moment's notice. Salar knows how many times he'd needed it.

The place was bustling with energy, and business looked good. While Aktar had spent most of his life in Pazh, and rightly considered it the center of the world, he always marveled at the vibrant Izari cities. They'd been successful trading ports since long before Pazh had taken them as vassals.

He tailored his inquiries to suit the person he was asking. He mainly posed as a visiting merchant, looking for his cousin Elysia. His parents had died in a fire, and he was looking to reunite with his cousin, the only family he had left. But her address was lost in the fire, so he only knew she was here in Attarsus.

He asked fishmongers, jewelers, money changers and the rest, with no success. He was beginning to grow frustrated by midday, questioning whether she was even from Attarsus. *One last try, then I'll stop for lunch.* The proprietor was a stout young woman selling fragrant oils from Marutha. She owned a few more curves than Aktar liked. He smiled anyway.

She smiled back. "I've got something I could oil you up with, honey."

Aktar raised an eyebrow. "Now that sounds interesting. But first, I was hoping you might be able to help me with something else. I'm looking for my cousin, Elysia. Do you know her?"

"The baker's daughter?"

He nodded. "You know where I could find her?"

"Well, she very rarely helps out her brother here at their stall, but you could ask him. You know Alexander as well?" Her eyes lit up. "But they don't get along."

"And where could I find him?"

She leaned a little closer. "Just follow your nose."

The words called his senses to action, and he nearly swooned as he isolated the aroma of fresh baked bread, sending his stomach into noisy protestations.

"Thank you, you've been so helpful. I'd like to surprise them, so don't tip them off. Let's keep it our little... secret?" He winked at her. "Now which of your oils would go well with some fresh baked bread?"

She feigned protest when he paid her, but accepted the coins after all. *Not sure how many fall for your act, but well done.* She asked him to come back later, so he just winked again and turned to follow his nose.

Several stalls down was a young man serving steaming garlic-encrusted flatbread to several happy customers. Aktar's mouth watered so profusely that he stumbled over his words when it was his turn to order.

"I've heard you make the best bread this side of the agora," he said, "and so far my eyes and nose are inclined to agree. My mouth can't wait for its turn."

The man laughed. Dark-haired and mostly Izari, but a hint of Pazian in him. Around the eyes. At least from one parent.

"My father's recipe won't disappoint."

"But how do you serve it steaming hot? It must have been baked hours ago?"

"You're lucky today. Luckier than me. My father is not well, so he was late to rise. I was up early for the first batch, and my father completed the second just now. It only just arrived."

"Then how does it get here, if you're busy, and he's sick?"

The man he assumed must be Alexander scowled. "My sister helped for once. If she helped more, maybe father wouldn't work himself until he's sick." His mood brightened somewhat. "At least she brought the bread. And she even went to make an offering for him."

"At the big temple?" Aktar indicated the acropolis with a jerk of his head.

"Father Attarso, of course."

"Ah, he watches over the merchants, as well as the city. Pardon my ignorance. I've been here many times, but never went inside. I've heard the statues are very beautiful."

Alexander scoffed. "You sound just like my sister." He shook his head. "Will that be all?"

"Yes," Aktar responded with another smile, handing over a few coppers. "Thank you for everything."

ᏼᏋ�6ᏋᏮᏋᏮ

Visiting the temples of the acropolis had been a mixed experience for Elysia ever since she discovered her passion for sculpture, and especially marble. There were no finer examples of the dizzying heights capable within the art form, with the work of great masters from a thousand years before.

She had first discovered the possibilities at the shrine of Aliata on the night of her dedication into womanhood, and committed her life to exploring that magnificent stone. But while she appreciated the dedication and devotion to the gods that elicited an outpouring of such beauty, at the same time she felt hollow. It was her duty to honor the gods, but she always felt like a fraud, like she was sleepwalking through a part in a play. She knew that her power came not from gods, at least not directly, but through the expression of her Talent.

*Was that Talent god-given?* She wondered if some thought so. In her heart, she believed everyone was born with some kind of Talent, just that few ever explored it far enough to discover how to focus and express it. And none in this day came anywhere close to exploring it as fully as these masters of ages past.

But while her faith was tenuous, her father's was as solid as the marble she loved. She came for his sake. His health was failing, and it worried her. She was spending as much time as she could with him, despite the warnings from Master Xelos. She veiled herself when she went between his house and her home, and even as she took the bread to Alexander at their market stall this morning.

Many women followed the waning Izari tradition of covering their faces outside the home, so she didn't draw any undue attention.

She carried the basket of bread up the steps to the main temple of Attarso, the king of their gods and patron of the city. Her father sent a sacrifice on the first day of every month without fail, and believed that this blessing was what kept his business afloat. Elysia challenged him on a great many things and often got her way, but on this one he remained steadfast. So she respected it, and on this day, with him sick in bed, she brought the offering to honor him, not the stone god. And a little extra, to pray for his health.

The temple was not very busy in the afternoon. The merchants tended to come before or after their work day, so the supplicants were mostly wives, old women, the lame and the sick asking for healing, forgiveness or other blessings. She walked to the right of the main hall, to one of the many alcoves housing shrines of Attarso in his varied guises. A priest looked to challenge her, but nodded when she held up the basket of bread. She gave him a small loaf, as was the custom.

Her destination was the third shrine. Standing inside the alcove was a statue that always made her father solemn, but she couldn't help but laugh. Attarso the Hungry, they called him. *Attarso the Fat is more like it!* In his blessing over everyone involved in the food trade, their king god was depicted as a rotund ruler at a royal banquet, his table overflowing with all kinds of food. He was jolly and laughing as he held up a cup of wine. The statue was so lifelike; it was hard to believe the food was painted marble and not real.

She approached the altar, removed her veil to show proper respect to an image of the gods, and knelt, her unruly hair spilling over her shoulders. She set to work on her offering with care and respect.

ᏪᎤᏪᎤᏪᎤᏪ

Aktar enjoyed the view of the temple complex as he mounted the stairs to the top. *Spectacular! These people may be our vassals, but we still have a lot to learn from them in the visual arts.* There were a half dozen temples to their various gods, but the largest by far was the temple of Attarso. It took pride of place in the center and was his destination, his eyes on the lookout for any young women matching the idea of Elysia he carried in his head.

He shuddered as he looked on the giant face of Attarso carved into the frieze above the steps to the big temple. He'd never been big on faith, but there was a power here, and one that demanded due respect. Pulling his hat down a little lower over his face to block the stony view, he picked up his pace.

Past the front row of columns lay a giant hall around the massive central statue of Attarso as king and lord protector of the city. He went inside and looked around appreciatively, enjoying the view as a tourist would. But no sign of the girl.

Doubling back, he noticed the corridor that traced the perimeter of the main hall. Inside were dozens of alcoves, each appearing to be a small shrine.

A priest approached him, carrying a small loaf of bread.

"Brother, are you lost?"

Aktar didn't have to feign confusion. "I'm a visiting merchant from Pazh, but I would like to ask the blessing of the father of the city on my venture. Where would be appropriate?"

"What is your line of business?"

"Grain," he added, looking at the bread.

The priest nodded, and pointed back the other way. "You seek Attarso the Hungry. Look for the image of our lord at the banquet. It is the third one after rounding the corner. But do you bring an offering... for our lord Attarso?"

Aktar jangled a pouch of coins, then withdrew one and placed it in the priest's hand with a slight bow of his head, before walking in the indicated direction.

⊙ℇ⊙ℇ⊙ℇ⊙

Elysia brought the bread up to her forehead with both hands, saying the prayer her father had taught her. Bowing three times, she laid it on the dish in front of the altar.

She repeated the action, with a more disjointed missive of her own, asking Attarso to restore her father's health and keep him safe. She struggled with the inner battle the words wrought, between her love for her father and her disdain for even thinking to ask this statue of a god for help. In the end, her anxiety won out and she actually felt a connection to the final lines of the prayer.

The sound of running footsteps from behind to her right shattered the sanctity of the moment, and she turned to see a cloaked man with a hat shadowing his face heading toward her. Suddenly feeling exposed, she smoothed the veil back over her face, but he'd already stopped, as if he recognized her. She scrambled backward in the grip of terror, trying to push herself up to her feet. He broke into a run. Her hands found the basket, and as he loomed over her she swung as hard as she could, connecting with a thunk on his forehead and sending the hat flying.

The muffled cry of pained surprise sounded almost familiar. "Ow! Elysia... what?"

*Simon?*

Looking at her were the hurt eyes of the man who had occupied her thoughts these past few days. A red welt on his forehead showed where she'd connected. She reached out to touch it tenderly.

"Simon, I'm so sorry, I thought..."

He smiled, putting his hand over hers and rubbing the mark. "I know I'm not familiar with all your customs... but I don't think this is a typical greeting?"

She tried a smile, but her heart was still beating too fast. "Master Xelos warned that I might be watched. I've been so careful... I was just here to help Father..."

"You're safe now. Master Xelos and I were both worried about you."

"You met him? Wait... how did you know I was here?"

He made a motion like painting a brush in the air, his face lighting up. "He showed me a little trick. And it worked! I can't wait to learn more!" He looked serious for a moment, then held out his hand. "With you."

She took it, and smiled, feeling comfortable once more.

He leaned in to kiss her, but she backed off, her eyes darting to the statue in front of her. He looked sweetly sheepish.

"Sorry. I forgot where we are. I... I missed you Elysia."

"I was worried you wouldn't be able to come back."

"So was I." He looked around cautiously. "Let's get back to Master Xelos." He pointed back to the floor. "But just in case, I think you should bring your weapon."

She scrunched up her face and gave him a playful shove. "If you're going to protect me, then *you* should carry it."

Grinning, he picked it up with a flourish. He nodded to a similarly dressed merchant who came around the corner, then replaced the hat on his head. Elysia covered her face with the veil, and hand in hand they walked out, heading for Master Xelos.

His hand felt so good in hers, putting her at ease for the first time since he first showed her his picture.

ᏩᏋᏩᏋᏩᏋᏩ

Aktar fought to keep control of his face when he spotted the young couple. She looked disheveled, but definitely the sister of Alexander. And the man, with his dark skin, was definitely Simon.

*Both of them! Persei will pay well for this.*

He nodded when Simon tipped his hat to him, but tried to keep his eyes shielded as they passed. To keep up the pretense, he walked past them several alcoves, stopping in front of a statue of Attarso holding a hammer in mid-swing over an anvil. Kneeling down, he tried to catch a view of them as they walked away.

He swore to himself, his mind racing. *Too risky to strike here and outnumbered. And they saw me, so I have to keep my distance if I'm to follow them. But that's my best bet.*

He dropped a few copper coins on the plate in front of the god. *Wish me luck.*

He stood and walked briskly to the exit. Lucky for him, the hilltop plaza was large enough that he caught sight of them just before they reached the top of the main stairway leading down to the agora. He picked up his pace when they vanished for a moment, reacquiring his target when he reached the top of the stairs. Keeping a safe distance he followed them down, through the agora, up a hill, and into a much more exclusive and wealthy area. When they stopped in front of one of the massive residences, he ducked behind the pillar of a neighboring portico, sneaking only furtive glances at them as they were granted entrance and disappeared.

He waited a few minutes, then passed by to get a look. The decorative carvings were beautiful, he'd give the owner that. Was it the girl? Her family? Things were getting much more interesting.

A man with the determined gait of a courier rushed down the street. Aktar hailed him, doing his best to appear confused. "Excuse me," he said in his barely accented Izari. "I'm looking for a Giannos? Is that his house?"

"Giannos? No. Not from around here, are you? That's the house of Xelos."

"Xelos?"

The man looked down the road, then back to Aktar, impatient. "Deals in marble? Sculpture? Statuary?" He shook his head. "There's no Giannos on this street."

"I'm sorry to have bothered you. Thank you for your help." The courier rushed off in a huff. Aktar coolly walked away, heading back toward the harbor with purpose.

*The plans have changed. I have much to report to Persei. If Simon's holed up here, we may need reinforcements.*

# XVI
ᏬᏋᏬᏋᏬᏋᏬ
## *Master*

The walk back was like a dream coming to life. Elysia's hand felt so warm, so right. Simon never wanted to let go. Gone was the stark fear that sent him racing through this foreign city to find her. And he had used his Talent to save someone he cared about!

But as excited as he was, they limited their conversation to the mundane: sights and sounds of the city, the sea voyage, and her father's health. Once they were safely across the threshold his tongue broke loose and he filled her in on every detail of his journey to Pazh and back again.

Or nearly every detail. He attempted to speed past his encounters with the women of House Lokuta, but Elysia probed further.

"So Persei sent this beautiful slave girl to seduce you?"

"Yes. He loves to surround himself with beautiful women."

She crossed her arms. "I guess you enjoyed yourself then?"

He groaned. "I'm not used to the attention from these beauties... no! In fact, I told her..." He looked earnestly into her eyes. "I told her that my thoughts were with another. With you."

That won back a smile. "And then you sent her away?"

"Not right away."

"Oh?"

"No! Not like that. I didn't touch her again—not at all! But I wanted Persei to believe that more had taken place. But it didn't! Actually, I was concerned about the girl. She seemed nice, and I didn't want him to have any reason to harm her on my account."

That bewitching half-smile was back, and somehow managed to

look both appraising and appreciative. He hoped that was good. His heart was tying itself in knots even with this slightest deception. Some of Mysena's advice had already kept him from blundering into the fire in this conversation, and he was certain that it would help again in the future. No need to share *all* of that right now. Nor mention Lokilla at all. And besides, Elysia appeared satisfied. He'd just have to live with the remaining guilt gnawing at him. He'd make it up to her.

"You're a good man, Simon. I'm glad I met you. And I'm glad you found me again today."

The moment was interrupted by clapping hands, and quickening footfalls as Xelos strode across the room to embrace Elysia like a doting grandfather. It touched Simon's heart to the genuine concern.

"Simon, thank you for bringing her back safely."

"Thank *you* for showing me how to find her. I can't wait to learn more. Will we be able to learn together?"

"Elysia is welcome to sit in with us, and I'm sure she'll track your progress with great interest." Xelos looked at her pointedly, and she blushed. "My steward has already set up a room for you, and your things are there. I don't want you to leave here until I deem it to be safe. Elysia, I sent word to your father that you'll be staying here for a while too."

"But with his illness, I need to help him! And if he's worried about me it could make him worse."

His voice was soothing. "Don't worry dear, I've already paid my physician to tend to him. He'll report back to us tonight."

She beamed, then hugged him again. "Thank you Master Xelos, you are so kind."

"It's the least I can do for my favorite student. Now as for my newest, you'll have much to learn and you need to stay focused. You must take care of yourself. Sleep after the evening meal, wake with first light, take meals with Elysia and myself, and spend the rest of the time in the workshop. Absolutely no visitors."

Simon nodded. He was no stranger to a regimented schedule. And at least he would be seeing Elysia every day while he explored his Talent. He'd go anywhere for that double opportunity, with this the most comfortable and safe place to do so.

"Glebric here will be your personal attendant." A thin, dark-haired Izari teen stepped out of the shadows, his eyes flicking over

Simon in quick appraisal before giving a deferential bow of his head. "If you need anything, let him know. He sleeps in the room next to yours, and will be with you all day, except when you're with us in the workshop."

*He'd make a good spy. No possibility of impropriety with this one around.* Simon would have to remember that, with the Izari known to be much more conservative in their views toward women. And Xelos was quite obviously protective of Elysia.

"You must be tired from your day, and you have already learned your lesson well. Come and eat with us now, and then retire early."

"Thank you again, Master Xelos, for this opportunity, and your hospitality."

"Simon, it is the least I can do. We need to stick together." That twinkle returned to his eye. "Especially if we're going to save the world."

Simon was impressed by how the cook made seafood taste exquisite with such simplicity, in contrast to the extravagance of House Lokuta. *If I ever have money, this is how I'll do things.*

He and Elysia were positioned on couches on opposite sides, giving him a great view of her eyes, smile and hair as they ate. She seemed so innocent and guileless compared to the more experienced women who had been throwing themselves at him. And that suited him perfectly, though he chided himself for comparing her to them in any way.

The meal gave Xelos a chance to question him extensively about everything from the exact details of what had happened in Pelusia to his meetings with Garas' allies, the Lokuta, and the Senate. He focused with particular intensity on anything to do with his art. It was strange seeing the curiosity of an excited child in a face so steady and wise.

"So the triptych was the first work of art of any kind you'd done since you were in school?"

"The only painting, yes."

"That's not what I asked. A sketch? A drawing? Something for yourself or at the request of another?"

"Nothing with any... power. Garas had me do lots of sketches for him. Of things he wanted done. Like the new fortifications to better repel the Scentari raiders."

Xelos gave him a knowing look.

"And tell me, what happened with those?"

"Well, the soldiers did a good job following the directions."

"How good? Think back on it."

Sudden realization. "Exact. They were able to do it exactly. I guess I did a good job? Made it easy to follow?"

"Easier than you think. It was a very subtle exercise of your Talent, and something you obviously knew nothing about. But let's just say you gave them an extra little push to make sure it was done right. What else did you do for them?"

Simon thought for a bit. "Maps? Lots of maps. I was making the maps as I went along. They praised me for their... accuracy. But there's no magic in that. Is there?"

"You tell me. What was accurate?"

Simon tried to search his memory. If only he had the maps to show them. "Everything was always right where I put it on the map. And then the strangest thing happened. On our escape from the Scentari we followed the path on my map... but I'd put some decoration on the scrubland." His eyes filled with wonder. "And the terrain was exactly as I'd put on the map. Like it was repeating my pattern over and over again... and that made it rough for the Scentari to follow. But I didn't... I mean, it's not possible for me to..."

"What were you feeling when you painted that map? What emotions?"

Simon avoided Elysia's gaze. "I was so afraid. Of the Scentari. Especially after what they'd done to our men. To the leaders. I wanted that to be our escape route, and for them not to be able to follow us."

"You have much natural Talent, Simon. You've done a lot already, before anyone showed you how to harness it or use it properly."

Xelos addressed both of them, as if to begin a lecture. "Every manifestation of Talent is different. Some require a more narrow focus, like a particular material or style. Some are more limited in scope. But you've already shown us several things yours can do." He counted them off on his fingers as he continued.

"First, your pictures helped another person to create something. Your diagram of the fortifications. Powerful instructions.

"Second, your Talent helped your maps to capture the reality of the situation around you, far better than a normal cartographer ever could. That was more of a latent use, that didn't require the same level of focused emotion. But can still be tremendously useful, with wide application.

"Third, you were able to lean on reality to subtly shape it to your desires, through your illustrations on the map. Nature conformed to your creation. And for that more powerful exercise, strong emotion was the key. There is much to explore in this area. And if you marry intention to that emotion, then there is no telling what you could create with your Talent.

"Fourth, you were able to capture the essence of the fear, the gravity, in fact the evil of what you witnessed at the Sentusi. To the point where it could affect those who viewed it, transporting them. Marry your Talent to pure emotion and the result can have great power.

"And finally fifth, with your work today, focusing your emotion and Talent to show yourself, or another, something that you wanted to know, but had no other way of discovering. You called upon reality to show itself to you, extending from something you already knew."

Simon realized he was looking at his hands in wonder.

"But this is just the beginning. I have a few ideas of what else might be possible, but your Talent is really only limited by your imagination. Within the natural bounds of your medium, of course."

Elysia looked at him with something beyond respect and admiration. Awe. Simon felt humbled, flattered and excited.

"Is this different from what you do?" he asked her, then piled a peppery tentacle onto his plate, feeling awkward for even asking.

She looked down at her hands. "My power is different... it seems so limited in comparison. Working with stone, or even wood... it's a lot slower. And I can only create solid objects that I see in the material... see in my mind."

Xelos looked at her, smiling mysteriously again. "Is that so?"

She looked startled. "What do you mean?"

"Well, you've never tried these things Simon did. You never even conceived of them. You've been so focused on capturing what you see, and bringing it to life in your sculpture. Or creating an ideal of something you can imagine and would love to see. But perhaps you should meditate on what Simon has done, and see if you can do something similar."

The excitement shining through her warmed Simon's heart.

"And you Simon, you haven't even begun to scratch the surface. There's so much you need to learn, and we must act fast if you are to help your friend."

"My friend?"

"The general. You wish to save him, do you not?"

"Yes, of course... but... I'm just one man. And likely branded a deserter now."

"Only you can put a limit on what is possible. I'm sure you'll figure out a way around that, with your Talent."

A thought bubbled to the surface, a question he'd been wondering about ever since his first conversation with Elysia. "But Shadush, his power... how can our Talent be so different from what Shadush used against us? It's not the same, is it?"

Xelos took a deep breath. When he continued his voice was full of concern. "His dark sorcery has great power, but you are correct. It is nothing like your Talent. Have you heard of the Damoz?"

"Those old stories about fallen gods? They used to scare me back in school."

Xelos snorted. "Yes. In Pazh the Damoz have become mere stories, bogeymen to scare children. Yet if you travel around the Near Sea, and beyond, all the different cultures tell stories of ancient beings of power living among us in this world. Some call them gods, others demons. They give them different names." He mopped his brow. "What if I told you they're real?"

"But..."

"As real as your Talent. Except instead of creating with magic, they feed on the energy of this world, bringing about destruction. From the power he has displayed, it appears this Scentari warlock, this Shadush, must have awakened Zaliakara, the Damoz of Flame. There are no official records of the presence of the Damoz in the entire history of the Pazian Republic. But if you go back, and farther afield, then some of the stories speak of them being destroyed, others trapped. But the descriptions are always consistent in one detail: the Damoz didn't do things themselves, but granted great power to those that would commit to them. Commit their soul in worship and through great sacrifice. If our understanding of how this dark magic works—and let me be clear, this is mostly supposition, we really don't know for sure—Shadush must have located Zaliakara and made such a sacrifice. And now he is a conduit for her destructive power. But it is exactly that—power that can only destroy."

Elysia interjected, "While our Talent can only create."

"Yes. Power that comes from the Damoz must destroy something. Take fire as an example. It either has to use natural flames, consuming their essence and growing in power, or—"

"Or it needs to burn something," Simon said.

"Yes, that is correct. The more he has to burn, the bigger the fire, or so it seems from the few existing references."

"But what if it's not material. What if it's people?"

Xelos screwed up his face in thought. "I believe all people have some measure of Talent… it is a part of life, of what makes people alive. So if a sorcerer, like this Shadush, is using the power of the Damoz, and consuming a large enough group of people—"

"Then it would be like storing up power," Simon said, "like saving up coins for a big purchase. He burned up more than two thirds of the 7th Legion, and all the officers. With that much power…"

"And unopposed even by an army, he has free rein to… to harvest more power across Pelusia."

"But how can we hope to stop him? My Talent is so feeble by comparison. How can I ever hope to match him?"

"Our power grows with our devotion to the craft, with practice, focus, and learning how to channel our creativity through our emotions. We combine these things to create something in this world. This is our offering to the gods. But this also means we are two sides of the same coin. In the natural world there should be a balance of both."

"So we're connected somehow?"

Xelos paused, reflecting. "Some believe that to be the case. In theory, yes. Things are never in perfect balance, and for much of the last five centuries there has been closer to no sign of either side. None of the Damoz have been seen in this time, and even the few misguided souls who claim to know their secrets and worship them in the shadows have little power to show for it." The stern expression returned. "But that has obviously changed now. And I have a hypothesis about this too."

Elysia and Simon leaned forward.

"The stronger one side grows, the more it will draw out the latent opposites."

*Latent opposites?*

Elysia voiced his question: "Are you saying that because Shadush brought this… Damoz back into the world somehow, and is growing in power, that it's pulling our Talent to the surface as well?"

Xelos nodded. "That's what I think. I need to discuss this further with some of my colleagues, now that we have some specifics to work from. It had always been only a theory…"

"Who are these colleagues?" Simon asked. "How many of you are there? How come people don't know about this?"

"All good questions. We are few and far apart, and are sworn to protect each other. Governments generally fear anyone who has power they can't control, so we keep our Talent a secret. There are people that actively seek out those with Talent in order to control them. So *we* keep an eye out for Talent. Most of us work somehow within the arts so we can have better access."

"What about our government?"

Xelos took a deep breath. "We rarely find anyone with Talent in mainland Pazh, or in the more established provinces. We have many theories why, but nobody can be sure."

"Theories?"

"Nothing conclusive. And absolutely nothing in writing from any Pazian source or in any known library. Which in itself is very strange. So this is all conjecture, and I don't like to say something is true unless I know it for a fact. Some believe a magical power in Pazh suppresses Talent. Others think the priesthood, or some other division of the government is actively keeping it at bay. Or even something in the natural Pazian character. You yourself know that creativity is far from prized among your people."

Simon found himself nodding. "All my life I thought my father was the one trying to stop my art. He supported the school in telling me what and how I could paint anything." He could barely choke back the tears. "I hated him for it." Elysia put a comforting hand on his shoulder, and Simon thought he caught a flash of concern in Xelos' eye. "But I couldn't have been more wrong. It was the schoolmaster that warned him to discourage me. For my safety?"

There was a new urgency from Xelos. "Were there any specific incidents in your childhood? What did the school do?"

"There was a contest. I was twelve. I… I wanted to create

something new, something different. Something worthy of the great masters. So I did. And I was so proud of my piece. But when I showed it to them, everything went wrong. They shamed me, called me an arrogant peacock. And then they made me burn it." His hands were shaking as he shared this out loud for the first time in his life. He'd never even told his mother. But now, looking into Elysia's eyes and seeing the hurt, the understanding... he felt a tremendous release, and closeness.

But something else nagged at the edge of his consciousness. Something important, but he couldn't place it.

Xelos nodded sagely. "So the suppression is at least somewhat institutionalized in Pazh proper. I must tell this to the others. Something is going on, and bears further investigation. But after leaving your Talent unexplored for many years, somehow things changed when you left. When you came close to the growing darkness. The Talent was drawn out of you, as if by a lodestone."

"So my being near Shadush somehow... woke this up?"

"That is something I myself had postulated would be the case. This lends the idea credence. Did anything feel different to you during that time?"

He nodded. "Dreams. I started having the strangest dreams... not quite premonitions. But when I think about them now, they all touched on some kind of hidden power... my Talent."

Xelos was nodding. "Fascinating. I'll pass this on as well. Have the dreams continued?"

"Yes... well, no. Not in the same way. Not since I got to Attarsus the first time. There have still been dreams, but more ordinary dreams, if still strange."

"If there is this kind of connection between the dark power and our Talent," Elysia said, "then if Simon is able to destroy this Shadush, will it affect him? Will he somehow lose his Talent, or be in danger?"

Xelos sat pondering for a long while. "I had never considered that. I... do not think that likely. It is truly a kind of skill, where practice and experience give you greater power and control, so I would guess that this boost you received by being close to the darkness is permanent rather than temporary. Of course we understand far too little about all of this. Some of my colleagues are trying to investigate older references, and how they tie into the myths. Stories from before the Republic controlled those areas, or before the Republic was even conceived. Sometimes *long* before."

Servants brought delicate cakes smothered in honey as the dessert.

Simon's attempt to bite one ended with him wiping sweet amber drips before they could make a mess on his chin. "So you think Pazh is somehow... dampening Talent? Are things different here in Attarsus, even under Pazian control? But this is such a center of the arts. What about your school, Elysia?"

Elysia looked embarrassed, and more than a little annoyed. "We don't have formal school here. My brother was sent to a tutor, but I'm... well let's just say the education of women isn't exactly prized here."

"Well at least you didn't have a teacher to discourage you."

Her expression was pained. "No, I had a Mother to do that."

"But then you found your way to Master Xelos?"

She shared a smile with her mentor. "Yes, and that was the greatest thing to happen to me. My father was trying to sell some of my early figurines, wood mostly. Votives of local gods. He found Master Xelos. Or should I say, *you* found him."

"I'm always on the lookout for more art. As a collector and patron of such things."

"So you brought me here, and for the past five years we've been working together."

"Five years, and you've learned so much," Simon said. "I wish I could have started five years ago."

It was Xelos' turn. "And now we need you to learn much more in a very short time, so we can prepare you for what is to come. As best as I can. Time is marching on. Get yourself cleaned up, and to bed. Lessons continue in earnest after the morning meal."

As excited as Simon was for the lessons to come, and to see Elysia again in the morning, he was asleep almost before his head hit the pillow.

Amazing how much better he slept in a clean, safe and comfortable bed rather than a swaying shipboard bunk or wagon, and avoiding disturbances like too much wine, strange women invading in the middle of the night, or someone trying to kill him.

After Glebric woke him, breakfast was a simple meal of sweet grapes and flatbread, and gave Simon time to ask Master Xelos more questions before the formal lessons.

"So you really think I can make a difference for Garas against the forces of Shadush?"

"You might be his only chance. They will be sending more legions as reinforcements, but that could take weeks or months for the redeployment, even longer if they choose to raise more troops. And if Shadush can sacrifice whole provinces while practicing his power, the legions may be no match for him."

"So how soon should I leave?"

"That will be up to you; how much you apply yourself, and how fast you're willing to learn."

Simon grimaced. "How am I going to explain my absence when I finally get to Garas? They'll surely have sent a message branding me a deserter. And how will I even get there? I'll have to find a ship, and merchants may be avoiding the area."

"Keep thinking of reasons why you will fail, or cannot even start, and you will surely be right."

"What if you used your Talent to draw up a message to Garas?" Elysia asked.

"You mean to bring with me? But to what end?"

"Saying that you had other messages to deliver along your way, and that's why you were delayed. And maybe the letter could cancel any other messages saying otherwise?"

Simon considered her words, trying to find a hole in the idea. "But surely I'd be found out..."

"Simon, do you want to help Garas, or not?"

Chastised, he remained silent.

Xelos stood up. "You can figure out the details later. Time for your training."

# XVII
## Learning

**X**elos led Simon and Elysia into the workshop.

"What is your Talent?" Simon asked.

Xelos glared at him. "Did you always question your teachers?"

"I'm sorry." Though the answer was indeed yes. Or had been before his father had forced him to stop challenging them at every opportunity. "I just…"

"You wondered whether I have Talent, or might just be good for teaching?" The twinkle returned, and he laughed. "A fair question. It really does not matter, as long as I can help you get results, correct?"

"I guess so."

"Well, in fact I *do* have my own measure of Talent. We all do. Actually, I believe Talent is buried deep inside every man and woman. Except it usually has no chance to be discovered, cultivated, and explored. But that is the general. Specifically, yes, a group of us with different forms of Talent work to protect each other, and indeed the world against destructive magic of any kind. Or at least has in the past, many times over. In my life we have been watching for signs, and learning as much as we can about what is possible. Until now."

He led Simon to a wall covered in sculpture, or rather of figures carved directly into the wall. Simon looked at the lifelike detail of hybrid men and beasts that appeared to be growing out of the flat surface. He felt a slight pull, similar to when he looked at Elysia's work. "So this…"

"Yes. My work. It pales in comparison to my pupil here." Elysia made to protest, but he silenced her with a wave. "It's true. My hand is great for the soft details, textures, even hair. Feathers! I can do it all, from the front. But I just can't get it to work in three dimensions. Try as I might, they can't break free of the wall into true life. Not like Elysia's work."

Simon looked at her, wondering. "True life? Does he mean…"

"Yes, sometimes my work can come… to life." There was a shy confidence to her smile.

Wondrous questions filled his mind, too many to ask. Especially with Xelos already chastising him. "I would love to see that!"

"In due time," Xelos said, on cue. "She can show you her work later. Much later. We focus on you first. But to set the tone, first a demonstration." He led Simon to another wall, where a row of what appeared to be sculptures were each covered by a fine cloth. Xelos withdrew one with a flourish. It was a light marble face, or at least the front half of the head, with the eyes closed and a large hooked nose. It looked foreign, but without color as a cue, Simon couldn't place it.

Xelos addressed the face. "Yalath, we need to speak."

The head quivered and the eyelids began to flutter, finally opening and with colorless pupils scanned Xelos before darting to Elysia and Simon. Simon jumped back in surprise, his heart beating in his chest. *The suspicion in the eyes was so lifelike!*

The lips opened and spoke in heavily accented Pazian: "I'm a little busy, Xelos. Who is that?"

"Our new student. I'd like to introduce Simon Baroba. From *Pazh*."

"Pazh?" The eyes widened, and appraised him fully. "What is your Talent, Simon Baroba?"

"Painting? Drawing too I guess?"

"You guess? Xelos, has he any training at all?"

"We have much to discuss, Yalath. I would come to see you in Jeppo, but we have no time. He has already been revealed to the Senate."

The mouth hung slack with shock. "The Senate?"

"Yes, and he showed them evidence of dark sorcery being used by the Scentari."

Yalath spluttered, struggling to form words. "Scentari with dark sorcery? Xelos, have you told the others?"

"I only now have the full details. But the danger is great. I'll contact you later. I need to attend to Simon's training before we send him to the East."

Yalath was incredulous. "Xelos, this is madness! He doesn't even know what he's doing!"

"Goodbye Yalath," Xelos said in a commanding voice, and the face shuddered and twitched several times before sagging into the frozen pose. "So Simon, what do you think? A useful little trick?"

"They're real people? Each of these?"

"Yes. And no matter where they are, I can speak with them. But in my case I needed to host them here so I could do the original creation. A little less flexible than what you did with Elysia yesterday. But I'm not completely useless." He winked.

"Could I do the same with my paintings?"

"It would make an interesting experiment some time. But first, there are techniques and exercises I would like you to try."

Xelos set the flow of what would become his daily routine. The morning centered on free and vivid painting of objects in the room: sculpture, tables, chairs, flowers and food, and even rays of sun streaming through the skylight. Xelos pointed out details Simon captured, and others he missed. It was very technical, but Simon relished the structured coaching, and every new element he could add to his work.

After a short break for lunch, they returned to the workshop.

"Close your eyes," Xelos said. "Now we will set the morning's work aside, and focus on working from memory. I want you to think of your home, back in Pazh. Get the image clear in your mind."

"I see—"

"No, do not use words. That is not your gift. Connect to the images. Look at them with the same attention to detail of the work this morning. See everything as if you were there right now. How does the room look in the midday light, with the light and shadow. The texture of every material. How they relate to each other in the scene. Do you have that?"

Simon nodded.

"Now feel. Standing in your home, what do you feel?"

Comfortable and warm, until a flower reminded him of his mother, and how much she loved flowers. An onslaught of loss, regret, and guilt at not having thought of her in so long... not even at his home. Then concern, for his father. *Was he safe? Did he get away...*

Simon opened his mouth to speak, but Xelos interrupted.

"Again, not with words, in your mind, let the emotions connect you to the image. The process is far more powerful when you have that emotional connection. Get both the details and the feelings clear, then start to work on the page. You can open your eyes, or keep them closed." Simon could hear the challenge of a gentle smile in his voice.

It was a revelation, connecting in a mental image as vivid as the scene of the battle, but even more realistic.

Elysia peered over his shoulder, watching in silence. When he finished, she smiled at him. "This is where you grew up?"

"Yes." An exact replica.

"It looks comfortable."

"It was... it used to be. And it still is. It should be. My father..." Regret welled up inside him, at the years spent in conflict and struggle that had pushed him out. "I hope to spend more time with him again in the future."

Xelos clucked his tongue. "Reminisce at dinner. Now is the time to work."

Xelos had Simon painting more scenes from memory with eyes open or shut. Scenes from Pazh and people he knew, every time pushing him to dig deep into his feelings and emotions about the scene.

"You have to ride your emotions down deep inside yourself, Simon," Xelos said. "Imagine the edge of a well, where the well is your creativity, where your Talent lives. The only way down is to catch a ride on your emotions and let them take you there. And once you grab hold, you can carry that inspiration out onto the page in your work. Picture that well."

Except in Simon's mind, an old stone wall surrounded the well, designed to keep him out. Stones laid by his father, his teachers, and under their guidance, by himself. Keeping him away from this font of power. But now the stones looked loose, and crumbling. With Xelos' voice to guide him, he chipped away at stone and mortar and dug his way through, just enough to get that connection flowing.

The flow became a torrent spurting out through the gap and

out of his grasp, too fast for his fingers to harness. What he captured on the page amounted to meager drops compared to the ocean of possibilities.

"I can see it… but I can't control it." He wrung his hands in frustration.

Even the twinkle in Xelos' eyes was frustrating, no matter how he tried to reassure Simon. "To see your Talent at all is a major step. And to open that flow. That's all I ask of you today. You'll have lots of time to learn to capture and control your Talent, and have it work with you, for you. Patience, Simon.

"Now for the next area, to close out the day. Elysia, you can keep working on that piece over there."

She walked to the far side of the workshop, while Xelos took Simon to an easel he'd set up with an empty board facing away from the day's work. Although surprisingly tired already, his excitement at another new exercise kept him going.

"You will need the ability to connect to your emotions. The deeper your connection, the more powerful your work. This also takes practice. Close your eyes again, good. Think back to that story you told us about that work of art you loved so much as a twelve year old, and the pride you felt in what you had created."

Simon imagined that piece, so vivid in his mind, of the gods he'd brought to life. He was still proud of it, and would be happy to show it to Elysia if Xelos asked him to recreate it. Simon nodded.

"Now imagine the faces of your teachers, their shock, their horror, their disdain at your audacity. How do you feel, you arrogant little peacock? Burn your work! Destroy the abomination!"

Ripples of confusion and horror washed through his body, but they were merely the precursor to a huge wave of anger that surged forth and overwhelmed him, hideous and powerful.

"Good, good… now let out that raw emotion, that pure feeling onto the page."

Simon's eyes snapped open, and he grabbed the brush, spurring it into furious motion. Nothing mattered but blacks and reds and purples splashed across the page in a maelstrom of emotion. Wave after wave of feelings flooded out through his hand and brush into the ugly monstrosity before him.

It left him empty and drained, with nothing left to give. He forced his eyes open and recoiled in horror at the hideous and distorted creature doubled over in fury on the page. Many times more vivid than the scene in his mind. *No, no, that's not me.* He thrust his body in front of the ugliness, to shield it from Xelos and especially Elysia. But Xelos watched him, not the page, with the same bemused expression. From across the room there was no rejection in Elysia's face, only gentle concern. Simon wiped the sweat from his brow, realizing only now that his hair was dripping.

"You are not done yet," Xelos said. He put a cloth over the picture without looking at it and led Simon to another similar easel.

He barraged Simon with a series of other emotional stories designed to elicit strong feelings, then would ask him to transfer them in the abstract to the page. He took Simon on a churning ride of raw emotions, from joy through grief and envy in quick succession. Such a contrast to what they allowed at his school.

By dinner, Simon was totally exhausted. He was used to physical labor with the legion, but this stretched him in completely new ways, using mental and emotional muscles that he didn't even know existed. His arm all the way up to his shoulder was alternately numb and cramping.

He ate his food in silence, without even the will to ask any further questions.

"You did well," Elysia said. "I know I was younger, but you've covered more in a day than we did in our first month together."

Simon could only offer an exhausted nod.

Xelos furrowed his brow. "This is a start, and you do have some natural ability, but you are a long way from me sending you off to challenge the Scentari warlock. We will pick up the pace tomorrow. Which means it is time for bed." He stood, and turned to leave.

Elysia stole a chance to clasp Simon's hand, offering the promise of something more. He smiled weakly in return, and she whisked it away before Xelos turned back to make sure they were following him.

"Sleep well Simon," she said with a smile.

He did.

ᏪᏋᏪᏋᏪᏋᏪ

Persei rode up to the command barracks after another long day of selecting recruits. A lot of veterans were re-enlisting. He was proud of what was shaping up to be a new, better 7th Legion. Especially with him in a more prominent position.

He left his horse with a stable hand and made for the officer's mess.

"Tribune Lokuta," a scribe said, catching his attention. "There is a letter for you, from Attarsus?"

He thanked him and took it, changing course for his quarters. Once safely inside, he tore open the familiar seal and read the contents. His worried frown turned to a confident smile as Aktar's sprawling hand informed him of the opportunity.

*This is my decision to make. What would Daymar do? Who cares? This is my mission. And as the general, he needs to be shielded from such matters.* His smile curled to a sneer as he wrote his response. *Any force necessary.*

He drafted two letters, one to a local gang leader in his debt, to send six strong and trustworthy men on the next ship to Attarsus, and the second to Aktar with very clear authorization to go as far as needed. To hire more local support if he felt it necessary. And even a few choice suggestions on how to smoke them out.

*You'll pay for crossing me, Benjai. You and those that support you.*

ᏅᏋᏳᏋᏳᏋᏳᏳ

The remainder of Simon's week followed a similar daily course, and as with military basic training he found himself growing accustomed to the pace. His hand still ached terribly at night, but each morning he was ready to resume the exploration of his Talent.

The hot bath Glebric prepared for him at night was a welcome retreat, though it was too short for his taste. He imagined inviting Elysia in to join him, but between Glebric's watchful eye and her respect for the customs of their host, he didn't see how it was possible. Should she find a way, his body would find some hidden reserve of energy to meet her. She began to visit his dreams, which made waking harder.

On the seventh day, Xelos had to skip dinner for a meeting with his colleagues using the talking sculptures. That left the two of them alone together at the table, even if they were surrounded by nosy servants.

A kiss was out of the question, but their hands met in secret. However brief the contact, it was like a jolt of lightning.

He kept his voice low. "Elysia, maybe we could… spend a little more time together this evening?"

She looked around nervously before whispering back. "With Glebric and the others around? Xelos is still in the house."

He let his finger curl around hers a little longer. "I just wish we could be alone."

"*You* need to focus on your studies."

"I am. Xelos was telling me the importance of appreciating beauty and its expression in nature."

He expected her to look away, but her gaze remained steady, a new wonder glowing in her eyes.

"You truly see me as a… beauty?"

His throat dry, his body feeling warm and heavy, he could only nod.

She sighed and brushed a flyaway curl from her forehead, tucking it behind her ear. "Are you sure Simon? I'm not one of those cultured ladies like the noble women of Pazh. Or even here in Attarsus. I know nothing of beautifying myself to attract a man."

He reached out and wiped marble dust from her cheek. "I'm not looking for that kind of shallow refinement. Your beauty shines through, when you let it."

She gave him a quizzical look, but her eyes still smiled.

"You have no idea how beautiful you are to me."

She looked thoughtful for a moment, then got excited with a new idea. "You just reminded me of something Xelos wanted me to share." He wanted so desperately to kiss her, damn the servants, but her mood swept him up. And the mention of the Master's name jolted him back into the present.

"What is it?"

"Have I told you what I see before I start carving?"

Now it was his turn for the questioning look.

"What do you see when you have a blank page in front of you?" she asked.

"A blank page."

"Hmm. That's different. Let me try and explain. Father told me the story of when I was a little girl, four years old. We used to go for walks, and one time we were in a park, the night after a storm. There were leaves and branches everywhere. I asked him 'Why is that mouse trapped in there?' He looked everywhere, trying to figure out what I meant.

"I pointed out one thick fallen branch, and showed it to him. I told Father how sad the mouse looked, and asked if we could get him out." A tear came to her eye.

Xelos' physician had been treating her father and he was almost up to a full workload again, but Elysia still worried about him, unable to be there to help directly.

"He was so good to me, always humoring me. So different from Alexander or my mother. I held that branch cradled in my arms like a little doll, all the way home. He gave me the smallest knife in the bakery to use. It was the first time I'd ever touched a knife, and he tried to guide and direct me, but... I was headstrong. I wouldn't let him interfere. The knife felt like it was made for my hand. And the hand just knew what to do. First I peeled off the bark, then the wood itself, chip by chip. I don't know if I'm explaining it right, but I was taking away everything that was not the mouse. All the wood around it, that trapped it there. Finally after many days of careful work when my Mother wasn't looking, I brought it out to them. Harry, my happy little mouse."

Her eyes grew wet, with a faraway look. "He was perfect. And Father said so the night I showed them. But Mother, she sniffed and made me wash up."

Simon loved seeing her this passionate, even if he didn't quite understand what she meant. "That's not how it works for me. Do you always see things like that?"

She nodded slowly. "Yes, well... not always. But in any piece of unfinished wood or stone, if I'm paying attention, I see something inside. It could be an animal, or a figure, or a plant. Or even a fragment or a part, like a hand or a foot or a face."

"But I don't understand, does that mean you can't choose what you make from a raw piece?"

"Well, I can choose whether to carve or not to carve, or which piece to start from... but I guess you're right. I've never thought about it that way. With my Talent I feel like I'm just releasing what's already there." She looked a bit embarrassed. "I guess that's not as impressive as what you can do. You can make anything come to life on that page?"

"I honestly don't know. I have to be able to think it, and feel it. At least that's what Master Xelos says. I haven't really tried anything different yet." He paused, reflecting, then spoke out his thought. "I wonder what limits there are to this? Maybe you can push yourself further too?"

"I don't know. I've only achieved perfection a few times."

"What do you mean by perfection?"

"Xelos didn't talk to you about that yet? Maybe we should wait?"

He smiled to reassure her. "I can learn from you too. Did you know you're my favorite teacher?" He winked.

She pushed him playfully, then tried to make her voice sound serious like Xelos when he scolded him. "Then focus, Simon. Listen carefully." They both laughed. "Perfection, at least with my Talent, means getting a sculpture so lifelike that the line between living and statue becomes blurred. And then with enough emotion I can give it that last little push. I call it... the breath of life. If I do it right, then the statue becomes a living breathing creature."

"It sounds incredible. Wow. I have no idea if I could ever do something like that."

Her eyes looked distant again. "It's the most amazing thing. It's like I'm bringing them into this world, like they're my children. It's joy and completion and... just the most wonderful feeling. I live for that feeling. I strive for it every day, with every piece. I wish I could do it on command."

"So what happened to Harry?"

Her face fell. "My Mother smashed him against a wall when we fought one time. I never forgave her for that before she died."

"I'm so sorry."

She squeezed his hand before standing up. "Don't be. It was the day she died that I first found perfection. And you know what? I think it was her departing soul that guided my hand. Like that was her way of apologizing, and finally believing in me."

He stood up with her, walking her to her room in silence. Glebric trailed just behind, like a late afternoon shadow.

"Thank you for sharing," Simon said, with his eyes trying to say so much more. He felt a whole new level of closeness to her, and wished he could take her in his arms and carry her to the bed.

Her eyes were full of something more as well, and he imagined her accepting his request in spirit, when she said good night before disappearing through the door.

# XVIII
## 6ᏋᏋᏋᏋᏋᏋ6
## *Plans*

Shadush looked over the faces surrounding the huge central campfire. With no light from the moon, the flickering flames drowned out the stars above. *All light and power from the flames,* or so the old Mijazi blessing went.

Though Mirasha had advised against it, and despite the growing awe and devotion they felt for his power with every successful conquest, he owed it to his people to give them a voice. The grand thane had always been elected, never inherited through birthright. Force brought him to power, but only with the will of the people. *Now, to show them a completely new vision.*

Kazash stood to his right, Mirasha and his sons at his left. Arrayed before him were all the other tribal leaders, the new and much more compliant priests of Mija, and his greatest warriors. And those new priests devoted to the Black Flame. He hadn't encouraged their formation of a new cult, but neither had he discouraged the conversion. It kept them further under his sway, hanging on his every word as their connection with a dark new god of redemption. And it gave him another card to play.

He rolled the words around in his mind as his men feasted on succulent joints of Pelusian cattle. He rose.

"My brothers. The greatest group of Scentari warriors ever assembled." There were grunts of approval and a few pounded their chests to accept his praise.

"With your blades and bows riding from the north, combined with the power sent to us by fiery purge," he said, cringing inside while keeping his eyes blazing with conviction, "we have struck deep into lands that the Pazians stole from us." The cheers grew louder and more raucous.

He waved his hand to the meat roasting on the flames before them, and jangled gold bracelets on his arm. "We have taken what we deserve from these dogs, laying waste to their cities. And it tastes good, does it not?"

"The meat, or the women?" shouted one, eliciting catcalls and graphic gyrations from a few of the younger generals.

He laughed lustily, as they would expect.

"We've all had our fill. As have our warriors fighting with us. It has been the greatest harvest in the history of Scentar." The fiery glow reflected off their proud and satisfied faces.

"The first of many!" yelled his eldest son, to cheers of approval.

He raised his hands to quiet the reaction. Kazash gritted his teeth, but nodded. Shadush avoided looking at Mirasha, but imagined her eyes burning into his other cheek as he started again.

"Here at the zenith of our greatest victory, I have a question for you. A choice. For my greatest and most trusted." A few heads perked up, curious, while most of the rest dismissed it as some trick of mere words. *No, I need your full attention.*

He held up his hand while menacing words spilled once more from his mouth with their spidery darkness, coalescing into a small black flame. A flame only visible for how it absorbed the light of the cooking fire behind it.

A wave of gasps passed through the group, with those who could see passing on their awe to those who couldn't, until Shadush was surrounded by an uncanny stillness.

"None of you need a demonstration. You have all seen this power in action." He clenched his fist, and when he opened it the flame was gone. "I only need your attention, because I am about to ask you something new, something difficult. It breaks with our proud tradition as masters of the steppe. But first, I ask you another easier question. Why is Pazh master of so much of the world?"

"Not for long!" cried his son, before a withering look silenced him. The others traded uncertain looks, none venturing to reply.

"Do they scavenge the world, taking everything they want by force?"

"Yes, like they did to us!" cried another of the young voices before him.

He shook his head. "They win by force. But they are rich, they can keep coming back, because they don't just conquer. They rule." He let the words settle in, but saw that he was still speaking above too many of them.

"They don't just take slaves and burn, they build roads, and walls, and new cities. They send their officials to rule over those they conquer."

"But they grow soft in their silk pillowed beds!" another warrior shouted, and many joined his laugh.

"Yes, they do. And we will not make the same mistakes. But I ask you. Would you rather steal a farmer's cow and eat it?" He paused for effect. "Or would you rather make him send you a cow every year for the rest of his days?"

Recognition and understanding spread unevenly through the group. He noted where it soaked in, and where it lagged.

One of the older generals tentatively called out. "So you say we should leave them be, and just take tribute each year?"

"Not quite. But from this point forward we will *take* each city, we won't destroy it. Only with their farms and cities and trade routes can they keep feeding us... forever."

Another warrior stood up, angry. "You promised us plunder and riches, and land to graze our flocks. Now you try to trick us into graves made of stone?" He spat on the ground. "Never." There were a few that stood up to join the dissenter, and others who reflected his view, but were too cautious to challenge their lord. With good reason. But he was done with burning his own people.

"You are absolutely right, Gufaz. And you and so many others who rode with my father, and our leaders for generations, you deserve the rewards you have earned. So I only ask you to continue on this campaign until we drive the Pazian yoke from all the people of the East. Then you will be given the lands to graze your flocks, and all the booty you can carry. Your fair share. That is your right, and my word is law."

Gufaz and the others returned to their seats, satisfied. But the others leaned in, more curious now.

"That is one choice. But choose this new path with me, and I will make you lords and governors of new lands and new people. Whole cities and towns will bow down to you and send you tribute. Your loyalty to our people, and your good administration will carve out a new Scentari *Empire*." The last word rolled off his tongue like sweet nectar. "The greatest the world has ever seen. We will match the might of Pazh when she comes back to be beaten down again and again until we can take the battle to her shores and make her home our possession. We will be masters of the world. This is a slave's meal compared to what is to come."

His words painted greed, hope and exultation across their faces. They were his. No need for a choice tonight. But he pushed them over the precipice of commitment. "Who is with me, for Scentar?"

As one their roar of "Scentar!" filled the plains with each shake of his fists, the hands of a man who would be emperor.

෧ଛ෧ଛ෧ଛ෧

Elysia approached Xelos in one of their rare moments alone. She didn't begrudge Simon the time. He needed the direct instruction so much more, and she certainly enjoyed having him around. But she did miss the time she and Xelos would spend in conversation.

This time she had something she wanted to ask him.

"Master, why Simon?"

"Hmmm?"

"Why does it have to be Simon that faces this Shadush? And alone? Don't you and the others have someone more powerful? More experienced?" She tried not to let the fear enter into her voice, but obviously failed when his eyes crinkled with concern.

"I know you have come to care for him. But he is the only choice right now."

"But he barely knows what he's doing. And how can he use his Talent to fight?"

"The potential uses of your Talent are only limited by your imagination. By your creativity. You know that. Do not presume to know what Simon is capable of, or not."

He paced around the room.

"Simon has been closer to the darkness than any of us, and this has awakened something in him. I don't understand how it works, but it appears Yalath was correct, that proximity to the use of dark power somehow draws it out. If this is true, then Simon is the only one who has been prepared to accept this challenge."

"But couldn't we send someone else to be close, to grow in power? Someone whose Talent is more refined?"

"How would we get them that close? No, Simon again has the advantage. Stationed with the legions he can get close enough to strike, and with what I teach him, his further growth will give him a chance."

"I could go with him."

He set his jaw. "Absolutely not. The legions are no place for a woman. Simon will not be able to keep you safe. I could not bear for something happen to you."

For the first time in her life she felt anger toward the kind master. "So you won't risk me, but ask Simon to go to what might be his death?"

His pained expression only angered her further. He looked older, weaker. "I'm sorry. There's no other way. My word is final."

Without looking back, she stormed off to her room.

๑ළ๑ළ๑ළ๑

"Can I paint you?" Simon asked Elysia.

She blushed and looked with embarrassment at Xelos.

Simon covered quickly, not wanting to give the wrong impression. "Not as some... model. As you are now. So that while I'm away, if I need to know where you are, I already have a picture ready to use with my Talent."

Xelos nodded. "That is a good idea. You're starting to think proactively, Simon. Preparation gives you so many options to use your Talent. Do a good enough job, and there might be a few more tricks you can learn. Perhaps I can even sculpt your head so we can contact you." He left the room for some important business, leaving them alone but for Glebric and another one of the servant girls waiting at the open doorway. Both had instructions to face away while Simon or Elysia was working, but Simon imagined them listening for the slightest whiff of impropriety.

Simon chose a small wooden board that he could keep with him in his pack. He'd work on her image now, since he had her available, then add the window after.

Elysia looked shy as she sat on the stool before him. She smoothed away a few flyaway hairs and settled into a slightly unnatural pose.

"Make sure you're comfortable. I'll need you to stay that way for a while."

She took a deep breath, and the movement of her chest drew his gaze down for the tiniest moment, but she intercepted his look and pursed her lips. She crossed her arms in front in silent challenge. Simon sighed and inwardly cursed himself.

*Focus, Simon!*

To keep that focus, he started with her eyes. Every time they connected, he felt like she looked deep into his heart, and took a piece of him back with her. Those striking eyes made him want to give himself over to her completely. They were smiling, challenging and calling out to him without speaking a word.

He did find that as he started to look at her in this new way, through his artist's eye, it magnified her beauty. Every detail, every line and quirk became a work of art, a delight.

Other than his quick sketch to locate her that first day back in Attarsus, he'd never painted a living woman before. And she was so full of life, staring at him intently while he did his work. It was headier than the sweetest wine. With every brush stroke he poured out his feelings for her onto the blank board. As the curves of her eyes and lashes came to life on the page, he was captivated.

His hand moved faster and faster, taking on a life of its own as more features appeared. He could see her straining to keep her eyes forward, her curiosity spurring her to peek before it was ready.

As he added the soft curves of her lips, a tingling warmth touched his own, a memory of every time theirs had met and connected. He closed his eyes for a moment, savoring the sensation. When he opened them, she ever so slightly bit her lip. *Through the connection of his Talent, could she could feel it even as he did?* The idea sent a thrill of excitement down his body.

With the brush as an extension of his hand, it returned to the paint again and again, each stroke deepening the bond with her. There was a slight flush of color on her otherwise pale skin. Her arms relaxed, letting her hands settle in her lap. She grew in confidence as he drank in every detail. As his eyes and brush moved down her bare shoulder in the picture, she twitched at the sensation as if he had touched her there.

It was transcendent, this sensual connection melding with the exercise of his Talent to create a work of such beauty. Time spiraled by in a dreamlike flow, until finally, bathed in sweat, he completed the final stroke.

They exhaled in unison, as if they'd just finished a run up the acropolis steps on a hot summer afternoon. He beckoned her over, and she stumbled briefly when her feet touched the floor. Without a thought he stepped forward and offered her a hand, reestablishing the connection. He guided her around to view the picture.

She gasped, then squeezed his hand, laying her head on his shoulder, the servants forgotten for a moment. "This is how you see me?" She gazed into his eyes with a soft, dreamy look, and his legs melted.

"Yes, I wasn't sure I could capture how beautiful you are to me... but I think this does." She leaned up to kiss him, turning away only at the last second. She sensed it too. Glebric was staring straight at them from the doorway, his mouth agape. Instead she gave Simon a sisterly peck on the cheek.

*Damn the eyes everywhere!*

They leaped apart at the sound of steps approaching down the hall, moments before Xelos walked in. Simon's hand dangled next to him, suddenly lonely.

"So will it work?" she asked.

"To find you?" Simon said. "If last time is any indication, yes. I just need to make it into a window and focus on the need to know where you are. My hand will do the rest."

"What else can it do?" Elysia asked.

"I have several theories," Xelos said. "You can find her, or possibly even communicate with her."

"Like with your talking sculptures?" Elysia asked.

"Possibly, but... the key to all this is creativity. Being attuned to your Talent. That's why I am having you focus on feeling, on connecting to what is possible, rather than specific demonstrations of capability." His face grew more serious. "I don't want to prejudice you. To stop you from figuring out what is possible for *you*. So while a test like this would be useful... it might lock you into a particular line of thinking. And if you used this one as a test you'd need to make another. This would be bound to her current location, and if she were to move to even another room it would likely break the connection. Save it for a time of great need. And trust that inspiration will lead you to the solution for that time and place."

Simon had been starting to question Xelos' methods, so the explanation was reassuring. And this was already his favorite piece. He'd hate to spoil it in any way.

Xelos continued. "But it is possible that you might impose your will on the scene and communicate with her visually. Of course this is only conjecture, since my power is different, working as I do with three-dimensions, even limited. I have not met another with a power quite like yours."

"So there aren't others like me?" Simon asked.

"Not that I've met. There are stories of course, but a curious lack of mention in written accounts. And of course now it is too dangerous to record them in detail. All we have are fragments couched in myth. Without the direct connection we can't separate fact from fiction. All we have are oral accounts, and hypotheses of old men like myself."

"How many others do you know, personally?"

"Four closer to my age, and three before them that have already left this world. And over the years, seven of their wards, or apprentices, if you will."

"Is Elysia your first apprentice then? And I'm your second?"

The master's jaw clenched, and he shifted uncomfortably. Elysia caught Simon's eye with a slight shake of her head.

Xelos gazed out the window. "There are too few of us, and we have to be extremely careful. Enough questions. Time to get back to your studies."

# XIX

ᏕᎬᏕᎬᏕᎬᏕ

## *Partners*

Simon wasn't sure about Elysia's idea of forging his marching orders, but Xelos declared it a good project. And Simon *was* very excited about the chance to collaborate with Elysia on the seal.

The Master had provided him with several sheets of the fine vellum used for official orders from the Senate, along with an official scroll of recent orders to the garrison of Attarsus. The presidential seal was cut through but fully present, for her to use as a model. Xelos was already more than he seemed, and Simon wondered what other secrets lay beneath those twinkling eyes. And whether he'd have sufficient time to uncover them.

Starting with the easy part, Simon drafted the words he and Xelos had agreed upon. He'd been officially excused for late reporting since an attempt on his life forced him out of the city. He was sent via Attarsus, to deliver another message. Since he remained a legionary of the 7th, it was up to Garas to readmit or discharge him as he saw fit. Any other preceding or subsequent news or orders regarding Simon were to be disregarded.

With mixed emotions Simon wrote out the letter in his own hand first, knowing that Garas would likely keep him, and thus he'd be kept apart from Elysia until the situation was resolved. Xelos had insisted that Garas be given the option, in order to distract him from the overall strangeness of the missive.

Elysia worked very quickly on her copy of the seal, first in wood, then in wax. Xelos wanted to show her a new technique he'd learned from a goldsmith from a far off land south of Marutha.

Simon continued testing his Talent on practice runs using cheap locally made papyrus. He fixed the text in his mind, then reviewed the script of the senatorial scribe, trying to merge words and style on the page. His first few attempts felt flat, like he was simply copying the style by eye. He balled up the papyrus and threw it in frustration.

"Master Xelos, this isn't art, this is writing. I don't think I can do it."

The bemused eyes took on a keen edge. "Is it not visual? Taking pen to a page? The lines are symbols, pictures, abstractions that your mind parses into language. It is just as much art as your draft work or mapmaking. Your mind is getting in the way." The expression softened. "Give it another try."

After cracking his knuckles and taking a deep breath, Simon laid down a fresh page.

"Feel the flow of the hand. See the lines as an intricate web of design. Channel your concern for your friend Garas."

Simon mustered his feelings and released them into his hand. The first phrase leapt out of his mind into the ink on the papyrus, the quill moving of its own accord. Simon smiled with excitement as it ran through the next line until… his concentration shattered as he looked back to his own writing. As he tried to return to the page for the next section, the thread of magic slipped away and the connection was lost. The words turned flat once again. Huffing, he slammed his hand on the table, shaking the ink bowl.

"I… I can't keep my focus in three places at once. The words, the scribe's hand, and the pen… and I can't very well memorize the entire message."

Elysia stood up from her work and walked toward him, her brow knotted. She patted him on the shoulder, and the touch calmed him considerably.

"I have an idea. What if I were to read your writing to you, as you finish each line? Would that help?"

Simon brightened, nodding. Xelos nodded as well, with a smile that looked like… pride?

"I'll stand behind you." She lowered her voice to a whisper: "so you won't be unnecessarily distracted."

"Wait," Simon said. "You can read Pazian?"

"Mother didn't care much for my education overall, but learning to speak, read and write both languages was important to her."

She picked up his text and took her place behind him. She read it twice out loud to get the flow, while Simon set the Senate order on a stand so he could see it clearly while he wrote.

"Ready?" she asked, her breath warm on the back of his neck. His mind painted a bewitching picture of her looking over his shoulder at his work. Driving the image away, he focused on the pages in front of him.

"Ready."

The second test run was a complete success, after figuring out an appropriate pace so that Simon could harness the flow of his Talent. Within the hour they had a completed copy that looked as official as their example. When Xelos finished scrutinizing it for flaws and gave his nod of assent, Simon let out a hoot of joy and Elysia jumped into his arms, hugging him tight. He leaned in to kiss her but she pulled demurely away and skipped back to her work.

Simon flushed, chastened. "I'm sorry, Master Xelos. I was overcome with excitement."

His voice was stern. "A trifle compared to what you'll need in order to confront Shadush. And Elysia still needs to complete the seal. You can continue yesterday's lessons."

When they were all satisfied with Elysia's wax version of the seal, Xelos took it from her and placed it in a large square pot. He lined up several thin metal tubes, leading from the side of the wax to little grooves at the top of the pot. He poured in plaster until the pot was almost full, covering everything except for the openings of the tubes. Simon looked on in confusion. Xelos held up a hand to forestall any questions, and took them to dinner.

The next morning after breakfast, he showed them the rest of the process. First, he poured hot copper in through one tube until it was almost full. The three of them peered in, and Simon gasped as it began to drain down with a sizzling sound. The smell of melting beeswax swirled out of the other empty tubes, followed first by drips and then a steady stream of hot wax. Elysia's eyes went wide with wondrous comprehension, and Simon smiled with her.

"This is incredible!" Simon said.

"Just goes to show that we can learn from everyone," Xelos said, pouring in a little more copper, "especially those from far off places. I'm always on the lookout for new techniques, and all this from a simple goldsmith. Remember that. Never stop learning! Now back to your lessons while we wait for this to cool."

The words opened up a new world for Simon. Pazh had always been the center of everything, and from birth he had been immersed in a vision of complete Pazian superiority. But now he recognized a more nuanced and complex reality, with powers that could challenge the Republic, and ideas beyond their imagining. He vowed to see more of this world after his duty had been discharged. Perhaps with Elysia?

Once it cooled enough to be handled, Xelos showed them how the plaster could be carefully struck away and the tubes removed. Remaining at the bottom was a perfect copper replica of the seal, which he doused in cold water for further hardening.

"Elysia, I think the honor of the test falls to you?" He handed her the stick of red sealing wax and the copper seal.

She held the stick against a candle until the wax bubbled and the drips fell onto the test letter. When she pushed the seal against the blob, wax squeezed out all sides like petals on a flower. Xelos waited a few moments, then nodded and she revealed the result.

A perfect seal.

Elysia grinned at them both, and Simon couldn't help himself from joining her with a laugh. Xelos rolled Simon's letter into a scroll and held it out for her to do the same. Once complete, she went down to one knee and proffered it to Simon with mock formality.

"Legionary Baroba," she said, her face deadly serious, "you are charged to deliver this to General Garas Numeno in Tamar." As he took it, she dissolved into a delighted giggle, and even Xelos laughed. He clapped them both on the shoulder.

"Good work. You can take a break until after lunch. I have to speak to some of my colleagues."

Simon stored the letter on a high shelf, away from the rest of their work. They left the workshop together, and Glebric, as always, followed two steps behind them, his eyes tracking their every move. Riding a wave of elation after their combined victory, Simon boldly embarked on another project he'd had in mind for several days.

"Follow my lead," he whispered to Elysia, without turning toward her. He walked ten more paces, then fainted.

"Simon!"

He looked up at her, feigning weakness. Glebric crouched next to her, eyes wide. Simon made his voice a croak: "Glebric... please... go... for... help."

Elysia picked up on the ruse. "I'll take him to his room, you go fetch the physician."

Glebric wore a deep frown as he looked from her to Simon and back to her arms. "Are you sure you can manage?"

*At least he's concerned. But for me, or for her?*

Elysia put her arm around Simon for him to lean on as he regained his feet. He managed a few stumbling steps.

"I think so," Elysia said, "Now go!"

The young man bolted for help.

As soon as Glebric was out of sight, Simon picked up the pace, rushing them forward, while leaning on Elysia in case they encountered anyone else. Which was for the best since they came across a servant girl around the next turn.

She fretted at Simon's discomfort.

Elysia waved her off. "Just a fainting spell, don't worry. I'm just helping him to his room. We've already sent for help."

The girl nodded and continued on her way.

Simon smiled at Elysia. "Maybe you chose the wrong art form? The theater is missing out!"

She laughed. "You're one to talk!"

He silenced her with a kiss, her lips responding against his. Flames ignited between them as they stumbled into his room, closing the door. He pressed his body against hers and she eagerly accommodated him, echoing his own need.

His voice was a husky whisper: "You don't understand how hard it is for me to be so close to you, yet unable to touch you..." His hands reached around her back, caressing the sleek muscles along her spine. Each rising and falling breath brought his chest in tantalizing contact with the mystery of her breasts. His mind exploded with desire. His lips sought hers again as he fumbled to remove the light wool barrier keeping him away from her skin.

"Oh Simon," she panted, matching his intensity. "We shouldn't... not... in..." A seeking dart of his tongue silenced her with a delighted gasp.

She clutched his back and pulled away. "How long do you think it will take Glebric to find the physician?"

"I don't care!" he said with a smile, lifting her up. Her arms and legs entwined around him as he sought out her lips again, passion overtaking him. He lowered her to his bed and pressed himself against her.

Her body was willing, but still her voice betrayed anxiety, in between gasps of pleasure as he kissed up and down her neck. "I don't know what Xelos would do if he caught us."

"The physician is with your father this morning. Glebric will be running around for a while to find help." He winked at her, then traced a line along her lips and chin, up to her ear and hair.

"We should have a few minutes at least," she said with a thoughtful look. She reached under his tunic to stroke his chest with her finger. "But still, we need to be careful."

She grabbed him by the sides of the chest, her arms stronger than he'd imagined, guiding him onto his back. "I can return to the floor faster this way, don't you think?"

He could barely think, with her propped up over his chest, her lightly covered breasts so close to his face. She traced his chest with one hand while the other reached behind his head, directing his lips up to meet her need. He felt himself stiffen underneath her and she caught his eye, surprised.

"Is it supposed to be that... hard?" she asked.

"I... uh—"

He was cut off by a knock on the door and Elysia vaulted to the floor at his side, cracking her knee against the frame. She said something that sounded uncouth in Izari. Simon faced the wall, trying to cover his flush. Elysia leaned over him and started weeping. The door opened and he sensed her turn to the visitor.

"I... the physician is away." It was Glebric's unsteady and heavily accented Pazian. "With your father this morning. Is Simon better?"

"He's quite flushed, I think it's some sort of fever. He'll need to rest."

"Can I help?" Glebric asked.

"I'm just worried about him. It was quite an intense set of lessons today. I fear he might have overdone it. Can you fetch him some water... and wet a towel. Nice and cold."

Glebric bowed and raced off.

When the door closed, Elysia dissolved into peals of laughter. "This is almost too easy."

Simon rolled back to face her, taking her in his arms. "I don't know why we waited so long."

"But what will Master Xelos think? I don't like lying to him."

Simon put the back of his hand to his forehead. "This project took a lot out of me!"

She stood up, hands on her hips. "If you remember, it was *my* work today, you did yours yesterday."

"Come here and I'll make it up to you," he said, pulling her by the hand to join him again on the bed. Silky curls slid over him, soft and seductive, exciting him instantly after the sudden interruption.

Her lips were soft against his cheek. "He'll be back too soon."

"Then let's enjoy every second. You're the most amazing woman, Elysia. I can't bear the thought of leaving you."

"But you have to go. You have to save Garas. It's the right thing to do, and I would do the same in your position."

He laughed. "Well in *this* position, I'm going to..." He drew her in for another kiss, and she melted into his enfolding arms, driving him wild with the need for her.

A lucid thought bubbled up through the boiling cauldron of desire that inflamed his senses. He propped her up and her hair fell across his face. They both laughed and he tucked the sweaty curls behind her ears.

"What is it?" she asked, her eyes beautifully inquisitive, with that curiosity he found so attractive.

"Come with me! To Tamar. We won't have to be apart. We can face Shadush together, with our combined Talent."

She started to speak, but sighed instead and backed her feet onto the floor, keeping her hands in his. "I... I can't." When she began to turn away he urged her back with a squeeze on her hand. She looked him full in the face, a tear in her eye. "I want to... but I... Father is here, and unwell. And Master Xelos doesn't have anyone else."

Simon let her hands fall, rejected. "You would choose them over me?"

She grabbed his hands again and leaned in, imploring him. "Don't make me choose. I have my duty as a daughter. And I still have much to learn. I don't know anything about fighting. And besides... where would I stay while you lived in the legionary camp?" Her eyes turned hard as she stood up. "I've heard about those… those women who follow the legions. You wouldn't have me stay with them, would you?"

Her point made him feel foolish. "No, Elysia. I'm sorry. You're… you're so much more to me than that. I wouldn't have you sully yourself with them. It wouldn't be right. Please forget I asked."

She squeezed his hand reassuringly and placed a light kiss on his mouth. "No, I understand. I don't wish to be apart from you either. But what is the point if I won't be able to stay with you. But…" She looked wistful. "I would love nothing more than to explore new lands with you Simon. I've never been outside of Attarsus, not even to the other islands, and the stories Xelos tells me… there's a whole world out there." Her eyes burned deep into his soul. "Promise me you'll take me to those places someday?"

"I promise." Smiling, he kissed her hand to seal it.

Glebric burst into the room at that moment, carrying a tray.

Elysia took it from him. "Thank you for bringing this." Glebric beamed. *But was it relief or something more?*

Elysia brought the cup of water to Simon's lips with the care of a nursemaid.

He drank deeply and nodded to Glebric. "Thank you, Glebric, I'm in your debt. You're a great friend. I feel much better already."

# XX

## Inspiration

Elysia herself came to wake him another morning, with Glebric trailing her nervously into the room.

"I think I've got it, Simon!"

Groggy, he mumbled a response. He had no idea what she was talking about.

She stood with hands on hips. "To get you to Garas quickly?"

The morning rust shaken off, he pulled the simple sheet over his lower half. Glebric turned away with a gasp, but Elysia smiled slowly before continuing.

"Come, I'll tell you at breakfast with Xelos."

She allowed him a few minutes to dress, then they made their way to the dining room. Elysia was skipping along, barely able to contain her excitement. Once seated, with the servants out of earshot, she leaned in conspiratorially.

"Zeno."

Simon looked at her with utter confusion. Xelos leaned back, nodding thoughtfully. "Are you sure?"

"Yes. I think I'm ready."

"What are you two talking about?" Simon asked.

"Do you remember in my own workshop, near Father's house, on that first night? The winged horse."

Realization hit him. *If he could fly...*

"But it's just a statue... can you? Doesn't it have to be new? In the flow?"

"Well, I've never tried... but I don't think so. I only have to finish it, and be in the right frame of mind. Or of feeling."

"But Elysia, isn't he your favorite?" She nodded. "You'd do this for me?"

She looked quickly to Xelos. "For the world. To defeat darkness." She looked back to him, and her eyes told him more.

"But... could he even fly? And how would I fly him? Would he listen to me?"

It was Xelos who responded. "All good questions, Simon. Obviously you'll need to test things. But this is a good enough idea that you should start working on it right away. Make it today's lessons. You can leave after breakfast. Keep your faces covered, and I'll send you each out with a guard. But first I will have Glebric and others go to the market to draw off any watchers."

Elysia looked horrified. "We're being watched here? Your house?"

"I believe so. There has been too much... shall we say... suspicious traffic on this street of late." He shook his head sadly. "But today would be good. You never can tell if it will work right away. You will not be able to bring Zeno back here, not without arousing suspicion. Actually, if you are both heading over there, you should take some supplies to have them ready for Simon's ultimate departure. Better not go back and forth unnecessarily."

"What supplies?" Simon asked.

"Some gold and materials mostly. For your journey. Although being able to fly will change what you need. You will need saddlebags, but that will also let you carry more. Hmmm. I will have everything brought up. That reminds me of something else I must share with you. Simon, are you in the right mind to remember some details?"

"Yes, but..."

"Then let me show you now, unless you are not done eating."

After sending off a servant with instructions, Xelos took them to his talking sculptures. With a deadly serious expression, he unwrapped them all.

"What I am about to tell you both, you must swear never to write down. If you are successful with Zeno, then when you do leave, Simon, you'll be going into great danger. You may not come back. You may be captured... which could be worse than death, and very dangerous for all of us." He looked them both in the eye. "Do you swear never to let these names cross your lips again, unless you need to go searching for them?"

Simon tried to protest. "But after I finish in Pelusia, I'll come right back here."

"Who knows where the winds of fortune will blow you, Simon. I am old, and younger men than me have been stricken by illness. Or you may be redeployed with the legion, or driven to another land, or sent on some further errand. My brethren wish you to know of them, so you can contact them again in a time of need. Repeat each after me."

Starting with Yalath that he'd already spoken to, Xelos named the four colleagues, and the cities they resided in. Both Simon and Elysia swore that the names would go with them to the grave.

"But how will I find them?"

Xelos smiled. "Take your time. Memorize their faces. I would have you paint each of them into this world, just in case. You can do that tomorrow, or whenever you finish with Elysia's big project. But it would be too risky to carry those pictures with you. When you head to their city, you paint them again and use the window exercise to get some sense of where to find them. Perhaps even contact them that way. Even though you do not know them, your need would be great and emotions strong in any event."

The servant arrived with a full satchel, a set of saddlebags, bridle, and a horse blanket.

"Ah, good," Xelos said. He retrieved the letter for Garas from a shelf and placed it in the satchel. "Gold and silver, dry food, basic survival equipment. And painting materials for you. It is with misgivings that I send both of you out from safety here, even for the day, but at least you can kill two birds with one stone."

He asked the servant something in Izari, and got a response. "Good. Glebric and the others have left, so you should seize the chance now."

"Thank you Master Xelos, you really do think of everything."

Elysia took the satchel, while Simon took the heavier horse gear. Despite his misgivings, he was exhilarated to go outside for the first time in weeks. *Especially with Elysia.* The two guards joined them at the front gate. *And of course a guard.* But he welcomed the opportunity, even with company.

He would go first to the right, while Elysia and her guard would leave a few minutes later, to the left. They'd meet up at the agora and then make their way to her private workshop.

The gifts made his departure much more real, and imminent. "When should I leave, Master? I have so much more to learn. I'm far from ready to face…" He looked at the guards. "Especially since he's getting a lot of live practice."

"You still have a long way to go. But you will never be fully ready. You just need to practice. Once you have control, if it truly becomes second nature, and the Talent comes as easily as breathing, who knows what is possible? Maybe you will not even need the material? I regret that there is not much more I can teach you."

The thought unsettled Simon as he walked out. Xelos was so wise, and knew so much more than they did. But so much was conjecture and theory. Always leading to more questions. Outside these walls how many times, if any, had Xelos used his own powers to affect the world in any way? Certainly not in battle.

Simon smiled in silent thanks when Xelos embraced Elysia like a granddaughter. Simon felt more at home, like a family, than he had in many years. It would be tough when the time came to leave both of them behind. Even if her experiment did work, he'd be bringing her back here tonight. There would be no goodbyes today.

### ᎶᏋᏋᏋᎶ

Aktar inspected the group he'd assembled. The men from Persei had arrived last night, and with three more local brutes harboring no love for art-loving aristocrats like this Xelos, it made ten in all. They all concealed short swords, clubs, and sturdy ropes to bind captives as necessary. Four of Persei's were pure muscle, but the other two were former acrobats with specific skills for getting into places quietly and unseen. All of them dressed like the kind of local ruffians that kept most honest people behind the gates of their homes at night. And in this case, with good justification.

*More than sufficient. Persei doesn't mess around.* And of course, there was no way to trace any of them to the Lokuta if they were found.

He went over the plan once more with the group. Barring an unforeseen delay, tonight was the night.

### ᎶᏋᏋᏋᎶ

Simon went first, brushing away the cobwebs draping the stairs down to Elysia's workshop.

"When were you last here?" he asked.

"Not since you returned," Elysia said, mock accusation in her eyes. "They'll miss me."

His head whipped around, startled. He kept his voice a hush so Xelos' guard wouldn't hear them: "Are any down here... alive?"

She laughed. "No, but I do miss seeing them every day. I feel like they miss me too. These are from years of my work, and most of my favorites are here."

Once they were safely through the door, Simon dismissed the guards with a silver each. "We'll be here a while, so why don't you find a place to wait nearby. You're more use keeping watch on the street. You could get some bread from her father's shop if you're hungry. We'll come find you when we're ready."

They looked happy to leave rather than sit around in a dusty basement full of odd statues.

When Elysia finished barring the door behind the departing guards, Simon whisked her off her feet into an embrace. His lips were fierce as they found hers. She made to protest but quickly surrendered to his urgent heat, stretching up to meet him as he backed her up against the wall.

His lips moved from cheek to ear to neck, tracing the lines he'd so sensually painted days before. "I've been wanting to do this again. You found us the chance."

His words snapped her out of passionate oblivion, and she pulled back with an angry flash in her eyes. "Simon! That's not why I suggested this at all!"

Stumbling back from her outburst, he felt a sharp jab in his back. He turned instinctively to face the attacker. It was a heavy sculpture of a dog, now wobbling on its base. He steadied it, then tried his best to look innocent.

"No? I had thought you missed my lips and hands as much as I missed yours... maybe more?"

She huffed with mock indignation, but was gentle as she stepped forward to guide his hands on the sculpture, moving it to the right place. "You know we have work to do. Maybe if you can focus long enough we'll have a little time later?"

That slightest narrowing of her eye sent shivers of anticipation down his spine. At least he hadn't totally blown the chance. Being so close to her... finally alone... was intoxicating.

"So what should we do first?"

"We don't have any protection for Zeno, but what if you were to paint on him? Make him... more protected somehow?"

"Like armor? Or scales?"

She shrugged, leaving it up to him.

He examined the horse... Zeno, and let his mind go free, imagining possibilities. She'd already created a horse that was not just a horse, and that should be able to fly with those majestic wings. He stroked the noble face, the intricate texture of the mane, and the smooth flanks. It stood slightly larger than the average horse, and the wings outstretched would practically fill the room.

"How long did you study horses to get him so perfect? It's really amazing."

She smiled. "Every chance I got. I would go to the market, or watch the carts come in through the gates. And one of Alexander's friends has a father who raises horses. The son was always asking me to come and visit. I never went for him... but the horses! They were so beautiful, so inspiring. After I saw the block of marble with Zeno inside, it was all I could think about for weeks. Seeing and riding the horses got it clear in my mind."

Her excitement made him smile, even though he was skeptical of her idea. "I'm still not sure if it will work though, to paint your piece... will our Talent really combine like that?"

"Xelos is always telling us to break free from limitations, and push the bounds of our work to see where it can go."

A thought occurred to him. "When they come to life, do they look exactly the same? The color of the stone?" She nodded. "Well at the very least, I should give him some color. A marbled horse would attract too much attention. And I can't think of a way to armor him that won't look too strange."

She looked at him like he'd said something stupid. "More than a horse with wings?"

"Oh, I've already thought of that. I can use the blankets to cover the wings when we're around people. Make him look like he's carrying things for me. In fact, I was even going to see how they fold down when not in flight. If they're like a bird's, they might fit alongside the saddlebags." *Cover... cover...* It gave him an idea. "Maybe I could put some armor on the parts that won't be as noticeable? If we're worried about him being shot at while we're in the air, then protecting the belly would be important, and it will be in shadow, and partially covered by the straps of the saddle and not

214

too noticeable. I'll see what I can do."

"Can you keep him mostly white then, but give the mane some color?"

He looked at the veins of green and gray that speckled the marble. To get a piece this size her father had to settle for one that was far from pure in color. "It would be too much to cover these with white, but would you settle for me making them more brown or gray to look like a natural coat?"

She put her hand on the hard marble mane. "I'm sure you'll make him beautiful."

"So what else do you need to do?"

"I'm going to work on some of my other pieces to get into the flow. When you're done I'll see what needs doing. To finish the work."

Simon set to mixing his paints, and she helped him to speed things up. Every time their hands touched he quickened his pace, wanting this done so he could steal a few more moments with her, away from the watching eyes of Xelos and his staff.

Xelos had included a variety of paint options in the saddlebags, though Simon at first worried about running out, with such a large piece to work on. By keeping things subtle like he'd explained, he was able to stretch it further. He made the hooves dark, and the mane speckled gray to cover the natural grain of the stone. With only a little light from slits high up on the wall to go by, he had no idea how much time passed.

It was more workmanlike than when he had painted Elysia, but there was still feeling to it. He tapped into her affection for the statue... for this Zeno that was waiting to break free of his stone prison. Every detail had to be perfect; the work was so delicate.

On the belly he painted subtle scales, but kept them the same color as the rest of the body—it was little lines of definition and shadow that added the perspective. In his mind they were clearly scales and harder than the rest. But would that come through in life? He'd have to see.

Finally, long after the light through the window slits had faded from gold to red to darkness, he stood back and beheld the sum of his work. He called to her on the other side of the room, where she pored over some smaller piece.

"What do you think?"

She walked over beside him and slid her hand around his waist, leaning her head on his shoulder. "Thank you Simon. For bringing him so much closer to life. He looks so... so natural. I think I'm finally ready." She put her arms around him, leaning up to kiss him softly. His arms waved around in the air beside her, not wanting to mark her with the paint on his fingers. She pulled away, looking at them with a laugh. "Don't wash up yet. Now it's my turn. And get some blue ready, like the sky."

"For what?"

"The eyes. But I have to finish them first. That's all that's left."

He watched her as he mixed the blue paint, marveling at how her delicate fingers worked with total concentration. With her little metal tools she sanded so gently that mere specks of dust came off. It amazed him how differently their Talent expressed itself: how she could remove to create, but he had to add. Yet both could result in the creation of something new, of something beautiful. Pure human expression.

Mere minutes passed before she called out to him. "Ready?"

With her standing close behind him, feeling the weight of her anticipation, Simon's hand started shaking. Twice he had to put the brush back down and take a steadying breath before he was calm enough to bring it to the whiteness of the eye. He closed his own eyes, vividly recalling horses he'd ridden with the legions and saying a silent thanks for that experience with the marvelous creatures. Xelos had said it was possible to create something completely from imagination, but Simon still needed a clear vision in his mind, or better yet, right in front of him.

When he was done, Elysia covered her mouth with both hands, her eyes filled with a happiness so intense it verged on tears. He started to put his arm around her, but she shook her head, recoiling slightly, and he backed off. She walked up to the statue as if she were approaching the real thing, speaking to him gently in Izari. Tracing the mane and ears with her fingers, then the face, she leaned in and hugged the whole head, bringing her eyes level with those of the stone animal.

It was a moment of such tender beauty, Simon thought his heart would burst with the love he felt for her, and through her for the animal. Her eyes were wet, glistening with happy tears. A single drop landed on the horse's left eye. His mind leapt to warn her not to ruin the wet paint, but the words died in his mouth when a pinprick spark of light flashed from the contact.

He wasn't sure what hit him first, the added warmth in the air or the unmistakable smell of a fine, clean horse, but his senses had prepared him by the time the animal blinked.

Elysia jumped with delight and resumed hugging the animal, joyful rivulets streaming down her face. A swishing tail showed Zeno's appreciation for the attention, and he nuzzled into her, the long hair of the mane flowing over her, no longer static marble. The colors of his coat blended naturally, much to Simon's personal delight.

Simon's jaw dropped when the wings stretched out to their full span, touching the ceiling of the workshop. Majestic, graceful and so natural... a living, breathing creature of myth. It set his mind wondering what else might be possible, what other fantastical beings had been lost to the mists of time. Might some have been the children of Talented masters past, or future?

Elysia was chattering away contentedly in Izari before remembering that she and her creation were not alone.

"Zeno, this is Simon. My very dear friend." Her eyes locked on his, sending out a very strong wave of emotion. "He helped me to rescue you from where you were trapped. To bring you into our world."

Zeno whinnied in what sounded like appreciation.

Simon was agape. "He can... you can understand us?" This elicited an affirmative snort. And she had been speaking Pazian to him. This was no dumb horse, but a thinking being.

He approached tentatively, but Elysia was encouraging. He stroked Zeno's mane in that way horses loved, and this one proved no different.

"Can... can I touch your belly?" Simon asked, trying to sound as respectful as possible. Zeno's eyes looked wary, but the horse inclined his head slightly as if to give assent.

Simon crouched down and broke out in a wide smile. The outlines of the scales were just as he'd imagined them. They were barely noticeable if you didn't know what you were looking at, but running his hand along the subtle ridges brought to mind the scaled armor worn by some of the auxiliary soldiers. *Might even be good enough to deflect an arrow.* Seeing his work come to life in three dimensions was a new kind of thrill, with so many possibilities to explore. *But not now.*

With that test out of the way, Simon's eyes studied the wings once again, now tucked deftly on each side, just as he'd imagined. *Like a bird.* Without thinking, he reached over to touch the wing, but with a flick it knocked his hand away like a tail swatting an annoying fly.

Elysia laughed. It was with genuine concern for the answer that he asked the obviously annoyed creature a question. "Zeno, will you let me ride you?"

Elysia stepped in. "Of course you will, right Zeno? I need you to take Simon somewhere far away, to help one of his friends." Her words tugged at his heart, and her face betrayed her own sadness. She looked to Simon, and to Zeno, and the tears turned sad. Both Simon and Zeno embraced her protectively with arms and wings.

"You could still come with us," Simon said, knowing she'd decline but wishing that she wouldn't. "You would be with two... friends."

She shook her head. "You know I want to. But Father... No, this is your road alone. But now you both have to promise me to bring each other back to me safely!" She wiped the tears away, but the forced smile didn't cover her true feelings.

"Well we're not leaving yet, so you can cheer up," he said, and leaned in to kiss her.

A light, yet firm tap on the back of his neck made him turn and almost hit his nose on the tip of Zeno's wing.

*Great, another chaperon?*

Elysia stepped between them. "You must both be hungry. You two get acquainted while I go get us some food." Her face lit up. "And I would love to bring Father down, to meet you both." Startled by the last statement, Simon didn't have time to object before Elysia slipped out the door and locked it behind her.

# XXI

## ᎾᎾᎾᎾᎾᎾᎾ
## *Attack*

Elysia's feet barely touched the ground as she bounded up the stairs and around the corner.

*Zeno is so beautiful! It worked!* And only because she and Simon had worked together, as partners in creation. The idea touched her in some deep, primal part of her being. She felt so close to Simon, craving his touch and lips every bit as much as he obviously did. Sighing at another missed opportunity, she promised herself she'd make it up to him when she brought down their dinner.

*Unless Father came too. Oh, when will we get time to ourselves?*

But she was so excited to tell her father about both Zeno and Simon that it was worth it. If Simon must go, then she wanted to introduce him to the other great man in her life before he left. And she'd have to bring Father to them. Coming in late at night did make him nervous, especially with Xelos' warning, and Alexander would scold her for being out too late. To bring a strange man with her? That would be too much.

*Not too much for Mother.* Her eyes misted up as she thought of how delighted Mother would have been in the same situation. This dashing young Pazian soldier. Yes, he was an artist too, and maybe a little thin... but tall! And his beautiful skin, like dark, living bronze, with its hard lines of muscle. *And he understands me. He appreciates my art.*

*And besides, Zeno needs the company. Who knows what kind of mess he'd make on his own down there among the sculpture? A newborn foal in a charger's body. And those wings.* She couldn't help but smile when she thought of the texture of the wings—living, moving wings—destined to soar over the sea. *Of course Simon couldn't come up, not yet.*

Lost in pleasant thoughts, she took no notice of her surroundings as she followed the nearly automatic route to her father's front door. She was on the threshold before she realized that there was no light coming from the windows, and the door hung ajar.

She opened it cautiously and as her eyes adjusted to the darkness, illuminated only by a pale streak of moonlight, the shapes were all wrong, with dark objects strewn across a floor that should be clear, and the shelf on the far wall empty and tilting to the side.

*Father!*

Panic-stricken, she stumbled through debris. Cutting through the familiar smell of fresh bread was a foul odor, sharp and acrid like... urine mixed with something metallic. Gagging and choking, she reached the counter mostly by touch and fumbled around to where the oven door was shut. She opened it a crack, and heat and light streamed out.

She screamed at the first horrible image: beside the oven door, just out of reach, lay the body of one of the two guards, head lolling to the side at an unnatural angle... from a deep gash still oozing blood.

Her head whipped away, gorge and terror rising together. In the light of the oven she could see broken plates and trays scattered across the floor. Beyond the debris lay another fallen figure, just inside the front door, scant inches from where she had stepped— the other guard, frozen in motion, hacked down before he could escape.

*Father? Father! Where are you?*

Not on the floor. As her mind caught up, she half-dreaded each new image, and gasped when she turned the other way. Another body—*Alexander! No, not Alexander!*—slumped beside the racks where they kept their dough, his eyes glassy and staring, mouth open in shock, tunic tattered and dark in four different places. Stab wounds.

Anguish cramped her stomach as she covered her mouth with her hands.

*No! No!*

She couldn't take her eyes from his face. That face that was so often stern and reprimanding, always the superior older brother... in death he looked so young, so scared. More the little boy she used to love playing with than the young man who disapproved of everything in her life, who only spoke with her to scold and berate. Now he was dead, and because of her, and those very choices he had opposed.

*But where is Father?*

Black dread threatened to overtake her, but she fought it, lifting a lamp from its place at the side of the oven, and lighting it with a taper from the fire. She shone it on the interior door from the shop to their home, a ruined mess of wooden shards clinging to the doorway like cold, dead hands. As she bolted through the dark opening, she stumbled on something slick and fell, slicing her knee on a piece of broken wood. Oil splashed from the lamp onto the floor, just missing her sandaled foot. But it didn't catch fire.

Favoring the painful wound, she limped to the back, seeking out any sign of her father, hoping beyond hope that she wouldn't find him lifeless, like the others. She searched room by room, finding nothing but destroyed furniture and every chest and closet thrown open, ransacked from a thorough search. *For her? But no more blood. No sign of Father.*

Uncomprehending, she hugged her knees on her slashed but empty bed, rocking back and forth with each of the terrors seen and imagined flashing through her mind.

*Blood—the bodies—Alexander!*

*All dead!*

*Father?*

*Xelos?*

*Simon!*

He was her lifeline; a beacon in the darkness of her thoughts.

She hobbled back to the kitchen, alert to every shadow, her eyes scanning for some weapon. A kitchen knife. She set the lamp beside the knife and steeled herself for one last look at her brother. She crouched down close to him, unable to avoid all the blood. *So much blood.*

"I'm so sorry," she said. "You... you deserve better. You were so good to him... to them. I will find Father, and the ones who did this, and they will pay." Reaching down with a shaking hand, she pulled his cold lids closed, and then his mouth, trying to give him some measure of peace. He looked better that way, more adult; once again the perfect son to both parents. Far better than she could ever hope to be. She kissed the clammy skin on his forehead.

In that fleeting moment, she sought a connection with those gods she barely believed in. "Attarso, Aliata, if you're listening… please take care of him. Help me find Father."

She stood a little straighter, with purpose. *What if the light brought back the killers?* She set the lamp on the sill of the oven, then closed the door, confining the heat and light once more. Gripping the kitchen knife in her hand and getting her bearings on the front door, still ajar, she snuffed the flame of the lamp and followed the thin trail of moonlight back toward Simon, Zeno, and the chance to find her father.

$$\text{ᎾᏋᏮᏋᏮᏋᏮ}$$

"Hurry up, old man," Aktar said as he prodded the baker in front of him, "if you want to see your daughter again, alive."

Aktar's arm was bound where he'd taken a slash from one of those guards. *Guards? In a bakery?* That still didn't add up. *Were they somehow expecting us?* It had set him on edge. He'd done threats and kidnapping a dozen times, and bloodshed was rare. A show of force was usually sufficient to get what his masters needed. A few bruises, a black eye, and usually the marks gave him his bonus themselves.

*But not this time.*

Still, he didn't let it show. He needed to be strong in front of the men, and the group moved confidently toward the house of Xelos. Even at night, nobody would dare cross them, especially with a few showing fresh wounds. His men walked in formation around the bedraggled old baker. The old coot had refused to tell them where his daughter was, even with some less than gentle persuasion. But no matter, they were pretty sure she was back at this house, and the hostage should be all the currency he'd need.

But the walk was giving him too much time to think. The day was ill-fated from the beginning, starting with the little incident with the slaves. His lookouts at the house had followed a suspicious pair in the morning, only to discover in the middle of the agora that they'd been following slaves. *Slaves in cloaks? Maybe servants?* It was a cool day, and this master seemed to treat his people well. It wasn't until the men got close that they realized the youth was too young—no soldier. But it remained another detail that worried him, and left an hour or more unaccounted for.

Still, with their eight they should be able to overpower any resistance. He sent the acrobats ahead with their instructions to get over the walls and be ready on the inside. Even if he wasn't successful talking or forcing his way through the front door, they'd be able to create massive confusion and turn the tide.

He shook his head as they approached the front gate, getting his first close view of the statuary. *Incredible! The detail work on the gods? Beautiful. Master Daymar would love it. It would be a shame to see it damaged if we have to force this. I'll have to get my hands on some more portable stuff inside.*

The sound of an owl hooted from above. He nodded and motioned his men into place. The other seven stood flush with the wall on either side of the door, out of sight.

Aktar stood with the baker in front of the heavy door, the point of his sword ever so slightly touching the man's back. "You say just what I told you, or you're dead."

The man nodded, and feebly rapped the knocker three times. It was shaped like a hammer striking a chisel. *Nice touch.*

The slit slid open almost immediately. Worried eyes peered through. "Yes?"

"I'm..." The baker's voice gave out. Aktar pushed a little harder, soliciting a muffled yelp. "Tell Elysia to run!"

The eyes went wide. Aktar swore, and grabbed the old man's mouth with his other hand. *Always damned plan B.* He put his face to the slit. "Listen. We know they're in there. Tell the girl Elysia that we have her father here. Either Simon comes out to see me in five minutes, or the old man's blood will be decorating this beautiful front gate. And don't try anything with the guards." He waved and the others stepped in behind him. "Me and my boys will make short work of them."

The slit snapped shut and he heard a flurry of voices and footsteps from the other side.

Aktar pushed the baker to his knees, his voice vicious. "Old man, you're making this hard on us. I might just have to take out my displeasure on your beautiful daughter." He laughed at the terror in the old man's eyes, and the pool forming below him. *That plus a few nice sculptures would be fair compensation for the extra trouble. And it wouldn't violate any of Persei's orders.*

Within moments a new pair of eyes peered out of the slot. Old eyes. *Xelos? Where is Simon, and the girl?* Aktar pulled the baker to his feet again, showing him clearly to the slot.

"Time is running out for the old man here. Trade us Simon and we'll be gone."

"I have gold," the man said, louder than needed. "Whatever they're paying you, I can double it. Just give us the man and be on your way."

The Attarsan men looked to him for direction, their eyes filled with avarice. The Pazians shook their heads. Aktar was impressed. Even with his longstanding relationship with the Lokuta, a deal was never out of the question. But he also knew the price of their enmity, and would rather live to enjoy his profit.

"We don't want your gold. You'd better hurry up."

The voice was little more than a croak: "I will not give you Simon."

"Then we have to do this the hard way." He nodded to one of the men, who put his hands to his mouth and made another hooting sound.

A cry erupted from behind the doors, and the eyes turned away from the slit. Aktar signaled to the men to be ready, and pounced on the opportunity for reconnaissance. The field of vision was very limited through the slit, but the scene was well lit and he got his bearings. Smoke billowed out from the left side passageway, and a group of guards rushed across his view in that direction. Two more guards were escorting a bearded older man in a fine tunic— *Xelos?*—at a run down a different hall, to the right, away from the trouble. Only two stood at attention in front of an elegant fountain, their focus on the front doors. From the nervous twitch of their swords, Aktar estimated them to be pretty green.

Movement from behind the guards—an open set of double doors—caught his eye, and with a flash and a muffled grunt one of them went down, a knife buried in his throat. *Good throw.* A body flashed by the slit at full speed, and Aktar heard the scrabbling of men on the floor beyond his view. He strained to get a better sightline, but had to rely on his ears, making out a choked gurgle and a sickening thud. Then new, much harder eyes peered out at him, narrowing with recognition, followed by the sound of bars being raised and locks opened.

He held up his hand, and the men stood at attention. He pointed to one of the Pazians and indicated the baker with his chin. "Stay with him at the entrance, and keep watch at the gate. It's a quiet street, but we don't want any surprises. And don't let anyone leave!"

His man nodded, binding the baker's hands behind him.

Aktar and his men charged through the door. He whistled as he took in the large square hall with its elaborate carvings. *Nice place.* But for now he needed to cover escape routes and keep control of the house. One guard was writhing on the floor, his hands too weak to remove the knife spilling his life's blood in a pool around him. The other was already dead, his head twisted at an awkward angle. He addressed the panting acrobat who had opened the door. "Good work. Your partner?"

"He started the fires, and will be busy with the guards that went that way." He pointed to the left.

"Take these three with you to relieve him. And then circle back through there." He pointed straight ahead through a double doorway. "I'll take the rest with me to find Xelos. He'll lead us to what we want. No witnesses." The men nodded and followed the smoke.

At first Aktar tried to keep his men quiet, but they were too slow, so he urged them to a run down the right side passage. They tried every door, finding each one unlocked and empty, other than the odd terrified servant or slave that cowered in their beds when threatened.

"Leave them. We want the master of the house."

After turning a corner in near darkness, a single lamp on the wall illuminated two grizzled men guarding a door between them.

"Master, they're here!" one called through the door before slamming it shut.

"Attack!" Aktar yelled, and his five surged to meet them. Though surprised at their numbers, the guards didn't appear unsettled. They braced for the charge.

The big man to Aktar's left smashed into his opponent with a loud crash. Aktar swung his sword down in a vicious arc at the other guard, then jerked forward, trying for surprise. Metal rang on metal as his blow was warded aside. He gasped as a blade caught his rib with a glancing blow, only his instincts deflecting it wide. Turning his parry into a slash toward the man's gut, his quarry lurched out of reach as another of Aktar's men barreled into him. Channeling his anger from the sharp pain in his side, Aktar dove in with an angry jab for the kill.

He stood up, rubbing at his rib and his hand came back bloody. More painful than threatening, but it still made him angry. The other three had made short work of the other guard, though the first was nursing a nasty gash on his off arm. Aktar silently thanked Persei for the numbers. These two were good enough to have been a problem. Clapping the men on the shoulder, he pointed to himself and then the door. He was the first to burst through.

The only light in the room came from a lamp on a table on the far right side, against the wall. A man held a hammer over his head—the old man in the finer tunic—and struck a blow at the wall, sending chunks flying off in all directions. *No, not the wall itself, but something attached to it. A... statue... of a face?* The old man looked briefly at Aktar then turned back to smash the stone again and again, faster now.

Aktar scanned the rest of the room. Some kind of workshop.

"Leave him to me," he said to his men.

He strode toward the man, picking his way past tables of sculptures, paintings, and tools. There were three other ruined faces in a row along the wall, and the whole room was filled with semi-finished works of art.

Xelos took three more blows at the statue as he approached, finally turning back to face Aktar when it was beyond recognition.

"Where is Simon?" Aktar asked, pointing his sword at the man he assumed was Xelos.

The voice was cultured, yet firm. "You will not be able to take him. They already left the city."

Aktar stopped his advance, fighting a sinking feeling. "Where?"

Xelos shook his head. "Safe. Lost to you. You failed. You will never find them now." The old man's smile was defiant, yet serene in the flickering light. Like a martyr ready to sacrifice himself for some higher cause.

Flushed with anger at the challenge in front of his men, he leapt at the old man, turning aside an ineffectual wave of the hammer with his sword. His blow struck true, driving through the old man's gut without much resistance. Aktar twisted it, wrenching it up into other soft organs. Xelos' eyes flared in pain, then he slumped forward. Aktar tossed the body aside like a rag doll before spitting on it.

*Parasite. Living like a noble with your art while other men do honest work.*

His men had finished searching the room but found no other exit, nor hiding places.

"Search the rest of the house. He's lying." But Aktar knew he was the one denying reality.

He looked at the shards of ruined statuary that Xelos had been busy destroying. *I come for the boy, and you defend this? Maybe Persei will make some sense of this puzzle. More likely Daymar.* He winced at the thought of reporting his failure.

᠖᠑᠖᠑᠖᠑᠖

Simon and Zeno eyed each other warily, silently competing to appear more impatient for Elysia's return. And the horse was likely winning, since part of Simon was madly rehearsing words that wouldn't sound completely stupid to address her dear father. Simon's only remotely relevant experience hadn't gone well at all.

The scrape of the key in the lock brought them both to attention, and Simon swore the winged horse also stood up a little taller as he looked at the door.

The Elysia that walked through alone looked like she'd been tossed through every part of the bakery. She was breathing heavily, with hair in matted tangles, her dress torn and discolored white, black and... red? *A knife in her hand?* Simon overcame his shock as she closed the door behind her, and he rushed to hold her.

Her eyes were red-rimmed, but resolute—fierce.

"Elysia, what happened? Where is your father?"

"Gone... the bakery... ruined. Alexander..." She looked lost for a moment, numb, then buried her face in Simon's chest, wracked by silent sobs.

His mind raced to make sense of this. "Where are those guards?"

"Dead," she whispered. "I saw them, Simon. On the floor. With Alexander. Father is... gone." The tears streamed down her face, but she was eerily quiet as he took her in his arms, trying to will peace into her heart after what she'd seen. Nobody was ever ready for the sight of a dead body, especially someone they knew.

"I'm so sorry. And they must be after me. It's all my fault."

That seemed to jolt some life back into her. "Don't say that! You didn't do this."

The horrible realization dawned on him. He hoped he didn't

show it in his face. He took her hands. "Elysia, I'll find your father. Xelos will know what to do. I'll go see him."

"I'm coming."

"No, it's dark out, and the city is not safe. And if we come across them... they killed two guards, and wouldn't think twice about killing you too. But obviously they don't know about this place, so you should be safe. Get some food from the bakery, and quickly, then lock yourself back in here. I'll come back when it's safe."

"But where will they have taken Father?"

"If my guess is right, to Xelos."

"But why?"

He couldn't avoid it. "To make Xelos deliver me to them."

"I won't let you give yourself up."

He tried to appear confident, smiling back. "I don't intend to. But I can't let them do anything to your father." He wiped flour and soot from her face, and her eyes still entranced him. So brave.

She stopped him. "But won't they recognize you? They must have a description, or even someone who knows you."

"What about a disguise?"

She looked around, bewildered. "With what? A statue?"

"Do you have a mirror down here?"

She nodded. "I use it to better shine the light on my work." She pulled a large square of polished metal out from an alcove.

He gathered his paints and sat down with the mirror revealing his anxious reflection. "Another experiment." It was very awkward at first, working in reverse. He managed to make her chuckle a couple of times as he jabbed paint into his nostril or lips, but she was ready with a cloth to wipe off the mistakes. At least he could do something to lighten her mood, because inside he was churning with anxiety. Channeling his yearning to save her father into each stroke, they began to come to life, leaving not just paint on his face, but the hair of a long gray beard.

She watched, entranced, as his skin lightened and aged in front of both their eyes.

"What about the hair?"

"I was hoping I didn't have to, but I guess you're right." He rushed through graying his hair, and even painted in some wrinkles for effect. The feeling of the power coursing through his fingers into instant reality was an addictive sensation. He wanted to do it again. But he shelved that excitement to stay focused.

She was shaking her head as he finished. "Wow. How will you get it off?"

"I'll figure that out later. I have to hurry. Do I look the part of one of Xelos' Izari friends?" he asked, twirling the beard. It was so real it even itched. He'd always hated beards, and had no issue with the legion rules outlawing facial hair. But now, looking at this foreigner in the mirror, he allowed himself a moment to celebrate. The world—even his own face!—was now his canvas, and he could leave his mark. Only the urgency of the situation stopped his mind from getting carried away with new ideas to try.

"It's incredible how different you look, but you definitely could pass for one of his colleagues." Elysia wrinkled her nose at the extra hair as he leaned forward to kiss her. "Maybe later. Be safe Simon."

Zeno nuzzled up to her protectively as Simon walked out into the night.

# XXII

## Fall

With his cloak pulled tightly around him against the chill, Simon dashed through the streets of this city he barely knew. Fortunately Xelos had assigned him to work on maps of the city from memory, and he'd enjoyed Elysia's help in correcting and refining them. While everything looked totally different in the dark, he didn't make a wrong turn.

It was the night itself that worried him. The streets of Attarsus weren't half as rough as those of Pazh, but he had to stand taller than he felt to dissuade the small bands of ruffians that might otherwise consider him an easy mark. It was lucky they couldn't see his face behind the hood of the cloak, and that the disguise didn't make him move like the old man he now resembled. He wished again that he had his sword rather than just a sharp knife. Not to mention his legionary armor.

At Xelos' street he slowed down to a normal pace to minimize suspicion. He walked on the far side, pulling his hood down and sneaking a glance across every few steps. Not many were out in the better neighborhoods at this time of night, and not a soul on this street.

His internal alarm went off when he approached the closed doors, triggered by an acrid smell tickling his nostrils. *Smoke!* He drew the knife, keeping it concealed in his sleeve. *The fire must be under control. No signs of forced entry.* Maybe he'd been wrong? *But where was Elysia's missing father?*

He couldn't think of another option, so Simon approached the entrance, his anxiety overwhelming even the beauty of the columns and the sculpture. But one image stood out—a central figure with a crown like a king. Attarso? *Father of the gods, help me find the father of my love.*

He crouched down slightly to bring his eyes level with the viewing slot, then drew back the hood and rested his hand on the iron door knocker. After taking a deep breath, he rapped the hammer against the chisel three times, the peal of metal on metal piercing the silence of the night.

Incoherent mumbling from behind the door was followed by footsteps. The slit opened, hard eyes boring into Simon's.

"Who goes there?" the man asked in Pazian, in a voice he definitely didn't recognize.

Simon's heart dropped with the confirmation of the breach. *Xelos! Now what?* "I… have a letter for Master Xelos."

"He's not seeing visitors. Call again tomorrow."

Simon scrambled to think of something. "It's urgent!"

"Then pass it through to me."

"No, I'm under strict orders to hand deliver it."

Now it was the impostor guard's turn to stumble.

"Aren't you a little old to be a courier? Fine, I'll fetch the steward. Wait outside."

The slit closed, and Simon put his ear to the gap, catching the sound of receding footfalls. He was about to step back to look for a way over the wall when moaning and shuffling came from floor-level beyond the door. Someone was moving toward him, calling out in muffled Izari.

"Hello?" Simon said, in Pazian.

"Help me!"

*It might yet be a trap.* Putting his lips to the edge of the slit, he called through barely above a whisper. "Who are you? What's going on?"

"Xelos is dead!" the voice cried out, the anguish penetrating the wood between them.

*Dead? No! I'm too late…*

Fury coursing through him, Simon banged his hand against the heavy wood. "He can't be dead! He can't be!" *But who was this messenger?* "Who are you?"

"Go for help. Find my daughter…"

The name was indistinct, but clear in Simon's mind. His heart wrenched as he heard the broken sobbing from the other side, then the man banging against the door. But no matter how hard either of them might try, they couldn't break through the inches of heavy wood that kept him a prisoner, and Simon unable to rescue him.

Simon squeezed out the words he'd been hoping to say to the man's face. "I came from Elysia, to save you."

"Elysia? Is she here?"

"No. She's safe."

"Keep her safe. Please... please protect her."

"I will, I..." The words were suddenly clear to himself, and leapt out unbidden. "I love her."

The voice was insistent, and full of emotion. "Then go to her."

"But I can't leave you. She loves you so much, and... I promised." He choked on the failure, not willing to give up. Not yet. Not when this man meant the world to Elysia. "I will get you out."

"No, too many men. Just promise me you will care for her."

He imagined this man, offering himself as sacrifice for the daughter he loved so dearly, and he felt so close to him... united in their desire to protect her. Simon closed his eyes and tried forming words through shaking lips to demonstrate how serious he was... and somehow offer solace and connection in what might be their only moment together. "F... Father... I'll take care of her." Tears streamed down his face as he made his vow.

"Then go! Go now!" the voice yelled, one final desperate command.

Muffled shouting. Running footsteps approaching. Her father yelled louder now. "Help! City watch! Save us! Xelos is dead!"

Angry voices. "Shut up old man!" An ugly thump against the door.

*No!* Determination burned inside Simon, and he stepped to the side, out of view of the slit just before it opened. His hand twitched on the handle of the knife, his arm cocked and ready.

The door burst open and Simon pounced on the ugly Pazian who emerged, sinking his knife into the exposed neck like it was a choice cut of meat. The man collapsed with a gurgling squeal, clutching the blade, and his short sword clattered to the ground. Simon pounced on it, then wheeled to see inside.

The silhouette of a second man filled the doorway. He shouted for reinforcements, then jabbed his sword toward Simon, who flicked it aside with his own.

"Now!" Simon shouted as if to an accomplice, which drew the man's eyes to the side for the moment he needed. Simon's thrust was true, catching the man above the kneecap. The man doubled over, giving Simon the chance to kick him in the same knee, sending him sprawling. The man howled in pain like a dying dog, writhing on the ground.

Peering inside the doorway, the surge of bloodlust drained away when Simon saw the crumpled form of Elysia's father lying against the inner part of the door. His search for a pulse or breath found none. He finally met this man, this cornerstone of Elysia's life, but moments after his death—a death Simon was powerless to prevent. Anguish at his failure welled up inside him, his whole body shaking, overwhelmed by the grim reality of so much death. *Her father, Xelos, and how many more servants? Dead because of me. All my fault.* And one more behind him on the street, dead by his own hand, sticky blood on his skin marking him with guilt. Simon gagged, choking back bile.

Running footsteps, louder and louder as they approached, jolted Simon out of his despondency. When the first face flashed into view around the corner, a surge of white fear forced his feet into motion, and he fled out the door, ignoring the sickening moans of the wounded guard.

Legionary conditioning kicked in as he ran full speed down the street. Nobody challenged him in the street, other than shouts from his pursuers. *Where to?* He couldn't lead them directly to Elysia. The old man's words flashed in his mind. *City guards! The agora!* It might be empty at night, but there should be some kind of guards, especially with the stairway to the acropolis.

A silent prayer to Attarso crossed his lips as he saw the two guards at the foot of the stair. He began shouting in Pazian as he approached them, hoping they understood.

"There's been an attack! Master Xelos has been killed! Thieves setting fire to his house! I tried to fight them off!"

The two guards looked at his sword, then at each other, and one raised a hand for him to stop.

His Pazian was halting. "You are a fast old man."

"You must hurry, call for more guards! I don't know how many they have."

The watchman nodded, then said something in Izari to the other, whose eyes lit up in shocked comprehension. He ran off.

The remaining guard looked over Simon's shoulder and drew his own sword. Simon's heart sank. *How many? Two on... Five!* The group of ruffians had reached the other side of the agora, and now were waving to the guard, gesticulating wildly at Simon as they ran.

The guard looked confused. "Why are they chasing you?"

Simon groaned, then took off in the only other direction he knew well, to the docks, and over his shoulder he saw the other five charging after him.

"Wait!" the watchman called out.

Rather than go straight on the open coastal road he tried taking more turns than necessary, hoping to throw them off while avoiding any dead ends. After the third turn he thought he might have lost them, but kept running full speed, not wanting to take any chances. The fourth turn led to a brick wall—*new construction?*—and he had to double back, his heart pounding from the mix of terror and exertion. He may have trained for this, but weeks spent mostly on boats and in workshops had taken off the edge.

The next turn brought him out to face the docks, still busy at this time of night with sailors loading and unloading, or ladies offering a little respite from their work.

"Hey Grandpa, I know what you're looking for!" one called out to him. He swore to himself, wanting to avoid any contact.

With his legs already burning, running around the city all night wasn't an option, so he made for the ships. The longest pier went out straight from the harbor before splitting off into two separate spurs. There were dozens of ships berthed, and they could provide at least a little cover. He didn't hazard a look back until he put one of the ships and its rigging between him and the shore. His pursuers were out in the open, looking around. The whore approached them, and he swore again.

Desperately looking around, he passed over several busy ships before spotting a smaller one near the end of the pier that looked settled for the night. The one watchman was busy cleaning something on the foredeck. Simon helped himself onto the ship and immediately headed aft. Before the deckhand could spot him, he eased himself over the stern and slid into the water with the sound of gentle waves lapping against the hull.

Simon had always enjoyed swimming, but never at night, and not with people hunting for him. He felt much more comfortable in the water, knowing nobody had seen him go that way. First he swam under the pier, then jabbed the sword into the dock post to free up both arms for holding on to slick wood. From that uncomfortable position he strained to watch through cracks between the boards overhead. Two men passed above him, going faster than mere sailors at this time of night. They approached the ship he'd boarded, and shouted to the sentry. Simon froze.

"Did you see anyone come this way? An old man running?"

"Old man?" He laughed. "Dock's been quiet. Just me."

After they ran on to the next ship, Simon relaxed a bit but waited to make sure they were gone. Was it ten minutes? Thirty? An hour? The water was cold, and the fear made it colder, but he hung on, conserving his energy and letting his arms give his legs a rest.

When he hadn't heard anyone for what seemed like half the night, and his spasming arm muscles were threatening to revolt, he decided he was safe. Shivering and numb, he uncoiled himself, retrieved the sword, and very slowly swam under the pier and past two ships, silently making his way beyond them to the coast road. It was difficult enough to keep afloat while holding a sword, and for once he was happy not to be wearing his full armor.

The cold, wet cloak stuck to Simon like an unwanted second skin as he crept out of the sea, over the rocks and onto the coastal road. The clouds had parted and the moon looked to be at its zenith, but he could only guess at the time. The moments flowed together like drops of water falling in the sea, leaving him disoriented and shivering as he took brisk steps toward Elysia's workshop.

His mind struggled with the weight of so much death and failure. Not only had he failed to return with her father, but he'd been inches away and powerless to stop his murder. *Will she hate me? Will she cast me away? Will she break down with the shock of her world collapsing around her?* But he had promised her father, and now he would take her away from here... from the violence and death that he had brought into her life. If she would still have him.

*And how could she?* Right now he hated himself. The monster he'd become, butchering another man. *How can I call myself a soldier, when killing feels so abhorrent?* Even revenge didn't justify it. His stomach churned and he fought off the urge to vomit.

How could he face her with such news? *Will this be my role in life evermore? Messenger of death and destruction?*

The imminent challenge of self-preservation took precedence as he got closer. He stuck to the shadows, knowing the attackers must be watching the bakery by now. It was their only remaining lead. He went the long way around to avoid the streets that intersected at the front corner. The side street was totally empty, engulfed in shadow.

Praying silently that Elysia was safe in the workshop, he approached the door. A sudden fright overtook him. *What if she's gone?* Then he'd have none of his supplies, forced to flee the city alone, penniless, and on foot. Especially since the city watch might also be looking for him, taking his flight as guilt.

Maybe she'd be better off if he just left? He stopped his hand just before knocking.

*No, I can't leave by myself. I have to keep her safe.* They would still hound her as a link to him. She wouldn't be safe anywhere, but at least he could help as long as she was with him.

His knuckles rapped softly in their agreed pattern. 1-2-3, 1-2-3, 1-2-3-4. Drips of cold seawater trickling down his legs measured out the beats as he waited for a response. *Please Elysia, be there.* He repeated the pattern, just to be sure.

Still no answer.

He felt so alone, so cold, without a friend in the world. He looked up the stairwell at the empty shadows above, wondering where to go.

The scrape of the bar lifting on the other side of the door was the sweetest sound he'd ever heard.

He rushed through the gap into the darkness beyond. When the door clicked shut, he was blinded by sudden light. He covered his eyes. She must have hooded the lamp.

"Sorry," she said. "Simon, what happened? You're soaked!"

He slowly removed his hands, needing to see her, but reluctant to meet her eyes. Her worried face turned grim, echoing what must be reflected in his own, and she started shaking her head.

"I'm sorry Elysia. I'm so sorry."

"They have Father?"

Tears welled up in his own eyes. "I spoke with him. I heard his final words before…"

"No, Simon, no…" She slid down to her knees, her eyes losing their life, head shaking in disbelief.

"He was their prisoner. In Xelos' house. Just inside the door. I tried to get in." His words fell useless, like stones onto the floor. Her face was as still and cold as one of her sculptures.

He sat down in front of her, taking her icy hands in his, trying to will warmth and life back into them, and her. *How can I help?*

He remembered what not to do: how his father had announced his mother's death.

He'd come home from the day's lessons to check on his mother. She'd been sick, with the ordinary kind of illness common in winter, especially in the crowded apartments of Salamis. Both he and his father fought it off, but mother had been laid up for a few days. Nothing serious, she'd said the night before.

The shop was closed, his father at the counter downing the dregs of a jug of wine, with several others lying discarded around him. His hair was a mess, his cheeks sunken. It was the first of many times Simon would see him like this, but he never forgot that particular moment. It had peeled away that cloak of invincibility a child wraps around the idea of his father; stripping away the authority, leaving only pain, sorrow and anger underneath.

"Where were you?" his father asked, his speech slurred.

"My lessons of course." He was more comfortable standing up to his father and clashed with him frequently, but he particularly bristled at the challenge from this drunk caricature of the master of the household.

His father spat at him, eyes filled with burning accusation. "She's gone! Little that you care!"

The moment seemed an eternity, his satchel falling to the floor in slow motion, and his mind filled with a white blast of anguish and total loss.

Everything hit him in a rush, his mind screaming defiantly at the impossibility of what his father had uttered. *No!* She was only sick last night, even this morning. *No!* He ran from the shell of his father to the bedroom to confirm the horror. There lay the body of his mother, still and pained, her face contorted in one final cough, with a rivulet of drying blood running down from her lips to stain the sheet beside her. Her eyes were closed with the exertion, and Simon didn't know if he could bear to see them. He dropped to the floor beside her bed, weeping as he grasped her hands.

Now he held Elysia's hands, only she was the one dealing with the loss by retreating deep into herself. She stared through him with glassy eyes, unseeing. Somehow the memory of his own pain emboldened him to continue.

"He wanted me to go for help, to find you. I told him I came from you, and…" He steeled himself, hoping to break through the wall that had formed so quickly around her. "I told him that I would take care of you."

There was a spark of recognition in her eyes.

"And he was so brave! After he heard that, he shouted for me to run, to get help! He gave himself up… to make sure I kept you safe." It sounded better in his head. The words fell flat again. Burning shame filled him, that the man had partially sacrificed himself for Simon. Even if it was really for her.

"I don't think they meant to kill him. But I… when they opened the door… I killed the one, or one of them that was there." Revulsion welled up in his throat, as he faced his violent action, rather than inaction. "I… sank my knife into his neck. I… I killed."

Her lips moved, her voice like ice: "Isn't that what soldiers do? Bring death?"

Shaking his head, he felt warm tears in his eyes. "No. I'm no killer. I'm barely a soldier. I… I had never taken a life. But hearing them harm your father, I wanted to avenge him. To rescue him. But I failed."

He let her hands fall, reaching up to his own face, wrenching at the skin in self-loathing. *Smooth? No beard?* Some part of his mind recognized the fact that it was gone. *Washed away?* Even in the midst of these powerful emotions, that spark of curiosity came to the fore. A curiosity that spurred him on to save them, for future exploration, urging him to move faster, to get her out of here.

He stood up. "We have to leave Attarsus. Tonight." He winced at the command in his voice.

Her accusing look was somehow more comforting. She needed to let it out. Even a display of hostility was better than stony detachment.

"What about Xelos?" she asked.

The reminder tore open his own wound, and raw grief poured into him. Their mentor, who had shown him a glimpse of what was possible and given him a home… was dead. Butchered because of him. He couldn't tell her. She was already suffering so much. That burden might crush her. "I didn't see him. I…"

"Why didn't you look for him? We have to make sure he's safe!" She started to stand up, her concern spurring her back to life, to action.

He put his hand on her shoulder. "No, we have to leave Attarsus. It's not safe... they're trying to get us."

She wrenched away from his touch. "Then he is also in danger. We have to..."

The only way to save her was to crush her hope. "Elysia, I'm so sorry. I was too late. Your father said... said... they killed him too."

Her face collapsed, all emotion draining away, like the flame had been blown out. She slumped back to the floor in a heap, burying her head in her arms. But she remained eerily silent.

Simon had no idea what to do. Her whole world had been destroyed. Would it crush her will—that beautiful will she channeled into her work? And how could he get her out of there?

Zeno seemed to shrug, its eyes sad. *I wonder how much it—he—understands.*

"Zeno, can I get you ready to go?" He gulped. "I'm afraid the city watch may be looking for me too... at least the old and pale version, with the beard. Luckily that seems to be gone." Again he rubbed his smooth face. "But still, we have to leave. We're not safe. The attackers are still looking for both of us."

Zeno nodded, and allowed Simon to strap on the saddlebags. Elysia had obviously been back to the bakery; there was a surprising amount of food that she'd gathered. Hunger hit him hard—he hadn't eaten since the morning—so he grabbed a hunk of bread and devoured it. He'd been going all day, and his muscles cried out in protest at being forced to function at this late hour, after such extreme exertion, but he willed them on.

Withdrawing modestly to a corner, he took off first the cloak and then the rest of his clothes and did his best to wring them out. They were still damp when he put them back on, but at least they weren't dripping with seawater. Or blood. The swim had washed away any evidence.

He packed away the rest of the food, as well as his painting materials and as many of her carving tools as could fit. Still she huddled on the floor. Simon explained the blanket to Zeno, who furled his wings so Simon could cover them. "You'll likely thank me for it, with the chill in the air." He stroked Zeno's flank.

With no scabbard to wear it in, Simon wrapped the short sword in a cloth and hid it under the blanket as well, hoping he wouldn't need to draw it quickly. Or at all.

"Ready?" Simon said to the majestic beast, stroking the mane. Zeno snorted his assent. "I don't think we should fly until we get outside the city. It's too dangerous, and I wouldn't want to attract attention."

He bent down beside Elysia, putting his hand on her shoulder. "Elysia, I can't bring them back. But I have to protect you. I vowed to your father."

She didn't move.

"Please Elysia, I can't let anything happen to you. I know I failed. I know I brought this on... on everyone. It's all my fault. I am so... so sorry. I would give myself up in a moment to bring them back.

"But I can't. They're gone. All I have left is you, and my promise to your father. Come with me. Blame me if you have to. Even if you'll never speak to me again, I have to get you out of here. To safety. If they caught you now, I'd never forgive myself. It's not just my promise..." His own sobs cut him off. "Elysia, I... I love you."

Did he imagine it? Or did she shudder ever so slightly under his touch?

Zeno nuzzled her, reanimating her further. Without a word, she gathered a few of her smaller sculptures to stow in the bags, opened a drawer and took out several wrapped items and packed them as well. She led Zeno to the door.

*What have I done?*

Simon followed them up the stairs onto the street.

"You should ride," Simon said to her, breaking the silence. She allowed him to help her mount Zeno, but still wouldn't meet his eyes. She rode side-saddle, and he took the reins, leading her along the street away from the bakery, the workshop, and her life.

At the next intersection he looked to her for direction. "Which gate should we take?"

She said nothing, only pointing the way out of this city of death.

# XXIII

### ᏸᏋᏸᏋᏸᏋᏸ

## *Flight*

Their walk out of the city passed in silence other than the steady clap of Zeno's hooves striking the road. There were few people out, and those they passed avoided looking directly at them. Simon was thankful for that, but it left him alone with the agony of his recriminations. Unable to save two old men, how could Xelos ever expect him to challenge the Scentari warlock?

And now it was like he had traded the statue of Zeno for a new one of Elysia. Hopelessness clung to him like his wet cloak.

He'd worried that the city watch might challenge them at the gate, but when he got closer he realized he'd misplaced his concern. While the gates of Pazh were grand, majestic and designed to repel attack from a land-based force, those of Attarsus were simple wooden doors. The true walls of Attarsus were built with ships in the sea, not with stone. The guard barely acknowledged them as they walked through, with the handful of farmers passing in and out to the farms and hilly pastures of the rest of the island.

They stayed on the coastal road to the east, and when they were a few hills away from the city and out of sight of the walls, Simon brought them to a halt. He found an apple for Zeno, who accepted it graciously. *At least we're getting along now.*

Simon broke the silence. "I don't think it's safe to stay on the island. Zeno, do you think you can carry both of us?" Zeno sniffed at the air cautiously. Simon's insides twisted. The idea of flying had entranced him from the beginning. But now with the reality looming before him, of soaring over the angry seas in the dark of night, it was terrifying. And this mount had never even tried carrying himself into the air, much less with two passengers and their gear. The whole idea seemed so much folly.

"I guess you need to try first?"

Elysia at least was cooperating, dismounting without his help. Simon removed the blanket and wrapped it around her while fighting against the chilly sea breeze biting through his own damp clothes. Her body yielded to the comfort even though her impassive expression remained.

Zeno stretched his wings tentatively at first, and began shaking them off as if they were covered in dust. Simon's curiosity won the struggle once again, and he watched in fascination as Zeno prepared to test his capabilities. The first tests were of the legs, progressing from a light trot through a canter and finally a full gallop. Simon's own muscles ached in sympathy, having been through their own trials tonight after weeks of light use. He could only imagine how it would feel to be gifted with a fully grown body on your first day in this world.

When fully extended, the wings shimmered in the moonlight, stretching far wider than any bird Simon had ever seen. Simon nervously checked all directions for potential onlookers, but found none.

Zeno's first few attempts to leave the ground were awkward failures. He spread his wings while running full speed down the hill before taking a short hop at the end, soaring no more than a foot or two before touching down. Simon's heart sank. He couldn't imagine the horse itself gaining altitude, much less the three of them. Even Zeno began to look discouraged, but the spectacle seemed to coax Elysia back to life. She crossed to her new friend.

"Zeno, I know you can do it," she said. "You were born to fly." Her conviction gave the horse new confidence. She pointed out a big hill. "Why don't you try running down that hill, and stretching out to soar as you go up that rocky part... like a ramp?"

"Or maybe more flapping?" Simon added, feeling stupid as soon as he said it. But at this point he'd try anything. "Like geese?" Who knew they'd have to help teach the steed to fly?

Zeno appeared more interested in Elysia's idea and walked slowly to the top of the hill, turned, and started a full gallop down toward the ramp. Elysia was cheering him on as he approached. He even started flapping his wings a bit, Simon noted with satisfaction.

His final flapping leap sent him airborne, and climbing! Elysia clapped her hands and hugged Simon in delight. He held her tight, sharing the elation and craving that closeness more than anything. *Maybe this plan isn't so crazy after all?*

Zeno circled around them, still awkward and unsure. It was a spectacular sight, seeing something so large truly flying, with grace and elegance that magnified as he quickly gained in skill. Simon would swear later that the horse seemed to be smiling at them as he showed off progressively more daring stunts.

Simon sighed with relief as Zeno glided in for a safe landing, slowly spiraling down to a stop before them. *Not even winded.* Elysia rushed over to embrace her creation, jubilant.

*Zeno made it look easy. Maybe it won't be so scary once we're up there?* Though his stomach worried that it might be even worse than he imagined.

"It's going to work," he said.

"Zeno says he's ready," Elysia said. "I never doubted that he'd be able to save us."

A fresh torrent of guilt assaulted Simon. But did he only imagine the barb? Was she still reacting to the horror of the night? Or just trying to show her confidence in her creation? *At least she's talking again.*

Simon helped her mount again, then climbed up to sit behind her. They had to sit pressed together to keep their feet in front of the wings. She felt so warm, stirring his desire, but she remained oblivious, focused as she was on Zeno's coming attempt to carry them into the sky.

Simon took the reins, more out of habit than any feeling that he could control Zeno with them. He'd heard that the best riders among the Scentari commanded their mounts with only their voice, but he had thought it was only a myth. Now he wasn't so sure, with Zeno responding only to Elysia's requests. He couldn't imagine using a switch or bit to get this one to do anything—it would be like beating your own friend—and certainly not while in the air.

With no better way to store it, he held his sword in his other hand.

"Are you scared?" he asked her.

Her eyes shone with anticipation. "I've dreamed of this moment for years."

"Was I a part of those dreams?"

"No," she said, but then her face softened. "But I'll let you come along for the ride. Just don't poke me with that thing."

He was mortified, until he realized she meant the sword. "I'll have to find a scabbard somewhere along the way. My hand will get pretty tired if I always have to hold it while we fly."

"Let's go," Elysia said to Zeno, scratching his mane between his ears.

Zeno cantered up to the top of the hill, pausing for a moment at the top. Simon held his breath. Elysia chuckled as Zeno galloped down, gaining momentum with every stride. The wind caught her hair, streaming it back into his face, so Simon couldn't see a thing as they raced toward the bottom and the ramp. Zeno took off with a leap.

Simon braced himself for impact, but instead a yawning weightlessness engulfed him—like he'd left his insides on the ground behind them. They were rising! Zeno's wings flapped furiously, but they lurched higher and higher. Looking down, he shuddered at the gulf between his hooves and the receding ground.

He was flying. *Really flying!* The thrill banished all traces of exhaustion.

Elysia squeezed his leg. "Isn't it incredible?" Her voice was pure joy.

He handed her the reins, and used his now free hand to brush her hair out of his face. He'd have to recommend she tie it up.

Without her hair shielding him, the wind buffeted his face with the full impact of their speed, making him gasp and blink. They climbed faster and faster, the air warm on his skin as they rose, Zeno's wings spread wide and soaring on waves of air.

Simon looked down and lost his balance, desperately grabbing on to Elysia's waist to right himself. His head swam, light and disoriented, but thankfully not sick. Trying again, he located the walls of the city far below, no bigger than a child's toy tucked in along the rocky coastline. He could see the whole island, with rolling hills and pastures, farms, and even the rocky peaks at the center. A perfect painting in the late night moon, from a vantage point no man had ever experienced.

"It's beautiful. Can you imagine how it would look by day?"

"Thank you for sharing this moment with me, Simon."

"I'm just happy to see you smile again. I thought I'd lost you."

"No, I... I'm sorry. It's just... It's not your fault. I don't blame you—you did what you could." Her tone turned fierce. "But if it takes my dying breath, those beasts will pay for what they've done. The ones who did it, and the Lokuta who hired them."

He was a little shocked by the turn, amid the wonder of flight. But her steel brought out his own conviction. "And I will be by your side through everything."

"I know. Thank you. But first, we have to do your duty, to help Garas. And if..." She choked up again. "If Master Xelos is right, we're helping the whole world."

Simon's worry that Zeno wouldn't have the energy to fly them to land again proved misplaced. Their steed was enjoying the flight even more than they were. After the rush out of the city and the exhilaration of soaring into the air, the sheer scale of the path before them began to become clear. Simon's mind needed time to sort out the details.

Attarsus was one of hundreds of islands of varying sizes in the Izar Archipelago, and hopping to the next in little more than an hour was good enough for their first flight. They chose a small, uninhabited islet as the site of their first camp, to rest and recover.

As exciting as the flight had been, the firm earth under Simon's feet was comforting. They found a sheltered spot of beach in the shadow of a rocky cliff and made it their base for what remained of the night. Nature provided them with unexpected and easily accessible bounty: eggs stolen from the nests of seabirds hiding in clefts in the rock face, along with a large green turtle that Simon found quite alive but half-buried in the sand. A curious creature, but ultimately very tasty. Zeno left them alone for a short time to graze on top of the hill. That was new too, a mount that didn't need to be tied up, and would find his own forage.

Elysia had set up their baggage in a nook beside the cliff, and laid out their one blanket. She also collected quite a pile of driftwood, looking right at home carting around such a weight. He guessed that she was no stranger to moving heavy materials for her craft. She set aside a few pieces.

"Birds," she said as an explanation.

He showed her how to start the fire. She was a quick learner—telling him she was used to tending the oven and hearth fires in their home—and soon took full control of those duties.

She grimaced when he used his blade to stab the neck of the

unfortunate turtle. It didn't spoil her appetite; her eyes filled with hunger as he cooked the pieces in the shell. It certainly proved handy that the creatures came packaged in ready-made plates and pot. After making do with just a little bread in the past day, the aroma of roasting meat sent his stomach into wild gyrations of hunger.

"I'm glad you can cook," she said to him as he handed her the first piece on a makeshift turtle-shell plate. "I'm afraid I never paid attention when Mother tried to teach me."

Simon smiled at her. "Lucky the legions teach all of us basic food preparation. I hope it's cooked." They blew on their own pieces in unison and gingerly took their first bites.

"It's actually good!"

He wrinkled his nose. "That's probably just the hunger talking."

"No, it really is good. I'm sorry I doubted you."

"Well at least we can rest with a full stomach tonight, what's left of it. We should sleep as long as we need to. It's been a long day. But I'm more worried about the water. I didn't see any streams here, and we're going to need to stop for supplies. It's going to be days across the sea to Pelusia."

"How do you know which way to go? The sea is so vast. I've never been off Attarsus before. And we have no map."

He grinned and tapped his temple. "This Talent may come in useful once again. After we eat you should have a rest, but I'm going to try my hand at a map. I can get the overall sweep of things from memory, and the major islands, but I might need your help for the little ones. Do you at least know these islands well?"

She nodded. "Xelos had a beautiful mosaic map, and I used to ask him the names. My dream was to visit them all." She looked down. "That seems so small now. This world is so big, and we're so alone." As she gazed out across the water, her eyes turned cold again.

He put his arm around her protectively, and this time she didn't resist. "Not alone. We have each other." When he leaned in to kiss her, an angry snort from behind made him jump. She laughed, welcoming Zeno back to their little camp. "And Zeno of course." The horse curled his wing around Elysia and Simon could only shake his head.

Elysia did her best to scrub the turtle shells clean after they finished eating to save for future use. Simon found a good flat rock to use as a table for his work and spread out his paints. Elysia watched him start, but he urged her to lie down, seeing the exhaustion creeping into her face, and she acquiesced. When she lay down on their blanket, Zeno nuzzled in beside her, covering her with a wing like a feathery blanket. They both looked so peaceful, untouched by the horror of the past day.

Simon smiled and set to work on his map.

Soaring over the Near Sea, wind ruffling his hair and his arm around the woman he loved, it was easy for Simon to forget for a few fleeting moments the potential doom that waited for him in Pelusia. Especially at sunrise and sunset. He'd never seen anything so beautiful as the sun's rays setting fire to the shimmering mirror below. If only he could paint while he flew, he'd capture that beauty for a lifetime.

They'd built up confidence in Zeno's ability to fly longer distances by hopping from island to island over the course of the first few days. He'd even figured out how to catch warmer streams in the air and soar great distances without flapping his wings even once.

They were approximately in the middle of the long flight to the coast of Pelusia. Simon had done his best estimates based on their speed in the early part of the voyage with land as a reference, but too much was uncertain with maps painted from his memory and the changing winds. Yesterday morning they'd left just before dawn from Nasos, the furthest northeastern island of the Izar Archipelago. Simon's best guess was about three days, with no sign of land yet.

They had, however, seen a flotilla of galleys far below them, and Elysia's eyes grew wide as they showed how high up they were. While impossible to tell over the vast surface of the water, with that point of reference—the ships looking like tiny crawling ants—it staggered the mind. *Could they be the Pazian legions sent to relieve Garas?* Simon was awed by how quickly they left them behind, soaring much faster through the air.

Before striking out across the open sea they'd found their way into enough towns to get proper supplies of food and water, additional clothes and other necessities like better bedrolls and a makeshift saddle. And a scabbard so he wasn't forced to hold the sword for hours at a time. Settling those logistical details had been a big relief. Those were the sorts of things that kept him up at night, which is exactly what working in the camp prefect's staff required. Now he applied his skills to ensure their survival.

Another source of worry was Elysia's state of mind. She was quiet too often for Simon's liking. She would sit by herself much of the day, whittling away at driftwood, her face expressionless. Sometimes she wouldn't respond to a question until a minute later, if at all. Not that he had any idea how to talk her through it. He knew she was grieving, but expected her to need to talk through the loss. His own heart still ached at the memory of losing his mother, even after three years.

Or was he thinking too much? Each day revealed more and more of Elysia's usual joy and curiosity.

Being forced to part from her again was the biggest weight on his mind. She'd never had to take care of herself, had never been out of Attarsus, and now would be alone in a strange land. They were almost the same age, but he'd served in the legions and traveled so much already, while she had been almost completely sheltered. Until now.

That looming separation was a point of argument. Elysia maintained that she and Zeno should stay in Tamar until Simon was released, at least until they redeployed. She could find an inn and stables and keep out of sight. Maybe even do some more sculpture if she found some quality stone.

Simon feared the worst, in details big and small. He didn't trust the clientele of a random inn to be safe for her. And what about keeping Zeno a secret? Nor was there a place for her anywhere near a barracks full of single men. And that's if the city was safe at all. He was worried enough about the Scentari coming to attack Garas and the rest of the remaining defenders. For all they knew, the city might have fallen already. If he had to worry about her being in the city too, he didn't know if he could handle it.

In their arguments, he'd seen a whole new side of her. Headstrong. Determined. The side that brought her into conflict with her late mother so often. He admired and respected those qualities as much as her creativity and curiosity, but right now they were sending her down a road too dark for him to bear.

He was working up the courage for a counter proposal. She hadn't responded to his last attempt to get her attention, sending him spiraling in introspection. He needed to get the details settled.

With her hair tied back over her left shoulder, out of his face, it left her right ear exposed. He leaned in to kiss it lightly. She hunched her shoulder and turned her head enough so that she could see him with one eye. "What?"

"Just needed to get your attention. I have an idea."

"I'm not leaving you alone in Tamar, and that's final."

He winced. "I know, I'm not trying to move you."

"I'm listening."

"What if I deliver the letter to Garas, and then ask him to discharge me? I'd be able to leave with you. And get vengeance on Persei and his thugs."

She shook her head. "And leave Garas at the mercy of the Scentari? No, you're going back to help. And you'll stay as long as you're needed." She looked forward again, trying to end the conversation.

He brought his lips to her ear once more, tickling her. "I'm not finished. I'm just worried about you. So how about a compromise. Before we go to Tamar, and Garas, we fly inland a bit and scout around. If there's no Scentari troops in the area, then you can stay for a few days at an inn, until we find a better place for you. It's a shame none of Master Xelos' contacts are in Tamar."

She nodded, agreeing so far.

"But if the Scentari are anywhere close, you'll drop me off within a few hours walk to the city and then take Zeno with you to Yalath in Jeppo. That's our closest contact."

She started to protest, but he silenced her with another kiss, this time on her neck. "I won't be much help to Garas in a battle if I'm worried about defending you."

She strained to turn her lips back to meet his. Just as they touched, Simon felt a whack on the back of his head and spun around as quickly as he could balance. Zeno's tail flicked back and forth behind him, in warning.

Elysia laughed and stroked Zeno's mane. Simon rubbed the bruise and scowled.

"So is that a yes?" he asked, his voice pleading.

"Fine."

# XXIV

### ᎯᎯᎯᎯᎯᎯᎯ

## *Tamar*

In the end, Simon got his way. He wished he hadn't.

They'd made better time than he ever imagined, spotting land before dusk on the second day. Hilly country north of Tamar, if Simon was right. It would have been a week or more with good winds on a ship. They were both tired and sore after almost two full days in the air, with even Zeno showing signs of fatigue.

They made their camp in the highlands away from the main road, barely kept their eyes open through a quick meal, and collapsed into dreamless sleep.

First thing in the morning Simon reviewed his map, committing it freshly to memory since it was impossible to hold in the air, and urged Zeno to climb as high as possible. Simon marveled at how the trees looked like blades of grass, and imagined that from the ground Zeno would be mistaken for a large bird. Drinking in every detail, he was amazed at how accurately his map matched the reality below them. It really was like flying over a map, rather than land. It thrilled him like a child making a new discovery.

The sun was still rising in the sky when they first got a view of the villages and towns leading up to Tamar, and then the city proper. To give the city a wide berth, they swept inland to the north and then east. Simon and Elysia split up the duties of scanning the ground ahead, with him taking the left, and her the right. They'd been at it for hours, and were thinking about turning back when she cried out.

"Aliata preserve us!"

Simon's head jerked to the right, matching her line of sight. He gulped. What looked like a great wave of beetles moving across the plains could only be one thing. Riders. Thousands of them. Headed toward Tamar.

"Ask him to take us a little closer."

Zeno swooped lower, allowing Simon to make out more detail. "They're coming for the city." He pointed to the back. "They're not going full speed because of the wagon train, and a lot of people on foot. Slaves and camp followers, I'd guess. That's not a raiding party, it's an invasion force." He bit his lip, wishing he had more details for the general. "They'll be there in the next few days, maybe even tomorrow. And Shadush must be leading a force that size." He hugged Elysia around her waist. "You have to get me back to Garas, and then get out of there before this gets ugly."

Zeno banked and turned back. Simon felt sick with worry. *Too soon!* It was the right thing to do to send Elysia to safety, though he desperately wanted to keep her close. With an attack imminent, he had to think of what to tell Garas, and how to explain what he knew. And figure out how to use his Talent to help. Too many worries and not enough time.

They landed on the edge of a small wood, away from prying eyes. Simon guessed they were about an hour's ride east of the city, off the main road.

"We'll take you at least to the gates," Elysia said, more command than question.

"No, Elysia, you should leave from here."

"I'm not the one in the hurry, and doesn't every hour count when there's an army almost at your doorstep? Besides, you don't even know for certain that Garas is still here. What if he moved? Or worse?"

He pursed his lips. *But she has a point.*

"You know I'm right."

"Just let me do the talking." And he had to admit he was happy for any excuse to delay their parting for a few more hours.

The ride was uneventful right up to the east gate. Elysia was enchanted by the different style of architecture and carving of the exterior walls, to the point where her enthusiasm broke through Simon's worries and engaged him in appreciating the artistry. When they got close Elysia drew up her hood and rode behind him.

The guards challenged him at the sealed gate.

"What business do you have in Tamar?"

"I've been sent to General Gar... Numeno. I have a letter from the Senate."

The guard looked skeptical. "Then why are you coming from the east?"

"It's a long story, and one for the general's ears only."

The guards spoke to each other, then the gates opened with a great creak, just wide enough for one of them to look through.

"Show me the letter," the guard said.

Simon produced it, his hand sweating. It was a good copy, but his heart knew the truth of the forgery.

The guard looked it over, then at Simon. "Open the gates!" The reinforced wooden doors opened the rest of the way. "General Numeno is at the garrison barracks."

Simon nodded his thanks as he took back the letter.

He remembered the way to the inn where he'd stayed the night in Tamar, not far inside the east gate. It was respectable enough, and he set Elysia up in a room, with Zeno in the attached stable. He had to shoo away the stable boy, warning him that Zeno was bad-tempered and liable to kick him, and the horse had supplied an almost human snarl to corroborate the warning.

He escorted Elysia up to the room, dropping the saddlebags on the simple table.

"Have a good rest here, I'll have them bring you some food. But don't go down there alone. This place is clean enough, but... it's not safe."

She put her hands on her hips. "I'm not a girl. I'm barely younger than you."

"But no woman, local or otherwise, should be on her own in a time like this. And certainly not on the streets at night. I'll do my best to come back as soon as I can. I'd rather you left now. But if I'm detained, I want you to leave the city tomorrow morning."

She folded her arms over her chest. "You're not my commander."

"No, never." He grinned at her. "But do you know what I could be?" He swept her off her feet, kissing her passionately. She matched him with a new intensity.

"We're finally alone," he said, his voice heavy. There was nothing left to interrupt his desire, and his blood thickened with the wanting of her. He carried her toward the bed, but set her down beside it. He unbound her hair, letting it fall in luscious curls onto her shoulders, framing that beautiful face.

Her hands unclasped his cloak, and then he did the same for hers, exposing her dress underneath. His mind worked over how to best remove it, with the clasps at the shoulders and belt at her narrow waist.

"Is this what you call rest?" she asked, sucking in her lip with a suppressed smile.

He kissed her again in response, his hands fumbling to untie the cord, while hers deftly removed his belt, leaving his tunic hanging freely. She pulled it over his head, exposing his chest. He closed his eyes, savoring the warmth of her hands as they traced the lines of his muscles.

The intensity in her eyes gave him pause. She looked down self-consciously, before taking his hands in hers, and guiding them up to her shoulders. Her smile beguiled him as they worked together to open the first clasp. The fabric slid down her slender frame, settling tantalizingly over her right breast. With the other clasp released, her dress fell to the floor, exposing two perfect little orbs that he ached to caress. Her hands led his down, and he got his wish, losing himself in the sensation. She purred, leaning her lips in to his, fusing them together in sweet passion. His hands stroked their way down her sides and the gentle curve of her back, pulling her against him, so warm and soft. He swept her up, her legs curling around him as he carried her to the bed, uniting in a blissful dream.

Simon's heart was still floating as he walked alone through the streets of Tamar, heading to the barracks. He passed numerous soldiers on his way, and more than a few that looked familiar. They were definitely on edge but not high alert, mainly going about their daily business. Many of the houses around the actual barracks had been converted for military use, likely vacated by citizens departing once the threat became obvious.

Despite the ill tidings he carried, Simon still felt light, unable to keep the smile off his face. He held on to a secret hope that he would be the next to flee, with Elysia. To depart for beautiful new lands where they could be together all day, exploring their Talent, and each other. That thought stirred his blood immediately, so soon after their intimate encounter. He hadn't imagined for things to go that way, but parting after such closeness was painful, and she had felt the same. Their lovemaking had been a wondrous blend of animal need, tender curiosity, and sweet delight. He shifted his tunic uncomfortably, wishing once again he still had his armor, this time for concealment. He strove to get his body under control as he approached the doors.

Two sentries crossed their javelins in front of the entrance when he tried to pass.

"No civilians," one said.

Simon laughed, unfortunately out loud.

The second guard brought the spear to bear on his chest. "Don't test me, boy."

Simon was out of practice after just a few weeks. He saluted stiffly. "Legionary Simon Baroba, aide to General Numeno, reporting to see the commander."

The first guard looked sideways at him. "I guess I'm an aide too then. Why haven't I seen you around here? And why are you dressed like an Izari merchant?"

"I was on a special mission to the Senate in Pazh." Simon produced the letter from his satchel and held it out with authority. "By order of the Senate."

That snapped them to attention. The second guard inspected it, consternation creasing his face. He saluted quickly, nodding for his comrade to do the same. "Sorry Legionary, we... can't be too careful around here. Those Scentari could attack any time. And word is there are spies among us."

The other guard shushed him.

"Thank you," Simon said, smoothing over the bad start. "You've done your duty. Which way to the general?"

"He should be in the main hall, down the corridor to the left. Through the double doors."

Simon saluted and followed their directions. The doors were closed, and locked. He knocked. A few moments later an unfamiliar scowling face around his age looked through the doors.

"The general said he was not to be disturbed."

"Tell him Legionary Simon Baroba has returned from Pazh."

Simon thought he saw the briefest flash of anger before the face broadened into a controlled smile. "Baroba? Welcome back. The general will be happy to see you. Follow me."

The young man led Simon through the double doors into a large dining hall. Garas was at the head table, poring over maps and ledgers with Kyso, Karr the garrison commander, and a few others. All in full armor, ready for action. Simon's heart leapt to see his friends safe. He wanted to rush to embrace them, but feared to further breach military decorum.

Kyso was the first to look up, and nodded conservatively to acknowledge him.

*Same old Kyso.*

When Garas met his eyes, he stopped mid-sentence. "Legionary Baroba!" Garas said, motioning him over.

Simon saluted, and all eyes watched as he crossed over to clasp arms with Garas. His commander's grip was strong but transmitted strong emotion, while his face remained an impassive map of scars and creases. Simon had to keep a tear in check.

"So you faced the Senate and survived?" Garas said, uncharacteristically jovial in his tone. The others laughed.

"I did, sir."

"And took your sweet time getting back here?" He searched Simon's eyes. "You're late. It's been over six weeks since you left us. Three since we got word from the Senate."

Simon produced the letter.

Garas looked at the seal, then at Simon, and straightened. "From the Senate," he said toward the others. He cracked the seal carefully, and unfurled the message. His lips moved slowly as he read through the letter, and Simon followed along in his mind. When he got to the end, Garas harrumphed, looking at Simon strangely. "You'll have to tell me later about this special mission." He eyed Simon's cloak with obvious distaste. "You look ridiculous. I don't know why they sent your kit separately, but it arrived in a chest, a few days ago. Part of the special mission?"

Simon could only nod, keeping his confusion to himself.

"Harron," he called to the young man who had answered the door. "Show Baroba to my quarters so he can change. Tell the cook he'll be dining privately with me. I have much to fill him in on." He clapped Simon on the shoulder. "Good to have you back, there's much to discuss."

Simon shifted his weight between his feet, agitated. He tested the waters first. "One more thing. Have your scouts reported lately from the east?"

Garas looked to Kyso, who answered for him. "They reported nothing out of the ordinary."

"How far do they range?"

"A half day's ride."

Simon nodded, his face grim.

"The Scentari are moving on Tamar in force. They'll be here in days, maybe even tomorrow."

A collective gasp went up from the room.

"How do you know this?" asked the garrison commander. "Didn't you just come by ship?"

Simon's throat constricted, but he forced out the words. "I rode in from the east. I…" He looked to Garas. "I'm afraid I can only tell the general about the details." *And I'm not sure what to even tell him.*

"But you're certain?" Garas asked.

"Yes. Many thousands."

The garrison commander went white, while Kyso started making notes, and the aides started whispering amongst themselves.

"And I believe their leader…" Simon said, "is with them."

Garas' eyes burned into Simon. His tone changed to that of the general. "Go change, now. We'll talk while we wait for dinner." He turned to the others. "We need the garrison ready. Kyso, double the scouting parties to the east, and have them ride half again as far. With strict orders to flee at the first sign of the enemy. We need to know exactly where they are and when they'll get here."

Harron looked very uncomfortable as he brought Simon to Garas' quarters. He had sent servants ahead and they met him at the door, carrying a heavy chest. They delivered it and Harron closed the door, leaving Simon alone.

He opened the chest, and the surprise inside was like meeting an old friend on the street. *My armor? Thank you Lokas!* He had no idea how they'd organized getting it to him, but he wasn't complaining. He discarded the cloak and tunic, realizing behind closed doors that it smelled strongly of Zeno. Donning his legionary tunic and armor was not just a physical reminder of his duty and belonging, but also security, as if he'd been naked all this time without it. In a way he had been, and lucky not to have needed it at Xelos' house.

Harron showed him to a small room next to the dining hall,

where Garas waited. There were two cups in front of him and he offered one to Simon.

"Thank you Harron. That will be all." The young man saluted, and left in a huff.

"He's afraid you'll take his job," Garas said.

Simon was surprised. "Why?"

"Well, let's just say that I *have* missed you, more than I thought. But I still think I made the right choice to send you. Even if General Daymar Lokuta is supposedly on his way to relieve me."

Simon spat out his well-watered wine. "Daymar?"

"Not my preference, but I'd take my mother in command with three full veteran legions. And a reconstituted 7th to make a fourth. At least Genaro is his second, to guarantee at least some competence." Garas took a long drink. "But if your information is correct, we may not live to see the reinforcements. So what do you really know?"

Simon looked at his hands, clenching and unclenching them. "I saw the Scentari. They're coming."

"With your own eyes?"

"Yes."

"Then how are you so far ahead of them?"

"I rode my horse into the ground. And they have a baggage train. It's no raiding party. They mean to take Tamar."

Garas sat back in his chair, brooding. "Can you tell me why you were out there to the east?"

"They wanted me to scout ahead, to locate the Scentari leader."

"So you could paint his portrait?" Garas looked pained, muttering a few expletives. "Simon, I'm still Garas Numeno. I know you too well, and I've served *far* too long for you to try to get this past me."

Simon opened his mouth to try to explain, but Garas cut him off again.

"Lokas filled me in. You had to run. From the Lokuta no less? I told you not to piss off Persei, but you went and did it anyway. And this letter?" He waved the forgery in front of Simon's face. "What is this? More of your work?" He turned it over, running his finger over the seal. "It's a damn fine job." He pointed his finger at Simon. "I should have you locked up. For insubordination. Fraud. Or desertion? This is a legion, Simon. You can't come and go as you please. Should I send you away? Are you truly fit to serve?"

Simon's mind warred against itself while Garas paced around the room. One side was screaming to seize this way out, this exile, and be done with the legions and Pazh. The other cried out at the injustice, when he had already given so much for the legion, for duty. So he said nothing.

Garas stopped and let out a long sigh before speaking again. "I guess your artistic talents are more varied than we thought? Lokas did say your painting was pretty special, and made the difference."

His brow creased with concern. "I'm not sure what's going on with you, but Lokas was worried too. That I put you in danger. I'm sorry if I did. But it was for the good of Pazh. So let's drop it. I don't care where you've been, or why. You're here now, and I'll accept this forgery for the sake of discipline and the men. The Senate doesn't need to know. You're back under my command, as my aide, and will follow my orders. We'll find you a room here."

"I have one more thing I need to do in the city."

He was met by a stony stare. "It can wait. We have too much to discuss with the staff."

In his mind, Simon saw Elysia through a doorway that was slamming shut. He tried to drive away the painful vision.

"I don't understand this dark magic," Garas said. His eyes pleaded with Simon. "You know more. You've witnessed its power. And you've seen them approaching in force. Do you have any ideas?"

He had none, with his mind still clouded by visions of the woman that waited for him halfway across town, but felt a world away. "No, I'm sorry."

"Then you'd better get thinking. That dark fire is going to scare the wits out of my men, and with good reason. The gates and even walls will be no match for it. So if you don't have any ideas, maybe you should head down to the temple of Tamla and pray for rain."

"Rain?" That got Simon's mind working. He stood up. "How many days out is the fleet?" There was no way he could reveal that he saw it too.

"Who knows with the weather this time of year. A week or more at the outside, why?"

"We saw the bad weather coming. It might just buy us the time we need. Where is the temple? Is it the highest point in the city?" *If only I could do the reconnaissance from the back of Zeno.*

"I wasn't serious, Simon."

"We may need the help of the gods in this one. Do you have maps of the city? Or any drawings of the defenses?"

Garas nodded his approval. "Now you're talking." He took out several maps and pictures, which Simon pored over. They weren't to his standard, but gave him the chance to piece together his thoughts.

"These pictures are useless. I'll have to go out and do my own, to see what we're working with. But I've got a few ideas. I can start now." It would give him one last chance to see Elysia before he had to send her away.

"Could you draw a picture of Shadush, to show the archers?"

"I think so. Tribune Lokuta described him in great detail."

"Do that tonight, and any diagrams for your special defenses, so we can show the troops. Then get some sleep. I'll send Kyso with you in the morning to survey the defenses and you can show your pictures to our men so they can build them wherever needed." He actually smiled. "It's good to have you back."

# XXV
ᏮᏋᏮᏋᏮᏋᏮ
## *Preparation*

As much as he wished to, Simon couldn't bring himself to flout Garas' orders and return to Elysia. And with Kyso accompanying him, he couldn't even try to see her off at dawn. It was for the best. She'd be safer away from the city, even if his plans worked. If the Scentari did penetrate their defense with sheer numbers then the city would be a bloodbath with fighting in the streets.

Immersing himself in his art let him banish thoughts of her for now. First he worked on adapting his horse defenses for city use, an idea he'd been considering since he left Garas. It was harder to brace them on cobbled streets than in grass and scrub out in the wild, but he'd come up with innovative designs to show the legionaries so they could build them.

With that done, he closed his eyes and centered himself, recalling everything Persei had told him about Shadush, with only the urgency of the situation banishing the accompanying image of Lokilla listening deliciously close to him. Relaxing his mind, he let the words of the description flow, coalescing into a vision of a powerfully built Scentari war leader, short but well-muscled, his intricately braided mustache framing the fearsome expression on his ruddy face. The bearskin was pure invention, as he'd never even seen a picture of one, only heard descriptions. Even in his mind, this was a formidable opponent whose power sent a shudder down his spine. He brought his brush to the board and began to bring this vision forth into reality. Working without color, the features poured out faster and faster. The physical part was effortless after all the practice with Xelos, but tapping into his Talent remained emotionally draining.

Gazing down at the finished picture, the grand thane's eyes blazed back at him with unsettling life that was all too real, and he forced himself to look away.

The exertions of the day had taken their toll, so Simon undressed and went to bed, hoping that the face of Shadush would not haunt his dreams.

There was a definite chill to the morning air as Simon and Kyso began their rounds. Simon attempted to steer them on a route taking them past the inn, but Kyso overruled him. Since Kyso was his senior officer, and one who demanded a high degree of order, Simon had to concede. In his mind, Elysia looked sad as she rode through the gate, but peace settled in his heart knowing she'd be safer with Zeno, far from here. Hopeful of catching one last glimpse, he kept an eye out for a lone woman with a horse.

Simon carried his completed designs, as well as reams of fresh papyrus for pictures and maps. Kyso was impressed with the plans, and would explain them to the legionaries assigned to set up the defenses inside each gate. They'd start with the access to the most major roads and work their way back from there. If they had time, they'd do the same inside the entire inner wall, in case the Scentari used their power to burst through another point.

Kyso sniffed the air. "Still think it will rain?"

"We'd better hope so."

Kyso led him to the temple. Pelusians did not build their cities around a central hill like the Izari; whether by design or because of the flatness of the plains, Simon didn't know. The temple of Tamla, their god of weather, was the next best vantage point. It rose to a four-story tower, and Simon intended to use that as his base for getting a good drawing of the city. Of course he also needed it for a different purpose than Garas and Kyso expected.

The top of the tower was open to the elements, with a large basin in the middle, and at the four corners stood bronze statues of the god, each holding metal rods up to the sky like bolts of lightning. The priests had protested when Kyso demanded they be allowed up there, but mention of the impending attack silenced them.

After the heights he'd reached riding Zeno, Simon considered the view from the top of the tower rather pedestrian. Kyso, however, looked a little green while trying to keep his eyes either on Simon or down on the floor. He was uncharacteristically nervous and chatty while Simon worked. Simon appreciated the company, and the chance to engage his mind so he wouldn't worry about Elysia. And since he was merely copying what he saw, it didn't hurt his focus.

"What an honor, to address the Senate. And all those generals. Were you nervous?"

"Absolutely. But they're just men, Kyso. Men with power and mostly from great families, but men all the same."

He sketched out the overall layout of the city, and compared it to the inferior maps Garas had been forced to work with. *I could do better in my sleep.*

"Did you meet General Lokuta? Is he a… superior commander?"

"He's better than Persei, yes. They invited me for dinner." Kyso's eyes went wide. "He's very comfortable in the political arena. Much more subtle. Ambitious. I could see him being president someday."

"He served under some good generals. I pray he has learned much. Although with three legions! Soon to be four! What a force!"

"Let's hope we live long enough to see them."

As the map took shape, Kyso pointed out strong points in the fortifications on each side, as well as ideal troop positions, firing angles for the archers, and ideas for securing the port. Soon Simon started on drawings of the city in profile, matching their current view. He planned to do four, one for each of the cardinal points. Tamar was a busy mercantile city, even under the threat of attack. From up here, Simon could see the steady stream of people flowing in through the south and east gates, and a larger one heading out the north. Civilian preparations were well underway.

"They don't have much faith in us, do they?" Simon said, pointing out those who were leaving.

When Kyso looked out to where Simon indicated, he took a staggering step and clapped his hands over his mouth. Simon helped him sit down.

"Have you ever been up this high? You don't have to stay here if it's making you sick. Why don't you take the drawings around to the teams to get the horse defenses ready? And take this map back to Garas. I'll stay here until I finish."

With a sigh of relief, Kyso kept his eyes on his feet and hurried down the stairs, his knuckles white as they clutched the pictures.

Simon chuckled to himself. *He'd probably die rather than ride Zeno.*

Without Kyso looking over his shoulder, Simon set to his real work. In his realistic renditions of the city, he augmented the walls, making them thicker and stronger. Next he painted in a dark and stormy sky, with torrential rain blanketing the city, and lightning crashes that lit up the surrounding countryside. He poured his emotions into the work, feasting on the darkness of his mood, the sorrow of the loss of his friends, and his separation from Elysia. It flowed in a torrent of feeling onto the page.

In the view to the west he added the image of the flotilla of galleys crowding the mouth of the harbor, a tailwind filling their sails and rushing them into Tamar. Adding them to the picture suffused him with hope and relief, a welcome antidote to the darkness of his stormy work.

He had no idea if his Talent would have any impact, or when. But at this point he didn't have any better ideas.

Garas addressed the men later that afternoon after meeting with Kyso and Simon. He announced that Simon would be his personal aide, assisting Kyso to coordinate the defense, which earned a furious stare from Harron. Garas waved Simon and his map forward, giving him the floor to share the plan Kyso had devised with input from Garas, but Simon had illustrated.

Simon threw himself into the details with confidence. He pointed to the three main gates. "They're likely to attack with their dark fire at one of the gates. We know it can damage stone, so wood stands no chance. But we believe they should only be able to attack one gate at a time. Our men have a huge advantage on foot in tight quarters, so we'll set up traps on the wider avenues to hobble the horses that burst through in the attack. Archers can also cover those areas. I've started on drawings showing what to do."

The staff looked them over. At least one grimaced. It would be very painful for any horses that tried to cross, and their riders would be defenseless once thrown.

Kyso stepped forward to add his thoughts. "We have already sent our men out to warn anyone remaining in the surrounding lands. Citizens should either flee or withdraw inside the city. After we gather in all the food we can, we'll shut the gates."

Simon continued: "We start immediately on these preparations, but I'm hoping we won't need them for a few more days. There's a big storm coming, and if there's one thing that might protect us from their fire, it's rain."

Karr challenged him. "How can you predict the weather? Are you some kind of weather wizard sent to defeat this warlock?"

Simon glared at him. "No, but I've been further afield, while you've been stationed here. There are storms coming."

Garas stepped in. "Simon has more experience with these Scentari than any of us. Our archers will have orders to shoot anyone who looks like a leader, dressed more importantly than the others. Simon?"

Simon set his picture of Shadush on the table. "Their grand thane, this Shadush, is shorter than most, and wears a bearskin robe over a decorated breastplate. He is the key to everything. If we can take him out, that could save us all. I've shown this to the captains of all the squads of archers."

"The Scentari have just begun to acquire the experience needed to take a city," Garas said. "They've only succeeded so far because of their sorcery, and only faced green garrisons. We have the survivors of the 7th Legion, more knowledge of our enemy, and time to prepare. If we can hold out for a week, until the legions arrive, we can crush them."

A messenger ran up and spoke directly to Garas, who swore before he'd finished hearing the message. The general addressed the group: "Our scouts found them, and their outriders chased our men all the way back to the city walls. Still not the main force, but they could be here any time. Get to it. Dismissed."

ᎶᏋᏮᏋᎶᏋᎶ

Kazash fidgeted, his brows drawn together as he rode up beside Shadush, in the middle of the Scentari force.

"My lord, I have word from the outriders. The city is well defended. And they appear to be expecting us. Our riders can't get within bow shot of the wall. They turn us back with their arrows, and we're taking losses. The men want blood. Are we ready to attack?"

Shadush didn't even show passing concern. "As soon as I get there, we will."

Kazash hesitated. "My lord, we can't guarantee we can protect you when you go to burn down their gates. Not with their archers. How will…"

"I wish to test my power further, from afar."

Kazash nodded, but didn't appear convinced. "Will it work?"

Shadush's anger boiled, and wondered if it showed in his eyes. He tried to stay steady. "Do not doubt me, Kazash."

"Never." He bowed low. Too low. Shadush was getting nervous, but didn't dare show it. There should have been reports of the Pazians landing by now. That's why he'd decided to start on the ports. The last remnants of the legion he'd destroyed must be cowering inside these walls. Which made this a likely landing point for when reinforcements did come. There was strategic value here. And regardless, it would open sea trade and access to its riches.

Already second guessing himself too often lately, this gave him another chance. He felt so tired. And a sense of foreboding. Strange dreams haunted him last night, disturbing his sleep even if he couldn't recall them when he woke. Lying awake he counted his mistakes, wondering if he'd made too many. He should have turned this way sooner, instead of appeasing the men by taking out the new towns that lay in their ancestral homeland, reclaiming prime farmland as pasture for their flocks when this was over. If it ever came to an end.

"Double time," he said. "Leave a small force behind to cover the wagon train. I want to be on them tonight."

Finally Kazash smiled. He was good, and partly because he had a mind of his own, and the balls to challenge him in private. They both itched for a real battle.

"Good thinking my lord." Kazash sniffed at the wind. "A storm is coming."

"*We* are the storm."

⚭⚭⚭⚭

Simon and a team of legionaries were busy tying sharpened wooden stakes into the frame he'd devised, making use of the last dim light of dusk. It was tough work. They'd brace each one against the side of a building or any other obstruction so it would stand up to the force of a charging Scentari horse. He grimaced at the savage potential of his design, and was thankful Zeno would never have to face one.

A drop of water hit his ear. When he looked up, another hit his nose. And another.

"Finish up quickly," Simon said. "Tamla be praised, the storm is here."

Then the skies opened and the deluge began. Rain had never felt so good falling on his armor.

Simon found Garas and Kyso braving the elements at the top of the highest tower on the wall. The rain was coming down by the bucketful and their heavy waterproof cloaks were losing the battle to keep them dry. It was cold early winter rain, married to the ferocity of a summer storm. Any colder and it would be snow.

Garas' grunt was barely audible over the sound of large drops hammering the surrounding stone. "Looks like you were right, Simon. Thank any gods, heathen or otherwise. And not a moment too soon. Look." He pointed out into the gloom, but through the sheets of rain, everything was a blur of dark colored hill and plain.

"What is it?" Simon asked.

"They're out there. The main force. Wait for it."

Blinding white flashed in the clouds above them, illuminating the Scentari massing in the field. Simon gasped, and the following thunderclap shook the city walls. "That's the force I saw."

"Thousands of them, and looks like they're preparing to charge."

Simon looked surprised. "In this weather?"

"Not sure about the urgency on their part. Maybe they know the fleet is coming? Kyso, is everything ready?"

"Yes. The archers will keep their bows covered until the riders come into range. As long as they keep firing, it should only affect their range slightly."

Garas pondered this for a moment. "Still, the enemy have to breach the gates or wall before we have any real trouble. And I'd like to see them try that dark fire in this weather."

Simon hoped that Elysia didn't need to test the magic of Zeno's wings in it either. She had ample time to get far away before the storm hit. The thought of being up in the air, buffeted by these primal forces of nature—even those that he had personally summoned—made Simon more than a little queasy.

# XXVI
ᕗᕗᕗᕗᕗᕗ
## *Rain*

The first drops of rain had dampened Shadush's mood, and he stormed violently around his camp. His men were cold, soaked and bedraggled, and he'd missed his chance to take the city by surprise. Now they knew he was here, and he was reluctant to try and use his power, for fear that the rain would disperse it. While the water weighed down his bearskin cloak and beard, the pent up power churned inside him, begging to be released on his enemies.

*But where can I do a test?*

He rode through his forces, the dull hiss of falling rain drowning out all the other familiar camp sounds. The eerie quiet made him feel shut in, enclosed.

The ranks parted as they saw him coming, most showing signs of confusion or even worry at the sight of their leader moving away from the front. *Let them wonder. Just don't let them see my power desert me.*

Where was Mirasha when he needed her? She'd have an idea. He cursed himself for making her stay with the wagon train, then again for becoming reliant on her counsel.

Finally he reached the back of their lines, and one concerned rider raised his hand.

"You may speak," Shadush said.

"My lord, let us accompany you... wherever you are going."

Shadush's anger burned, his fingertips sizzling as the dark rage met the sheets of rain. "Do I look like I need your escort? If I did, my blood riders would be with me. No, what I do now, I must do alone. I must pray to our deliverer, and any that watch will be turned to ashes like the Pazians we are here to destroy!"

The riders bowed their heads in fearful shame, letting him pass.

His horse protested as he pressed forward into the darkness, away from the men, but he urged the beast on at a careful pace. The last thing he wanted was for the horse to turn an ankle in a hole and throw him to the muddy ground. They made their way to a small copse of trees he'd spotted as they passed earlier. Cold raindrops dribbling down his neck and under his armor marked the time until he finally arrived.

He dismounted and tied the horse to a tree. No telling what it might do if spooked, and he'd hate to make his own soggy way back through the mire.

With the trees at his back, he basked in his anger. Anger at the weather, the insult of the Pazian former overlords, the thought of anyone seeing him as weak, and his dependence on this power. Streams of fury surged into a frothing mass of evil in his heart, coursing hot through his veins and into his hands. He no longer needed the incantations to focus the energy, his will was enough, and he released the fury toward one solitary tree, away from the others.

Superheated steam scalded his palms where the driving rain quenched the dark fire. He cried out in agony, and his power winked out like an ordinary candle. Clenching his fists only intensified the pain, so he opened them to what he hoped would be the healing balm of the falling water. The cold drops still caused discomfort, but it was better.

Chastened and very alone, he shook his hands in anger at the stormy sky.

*There will be no attack this night.*

ᏇᏋᏏᏋᏏᏋᏇ

Another flash illuminated the Scentari forces as they pulled back, and a few of the archers on the battlements cheered in response, but the sound was muffled by the rain. A booming crash of thunder broke through the dull wall of sound. Garas held up a hand. "They're not leaving. Watch... they're just setting up camp."

The next flash didn't come for several minutes, but in its light Garas' prediction was shown true.

"Go get some sleep," Garas said. "We'll need the rest for the battle to come. When this weather breaks, if not before." He said something to the sentry, who saluted. "Come. The gods have granted us at least one more night."

Simon said a silent prayer as he descended the slick steps back into the city.

ᏓᏓᏓᏓᏓ

Shadush woke with a start, emerging from another nightmare, his second in as many nights. The rain was still drumming on the roof of his tent, even harder than when he'd gone to bed. Lifting his tent flap, he swore when he saw the sky. It should be day, but angry clouds and rain made it look like dusk.

"How long did I sleep?" he asked one of the guards outside the flap.

"We're the fourth watch, my lord."

Shadush rubbed the rest of the sleep from his eyes, with hands that still felt raw. He'd been sleeping half a day, so exhausted that the dreams didn't even stir him, though they tormented his mind. This campaign was taking a toll on him. And nature had sided with the Pazians, for now.

"Father!" he heard Mirasha call out. The oil-slicked skins she wore looked to be keeping her remarkably dry. And in better spirits.

"I thought I left you with the baggage train?"

"You did. But your lethargy allowed us to catch up." Her voice turned accusatory. "Why didn't you take the city in the night, as you'd planned?"

He grunted, and led her into his tent, away from prying ears. His body ached. "It's the rain."

"Are you getting weak? You've been given this much power and you let the weather get your measure?"

"It's not a little rain. It's like the gods are pouring the sea on our heads. To preserve this city? It's a bad omen."

She looked angry. "This is no omen. But it might be a test of your leadership."

"But the dark fire is doused by this heavy rain! It shows no sign of stopping. It can't keep raining for days. It's unnatural."

"Unnatural like dark fire?"

"What? Are you saying this is magic?" He was still coming to

270

terms with the power he wielded. To think of others opposing him with magic of their own terrified him.

"You're more powerful."

"Not if I can't use it in the rain!" *Is she even listening?* He threw his hands up and stormed toward the door.

"Then use it out of the rain."

His head snapped to look at her. That deep intelligence in her eyes unsettled him. He hated being dependent on the advice of this young woman that was also his daughter. So desperately did he want to ask her for a solution that he almost cracked, but instead forced his mind to come up with its own plan.

*A moving tent? No, it would be riddled with arrows by the time it reached the gate.*

*Siege engines? The Pazians use them, but how to construct such a thing? And these plains are filled with farms, not forests. Not enough wood.*

She stood with hands on hips, as if waiting for his mind to engage. His frustration burned hot and dark within him, barely contained.

*Like it's boiling just below... the surface!* He broke out in a knowing grin.

"A tunnel. Below the surface. Use the earth to cover us. We can set up a tent over the entrance, dig down, and then my power will blast the way through until we're under the walls. And then I can bring them down. They won't know what hit them."

She looked satisfied. "Maybe you do deserve a crown, after all."

He raised his hand in anger. "I ought to..."

"What? You would dare harm your daughter?" He drew back and she laughed at him. It was one of the few sounds that could dissolve his anger, and it did, even if everything was different. He detested the triumph in her eyes. The influence she had over him. She was his link between power and humanity, like a chain pulling him forward, deeper into this conflict.

"Where is Kazash? We start digging, now."

ᏫᏬᎬᏬᎬᏬᎬᏫ

Kyso looked puzzled as he and Simon watched the Scentari tents, while the afternoon rain droned on as steady as ever. "What could they possibly be doing?"

"Trying to keep drier than we are?" Simon said.

"Their tents are just outside of arrow's range. Nobody ever sets up camp that close. If we were to send riders bursting out the gate—"

"You're right, it doesn't make sense. Maybe they're hiding their own riders inside the tents?" He'd seen that in his dream last night. Except they were made of flaming shadow. The darkness had felt closer than ever before, more sinister, and far more powerful. He shuddered at the memory.

Kyso squinted, trying to get a better look. "They do have their horses inside. Perhaps ready to charge the moment this lets up."

Simon cupped his hands out in front and they filled up immediately with water. He took a drink. "Doesn't show any signs of stopping. Maybe it will hold until the fleet arrives?"

"Not if they have been caught up in the same storm. With strong winds coming in from the sea, they will be lucky to get all the ships here in one piece. It is bad enough living through this on land."

Kyso did look a little green. Simon put a reassuring hand on his shoulder.

"Don't worry, my friend, nobody is asking you to be a sailor."

His words elicited a rare smile from the normally laconic tribune.

᧞᧞᧞

It was hot work, down in the tunnel. But it gave Shadush a place to vent his anger and frustration, and every step took him closer to proving his point. Tamar would fall, but into their hands, not into ruin. And he would be the agent to make it happen.

Kazash of course had opposed the idea. Not safe for the grand thane to be experimenting under wet earth that could collapse upon him. But was there more? A flicker of ambition present? Was the protest just a show? No, it must have been sincere. Kazash ultimately relented and carried out the order. The hand-picked gang of strongmen dug the initial entry point down from the center of a supply tent to a depth of two and a half heights of a man. Shadush had reckoned that to be deep enough so it wouldn't collapse on top of him, while still allowing him to see the roots of the city walls. His men used the resulting earth to build a short wall around the hole to keep the water out.

He had his youngest son Yagrash trail behind him at a safe distance, as a messenger to the surface if he needed one. The runt of the litter, Shadush had no great love for this boy of eleven. He would never be a great warrior, so was expendable. But he could be trusted. And he feared his father. He might be the difference between life and death if this went wrong.

The first part was a test. Down in the hole with loamy walls surrounding him, Shadush became one with the darkness. He drew it into himself, into his soul, where the power thrashed violently, yearning to find purchase in this world. He pictured smug Pazian aristocrats, fat on the backs of slaves, and his people debased. Hatred roiled, flowing out through his fingers, igniting the air in the darkness and spreading to the earth before him with a crackling hiss. The soil didn't burn; it melted, with the moisture escaping as puffs of steam and the dirt crumbling away like ash blowing in a wind. After his first focused blast he stood sweating before the beginnings of a tunnel.

He summoned Yagrash and gave him the bearskin cloak to return to the surface. So far, it worked even better than he expected, but there were many more hours of hot work ahead.

Through experimentation he quickly learned the optimum range to avoid the searing steam while maintaining good progress. It was the boy's job to count out the distance using their traditional measure, a pair of long spears separated by a rope the span of a horse. They couldn't be sure of the distance required, but between one hundred and one hundred and fifty horse-lengths should bring him to his destination.

When it became routine, Shadush's mind wandered while he exerted his will on the defenseless earth before him. They moved at a steady pace, each horse-length bringing them nearer to victory. The further they went, moving forward behind the corona of hungry darkness, the more the damp heat intensified.

Though these walls of crumbling soil were very different, being below the earth drew him back to his only other experience underground. To that ancient place where everything had changed. The memory clawed at his mind for attention, try as he might to resist its power.

When his men had discovered a strange cave in the wastes of northern Scentar, they had reported it to him, but without knowing really what it was. A tomb? A temple? Hewn out of the rock inside a scar in the ground, it was a place of evil. He knew that now. To be honest, he knew that then. Even before he set foot inside. The horses certainly knew. They had to be tied up or they would have bolted. Something they never do.

Away from the massed army, responsibility, command, family and officers, his mind could reflect on what he had done. What he had sacrificed. Duty and revenge had triumphed on that day, over everything else he held dear. He had walked willingly into the void. And gained so much.

But at such a cost. Tears welled up in his eyes. Was there some way to keep this power, yet undo the price? To reclaim what it had taken from him? Or was his daughter lost to him forever?

He clamped his eyes shut and stilled his mind, as the dark flames continued to surge from his hands. *Begone, these idle thoughts. What's done is done. We are about to see the first of many new triumphs. As we take not just what was lost, but carve out a new empire for Scentar.*

It was at that moment that his power burned away the earth to reveal solid stone, and above it, mortar and the base of a wall.

And if the boy's count was right, at 132 horse-lengths his toil brought him to the end he sought.

He stopped for a moment and pondered. *Could I go further? Around and under? Into the city? Would the extra time be worth it? But would any of my men dare to go through this tunnel, and come out in the rain beyond? They could drown. No.* The cavalry charge and the surprise of the wall collapsing on itself would seed enough chaos in the defenders, and win the day.

"Yagrash!"

His son cowered before him.

"I'm through. Run back and ready the riders for the attack."

As night fell, Shadush outlined the final plans and preparations to Kazash, who was champing at the bit in anticipation of the battle to come. The grand thane rested in the tent at the tunnel entrance, waiting for Mirasha to come for her part. His power needed to be fed after so much use, so feed it he would.

Her voice roused him. "I've brought the slaves you requested. Four of them. Pazians. What are your orders?"

Shaking the weariness from his body, he donned his discarded bearskin to ward off the damp chill of the surface. "Good. Bring them in."

Four bound and bedraggled Pazian men were led into his presence. They were soaked through from the relentless rain.

"They'll do. You," he said to the first of them, a blond, slightly pudgy man. *Maybe a merchant?* "Into the tunnel." He pointed into the darkness.

The man shook his head, his hands palms up.

"I should have learned more of their language. I will yet. It will be useful as I rule their former vassals. And to give orders to my slaves." He snarled at the man. "Into the tunnel!"

The guards pushed the man forward, and he peered over the edge, his eyes opened wide. He started wailing as he wet himself.

Shadush rolled his eyes. "Have it your way." With a flick of his finger, dark flames ignited in his open palm. The captive shrank back, trying to escape through the guards, who held him tight before themselves. Shadush recognized the fear even in their eyes, but it was nothing compared to the terror in the Pazian's. The other three men whimpered in a pitiful huddle.

The flames danced and played in Shadush's hand, before his mind bid them leap forward to set fire to the pudgy man's chest. As the power welled up inside Shadush he could barely make out the agonized screams of the man being consumed by the flames. It was ecstasy every time, though noticeably weaker than in the past. When the captive was reduced to a pile of ash, Shadush only felt his appetite growing.

He pointed to the tunnel again. "Who is first? Go!"

Two of the Pazians scrambled over each other toward the hole, with the first tripping and going down head first. His muffled complaints from the bottom indicated that he didn't do any irreparable damage. The second climbed down after him.

But the third was a quivering mass of abject terror, surrounded by the acrid evidence of his bowels.

"Savages," Shadush said for the benefit of his men, who laughed. "Time to clean up."

The dark fire arced over the body of the other captive, turning what was barely a man into a smoking pile of ash. It smelled disturbingly similar to wild boar roasting, far preferable to the aroma of his excreta.

Yagrash and his drummers arrived, and Shadush bid them follow him down into the tunnel.

Mirasha leaned over to him, giving him one last embrace. She whispered in his ear. "Succeed, and you will have your crown. Fail, and I will have to find another." Her threat was punctuated by a sudden void inside him, with his power wrenched away for an instant before flowing back.

Fighting against the surge of fear, of the loss of control, he hugged her for the sake of all those watching eyes.

*My plan is sound. You will not take this away from me, not after all I have sacrificed. I will be victorious. Then I will bend this power to my will, and deal with you.*

The two remaining captives were given torches to light their way through the dark passageway. He wondered idly what was going through their heads, if their fear left them any room for rational thought.

The plan was simple. When Shadush signaled Yagrash, he'd start a slow beat of his drum, and each man down the line would match his beat, carrying the order down the tunnel and back up to the tent on the surface. After the fifth beat the riders would charge, and after the fifteenth Shadush would unleash his power.

And then run back to join the attack.

The thrill of consuming two more lives coursed through his body, and had pushed aside any fear of side-effects from unleashing his power into the wall. While the tunnel seemed solid enough as they trudged through it, these were forces he didn't really understand, or control. The drummers looked almost as scared as the two captives, who would stop every few feet, requiring another sharp reminder from his spear to keep them moving.

When they reached the end, they turned to Shadush in confusion. He held his hand up, and started backing away. Shadush laughed at the relief on one of the faces, while the other started calling out in unintelligible Pazian speech. Shadush was surprised at how far back he was able to go with them still in his sight. The torches made a big difference in lighting the way, but also made breathing difficult, as if the fires consumed the air he needed to breathe. He coughed, and a wave of panic shot through his body, but he fought it, forcing himself to take a deep breath. It tasted like smoke, but settled his nerves. The two slaves, barely visible, prostrated themselves before him, beseeching. He shook his head. *Should be far enough.*

He turned and was surprised to see Yagrash right behind him.

"Begin the beat."

Yagrash nodded and struck a mighty thump on the hide-covered drum he carried with him. Another beat echoed further down the tunnel, and then another, until the sounds disappeared into the distance. Yagrash struck again, the sound reverberating in the darkness.

The two slaves screamed in unified bewilderment.

*Six.*

The ground beneath his feet pulsed rhythmically, each beat building toward a crescendo.

*Thirteen.*

He extended his hands toward the two slaves. They jumped up, cowering against the end of the tunnel.

*Fifteen.*

The blast of power erupted as a screaming vortex that expanded as it surged through the air, striking the captives and exploding upward in a fireball of immense dark energy. A wave of angry hot air screamed toward Shadush, knocking him back off his feet. The crashing roar was the last sound he heard before absolute silence, and the tunnel plunged into darkness. One small light flickered and shrank, moving away from him down the tunnel toward the surface.

His hands fought frantically to push himself up. Was that Yagrash running with his torch? Or one of the other boys? Shadush slipped and landed painfully on his knee. The light continued to fade until he could see nothing, while increasingly intense vibrations shook the walls around him.

Something struck him in the eye. Dirt. Small rocks. From above. The ceiling was collapsing. Sharp pain and...

# XXVII
## 6ᘓ6ᘓ6ᘓ6
## *Breach*

Shouts rang out along the wall, snapping Simon to attention. He squinted but couldn't make out anything through the gloom and rain. "Kyso, do you…"

"Sound the alarm!" Kyso yelled, pointing at what looked like a storm cloud emerging from the darkness. A wave of riders undulated toward the wall. Kyso sent guards running in both directions to pass on the message. The pouring rain muted all sound, even from the approaching horde.

"Do you want me here, or with Garas?" Simon asked, deferring.

A thunderous explosion shook the wall they stood on. Simon's stomach turned to water at the sickening crack, like the bones of the city had snapped beneath them. He looked on in horror as the tower swayed and toppled toward the onrushing riders, now clearly visible. Their runner in that direction disappeared over the edge. *No, not again! How?*

The collapse of the tower sent a ripple through their portion of the wall, which listed badly outward, but held. Simon grabbed the suddenly queasy Kyso.

"We have to get to Garas. Come, I'll help you. Close your eyes if you can't take it. I'll guide your feet."

"We have to go to the north tower gate."

"I know. I drew the map. This is bad." Simon looked out at the crashing waves of riders, the first of which were about to reach the chaos of the destroyed gate tower. "And we have to hurry. They have their breach."

Kyso righted himself, and shook off Simon's help. His voice was weak. "I think I can manage if you run first, if I just keep my eyes on your back."

They ran. Simon tried to get the archers to move south to cover the gate, but was met with irritated stares. They were already shooting down into the darkness. His stomach sank. Riders surrounded the wall in both directions.

Kyso stepped in with his authority. "New orders. Cover the breach at the east gate, taking out as many of these savages as you can." The men saluted and ran as quickly as the slick path would allow. They repeated the instructions at every archer placement.

"What if they're also attacking the north gate?" Simon asked.

"Then we are dead."

Simon's worst fears were not realized. At least not so far. A large number of Scentari were taunting the archers at the north gate, but making no move to attack it. Yet.

Kyso was grim. "They're showing a high degree of organization. If I were their leader I'd target the other gates from the inside. That's if they can't repeat their trick to take out the gates entirely." He warned the officer in command of the north tower to be wary of such an attack. The officer paled and set to alerting his men.

At ground level, with Kyso much more sure-footed, they ran. The streets were almost empty, with the few citizens remaining shut tight in their houses. Small groups of legionaries were setting up positions behind the defenses Simon had designed. They looked ready for a fight. *Too ready.*

The squads of men moving out into position were progressively larger as they neared the barracks. Garas was fully armored and directing a large group with his usual gruff authority.

"Tribune, what news from the east wall? The gate has fallen?"

Kyso snapped a salute, and Simon copied him. "The gate is in ruins, and they have their breach."

"How is this possible?" Garas asked Simon.

"I don't know. It seemed to come from inside the tower. Or beneath. The riders still hadn't reached the wall."

"So that is their main attack?"

"Yes," Kyso said. "And I've diverted the archers in that direction. But they weren't doing it on their own. They have riders along the full length of the walls all the way to the north gate, and a large host there. Waiting. I believe they're drawing off our numbers from the real threat. They will try to open the other gates from the inside to open up multiple fronts."

Garas swore. "Any idea how your traps are doing holding them back inside the east gate?"

"We didn't see. That's all we know."

Garas directed the largest group to reinforce the east gate, and the rest to intercept any attempt by the Scentari to head for the north or south gates. He held back the auxiliary cavalry to face any small groups of riders that broke through.

"We still have the advantage, men. We can fight in a city in formation. The water is up to our ankles in places. Hold the line! Their horses aren't as effective and the roads are slick. And they'll have a hell of a time getting them through the rubble and our defenses. We're the best of Pazh! We shall not fall!"

The ranks saluted and ran off under their centurions' orders.

He looked to Kyso. "Tribune Scribora, you take charge of the defense of the main group at the east gate. As soon as I've set the rest of the reserves in motion I'll join the group blocking them from reaching the north gate." Kyso saluted and ran off, leaving Simon and Garas alone.

"Any sign of the warlock?" Garas asked.

Simon shook his head.

"Could he do this from a distance?"

"I don't know."

Garas looked uncertain, reluctant. His voice came out a mumble. "We need your... power."

Simon felt naked before the commander. "My..."

"Lokas hinted it to me in his letter. I don't want to ask you to do this. But if he's running around using his power, we're all going to be corpses. Unless you do something. Again."

It crushed Simon to see his commander so pained and vulnerable, admitting he needed to lean on Simon's power.

"I don't know."

"Simon. You're not a soldier. But you have this ability. You brought the rain, didn't you? I'm ordering you to try. You may be our only hope."

He nodded mutely.

"And if you have any other ideas, we could use them."

Dreams came rushing back to him. Of what he had to do, or at least try. "I just might be able to find him."

"What are you waiting for? Whatever you can do to take him out. Go!"

Simon saluted, and ran into the barracks.

Could he even do this? He did have the picture of Shadush that they'd sent around. If it was good enough, he could try to use it to locate him.

*Elysia!* Her picture was also in his room. He had to let her know what was going on. It might be his last chance. If the Scentari overran the city, he would be among those who fell, forever silent. *I can't leave her like that.*

He found his small room and laid out his materials with shaking hands. Thoughts raced through his mind, of worry, panic, death and blood. It took all his willpower to still his mind, breathing deeply to regain some clarity and remember Xelos' lessons.

*First things first.* He looked back at his painting of the city, and the rain. *Time to make a change.* He painted over the rain on the port side of the city, making it clear for a landing, and painted the ships coming closer. *Hopefully that little nudge will speed our boys along.*

*Next, Shadush.* He focused on the image before him, letting it burn into his brain. Emotions swirled around within him: anger, fear, revulsion. Basking in those feelings he closed his eyes and let his mind go, allowing a lightness to overtake him, as if his consciousness was floating up out of his body and searching the world for the villain in his mind. He set his brush to the dark paint and let it flow.

The strokes came slowly at first, but built up to a frenetic pace. Finally he opened his eyes and was completely confused. Only part of the grand thane was still visible, the rest covered in darkness, like earth.

Simon snapped his brush in frustration. *Gods, what does this even mean?* Simon looked at the light of the oil lamp illuminating his page. *If only it were daylight, to see better where he is.*

*That's it! Light!*

Simon painted a ghostly glow on the body of Shadush, lighting up the lower half that was most obscured. As he did so, his hand moved unbidden to add more detail, and subtle differences lost previously to the darkness. Even with the light, it was murky, with patches of green mixed in—*under water!* He was half-buried in the ground, in a dark pool only slightly exposed to the night sky. Simon urged his hand onward, adding light to the beard and face of the grand thane, marking him both high and low so they could locate and eliminate him. Shadush was in a bowl-shaped depression below the ground, but open to the air. He must have been close to the gate, and the explosion somehow got to him? His eyes were closed. But somehow Simon knew he wasn't dead.

Simon's stomach churned as he realized he'd have to go back to the walls to look for him. Putting himself right in the middle of the danger again. Sighing, Simon took out the picture of Elysia.

A tear came to his eye as he looked at her beauty, captured in that happy moment. *I have to get her a message.*

With very different emotions he focused himself for another exercise of his Talent. Love, gratitude for her safety, and the desolate fear of never seeing her again. This time he opened his eyes as his hand moved with the flow of revelation, showing a room with a window, a too familiar bed....

*No!*

He dropped the brush, his hand quivering and heart racing. She hadn't left. She was still at the inn.

ᏬᏋᏬᏋᏬᏋᏬ

Wet choking coughs wracked Shadush, bringing him round. Spluttering and immobile, his whole body screamed in terror. His beard was immersed in water up to the line of his mouth. The smell of rain and wet earth filled each breath through his nostrils. He saw only darkness, with rain battering his eyes and his ears filled with the steady splash of raindrops into the pool around him.

His arms and legs couldn't move... frozen in place, covered in... earth? Panic seized him. *Where am I?* Forcing his eyes open to a squint, he looked up, and the darkness was less complete overhead. *A well? How?*

Disjointed visions flashed through his mind. The captives. Dark fire. Explosions. Darkness.

Realization hit him like more stone crashing down on his head—the ceiling had collapsed. He was stuck many feet down in the earth. And the rain was filling up the hole.

His mind scanned through solutions. *Power? Only if I want to boil myself alive.*

*Call for help?* No. He couldn't be sure that one of his men would be the first to find him. And what if it was a rival who worked with him out of necessity, or fear? The gods knew he'd made enough enemies within the tribes.

*I must get myself free.* First he tried his feet, but they were stuck fast. His hands could move slightly within their own space, but it would take a while to get them out. Moving his body in the quagmire caused the pool of water to bubble and then drain down several inches, buying him valuable breathing time. He exhaled through his mouth in relief.

Suddenly there was a presence in the well, watching him. His eyes darted around frantically, but there was nothing to be seen. Just cold earth barely visible, and this water around his neck. He fought the urge to cry out against it.

Minutes passed, with nothing but awareness of the presence, and he kept himself busy wiggling his fingers to try to buy himself more space so he could get his hands free. Inch by inch he made slow progress, rotating his arm to free enough space to slightly shake it. *I will not die in this foul pit. Not on the night of my triumph.*

The rippling darkness of the pool lit up with a murky green glow. He looked up, but saw nothing that could be reflecting. No, it was coming from under the water, but he could still barely make out his legs.

Suddenly the pool lit up like a bonfire, and forced his eyes shut against the blinding whiteness. His eyelids were still bright, as if looking straight at the sun through closed eyes. Shock and wonder filled him. He tried to turn away from the source and cracked open one eye.

The light reflected from the surface of the pool, but not from above like he expected. It came from... his beard glowing, and now his face too. Ghostly white light was spreading in a line, shining outward to illuminate the pit. Squinting, he opened both eyes to get a better look. His drooping, soaked mustache lit up like a candle. But with no heat. It was unnatural, and terrifying, but he couldn't look away. As he peered down through the water he saw the lines drawn down to criss-cross his breastplate, shedding light even within the murky pool.

He was at the bottom of a deep bowl-shaped depression that was wider toward the top. His body was plugging the hole, allowing the water to fill up like a washtub.

As quickly is it appeared, the presence was gone, and though the light stopped advancing, it remained. The illumination gave him renewed will to get himself out. He continued the slow work of extracting his arms from the walls.

Alone once more, he was reminded of what he'd met in that dark temple, that had started it all. Of that unseen being of immense power who had offered him an unfathomable bargain. Had shown him visions of burning Pazians, sating his lust for revenge. Promising the world. *If* he was totally committed. *If* he would pledge himself to the power. But at what cost?

He had purchased the power, but didn't fully comprehend what he had acquired. And it wouldn't even help him get out of a hole. He felt so alone.

He wondered where his daughter was now. Mirasha. Or was there anything left of her inside that body? His salt tears joined water of the pool below. His precious daughter. He had loved her as much as life itself. So devoted. She had begged her father to let her play her part in his grand plan. She had assumed it would be a marriage to bind some important tribe or warrior to his cause.

But instead *she* had been the price for his power. The demand made by that being. And he had consented, bringing her to the dark temple, like a ritual sacrifice led to the slaughter. He had been willing to give her up for the sake of his revenge.

He had balked at the end. Was willing to walk away. Give up on his dreams. He had shown weakness. Love.

But she hadn't let him. His daughter had stepped forward, willingly sacrificing herself so that he would have the power to free his people. Her people. She had entered the flames and he cried out at his loss.

Only she hadn't been consumed.

She had been... inhabited. By the dark power that had promised him so much. An ever present reminder of what he valued the most. What he had offered on the altar of power. And that reminder drove him on, and on, to justify his sacrifice. Her sacrifice. His loss.

Once more, he vowed to beat the Pazians and use this power to find a way to free her. To have it all.

*I will not die here.*

He kept digging.

ᏪᏋᏪᏋᏪᏋᏪ

Elysia rummaged through her things for the hundredth time, getting ready in case she had to leave but not knowing what to do. She'd heard the loudest thunder of her life, like a lightning bolt had hit one of the buildings nearby. She was curious to see the extent of the damage, but not enough to venture outside the inn in this storm.

She'd been ready to leave since the morning after Simon had left, gone as far as the stables, with Zeno saddled and ready to go, but she'd balked, despite even Zeno's urging. Despite having the most vivid dreams, of darkness approaching, and herself at the head of an army of statues ready to fight. Like she had some part to play. Did that mean Shadush was as close as they feared, now drawing out her own power? She should get away.

*No.* She couldn't bear to leave without seeing Simon one more time. Not after what they'd shared. He'd been gentle, and strong, and... she closed her eyes, recalling the warmth of his touch all over her body. She tingled, longing to feel him again. She'd never imagined the day she'd give herself to a man, but he had been so wonderful, so attentive, so understanding. She loved him, and she couldn't leave him, even though he'd made her promise she would. Would he ever trust her again?

But the thought of flying alone to another new country was not something she wanted to face. Not yet. Not unless she had to.

Instead she'd returned to her room and worked on the pair of driftwood birds she'd started carving on the beach. It was therapeutic. They weren't sweet little songbirds, instead they featured sharp beaks and lines as hard and savage as her pent up anger. Only her work helped her cope with her Mother's death five years before, and they hadn't even been close. Losing the two most important people in her life, and her brother, had brought her to the brink. She mourned their passing. The loss of her quiet life. Of everything she knew. Her Talent was all that remained.

Letting her hands reveal the forms hidden inside the wood, forms only she could see... it kept her sane. She could lose herself for hours at a time in her connection with the wood. Until the feelings came back to haunt her. But that let her focus her work, to dedicate it to them, one bird for each of the two pillars in her life. Both gone, but not forgotten. Never forgotten.

Now with only Simon left, she couldn't leave him too. Not if she had a choice.

So she waited, taking only one meal each day in the dining room, by herself. She kept her cloak huddled around her, drawing a few curious looks, but she didn't want these people to see her. The few that were still in the town. She'd heard that most had left, like Simon had bid her.

Now she found herself waiting in the room, in the midst of this endless storm, with the two completed birds standing on the window sill like little guardians.

She started to unpack again. Was she crazy? She couldn't go out in this storm anyway. Nor did she want to. But with nothing left to carve, her hands twitched. Skittish and bored, she needed a change.

She felt her skin prick, as if someone was watching her. Her head whipped around, to the door and window, fear seizing her mind, but nobody was there.

Staying in this strange room all day was making her crazy. She was sure of it. Now was the time to leave… if only she had word from Simon. No, she would wait one more night.

*Back to bed?* She turned and the sight made her jump. A line of blood marred the formerly clean sheets, growing and moving toward her. She caught herself before she screamed, not wanting the attention. But what was it? Not lines… letters? Pazian letters spelling… her name! *Simon!* Her heart leapt at the connection. She read the message as each new word formed.

*Elysia Zeno stables now!*

She rushed to her things, filling her pack again, with the two little birds on top. She would be there for him, and she would be ready.

ᎾᏋᎾᏋᎾᏋᎾ

Simon ran full speed through the wet streets, this time carrying his pack. *First, Elysia. Then, Shadush?* It was as much of a plan as he could muster. But he had to get Elysia away from the slaughter.

Shouts and other sounds of battle came from most directions. And the inn was too close to the east gate, where the noise was loudest. Simon unsheathed his sword, ready for anything.

Rounding a corner, he came upon his first view of the battle raging inside the city walls. Men of the 7th held a fragile line no more than two deep across the width of the street, from building to building. A hail of arrows joined the downpour falling on their heads. Blows battered into the shield wall like muffled drumbeats. And the defense was failing. There were no bodies behind them, which to the untrained eye might look like none had fallen, but to him they were being pushed back.

Simon sprinted for the left side of the group, behind their commander.

With a crash and a cry, the right side of the shield wall fell, and the formation crumpled in from the gap with the riders hitting them hard. Several legionaries fled. Rydar ran past him without recognition, the slits of his eyes impossibly wide with terror.

Their commander, a tribune, bellowed for them to hold the line, but his voice was drowned out by the rain, and the screams of the dying.

The rest of the line began to falter as Simon reached the tribune, and he recognized him. *Kyso!* Simon grabbed him by the shoulder, and had to deflect the instinctive slash that was the tribune's response.

"Your position is lost!" Simon said, their eyes locking in recognition, but Kyso set his jaw, determined to fight on. "Run with me! I found Shadush!" His voice was enough of a command to force Kyso into action.

Taunting screams of dying men being cut down in their collapsing formation would be sure to visit his dreams, but Simon shut them out of his mind and led Kyso along the side street to the inn.

The gate to the stables was barred, and Simon banged on it, shouting Elysia's name. Kyso looked back, his head on a swivel to watch for any riders who had broken through.

"Simon!" came the muffled response, then the sound of the bar being slowly lifted. The gate creaked open.

Elysia pulled him in and wrapped her arms around him. He kissed her fiercely, then remembered himself.

Kyso spluttered, furious. "Our men are dying out there, and you come for a *woman?*"

Simon stepped toward him, now angry himself, but Elysia interceded, keeping her voice surprisingly level. "Simon, who is this? What is going on? Zeno is ready, like you asked."

Simon settled his anger, but was still shaken at seeing the city's defense already beginning to fail.

"Elysia, this is Tribune Kyso Scribora. A good friend to me, and

Garas. The Scentari have burst into the city. I'm afraid it will fall, especially if their sorcerer is left unchecked."

Her eyes went wide. "He is here?"

"Yes. He used his power to destroy the gate we came in through."

Kyso was impatient, eying the door. "Yes, so where is he? The riders will be upon us any minute!"

"I… think we can see him from the air."

Kyso looked incredulous. "What, you mean to take us to the temple again?" He paled. "Not in this rain, and how would we get away if the Scentari surround us?"

Elysia looked concerned. "I don't know if Zeno can handle this weather." She was met by an indignant snort from behind her. Zeno nuzzled up beside her, and she stroked his mane lovingly.

She looked the horse in the eye. "Zeno, will you be able to carry all three of us? With those two in full armor?"

The horse puffed up proudly, and nodded.

"Simon, what is going on?" Kyso asked, anxious and impatient.

Simon walked over to Zeno and pulled off the blanket covering his back. Zeno stretched his wings, enjoying the freedom.

Now it was Kyso's turn to be wide-eyed with wonder. Simon smirked at the effect it had on his friend, especially as Kyso pieced together Simon's proposal. He started backing off, looking ill.

"No… I am not going up on that… thing."

Zeno snorted and turned his head away, indignant.

"His name is Zeno," Elysia said. "He's not a *thing*."

"And he's going to both save us," Simon said, "and help us find and neutralize Shadush."

"But how are we going to see him in the rain, and at night?" Elysia asked.

Simon grinned. "Don't worry. We'll be able to see him from a mile away."

# XXVIII

## Shadush

The street outside was empty, save for the echoes of horses galloping on nearby streets. The three of them filed out, followed by Zeno, who bristled at the falling rain before Elysia coaxed him to follow.

Simon looked to the right, where the street continued through a cross junction before ending at the street after that. "That's not enough room. And every junction is a danger point. We should start at the end there and come back this way to get airborne."

He helped Elysia up into the saddle. It would be tight with the three of them, but would have to do.

"Kyso, with me. Elysia, you follow behind. We'll have to make sure the cross streets are clear."

Zeno was remarkably quiet as he followed them to the junction. Simon took the left street, Kyso the right. When he peeked around the corner, Simon found his empty, as he expected. Kyso signaled him over.

Several blocks from their position, down the right side street, a group of legionaries were fighting a pitched battle and faring little better than Kyso's former squad.

Simon grabbed Kyso before he could dash after them.

"I know, they're my brothers too. Your men. But the best we can do for them is to eliminate Shadush. You know it's true."

Kyso stuck out his chin like a petulant child. "I feel like I am abandoning them."

"But didn't those heroic tacticians of old know when to retreat?"

"I should be calling for *them* to retreat!"

"What, and be slaughtered by the faster horsemen?"

Kyso's shoulders slumped, the fight drained out of him. Simon pulled him forward, urging Elysia to follow as well.

As they came to the junction where their street ended, they repeated their scouting pattern. This time two Scentari riders whipped around the corner just as Simon was about to do his check. Zeno reared up at the sudden apparition, his wings spreading out to their fullest like some menacing demon. The Scentari horses bucked and their riders needed all their skill just to stay mounted.

Simon pounced, charging from behind and putting the full force of his shield into knocking one rider from his mount. The man went down in a heap.

Kyso neutralized the other confused rider before he even saw him, cutting away his bow with a quick strike of his short sword.

Simon dispatched the fallen rider with a thrust through the neck that made a sickening squelch. The driving rain immediately washed away the blood from his sword as he drew it out. He was slightly disturbed at how easily he did this now. Yes, Elysia was in danger, but this was still another human. But necessary. They needed a long clear stretch for takeoff.

When he looked up, Kyso had also downed his man. He clapped the two horses on the hindquarters, sending them galloping back the way they came. They were more than happy to escape what must, to them, be a terrifying alpha horse.

"Good work Zeno," Simon said.

"Are you any good with a bow?" Kyso asked as they readied to mount.

"Never used this kind. You?"

"No. But these are both broken. I figured that if we're going to be mounted, they would have been useful."

"I'm just glad I have your sword at my side."

Kyso helped him up in the saddle, behind Elysia, and he returned the favor. Zeno didn't seem bothered by the extra weight, which made Simon feel a bit better, but he still wasn't sure this would work.

Kyso glanced up toward the tower. "How high do we have to go?"

"Out of arrow range. Can you do a quick calculation?"

"Their range should be reduced if they're aiming up, and of course with the rain. I'd say…" He looked queasy when he applied that to his own person.

"Should we blindfold you?" Simon asked, smiling.

Kyso thought about it seriously. "No, I will just close my eyes if it gets too bad."

"What are you talking about?" Elysia asked.

"My friend here doesn't like heights. Don't worry." He gave her leg a gentle squeeze. "I'll be your shield if he gets sick." He turned back to Kyso. "But I'd appreciate it if you would turn to the side. Maybe it can be a weapon against the Scentari."

Kyso blanched. "Just get this over with."

With no threats visible on either side, and the road clear in front of them, Simon nodded to Elysia.

"Go, Zeno," she said.

Zeno shook his wings out, the drops of water disappearing into the steady rain that was soaking them once again. He eased into his gallop, hitting an even stride as they passed the previous junction.

"Look!" Simon cried out. More riders were galloping down that way, sighted them, and turned the corner in pursuit. Simon held his shield on his back to that side, expecting Kyso to do the same—just in time, as an arrow nicked the corner and went clattering away.

Zeno hit full speed as they passed the inn.

More arrows whizzed by and Kyso jerked, cursing.

As they reached the junction with the main street, Simon gulped as he saw Scentari riders in both directions. One saw him and started shouting.

He squeezed Elysia tight, trying to wrap his body around her to protect her back.

The thudding undulation of the galloping approach ended with a final lurch into sudden lightness. They soared into the wet air, leaving the street behind. Kyso squeezed him so tight his armor jabbed painfully into his ribs.

Zeno spiraled up until they were clear of the rooftops, his wings flexing powerfully to gain altitude. Simon frowned. He'd been on Zeno enough to notice that their mount was straining with the extra weight, but made no comment. Kyso's stomach likely couldn't take it.

He kept his face close to Elysia's, observing her fascination as she looked down at the numerous fronts of the battle below. She pointed to the fallen gate tower, and the bodies littering that area. Bodies from both sides in equal numbers. His traps had been moderately successful, but sheer volume had overwhelmed their men.

"Do you see that, Kyso?" Simon said.

His only response was a moan.

"Did they hit you?"

"Grazed the back of my leg. Nothing serious."

"Your eyes are closed already?"

"Tight. Trust me. Better for you."

"Then I'll give you the overview. The Scentari have broken through to the south, and are already at the south gate. There is tougher resistance heading north, but now they're..." He hesitated for a moment. "They're outflanking them now. Even Garas."

Kyso tensed behind him. "We have to relieve him."

This time Simon's heart was with him. "Elysia, you see that group down there? That's Garas and his men. They need our help."

She whispered to Zeno, who changed course to head that way.

"But what of Shadush? Wasn't that his order? Isn't he buying you the time to do your duty?"

"We can't leave him. He's a good man. He's done so much for us."

They soared down toward that particular battleground, coming in behind their lines. Excited shouts from the first to spot them drew even more attention. Garas didn't appear as surprised as the others. He stared at Simon, shook his head, then pointed back up toward the wall. With a final salute, he turned his attention back to the battle.

A fresh chorus of shouts was followed by a volley of arrows. Several dull thuds hit Zeno's belly, and he jerked violently to the side, flapping his wings vigorously to reverse course before the order came. He continued to rise, with no sign of being hurt.

Simon's heart pounded in his chest. Kyso was sick over the side. With a dead voice, Simon gave the order. "Zeno, take us up high. Over the wall to the east."

Elysia patted his leg. "You're doing the right thing."

His tone was grim. "We'd better find that sorcerer."

They flew high over the wall, and it heartened Simon that their archers continued to rain death on any Scentari in range. In the plain beyond, the movement was concentrated to the north and south, with multitudes of riders waiting for entrance through the gates. With the south on the verge of falling, the city was doomed. But they could still strike a strategic victory for Pazh if they were successful in their mission.

"What are we looking for?" asked Elysia.

"You'll know it when you see it," Simon said, his eyes scanning the darkness below, starting from the area around the fallen tower. No riders, but a flickering light like a beacon fire shone through the rain, less than a hundred feet from the east tower on a line toward the Scentari camp. "There it is!"

"That light?" Elysia asked.

"Head for it, Zeno."

On closer inspection, the glow poured out from a large depression where the ground looked to have melted away, exactly like Simon's painting. They landed beyond the edge, not trusting the muddy footing. No sooner had Zeno's feet touched the ground, but the glow reached ground level, and two hands gripped the side, followed by a glowing bearded face. It was him.

"Kyso, down with me! He's coming!"

Simon vaulted off, and Kyso, much more gingerly, followed him. Elysia and Zeno backed off.

Shadush looked like a vengeful spirit returning to life as he gained his feet. Kyso and Simon exchanged nervous glances. They advanced on him slowly, spreading wide to hit him from two directions. Simon's hands shook, and Kyso was noticeably limping.

The grand thane drew his hands together in intense focus, and a knot tightened in Simon's belly, bracing himself for the dark assault. But the Scentari clenched his fists and roared in frustration. *So I was right about the rain.*

They were almost in striking distance when the Scentari surprised both of them by throwing himself down, palms on the ground.

Kyso looked to Simon, who shook his head, taking another step forward. Kyso held up a hand in response.

"Stop, Simon. He can do no harm as our prisoner. *We* are not savages." What was that glint in his eyes? Ambition? Pride?

Simon's mind screamed in warning. So much darkness here. So close. He had to be stopped.

"Bind him," came the order from Kyso.

Simon stood still, resolute. "You're making a mistake."

"He's the dark one!" shouted Elysia, who looked on in horror. "Kill him! He's too dangerous!"

Shadush whipped his head up to look at Elysia and Zeno. His eyes narrowed and he bared his teeth in a snarl.

Kyso waved them off. "Then I will do it myself." He approached the prone Scentari, who didn't budge. First Kyso removed the bearskin cloak, which looked exactly as Simon had pictured it, and a thinner garment that he used to tie the grand thane's hands behind his back.

Simon couldn't let this happen. *This is madness!* "Where are we going to take him? The city is falling!"

"Then we'll take him up on Zeno, away from here. Without their leader or his power, our reinforcements will make short work of the remainder. Just help me do it."

Simon stood, conflicted. Elysia continued to urge him to murder, the discordance of her kind voice beseeching such an atrocity jarring his soul. He was here doing his duty. Kyso was his superior, and had given him a direct order. But this man, if he was indeed just a man, was far too dangerous to be allowed to live.

"No, Kyso! Can't you see it's a trick? You think a proud warrior would go down without a fight? He's stalling." Simon took another step forward, his sword drawn. "This is bigger than duty to Pazh." His next words were barely more than a whisper. "This is for the world."

Kyso ignored him, pulling the makeshift bonds tight. The Scentari grunted in discomfort.

The eerie glowing face looked Simon in the eye for the first time. Evaluating. Appraising. *Recognition?* An evil grin. His bound hands burst into dark flames, sheltered under Kyso. The explosion knocked the tribune backward in a moaning heap.

Elysia screamed.

Simon charged, but Shadush rolled away, light as a cat, grabbing Kyso's sword from the ground beside him. He grinned as he faced off, circling away from Simon.

Simon was more scared of Shadush's hands than the sword, though the warrior was no stranger to a blade. He was armored too, with the breastplate covering his chest and heavy leathers studded with iron protecting his extremities.

Simon tried to remember his training. He hadn't been very good, but at least he could remember the lessons. Half a head taller than the Scentari, he had a reach advantage. With equally matched weapons that might prove decisive. *Keep your feet moving. Use the shield. No reinforcements available.*

"Simon," Elysia shouted. "Riders coming! Drawn to the light!"

Shadush attacked, and Simon steered the strike to the left with his shield. The Scentari dodged the counterthrust like he was expecting it. He might be smaller, but he was powerfully muscled, and in prime fighting condition. The next blows rang out blade on blade, and Simon knocked him back a few steps with a shield punch.

The Scentari charged back with a flurry of thrusts and short slashes. It took all Simon's strength to ward off the attacks with his raised shield, putting him off-balance with no opportunity for a counterattack.

A sharp pain in Simon's left leg—a kick—dropped him to one knee, his shield instinctively rising to face the standing enemy. Heat surged under the shield, and Simon screamed, sizzling pain shooting across his arm as steam obscured his vision. He and the Scentari both stumbled back several paces while the boiling cloud dissipated.

He threw down the shield, refusing to give the warlock any cover for his dark magic. His leg throbbed but was stable, so Simon engaged again, circling.

The Scentari's eyes flicked away to the incoming riders. He roared something in their guttural language.

Simon charged again, and after a feint, changed direction to catch Shadush solidly on the off arm. Shadush's follow-through grazed his armor, coming up just short as Simon dodged to that side.

When Simon backed off a half step, Shadush closed again and they traded another flurry of blows, neither doing more than nick the armor of the other.

Simon was panting heavily. *Can't keep this up much longer...*

Simon deflected a savage blow at the last moment, but the force made his bad leg buckle beneath him. Shadush grabbed his sword arm and blinding pain burned into the flesh. Shadush's sword arced forward in a killing blow, but darkness covered Simon's eyes before it connected.

A loud thud and Shadush's grip tore free.

Propping himself up on an elbow, Simon tried to look around, but the darkness still covered his eyes like a fog, clearing slowly to reveal a much darker scene. He could barely make out Kyso grappling with Shadush in the muddy grass, most of the magical light covered in mud and grime.

Simon regained his feet and watched for an opening, but they moved too fast. The much stronger Scentari overpowered Kyso, pinning him to the ground. One hand held down Kyso's neck, with steam sizzling from the point of contact. Kyso screamed.

Seized by fury, Simon charged at Shadush's exposed back, throwing all his weight into a thrust toward the head. The warlock turned at the last moment and the blade crunched through his temple. Simon yanked the sword free and stabbed it repeatedly into the neck, again and again, until his quivering hands could no longer grip the hilt. The dull magical glow illuminated the mashed inside of the warlock's lifeless head. Simon retched violently on the ground, revulsion overwhelming him.

Kyso writhed underneath the body, clutching his agonized throat and gasping for air.

"The riders!" Elysia screamed again, more urgent.

After rolling out from under the corpse and finding his feet, Kyso retrieved his own sword and grabbed Simon, urging him to face the new threat. Three more riders raced toward them, spears cocked and ready to skewer them where they stood.

Simon's arms hung limp at his sides, spent and unable to even raise his sword to face the charge. He looked on in mute horror at their approaching doom.

The closest rider was thrown from his saddle like he'd been shot by a siege engine. Then another. The third veered off, looking around wildly.

A brown projectile screamed toward him, curving impossibly to hit him square in the head. Down he went.

Kyso dragged Simon with him to dispatch the fallen riders, but found them already dead. Each one with a smashed skull.

Kyso looked up, confused. "What was that?"

Simon was sick again. He'd seen enough spilled brains in this battle to last him a lifetime.

Elysia rode over to them. Two brown birds with strong, pointed beaks perched on her shoulder.

The sight somehow calmed him in all the madness. Simon raised an eyebrow. "You did that?"

"No, they did." She smiled as she petted the birds, disturbingly unmoved at the three violent deaths.

Kyso looked between them, backing off a step. "You are a sorceress too?"

Simon ignored the question. "Why didn't you use them on Shadush? Or sooner?"

"I wasn't sure it would work, and didn't want to hit either of you by mistake. And..." She sought understanding in Simon's eyes. "It didn't work until... I felt there was no other option." A dark cloud came over her. "I imagined them being the ones who killed my Father. And Master Xelos. They'll—" Simon held up a hand in warning, looking pointedly at Kyso. She took the hint and her face softened. "Are you two all right?"

Simon nodded weakly. His arm was an oozing, blistered mess where Shadush had seared him, his throat burned with the taste of bile, and he could barely put weight on his leg. Kyso looked even worse with his armor, chest and part of his neck charred black.

"So what do we do now?" Simon asked Kyso.

"We have to cover that light unless we want to put her birds to the test against yet more riders. Who knows how many are still out there? Into the pit with him."

Simon nodded. "Don't you want some proof of his death?"

"We can always come back for the body later." Kyso thought for a moment. "But you're right." He bent down and took the Scentari leader's belt, and the bearskin. Then he and Simon dragged the body through the mud, rolling it a few times to cover the light, and with a final heave propelled it into the pit. It landed with a splash, sinking into the murky water.

Kyso considered what he saw, and nodded, impressed. "He must have used his power to tunnel under the ground. All he needed was a little shelter to unleash that evil." He rubbed at the charred armor on his chest. Simon inspected the ugly mass of blisters on his own arm. "He destroyed the tower from below the ground. Imagine what he could do to an army."

"Could have done," Simon said. "Thankfully we'll never have to find out."

Kyso looked to the sky. "This rain has been a gift from the gods."

Simon and Elysia exchanged a glance, and he winked at her.

"Well boys, let's get out of here," she said. "Where to?"

"To Garas. Hold on," Kyso said, looking at Zeno. He went back to one of the other fallen riders and cut a strip off his cloak. He mounted, then tied on the blindfold. "Now I am ready."

# XXIX
## Aftermath

**W**hen their circling ascent gave them a view back into the city, Simon sharply sucked in a breath. While they'd personally seen success, the battle had taken a bad turn on all other fronts. There were no longer many Scentari outside, with both north and south gates breached.

The battle still raged on in pockets, but far more Scentari surged through the streets unopposed. Even the archers were engaged in hand to hand combat against larger groups of Scentari on the walls.

"How does Garas fare?" Kyso asked.

No movement from the spot they'd left him, but too many fallen bodies. With a lump in his throat, Simon couldn't answer.

"The gates?"

He managed a response. "North, south, both have fallen."

"The port?"

Simon cast his gaze to the west, and his heart leapt in unexpected joy. Galleys and transport ships filled the sea all around the harbor, and the rain was letting up in that direction. Exactly like his picture.

Simon whooped in exultation. "The fleet! It's here! The city is saved!"

"We can help them!" Kyso said.

"*You* can," said Simon. "We're done. So is Zeno. We completed our mission. Shadush is dead and the magical threat has passed. Soon the city will be safe, with any of our brothers of the 7th that remain. I did my duty to Garas." His throat constricted.

"Take us back," Kyso said.

"Elysia is not going near the legions. Who knows what they'd do to Zeno?"

The horse snorted in agreement.

"Fine. Then find a place to put us down. Simon, you and I will report."

"No. We'll let you go."

Kyso was incredulous. "What? You are a legionary of Pazh. You will be a hero. You did what Garas asked and saved the day! We must report to General Lokuta and give him the news."

Elysia looked back at him, and mouthed Persei's name, her eyes burning with savage intensity.

Simon shook his head. *Not now*, he mouthed. She scowled, but nodded.

"We'll let you off at the tower," Simon said. "You can be the hero. I'm not facing the Lokuta. I'm getting Elysia out of here." He pointed out the temple tower. "See that, Zeno? Take us down there. It will be safe."

Kyso groaned. "How about somewhere lower?"

"You'll be safe there, and can find your own way back to the harbor."

Zeno brought them to the top safely. Simon helped Kyso to the top of the stairs before removing the blindfold. "Feel a little better to be on solid ground again?"

"You have no idea." He even managed a slight smile before his face turned serious. "Simon, we could not have done this without you. The legions will smash the Scentari. You will probably get a promotion."

"Not with the Lokuta around." He sighed. "Let's just say that Persei and I are no longer friends."

Kyso raised an eyebrow.

"If we meet again someday, I'll explain. But you've got work to do." Simon handed him the bearskin. "How are you going to explain how you beat Shadush and got back into the city?"

Realization dawned on Kyso. "Flying horses? Magical lights? They will think I am crazy if they do not get to see you."

He clapped his friend on the shoulder. "Then make something up."

Kyso spluttered.

"You'll think of something. But don't tell them the truth."

"Where will you go?"

"We're going to take a vacation." He looked at Elysia, who was inspecting the sculptures surrounding them with admiration. "How about somewhere hot?"

She shivered in the damp cold and nodded. "I've had enough rain," she said, coming over to them. "Though it finally seems to be letting up."

She kissed Kyso on the cheek. "Farewell Kyso. It was nice to meet you, considering the circumstances."

He was speechless, unused to women showing him any affection.

Simon clasped arms with him. "You're a good soldier, and will make a great leader someday. Go be the hero."

Kyso nodded, his face full of emotion. Then he stood at attention. Simon saluted first. "It was a pleasure to serve, Tribune Scribora!"

Kyso snapped a salute back. "And with you, Legionary Baroba. You are dismissed from the 7th Pazian Legion."

"Dismissed?" Simon said. "I was killed in the line of duty." He winked at Kyso, who looked uncomfortable, but nodded. The tribune carried the heavy bearskin down the stairs.

"Good man," said Elysia. "But a little serious."

Simon laughed. "You saw him on a good day. Don't get him talking about great battles and military tactics, or he'll have you nodding off."

She looked at his arm, and her expression changed to one of concern. "That looks awful. We should do something about it. You don't want it to get infected."

"Well, it's been washed very well." He scooped his good arm around her waist, turning her to face him. "I didn't get a chance to thank you yet."

She looked up at him innocently. "For what?"

"For saving us from those big bad barbarians."

"Glad I could help. It was... kind of fun."

"You call that fun?"

"This was the most exciting night of my life, Simon. Scariest. But fun."

"We'll I've had enough of *that* kind of fun." He leaned in and kissed her waiting mouth. Her lips were warm and soft. He felt like light was returning to the world. As if on cue, the sky lit up in the east. A new day was dawning over Tamar.

After a wonderful moment she released him, looking around furtively. "Not here. It's a temple. Shouldn't we give this rain god our thanks?"

"Since when are you so observant?"

"I... I'm just thankful you're safe, and we can leave. And doesn't it feel somehow holy to you? And what if there really are some kind of gods out there, listening? We know now that the Damoz are real."

Simon wondered then, for the first time, if indeed the rain god had somehow amplified or focused his power. He filed away that possibility for future consideration.

Standing self-consciously before the overflowing central basin, he raised a hand. "Thank you... oh Tamla for your... life-giving rain. Your rain that held back the Scentari so that help could come. Your winds that brought the ships safely to harbor. Thank you." He bowed his head.

A lone crack of thunder seemed to answer directly overhead, making him jump.

Elysia sent him a wry smile. "We may have Talent, but what if it comes from the gods somehow? Did you ask for his help in summoning the rain?"

"I... I guess so? I did say a silent prayer. And it was here that I painted the pictures of this crazy weather."

"Makes sense," she said. "So where *are* we going then?"

"Where I told *you* to go. Jeppo. Yalath."

Her eyes lit up. "Oh, have you seen their marble? I've heard it's some of the best!" Her excitement was contagious. And he could find painting supplies anywhere.

"It's almost twice as far as Attarsus, but south. Over land, which means we can at least get some proper sleep each night. And there's no real rush. Maybe we can enjoy the trip?" He took her hand, smiling. She smiled back, drawing in close to him for a wet embrace.

Zeno nuzzled his nose between them. Elysia laughed, the happiest most peaceful laugh Simon had ever heard. He joined in, stroking the interloper's mane. At least he allowed them one kiss before getting involved.

"One more thing. And maybe I should do this alone?"

Elysia stuck out her chin. "I'm not letting you out of my sight."

"Garas. Especially if he has fallen, I want to pay my respects."

"Do you think he fell with his men?"

"There's only one way to find out."

Simon was a little nervous about Zeno taking flight right from the top of the tower, without a running start. But the big horse was not perturbed. He spread his wings, walked to the edge, and without so much as a glance downward dove off. Down, down, down, with Simon holding on for dear life, his insides left on the ledge. They leveled off and aimed straight for where they'd last seen Garas and his men.

After the elation on the tower, the gruesome scene cast a pall over their mood. There were more than a hundred dead legionaries, most in formation, and many entwined in death with Scentari horses or their former riders. Men the same age as Simon, or even younger. Cut down in the prime of life. And for what? For the vengeful ambitions of some barbarian warlock? Such a terrible waste. In death the Scentari seemed more human as well. Why should they deserve to die for the folly of their grand thane? The scene raised too many hard questions for Simon. Questions he was nowhere near ready to answer.

Simon dismounted and searched through the lines for that one face. There were many—too many—that he knew in passing, and even a few by name. Jarom the Maruthan skeptic and Tark the practical Borathi lay twisted at each other's side in the end. He could so easily be among those lying there, dead. It was only this curious conspiracy of chance, timing, Garas, and his Talent that allowed him to be the one still standing.

He froze. It was the helmet of the camp prefect, distinguishable by its distinctive plume, red-black-red. He was a general in capability and the men followed him, but he still refused to put on airs and accept the trappings of the title. His face was unmarked, with teeth still clenched against obvious pain. By the angry marks on his arms and legs, he looked like he had been trampled, likely when the Scentari horse broke through their lines. Dark brown blood caked the side of his neck, where it looked like a spear had finished the job.

Simon put his own helmet down at Garas' feet as an offering, and knelt over this man who meant so much to him. With shaking fingers he closed the pain-filled eyes.

He fought back tears. "Mission accomplished, General. We

took out Shadush, Kyso and I. Just as you ordered." The tears began to flow, falling into the upturned helmet to mix with the now much lighter rain. "And you did it. You held them off just long enough for the fleet to arrive. Tamar is safe. Pazh is safe. The Scentari are a threat no more."

He paused, gathering his thoughts. "You served Pazh to the end. The Republic is in your debt. You died an honorable death... a heroic general. No man can take that from you."

Simon breathed deeply before continuing. "Thank you. I'm only alive because of you. Because you chose me. Took me out from the rest of these young men. I don't know how you saw something different in me. How I could deserve this."

Overcome with emotion, he took a long time to form his next words. "You... you were the closest to a father I'd known in years. I'm sorry I couldn't save you. I did everything I could."

He looked on the gruff mix of scars and creases one more time, capturing them in his mind like the map of a heroic life of duty and service.

"We will honor you, wherever we go. And I will write to your friends, and they will ensure that your memory lives on in the glory it deserves."

He leaned in one more time, and kissed the cold wet forehead.

"Goodbye Garas Numeno, hero of Pazh."

When he stood up, Elysia ran to him, tears streaming down her face. She hugged him tight to herself, and he sobbed into her shoulder. This time Zeno let them be.

After letting him settle his feelings, she looked into his eyes again with that frightening fervor. "What about Persei? He ordered Father killed. And Master Xelos. We know they were his men. He would be with the army. We could go after him now."

Simon shook his head. "I know how painful it is," he said, his voice rough. "But it's too dangerous. I promised your father I would keep you safe. Not let you die avenging him."

"I will make him pay, Simon."

"Someday my love. I promise. For now, I'm done with death. With darkness. I want to celebrate life, with you. Let's go."

They soared one last time over the east walls of Tamar, this time into the golden symphony of the morning sunlight, unfettered by rain and cloud.

Elysia pointed to the huge tent city laid out across the plain, with multitudes of regular people waiting for their force to return.

"What will happen to them?"

"They'll be captured and sold as slaves, the money divided among the soldiers. Some will be paraded around Pazh in the victory celebration first."

"That's horrible!"

"It's just the way..." The way of Pazh, but she was right. *Did those people choose this war? Did they fight it? They didn't deserve this fate. No man did.* "You're right. It is horrible."

Zeno banked south, toward a new life.

"Let's leave this whole world behind."

# *Epilogue*

As general, Daymar blessed Persei with the honor of leading a legion to round up the remnants of the Scentari force, the baggage train and the non-combatants. He had earned the right with his savage valor in leading the first group of soldiers off the ships and securing the harbor.

Persei fought with a ferocity far exceeding that of any of the men that followed him. For he fought for revenge. For the insult of an inferior race of barbarians that debased him as their prisoner. Who brutally murdered their captives in sacrifice to their dark power. A power so repugnant, yet so fascinating.

Persei wanted nothing more than to find the Scentari Grand Thane and skin him. Instead he had to settle for taking it out on his captain.

His unit pushed through to the east gate, clearing the streets before them with ruthless discipline. Where most of the opposition was savagely strong, but disorganized, they ran into a pitched battle led by a familiar tall rider. Persei recognized him as the warrior who held General Suboras just before his death. His blood boiled and he urged his men forward in a charge, crashing into the remaining opposition. Cutting, slaughtering, destroying them.

He made his way directly to the rider, his shield deflecting spear thrusts and sword blows, warding off any attack. His bloodlust drove him right through the horse, unseating the rider and sending him sprawling.

As he leaned over the Scentari dog, recognition flashed in those dark eyes just as Persei sank his blade in the man's neck, ending his life.

Persei seethed, furious that his frenzy had ended the moment too quickly. This dog deserved so much more pain, more suffering. He vowed to exact that punishment on the grand thane himself.

So it was with unusual anger that he greeted Kyso Scribora's report of the death of Shadush. Persei didn't want to believe it, but the familiar bearskin vouched for the truth.

After the mop-up, he had Kyso accompany him to dredge up the body from the watery pit, and they found it just as Kyso had described.

The corpse was a disgusting figure, muddy and bloated, with parts of it radiating an unearthly glow. The sight filled Persei with rage, and he kicked it several times in the side, and once in the mangled head. It did nothing to satisfy his anger, so he had Kyso and some of the men prepare the body to be taken back with them, while he led the rest of the legion toward the Scentari camp.

There would be no pity on this day. And he would take his rightful share of the spoils.

His men advanced, demanding surrender, but cutting down any who didn't comply. He personally dispatched a few of the old and the weak.

His eyes searched for something, anything that linked to the Scentari leader. Something was pulling him, drawing him. He'd know it when he saw it, though he didn't know how.

A few tents in the middle were larger than the others, and he made for them. Smoke billowed from the top of the largest. Drawing back the flap, he looked inside.

And saw her.

He'd found what he was looking for.

She looked up and their eyes locked. There was fear in that noble face. It aroused him. She retreated to the back of the tent.

He grinned, and made a show of stroking the armor on his chest over the scar she'd given him.

In the flickering firelight, even terrified, she was so beautiful. He removed his helmet and walked toward her, his hand outstretched.

She had spared him once. Now he would do the same.

Shadush's daughter would be his prize. And his revenge.

# Get Book Two:
# Blood of the Water

The story of Simon, Elysia and Pazh continues in **Blood of the Water**, Book II of Arts Reborn, to be released in July 2014.

To be the first to find out when each of Jamie's new books are released, get on the release e-mail list at:

http://www.jamiemaltman.com/newreleases/

# Reviews

Reviews are hugely important for independent authors, so if you'd leave your review or even just a star rating on the site you bought this book, or Goodreads, Jamie would thoroughly appreciate it. Mention it to Jamie and you might make his day.

# More by Jamie Maltman:

*Arts Reborn*
Brush With Darkness
Blood of the Water (July 2014)

*Short Stories*
She Had Eyes Only For What Could Be - a story of Elysia

# About the Author

Jamie writes from his home in Richmond Hill, Ontario, Canada, when he's not reading, traveling, watching or playing sports, or playing some kind of games with his wife and two young sons.

Jamie would love to hear from you:

Website: http://www.JamieMaltman.com
Facebook: http://www.facebook.com/byJamieMaltman
Twitter: http://www.twitter.com/jmaltman
Google+: https://plus.google.com/+JamieMaltman
E-mail: jamie.maltman@gmail.com

# *Glossary*

## PEOPLE

### *Pazian Legions*

SIMON BAROBA, legionary and son of a *mundati* merchant, aide
to Garas Numeno

JASUN SUBORAS, General and Governor of Pelusia, current
commander of the 7th Legion

— MARCUS SARRINAI, his uncle, Senator and former General
who defeated the Scentari and established the new
province of Pelusia

GARAS NUMENO, Camp Prefect, 7th Legion, veteran of 30
years in the legions

KYSO SCRIBORA, *suprati* Tribune, 7th Legion

— AKERI SCRIBORA, his uncle, first of his family to reach the
Senate, Garas served under him

PERSEI LOKUTA, *digniti* Tribune, 7th Legion, younger son of a
very wealth and storied family

JAROM, Maruthan Legionary, 7th Legion

TARK, Myraki Legionary, 7th Legion

BRELLAS, Tribune, 7th Legion

RYDAR, Kawanian auxiliary rider, 7th Legion

MALEM, Pelusian scout, 7th Legion

KARR MYKANDER, garrison commander at Tamar

HARRON, aide to Garas Numeno, 7th Legion

### *Pazh*

CAPTAIN MELCHIOR, Maruthan merchant captain of the
*SUNRISE*

— JAWAD, sailor on the *Sunrise*

— MYTAR, sailor on the *Sunrise*

CORELLUS, headmaster of Simon's school

GRANUS, teacher at Simon's school

MARCINUS, teacher at Simon's school

TYRON, wealthy *mercati* student at Simon's school

TARINA, a young female neighbor of Simon's

LINTARUS, MARCED, BURKHAN, neighbors of Simon

YARKSES, a merchant in the Great Forum

MARKUS SENTOLLUS, *suprati* Senator and decorated former General

— XANDER, his Izari steward

— GALCIUS, one of his slaves

GENARO MORICHEA, *digniti* Senator and former General

LOKAS LEPILLA, *suprati* Senator and famed orator

— POLAS LEPILLA, his uncle

DAYMAR LOKUTA, Senator and older brother of Persei

— LOKILLA, his younger sister

— MYSENA, a female Valtari slave

— GALAX, Gathaki bodyguard

— MYLAX, Gathaki bodyguard

— AKTAR, Lokuta family agent

DARAS VANATRI MARASSANO, decorated *digniti* former General

PATRO SUBELLIUS, *digniti* current President of Pazh

TYBERO BAROBA, Simon's father

PLINAS, priest, Keeper of the Secrets at the temple of Choron, cousin of Lokas Lepilla

GLEBA, a wine-merchant in Salamis


### Historical Figures

LUCAS MARCONA, former President and builder of the Basilica Marcona, 500 years prior

MARCOS LUKKEN, former President and builder of the Senate Hall 400 years prior

PORRUNA MACATOR, General and famous tactician who defeated the Western Macatri

POLLIAN, a famous *digniti* family

SUENAS VII, last King of Pazh, tyrant overthrown by the people when the Republic was established

## *Izari*

ELYSIA, young sculptress from Attarsus
— her father, a baker
— ALEXANDER, her brother
— ZENO, her creation
XELOS, master stonemason, from Attarsus
— YCASTROS, his steward
— GLEBRIC, a teenage servant
— YALATH, his Maruthan colleague in Jeppo

## *Scentari*

SHADUSH, Grand Thane, ruler of all the tribes
— MIRASHA, his 16 year old daughter
— YAGRASH, his younger teenage son
KAZASH, Cavalry Captain
MIJAZI, priests of Mija, Scentari fire goddess
— JAGAZ, Mijazi priest
— SORGHUZ, Mijazi priest
GUFAZ, a Scentari warrior

## PLACES

PAZH (people or language: Pazian), can refer to
— PAZIAN REPUBLIC (or REPUBLIC OF PAZH), dominant
    power in the Near Sea and surrounds
— PAZH, city of, capital of the Republic of Pazh
    — ARENIAL, hill and district of the city of Pazh, location of
      the Great Forum and home of most of *digniti* families
    — JANIAR, district of Pazh, home of some *digniti* and many
      *suprati* or wealthiest *mercati* families
    — MAZIAL, district of Pazh, north side of the main hills, out
      of the way and secluded
    — NARUNIS RIVER, main river running east-west through
      Pazh
    — SALAMIS, busy southern neighborhood of the city of
      Pazh, home to Simon and many *mercati*
    — VALLEY, district of Pazh along the Narunis river, home

to the poorest of Pazh in large apartment complexes
— mainland PAZH, the peninsula containing the city of Pazh
— MALAYUS, Pazian city on the southeast coast, originally established by Izari settlers
— MELAXA, city on the northwest frontier of the Pazian peninsula, on the border with the Valtari
— NAHUZ, Pazian city on the east coast, north of Pazh
— PELARI, most famous wine region in Pazh
— SAREA, city on the southwest coast, popular vacation town

## Pazian Provinces

BOR (people or language: Borathi) - province in the East, ruled by local female elected governor, with men as warriors and main child-rearers, women in most administrative and government roles, known for men and women dressing in similar formless tunics. Generally dark-haired, skin like fresh cut oak.

EGARAS (Egarasi) - southwestern province, past home of several past great empires, including the oldest in the Near Sea region, natives have dark copper skin and dark hair

IZAR (Izari), people of the Izar Archipelago, light to olive skinned, with a variety of hair colors
— IZAR ARCHIPELAGO, a large number of islands in the middle of the Near Sea, previously ruled by local councils as individual city states, but now Protectorate of the Pazian Republic, reached their height around one thousand years ago. Individual city-states still have elected councils, but the Senate can override their decisions.
— ATTARSUS, leading mercantile city state of the Izar Archipelago, also famous for the arts
— NASOS, most northeasterly island of the Izar Archipelago

KAWAN (Kawanian), southern province famous for swift horses and capable riders, supplies most of the auxiliary cavalry to the legions. Natives have tawny skin, dark hair and slit-like eyes.

MARUTHA (Maruthan), southeastern province based around a major river system, site of several great empires in pre-Pazian times, home to many ancient ruin sites. People are known for golden skin and often golden hair

MACATRI, tribesmen who previously held much of Marutha until wiped out by the Pazian legions, the western Macatri by Porruna Macator

MYRAK (Myraki), eastern province, generally swarthy and dark-haired

PELUSIA (Pelusian), northeasternmost province, famous for trading. Newest province in the Republic, the northern half was carved out of what was once part of Scentar before their defeat by the legions. People are typically stocky, with tawny skin and hair

— JAMAD, a frontier town on the north border, established after Pelusia became a Pazian province

— TAMAR, main mercantile city of Pelusia, famous for exporting red dye called "The Blood of Tamar"

— SAL DAR, provincial capital of Pelusia

— SAL PRATTA, military port of Pelusia


**Other places:**

BENJEA (Benjish), nation west across the Far Sea from Pazh, followers of the Benjish religion. Now a subject province of the Kingdom of Randesh

GANDARI (Gandari), nomadic desert people south of Kawan

GATHAK (Gathaki), barbarian people from northeast of Pazh, often hire themselves as bodyguards and mercenaries

MARASSANO (Marassani), warlike people east of Myrak and Bor

SCENTAR (Scentari), nomadic horse people of steppe north of Pelusia, whose land formerly included most of the present province of Pelusia

— SENTUSI RIVER, main river of Scentar and best winter forage grounds for their flocks

— NAHAR HILLS, hilly country along the border between Scentar and Pelusia

VALTARI (Valtari), tribes hostile to Pazh northwest of the peninsula over the mountains

# PAZIAN TERMS

## *Social Classes (highest to lowest)*

*DIGNITI,* those of the original 200 Senatorial families of Pazh who still qualify for the Senate, going back to the founding of the Republic

*SUPRATI,* families who are eligible to be added to the Senate based on family success and financial qualification

*MERCATI,* merchant class of Pazh

*MUNDATI,* working class and laborers of Pazh

*DISSATI,* the poorest of Pazh, families who have fallen from higher classes, or freed slaves who haven't worked their way up

FREEDMEN, former slaves who have bought or earned their freedom, generally become clients to their former masters

SLAVES, slavery is legal throughout the Republic, and children of slaves are slaves by default

## *Military Terms*

CAMP PREFECT, any army of one legion or more will have a camp prefect in charge of all logistical matters, including fortifications, supplies, and pay for the legionaries. Third in command to the legate and general.

CENTURY, a unit of 100 legionaries in a Pazian legion

CENTURION, commander of a Century. Elevated from the ranks of the common soldiers, and receives 1.5 times pay.

COHORT, a unit of 600 men, 10 cohorts make one legion. The first cohort contains the best veteran troops.

GENERAL, the current head of one or more Pazian legions. A single legion can be commanded by a legate, but the Senate can name a General of a certain region or to prosecute a specific conflict, but a provincial governor can assume generalship over a legion stationed in his province

LEGATE, always from a senatorial family, assigned as commander of a single Pazian legion. Reports to a general.

LEGION, the main numbered unit of the Pazian army, made up of 6000 legionaries (at full strength) and auxiliary cavalry under the command of a single legate. Referred to by their number, ex. "The 7th" or "7th Legion"

SQUAD, group of 10 legionaries. 10 squads make one century. A squad shares a single large tent and their tools and supplies.

TRIBUNE, a junior officer in the Pazian legions, always from a senatorial family. They serve for 1-5 years, and are paid better than centurions

## Political Offices

CENSOR, Senator elected for a five year term to review the financial position of current or future candidates for the Senate and other lower public offices. Also responsible for prosecuting illegal activities by previous officeholders.

GOVERNOR, Senator elected for a three year term to oversee one of the Pazian provinces.

PRESIDENT, Senator elected for one year with executive authority over the entire Republic. Has the right to veto any decision by the Senate, and to propose legislation. Can also assume generalship over any or all Pazian legions unless the Senate proposes an alternate by two thirds majority.

SENATOR, one of 500 men who serve in the Pazian Senate, subject to a minimum level of financial qualification. Any who are found short of that qualification can be suspended, and if not rectified within three years, can be expelled. New Senators are chosen by the Censor to replace any expelled, or who die without any male heirs, and they must prove their financial qualification and membership of the *digniti* or *suprati*.

VICE-PRESIDENT, Senator elected for a 1 year term, as second in command of the Republic. Automatically becomes President if the President should die or become incapacitated while in office. Can be sent as General by the President's executive order unless the Senate proposes an alternate by two thirds majority.

## GODS

ATTARSO, Izari god with many forms
— aka Father Attarso, patron god of Attarsus
— aka Attarso the Hungry, patron of food-related merchants
— ALIATA, his daughter, patron of young women and their coming of age
CHORON OF THE SECRETS, Pazian god of the hidden knowledge
DAMOZ, ancient evil beings that grant power to humans in return for devotion
GOD, Benjish single god
HARINA, Pazian queen of the gods, goddess of fertility and motherhood
HASUR, Pazian god of wisdom
MELIAX, Pazian king of the gods
— METRIA, a mortal dalliance in a famous myth
MIJA, Scentari goddess of fire
SALAR, THE IRON ONE, chief god of the city of Pazh, the army, and metalsmiths
TAMLA, Pelusian god of weather, patron of Tamar
ZALIAKARA, female Damoz of flame, unseen for a millennium

# Acknowledgements

Getting a book out of your head and into a computer in a form you're happy with takes a long time. And the process of getting that draft ready for anyone else took some help. I'm blessed to have some wonderful people that I worked with to make that happen.

Thank you to Richard Scarsbrook for being the first person I shared this with, out loud, and for finding something to like, and other things to work on.

Thank you to Natassia Velez for developmental editing input and asking a lot of very good questions that I had to answer for myself, if not address in the text for readers.

Thank you to my amazing readers Suzanne, Nolan and Valerie for various levels of review, copyediting, proofreading and sanity checking. And more encouragement.

Thank you to Keri Knutsen of Alchemy Book Design for taking a cover idea and making it awesome.

Thanks also to a couple of notable teachers and instructors: Richard Scarsbrook again for being the first local writer I'd ever had a serious chance to chat with, and to be inspired by, and Phyllis Salgo, the one English teacher in my highschool who cared more about creative writing than literature, and encouraged me in every direction I took that.

And thanks to my past and present writing groups for feedback and encouragement based on my short story and the beginning of this book. Hearing that you wanted to know what happened to these characters means everything to me.

And there are too many bloggers and podcasters out there to even name that had an impact on me getting this done.

A huge thank you to my mother, for introducing me to Narnia when I was three, reading it to me until I could do it for myself. Without you I don't know when I would have discovered Lewis and Tolkien and the love of fantasy that I carry with me to this day.

But thanks most of all to my wife, Monica, for supporting me through this crazy idea I had to finally start getting these stories out of my head so I could share them with others. I couldn't have done this without your support, and I'm so happy you were the first to enjoy it, even in a rough form. I'll keep writing for you.

— Jamie Maltman, Richmond Hill, February 2014